FAT LAD

Glenn Patterson was born in Belfast in 1961 and from 1989 to 1991 was Writer in the community for Lisburn and Craigavon. His first novel, *Burning Your Own*, was awarded the Rooney Prize for Irish Literature and a Betty Trask Prize. He now lives in Manchester.

*Also by Glenn Patterson
available in Minerva*

Burning Your Own

GLENN PATTERSON

FAT LAD

Minerva

A Minerva Paperback

FAT LAD

First published in Great Britain 1992
by Chatto & Windus Ltd
This Minerva edition published 1993
by Mandarin Paperbacks
an imprint of Reed Consumer Books Ltd
Michelin House, 81 Fulham Road, London SW3 6RB
and Auckland, Melbourne, Singapore and Toronto

Copyright © Glenn Patterson 1992
Glenn Patterson has asserted his right to be
identified as the Author of this work.

The lines from *The Plague* by Albert Camus
on pp 215-6 are from the translation
by Stuart Gilbert, © 1948 Hamish Hamilton Ltd.

The lines from the following songs are
by permission of their publishers:
'Sugar Baby Love' by Wayne Bickerton and
Tony Waddington, © 1974 Odyssey Music Ltd,
courtesy of Chelsea Music Publishing Co. Ltd;
'Nobody's Child', by Sy Coben and Mel Foree,
© Acuff Rose Opryland, and 'Over There'
by George M. Cohan, © Leo Feist Inc.,
courtesy of Warner Chappell Music Ltd;
'I Am A Rock' by Paul Simon, © Paul Simon 1965,
courtesy of Pattern Music Ltd.

A CIP catalogue record for this title
is available at the British Library
ISBN 0 7493 9890 6

The author gratefully acknowledges the
financial assistance of the Arts Council of
Northern Ireland in the writing of this novel.

Printed and bound in Great Britain
by Cox & Wyman Ltd, Reading, Berks

For Colette

1

– Goldfish? My granny had a goldfish once. It drowned.

The crack that lost him his virginity. Indirectly. A dreadful joke, if joke you could even call it, for there was no more to it than that: a drowning goldfish and a Northern Irish voice. And it was the voice, raucous above the babble, turned her head in the first instance, before the image congealed and made her smile and she began her evening-long drift round the tables of the Union bar towards its source. He watched her approach, knowing full well what lay ahead, amazed at how easy it was, when it came to the bit, to make the little betrayal in pursuit of success: *it's the way I tell them*; the green and white minstrel. Amazed too, though not for the first time since arriving in England a fortnight before, at the unexpected effects of this thing coming from his mouth, this Belfast accent, his sister's childhood nightmare. A stigma turned distinction.

Hours later, after last orders at the bar and drinks in someone's room and a smoke in someone else's, after faltering sex by the light of a reading lamp turned to the wall, it was the voice she came back to:

– I could just lie here all night listening to you talk, she said, confirming what he had already thought, while putting the dampener on any hopes he might have had of trying to improve on his initial, dismal, coital efforts.

Her name was Kelly Thorpe, a languages student from Leicester: *though my great-grandparents on my mother's side were from Ireland, which is where I got Kelly*. At Christmas she sent him a card in Belfast, with an airmail sticker in the top left-hand corner of the envelope. But by that time, the compromises of his fresher weeks long forgotten, he had fallen in with the Ex-Pats, a group of jaundiced exiles, sworn to renounce their birthplace and all its works, and Kelly's misconception about the countries' postal relations was no more ludicrous to him than the posturings of the earnest boys who stood every Thursday on the steps of the Union building, with their Harringtons, number one crewcuts, and armfuls of *Troops Out* papers, bellowing in best Home Counties accents:

– Support the revolution in Ireland!

Hugh McManus, final year law, guiding light and *ex-iest* of all the Ex-Pats, had harangued them, solo, one famous rainy Thursday, challenging them to define their terms – What revolution? What *Ireland*? – and cutting to pieces each glib formulation with a flourish of his free hand (for one or other of Hugh's hands was invariably entangled in the straps of a garish and voluminous vinyl shopping bag), till they, their hair sticking up like a teddy bear's sucked fur and the thighs of their jeans wet where the rain had coursed down off the plastic sheets protecting the papers, were reduced to shouts of *Paisleyite!* and *Fascist!* Hugh McManus. The son of Belfast's foremost Catholic solicitors. The brilliant Hugh McManus, shot to death last year at age twenty-nine by a gunman, or gunmen, unknown, following his successful defence of Father Fiacc, the Liverpool priest (dubbed Father Fear by the tabloids) accused of plotting to assassinate the Environment Secretary on a visit to a Merseyside garden fête.

Drew looked at his reflection, double-exposed (speccy eight-eyes) in the aeroplane window. Where did Hugh come from all of a sudden? The lips in the window rewound at speed and tracked in on the word goldfish. That bloody goldfish. Eight years and more after he could last remember having given it a thought, it had turned up in his dreams the previous night and was still there when he awoke this morning, going round and round in his brain as monotonously and pointlessly as it had used to in its bowl.

Grandpa Linden, who Drew knew only from photographs and yarns such as this, had brought the goldfish home with him a month or two before he died.

– Where'd you get it? granny asked.

– A wee man Big Alec knows is selling them cheap.

There was always some wee man Big Alec knew selling something cheap. No questions asked, of course. Grandpa Linden asked none then, but from the day and hour it came into the house it was clear to his wife that that goldfish was never bred for life in a bowl.

– They're a special strain, grandpa hazarded. From Africa.

– From somebody's pond up the Antrim Road, more like, she said, peering at the thing through cloudy water.

It was huge. Even at that early stage swimming backwards and forwards was out: round and round was all it could manage, or every once in a while, with a huge splosh as it performed a laborious about-turn, round and round in the opposite direction.

– We can't leave it in there, it'll die.

But they did and it didn't; not for a good many years anyway and certainly not in the way Drew's grandmother had in mind. But then, who ever heard of a fish drowning? Or rather, to give the thing its proper name, *being drowned*? For even when the goldfish finally did go (early April, mid-seventies, while Granny Linden took an Easter week in Portrush), it did not go of its own free will. Drew had pushed open the bathroom door one evening to find his sister Ellen kneeling on the oval mat, her arms plunged into the bathwater and the empty bowl on the lino beside her. She turned her eyes towards him briefly, then looked away into the water.

– Get out, Drew, was all she said and when he saw her next she was at the boxroom window, pressing her face to the glass, causing ripples of mist to expand and contract about the imprint of her lips. Again and again, expanding and contracting, till the curtains were yanked together and the ripples contracted one final time in a slow-dying grin.

The *fasten seat-belt* command pinged red as the plane emerged from the mizzle and banked right, putting stern dark hills between itself and the lough shore on the descent into Aldergrove. And only then did Drew accept what was happening. Only then, despite everything that had gone before in the six chaotic weeks since he had read of the vacancy on the staffroom noticeboard – the letter of application, written on an impulse, then and there, the interview, the discussions, turning to rows, with Melanie, even the week-long visit to arrange a flat the month before (his first visit in four years and the only one since he graduated not occasioned by a funeral); all had been conducted in a bubble of unreality which popped now with the drop in cabin pressure.

The plane roared in towards the runway, hitting the tarmac with a bump. Impact of incompatibles. It reared up, as though affronted. *Forget it*, Drew felt like saying. *Let's turn round.* But even while the thought was forming the plane was adjusting its speed and the second time there was no bump and he was back.

Only a year, he promised himself. Only a year.

No one was watching for him from the viewing tower, because no one knew when to expect him. Drew took renewed heart from his foresight in not phoning ahead. Start as you mean to go on. The less he depended on the family the better. He was nearly twenty-seven, after all, and well used to looking out for himself. He had come back, he thought now, and he hadn't *come back*. For how could he be said to have returned to something that wasn't there before? The Belfast he left, the Belfast the Ex-Pats forswore, was a city dying on its feet: cratered sites and hunger strikes; atrophied, self-abased. But the Belfast he had heard reports of this past while, the Belfast he had seen with his own eyes last month, was a city in the process of recasting itself entirely. The army had long since departed from the Grand Central Hotel, on whose levelled remains an even grander shopping complex was now nearing completion. Restaurants, bars and takeaways proliferated along the lately coined Golden Mile, running south from the refurbished Opera House, and new names had appeared in the shopping streets: Next, Body Shop, Tie Rack, Principles. And his own firm, of course, Bookstore.

The doors opened on the arrivals lounge and a notice welcomed passengers no longer to Aldergrove, but to Belfast International Airport.

A groan rippled down the queue as they saw the size of the bus pulling in, a small nineteen-seater.

– Imagine sending a Flexibus, the woman behind Drew said,

making *Flexi* rhyme with taxi, so that Drew wondered whether subconsciously she had established some analogy between function and pronunciation.

– All aboard the Pope-mobile, her friend said.

The bus driver fended off the jibes with a shrug of his shoulders. It was always the same when an English flight came in, never enough cover.

– All's I do's drive them, he said.

He wore gold-framed aviator sunglasses (though it was the middle of February) and rested a foot on the low dashboard as he dispensed the tickets: white sock, maroon shoe.

– There'll be another one in half an hour, he said through the closing folding door when the bus was full.

– Half an hour's a lot of bloody use to me, a man with two children said and the driver shrugged again.

Drew, who had made sure he was at the head of the queue, snuggled down in his seat, closing his eyes and wedging his knees against the seat in front. Just as the bus moved off, however, the person beside him stood to let an old man sit down. Drew had seen him earlier at the baggage collection point, smiling at everyone – his smile an erosion in the folds of his face – and marked him down as one to avoid.

– That's no day to be standing around outside, the old man said now and rubbed his thick purple hands together. They made a rasping sound like the pages of antique books.

– Just visiting? he asked.

It was as Drew had feared: a talker. He thought despondently of the long drive into town.

– Business, he said, turning to the window. An off-putting word spoken in what he hoped was an off-putting manner.

But it was the worst thing he could have said. The old man took him for English and insisted on glossing the entire journey with his comments.

– This here's a checkpoint, he said, when the bus slowed by a sign saying *Vehicle Checkpoint*; and a bit later, indicating the winter-stripped fields to the right and left of the road: We're in the country yet.

Drew tried telling him that he was Belfast born and bred himself, but the old man wore a hearing aid and only smiled his canyon smile and nodded while Drew spoke, then turned in his seat the second he was finished to point out some house or other they had just passed, and Drew gave up explaining.

Where the M2 curved across the Shore Road below Whitewell and levelled out for the run-in to the city centre, his neighbour shook him yet again by the sleeve.

– Here's a thing here'll get you, he said. See the whole of this stretch of road. See years ago? Even twenty years ago, I mean, even *ten*: All underwater. Would you credit it? Underwater.

He chuckled to himself, then stopped abruptly. His red-rimmed lids blinked a bleary film over the surface of his eyes.

– Ah, boy, you could have fished out here and everything once upon a time, he said and Drew watched, horrified, as tears teetered on his eyelashes and plashed on the purple, rasping hands.

Drew appealed mutely to the people standing in the aisles, but they were all engrossed in newspapers and magazines. What could he do? He did what he always did in such circumstances: unhooked his specs from behind his ears, wipe-wipe-wiped them on a pulled-down sleeve kept unbuttoned for that very purpose, put them on, took them off, put them on again; then in desperation he pushed a Kleenex into one of the aged fists and faced the window once more.

– God spare me this old man's double vision, he prayed. What is is all.

And at that point he saw the road swell magnificently to ten lanes then burst into splinters: Bangor, Docks, Newtownards, City Centre, Westlink, M1, The West.

It was already dark by the time he reached the flat. There was a Telecom package waiting for him at the end of the landing by the front door. He dragged his suitcases inside and ripped open the padded envelope containing his new Viscount phone. The line had been reconnected that morning, though he had quite a hunt before he found the socket – in the passage between the kitchen and living-room, of all places. He'd need a wall bracket. He sloughed the polythene wrapping off the handset and called Melanie. No reply. Friday evening. She'd be doing her shopping. He remembered he'd nothing in himself and wondered what to do about dinner. Phone out for something. But not yet. After reading the instruction leaflet for the central heating he set the thermostat and went into the bedroom to stretch out on the cold mattress. He woke at midnight and tried Melanie again. Still no answer. He fetched his specs and looked to see where the wall bracket would go, then decided it was too late now to eat. He made up the bed with the bedding he had bought last month and got inside. The smell made him dream he had fallen asleep in a department store.

*

Melanie balanced her glass on the arm of the chair and sucked a thread of lemon from between her teeth. Drunk. Good and drunk. Good, good. She let the phone ring. Good for me. She crossed the room for the gin, passing the hi-fi and starting a record up with her foot. The stylus bounced twice, like a stone on black water, before coming to rest in the middle of a track. He'd have a fit if he could hear that. *Dead* scared. She kicked the turntable and the pick-up skited sideways. A zip being undone. Plus applause. The phone stopped ringing. Good again. Good riddance to bad rubbish. She sat on one of the cardboard boxes clumped in the centre of the room. It sagged and for some reason that made her snigger, which in turn made her sink further inside, so that her bum settled on the boards of his hoarded notebooks, and she laughed louder and louder, laughed till she thought she would cry.

She had left the theatre early this afternoon to pack his things. He hadn't asked her, didn't know; she'd just decided on the spur of the moment. She was fucked if she was going to look at his leavings every day. Tomorrow they could go down into the cellar until such times as he sent for them. For so far as she was concerned, when he got on the plane today that was that. It wasn't as if she hadn't told him. From the minute – the second – the *milli*second – he mentioned it she'd told him. But he insisted: it was only for a year; in a year he'd be a manager and have his own shop. . . . Of course he would, and she knew where too: Derry, or Londonderry, whatever it was he called it, or some other miserable hole over there. And all that big talk there'd been through the summer of branches in

7

Paris and Rome. For a moment she almost felt sorry for him. The first assistant manager's position to fall vacant and it had to be there. Even Dublin wouldn't have been so bad. But she quickly banished all such conciliatory thoughts. He could have waited. Another post would have come along sooner or later.

A pair of tailor's dummies stood back to back in the corner by the window. Two mud-brown velveteen lollies licked into approximate human shapes (the prototypes on which her occasional freelance creations were modelled), locked in a struggle they were powerless to resolve.

She got out of the box and returned to her chair, pouring herself another drink.

They had been here twice before in the eight years she had known him. Twice before work threatened to part them. Her work both times and both times he gave up what he was doing and followed. (The tailor's dummies were a gift from him the day she got the wardrobe supervisor's job here.) But that meant nothing. There were no trade-offs. Everyone had somewhere where they could not or would not follow. And for her it was Belfast. Then too, it caused him no special grief to leave a place behind to be with her, for he had formed no special attachments in England. One place was much the same as another to him. Wherever he was was just where he happened to be. Arriving to pick him up from shopping one day, a full six months after they'd moved here, she had spotted him standing on a traffic island, trying to work out which side of the road he should be waiting on. She drove twice round the block before tooting the horn, all the time thinking how precarious he had looked, the grocery bags slanting in against his shins and calves his only ballast; and she remembered now, as she remembered then, a photograph, carried by all the papers after a fertiliser bomb (a *fertiliser* bomb! she'd never forgotten that: like corrosive baby oil) had exploded somewhere or other on the Irish border, of a car resting on its head in a ploughed field.

That was Drew for her, a piece of debris, blasted out of his natural orbit, always incongruous elsewhere. And that was why he could never leave it alone. He would deny that, of course, but it was true. None of them could, not even Hugh McManus, for all his cleverness and his declared antipathy. What was it

Hugh used to say? *Fuck Ulster before Ulster fucks you.* Well it had fucked him all right. Poor Hugh.

Melanie shuddered. What a dreadful place. Everything associated with it filled her with distaste. Christ, even this morning, their last morning waking beside each other, when she looked at his brown hair disordered on the pillow and, ready to forgive his leaving, reached down between his legs, what did he start on about? Some disgusting goldfish his granny used to keep, its nose and tail so close together in the bowl it was almost able to eat its own shit.

2

WILBUR WORRELL, DREW knew, didn't exist, but, looking at the shop again his first morning at work, he congratulated him anyway on another grand job. Wilbur had been dreamt up by the Bookstore publicity department to intrigue the press and tease rivals, jealous of the reputation the company was acquiring for the high architectural standards of its shops. Wilbur was supposed to spend his entire life crossing and recrossing the British Isles, scouring cities and towns for premises worthy of the Bookstore name. Drew saw him as a nervy, ulcerated little man, who survived on sandwiches snatched at the wheel of his car, a much-patched Austin Maxi (from choice rather than necessity) with 90,000 on the clock, second time around; who preferred guest-houses to hotels, slept in neither, and passed the long insomnious nights propped up in bed with a Pevsner. Among Wilbur's greatest triumphs were the listed buildings in Durham and Bristol and a Mackintosh in Glasgow. A toast was drunk to his health at the opening of each new branch and guests not in the know always gave him a generous round of applause. For a while, a year or two back, there had been a fad among junior staff for lapel badges with the message *I've seen Wilbur and she's black*.

The Belfast Bookstore was a slender, four-storeyed building on the south side of Castle Place, across the road and down from the new Head Post Office and the purpose-built newsstand around whose parapet ran the endlessly repeated, digital refrain, *Belfast is buzzing*. For many years it had been Henderson's Gentleman's Outfitters, one of a block of five shops created in the 1930s by the partition of an Edwardian drapery emporium. Even now, more than half a century on, the art nouveau façade of the upper storeys, curving in an elaborate bracket across the block, proclaimed the common lineage. But while time and changing proprietors had dealt its siblings increasingly solecistic lower floors (like the losing hands in a game of architectural Misfits), Henderson's, with its tall narrow windows and ornamental glazing bars, had managed to retain down the years something of the original's turn-of-the-century splendour.

The Bookstore conversion had been faultlessly sympathetic. Design consultants were flown in from England to oversee it and an eminent art historian was hired, at great expense, to supervise the restoration of the magnificent mosaic floor. For it was the Bookstore house style that there was no such thing as a Bookstore House Style: no absolute prescriptions about fixtures and fittings, no externally imposed (and invariably inappropriate) colour schemes of maroon or bottle green. Context and harmony were the keynotes. Even the appearance of the name changed from shop to shop, so that the company itself had become, in a strange way, transparent and in place of anonymous branches of an impersonal chainstore, the public saw only enticing shopfuls of books. Perhaps if there was a Bookstore trademark it was that: every shop, without exception, was packed to the rafters with books. Many people in many different towns took them for a local firm; some were even prepared to swear (market research had proved it) that their family had always bought books there, though the first shop was opened as recently as 1977 and the majority had appeared within the last five years. Advertising campaigns capitalised on the misconception. Each new shop was announced in the local press by a simple full-page photograph, an address, and, below that, two words: *Your Bookstore*.

Business boomed.

From its north London street-market origins as a used-books stall run by three Cambridge undergraduates in the long vacation, Bookstore had grown in just over a dozen years into a nationwide concern of some twenty-five shops. It was said that the three co-founders (whom all the staff, from managers down to Saturday workers, were instructed to call simply Karen, James and Phoebe) could sell up tomorrow and retire, millionaires many times over. But then, as Phoebe told the *Sunday Times Life in the day of* ... column recently, there'd be no point, since they'd only be down at Camden Lock again within the month, setting up another stall.

Bookselling, the company philosophy ran, was something you either had in you or you hadn't and James, who prided himself on being able to divine this at a glance and who, with Karen, made a point of interviewing all potential employees personally, decided the second he set eyes on Drew that he had it in him: the dark grey baggy suit (missing a button) and Doc Marten shoes; the rumpled brown hair and granny specs. *Bookish but approachable*, he wrote in the margin of the interview sheet, then, drawing an arrow, *Poet?*

Drew, of course, wasn't aware of this speculation (and indeed was indulging in speculations of his own about James whose razor-cut blond hair and natural fabrics suggested a punk mellowing into his funky thirties), but even if he had been he wouldn't have been in the least surprised. The same assumption had been made of him more than once when he was a student, a combination, it seemed, of the subject he studied, English, and the company he kept, Irish, like himself; so often in fact that he had eventually come to expect that it was only a matter of time before he did begin writing, though whether poetry or prose he had not yet been able to decide. His relaxed easygoing manner with visiting writers, which his first manager had remarked upon and which, for Karen at any rate, was the deciding factor in his getting the Belfast job, stemmed from this. He thought of himself as one of them and was often to be seen scribbling away in one or other of the Black n' Red notebooks (marked *W* and *P* respectively) which he carried with him wherever he went.

There was heavy fog lying, like underdone air, the Monday morning Drew started to work. It was a twenty-minute walk from his flat into town. Malone Road, University Road, Bradbury Place, Shaftesbury Square. . . . Buildings appeared to him one at a time, stripped of context, jutting into space, as though craning their necks. *Where the fuck are we?* . . . Dublin Road, Bedford Street, Donegall Square – West, North – Donegall Place. Turning a final corner, he followed for a time the course of the culverted Farset as it flowed, unseen, from its shrouded source to its ancient, city-christening union with the fog-bound Lagan, and then he was there. Belfast's Bookstore. A sign on the door bade him enter, but he was still a few minutes early and, not having been given his own keys yet, had to wait for one of the other staff members to let him in. First to emerge from the fog, her features clinging to her wetly, like spiders' webs on privet, was a tall, fair-haired woman aged, in common with most Bookstore employees, in her early-to-mid-twenties. She walked with her head and upper body held slightly back and her shoulders curved forwards, giving her an air of constant query and reminding Drew instantly of her name: Sian Miles. It was a technique he'd seen demonstrated on television once – fixing a person's name to some outstanding physical trait – and it had never failed him. (In more ways than one: people warmed to someone who took the trouble to remember their name.)

– Morning, Sian, he said.

Sian, who had been approaching him cursing her luck for being the one to get stuck with the new assistant manager, brightened a little at this. She had met him only once before, very briefly, and was expecting to have to go through the embarrassment of introducing herself again.

– Morning, she said. Been standing long?

– No, not long.

They chatted in the lift to the second floor and entered the door, between Religion and New Age, to the staff-only area. This consisted of two passages in an inverted T. The shorter, running from left to right as you came through the door, had the women's and men's toilets at either end, while the longer gave on to the staffroom itself on one side and two small, interconnecting offices on the other. The second of these, no more than an alcove off the first, was to be Drew's. There was space for a desk, a swivel chair, with its back to the through archway, and a bin. Shelves had been fixed to the walls on all three sides (there was no window) but even so the bulk of the paperwork had to be kept in cabinets next door.

Drew came through here to empty the contents of his carrier bag – desk diary, personal diary, specs case (brought everywhere and never used), the two Black n' Red notebooks, marked *W* and *P*, a bottle of Quink, four sheets of pink blotting paper and a Sheaffer fountain pen. When he returned to the staffroom, eight or nine people were assembled round a table strewn with trade magazines, publishers' proofs, the full complement of local and national dailies, and headed by the manager, Pamela Magill.

Pamela Magill was something of an oddity at Bookstore, having started in the trade years before the Camden trio, and consequently most of their employees, were even born. Her face hung in fleshy folds over a sharp peg of a nose which on her bad days (Pamela slouched terribly when she was tired) appeared to be all that stood between her and total collapse. She was also a confirmed smoker, a habit which Karen, James and Phoebe tried hard to discourage, especially in senior staff. But they made an exception in Pamela's case because the fact was *she knew her books* – the company's ultimate accolade – *bloody well*.

The fact was too that when news of the Belfast branch was originally circulated around existing shops, nobody with the necessary experience offered themselves as manager. Pamela had been poached, at a price, from one of the larger stores in the Republic where she still kept a home and a husband.

This morning she made all the remaining introductions through a haze of Carrolls Number One. Her dough-coloured hair was pinned in a topknot resembling a collapsed Yorkshire pudding and slid from side to side when she talked, so that it seemed every moment to be in danger of slipping round completely under her chin. Drew hooked on his specs and shook hands with each person as they were introduced, fixing them in his mind.

– When he's not in his cubby-hole, Pamela said, Drew'll be on the bottom floor, helping Matt – (Matt, twenty-ish, sports-jacket-and-tie man, blushes hearing his name) – with Classics, Poetry and, ah . . .

– Drama, Drew said quietly.

– And Drama, Pamela said, without acknowledging the prompt. Richard – (a scrawny Lionheart, Catweazel beard concealing spots, a rebellious state within the state of his face; he'd need to keep an eye on Richard) – is up on One from now on in Simon's Reference section.

Simon was Drew's predecessor as assistant manager. Drew looked round the table at the faces looking at him, trying to decide who had been Simon's particular friends and wondering how quickly he could strike up a rapport with them all. He had his work cut out for him: there were sixteen full-time members of staff altogether and half that number again part-time.

Sian smiled, a short quick smile, like a thick elastic band being forced apart then released. Drew smiled back. It was a start.

– All right, Pamela said, TV-tough. Go sell books.

Drew's morning was divided between the two offices, familiarising himself with accounts and general administration, saying hi to reps and any other passers-by (and there were several), who happened to drop in on Pamela for a cup of coffee and a cigarette. Every so often, picking up a sheaf of papers or opening a file, he came across jottings in Simon's loose, confident hand, advising on the payment of a certain account one time, explaining the procedure for re-ordering bags and bookmarks another. Simon was only twenty-seven himself and he'd been given his own branch. Dundee – huge floor space. And that after just six months as assistant manager in Chesterfield and five months here. A natural progression. James had said as much at Drew's interview for this job: *we usually find that after twelve months or so* . . . something along those lines.

Once, towards the end of the morning, he glanced at his ever-expanding list of things to remember and panicked at the thought of not being able to cope. But just then he turned up another of Simon's notes and he told himself if Simon could do it then so could he. In a short while he had lapsed into daydreaming about the big changes he would make to the place, imagining soaring sales figures and memos headed *From* James *To* Phoebe & Karen. *Drew L for Paris?*

He bought lunch from a wholefood shop in Lombard Street and, ignoring the still-damp air, sat down to eat it on the benches outside the Post Office. The morning's fog had retreated to the point where it was difficult to identify as fog now and not simply the negation of the middle ground, so that whatever street you happened to be in was at once everywhere and nowhere. Drew ate his chickpea pitta watching the people enter then leave his – no, not his, *their* – bookshop, then turn the corner and disappear.

Midway through the afternoon, while he was serving on one of the ground-floor tills, Matt held the telephone out to him.

– Somebody wanting you, he said. A woman.

Drew had tried Melanie a dozen times the day before without success. He checked an impulse to abandon his customer to Matt and finished the sale before taking the receiver.

– Hello?

– I thought it was today you started, the voice said.

It was Ellen.

– Oh, hello, Ellen.

– When did you get back?

– Just last night, he lied (there was no point starting anything on the phone).

– I said that to Derek, it would be last night. You should've called. Him or I would've come for you.

– I flew standby, he said, I didn't know to the last minute when I'd get on.

– I said that to Derek, Ellen said, that you'd come standby. It was more Daddy was worried, but you know what he's like.

Drew saw the perplexed eyes, the hands wrestling with one another, over and over, without resolution. He knew all right.

– Ah, listen, Ellen, I'll have to ring you back, I've a queue of customers standing waiting.

– You're on the shop floor? I thought you had an office. Are you not in an office?

– Not all the time, Drew said.

– Sure you should've said. But here, you'll come up some night for your dinner, won't you? Thursday, maybe?

– Thursday should be OK. I'll give you a call.

He put down the phone. Matt was folding leaflets to put inside customers' books. When there were customers. The till was quiet. Matt looked at Drew and smiled, colouring slightly.

– My big sister, Drew said, I'd've been there all day.

Thursday, in fact, was to have been his day off, but waking

that morning at his usual time he decided to go into the shop after all. He could do with the extra few hours to get ahead of himself with the paperwork.

He didn't get far, though. Pamela was in her office when he arrived and he spent more time looking over his shoulder, talking to her than he did looking at the papers on his desk. Not that it was hard to be distracted by someone who in the fifties had rubbed shoulders with the likes of Brendan Behan in her Dublin local, McDaid's, and whose husband had been there with *Brian* (as in O'Nolan, as in Flann O'Brien) *and that crowd* on the very first Bloomsday walk – *though there wasn't many could walk*, she said, *by the end of it*. Pamela's CV was a guide to the cities and booksellers of Ireland, winding up in the Cork shop where she had anticipated seeing out the remainder of her working days until Bookstore made their offer.

– I thought hard before accepting them, she said. I loved that place.

– How many square feet had you? Drew asked.

Pamela's topknot lurched first one way then the other.

– Lots, she said. I don't know.

She lit a cigarette, provoking a spasm of coughing which had her rooting in her cardigan pockets for a Kleenex and reminded Drew he had come here to work.

– Don't kill yourself over it, for God's sake, Pamela croaked, seeing him turn his face to the wall. Between the two of us it'll all get done.

He left work at half-four and caught a bus from the back of the City Hall. He had bought a bottle of wine at lunchtime and was sorry now he had. They wouldn't be expecting it. He tried to think did Ellen drink wine, but all he could remember ever seeing her with was a Dubonnet. God, how tedious it was to have to analyse every little action for fear of creating awkwardness or giving offence. He stared sullenly out the window. There was a new one way system operating in Great Victoria Street. Outgoing traffic was now directed on to Dublin Road by an *All Routes* sign just below Hope Street. His frown was cracked by the combination. An Ordnance Survey drollery, to be delivered, for preference, in an Ian Paisley voice.

He'd make a note of that as soon as he was at Ellen's. Have

a go at a humorous verse, maybe. All Routes. Rhymes with flutes, and big galoots.

The bus was climbing away from Bradbury Place on to University Road. Drew had passed this spot many hundreds of times when he was younger and yet he had never reflected on the significance of the pronounced slope here until the day Hugh McManus explained to him how the whole of Belfast city centre was built on mudflats, exposed, centuries before, by the retreating lough: sleech, in the local idiom, or, the word Hugh preferred, slobland.

On another occasion he and Hugh were in a bar together behind their university when three men started to snigger at Hugh's vinyl shopping bag.

– Poof, one of them said into his glass, in a broad Belfast accent.

Hugh sat down across from them and addressed Drew in a loud, unconcerned voice:

– We are fortunate, I see, to have in our company a couple of fellow natives of the slobs.

The man slammed his pint glass on the bar.

– Who are you calling slobs, you queer?

He wore his shirtsleeves rolled, revealing a King Billy tattoo on one arm and, on the other, an ornate device of crossed machine-guns, Vanguard flag and a bleeding red hand. Both of these were underscored by do-it-yourself efforts in green-faded ink: UVF, YCV, FTP, KAI.

– Tell your friend, Hugh said leaning across solicitously to the tattooed man's companions, to see a doctor. He's so bloated with bigotry it's breaking out on his skin.

They were lucky that day. Only the barman saved them, putting himself in the way of the three men long enough for them to reach the street. And, even then, Hugh nearly pushed it too far, turning at the door and snapping his heels to attention, smiting his chest and declaring: *God help the Queen!*

Drew was past the New Houses and heading towards the old estate before he remembered where he was. He got out a hundred yards down the road and walked back. Night had fallen while he was on the bus, catching even the stars unprepared. Without them the darkness was a black hole where the sky had been.

Twelve years ago when the New Houses really were new they were separated from the estate where Drew's family lived by several acres of waterlogged meadow. There was only the one street originally, with six sets of sturdy semis on either side and beyond them, in a slight recess where the rudimentary dirt and gravel road bulbed to let cars turn, a thirteenth, unmatched, pair – the show houses – finished before the others were half begun. All through that spring their rich creamy stuccoed fronts lured people across the meadow from the old estate to wander through the wood-smelling interiors, pacing out the extra yardage in the kitchens and living rooms, opening and closing the doors of the second toilets, talking of all the things you could do with the additional attic space. To this day many on the old estate dreamt of *moving up there*, as they still termed it, even though the meadow was long ago built over, making the two areas, to all outward appearances, one; and even though the owners of the New Houses themselves now aspired to the Georgian-style development which was spreading away from them southwards into the countryside.

Ellen and Derek had lived in the New Houses from the very start. Nineteen seventy-eight was also the year they were married and the house was their wedding present to each other. It had nearly broken them at the time, but they didn't care; they were both young, both earning and both happy to put off other things for a while. Like owning all their own furniture; like going on honeymoon. They spent their wedding night on a borrowed bed in their just-bought house at the top of the new street. They'd gone for one of the show houses in the end. They were a couple of thousand cheaper, of course, but also, as Derek and Ellen said, *they sort of stood out more.*

Despite all the building that had gone on around it in the intervening years, Ellen and Derek's house still stood out, although they mightn't have thanked you now for saying so.

Drew saw the telltale electric blue aura before he was halfway up the street and as he followed the footpath round a more prolonged, juddering brightness illuminated the whole house from behind. Holes pockmarked the plaster; a pair of driveway gates slouched beneath the front window, bound together with cord. He walked along the side of the house to the open garage door, shielding his eyes with his hand. Sparks bounced, crackling, on the concrete floor and the air was filled with the smell of burning flux. After a moment the crackling stopped, but as Drew parted his fingers there was a sudden resurgence and he was staring unprotected into the source of the light – the white-hot point of contact between a welding rod and two lengths of metal. He turned his back immediately, pressing down on his eyes, but when at last he drew back his hands and looked at them the after-image remained, sharp as sunlight focused through a magnifying glass, so that by staring long enough he might have been able to set himself on fire.

– Drew? a muffled voice called to him. Is that you?

Derek came towards him, a collision of B-movie alien and angel, with his Cyberman-welding mask and the soft, seraphic glow which seemed to swathe him from head to foot.

– Have you hurt your eyes? he asked. Come on inside and bathe them.

– I'm all right, I think, Drew said.

Little wraiths of smoke were appearing and disappearing on the edge of his field of vision, but the white spots had begun to diminish and Derek's glow was fading, like a cooling coal's. Derek set his mask and welding gun on the bench and took off his protective gloves.

– Well come on in anyway, he said, putting his arm around Drew's shoulder. The pungent smell was trapped in the fibres of his overalls.

– Good to see you home.

Home? Drew thought, but said nothing.

They cut across the back garden, more mud these days than grass and more scrap, it seemed, than either. Abandoned now by the rest of the family, the garden was an early casualty in the battle for space that had been raging more or less constantly in and around the house in the eight years since the engineering plant where Derek was working closed down and he set himself up in the garage, with welding machine and second-hand lathe, as D. *Hastings Railings and Gates (Efficient Service, Competitive Rates)*.

– How's business? Drew asked.

– Ach, you know, Derek said equably and looked up at the starless sky as though it was something up there they were discussing. You just keep plugging away, don't you?

His hair was going a bit at the crown, but other than that he had changed little since Drew first met him more than fifteen years before. Ageing held all the terror of a child's dressing-up game for Derek; his present guise was called Thirty-two and Father of Three. He kicked off his boots at the back step and held the door for Drew.

Ellen wasn't long in ahead of them. (She was back out to work again, as a wages clerk for a firm of stationers, now that Nathaniel was started school.) She was still wearing her rain-coat when Drew entered, but had managed to get an apron on underneath. She kissed her brother's cheek and hugged him on her way to the fridge.

– Excuse me a minute, Drew, she said, her voice competing with the sound of the television from the next room, I'll just get this started.

She threw a white plastic butcher's bag on the counter top and slit it with a knife.

– Pork fillet OK? You still eat meat, don't you?

Browned blood bubbled from the punctured lung of the bag.

– Yes, Drew said (though, in fact, he ate very little). Pork fillet'll be fine.

– I sometimes think I could live without it myself, Ellen said, but with the kids and all . . .

She turned a quick smile on him.

– You've a button off your jacket.

– I know, Drew said.

He always had at least one button off his jackets; it pricked the pomposity of a suit, even an Oxfam suit.

– It's meant . . .

– Sorry, Drew, Ellen said, stopping him with her hand and calling into the sitting room. Tina! I thought I asked you to do the potatoes?

– What?

The reply was shouted above the television's din.

– I said . . . Ellen shouted back, then rested a hand on the counter top. Turn that thing down! Now come in here when I'm talking to you.

The sound was dulled and Tina appeared, sulkily, at the kitchen door. She was ten now, going on eleven, and had a sour, putty-ball face with traces of Ellen and Derek rolled in. Her jeans were of a type (long since unfashionable in England) which Drew particularly disliked, with a Fred Flintstone motif on the leg.

– Well? her mother prompted. Say hello to your Uncle Drew.

– Hello, Tina.

– Hello, she replied and looked at him, nothing more to say.

Ellen had evidently forgotten what she had called her daughter for in the first place because she had taken the potatoes from the cupboard herself and was scrubbing them at the sink. Her coat lay in a heap now behind her.

– Where's the other two? she asked.

– In there, Tina said, nodding back towards the sitting room.

– Well, go and get them, for heaven's sake, Ellen said, then rounded on Derek who was reaching across her, washing his hands. Could you not do that up the stairs out of my road?

Drew was still stood with his two arms the one length in the middle of the kitchen floor.

– Can I do anything?

Ellen pointed to the basin of potatoes in the sink.

– You could peel those, she said at the same moment as Tina's two young brothers pushed each other into the doorway, yelled hello and ran away, giggling, to continue watching their programme.

– Laurence! Nathaniel! Ellen started to call them back, but let it go.

Drew suddenly remembered something.

– The wine, he said.

– Oh, good, said Ellen, did you bring wine?

– No, he said. I left it on the bus.

The dinner preparations were delayed while Ellen hunted for the potato peeler. Drew helped her search, pulling out drawers, opening and shutting cupboard doors. He found nuts, screws, washers, bolts, odd lengths of metal and a claw hammer, but no potato peeler. In one corner, behind the electric chip-pan, he discovered a parcel of newspaper which on closer inspection was found to contain two paintbrushes, stuck together in a bristly kiss.

– See Derek!

Ellen snatched the brushes from him and, in her vexation, slung them out the back door into the garden. She pinched the bridge of her nose to keep herself from saying more and when she screwed up her eyes a pattern of furrows, the inevitable contours of her future face, emerged with practised ease from beneath the pellicle of the present.

– Don't bother yourself with the peeler, Drew spoke quickly. A knife will do just as well.

They worked a minute or two in silence, then Ellen said:

– You really should have called up with Daddy, you know.

– I thought he was going to be here tonight? Drew said.

– He is, said Ellen. But, like, four days you've been back.

Drew threw the peeled and cut potatoes into a saucepan of salted water.

– I've hardly had a minute with the shop, he said and indeed it was ten o'clock most nights before he got away. I rang him Monday to explain.

– Only it's easy to forget, but he's sixty-seven now, you know.

– Ellen, Drew said, it wouldn't matter if he was twenty-seven or a hundred and seven. I've been busy. Anyway, I'm here a while, I'll see him plenty.

And as if on cue there was a rap at the back door and their father came in, stamping his feet on the doormat. He wore a turquoise anorak, belted tight at the waist, as though to keep him from falling out, and a greenish tweed trilby with a feather in the band.

– Hiya, Daddy, Ellen said, kissing his cheek.

– Hello, Ellen, love. I'm not late, am I?

– Not at all.

He nodded to Drew.

– Hello, son.

– Hello, Dad, Drew said and for a second he looked at his father the way Tina had looked at him. Then he held up his wet, starchy hands.

– Can't shake hands, he said, they're all slimy.

His father wagged his head. His nose and cheeks were meshed with fine, mulberry veins. Plugs of hair, the yellowy-white of soiled cotton wool, nestled in his ears. Ellen was wrong, there was no forgetting his age.

– Has she you on the spuds already? Our Ellen won't leave you standing too long with your hands idle.

And when he laughed his false teeth made their familiar tut-tut-tut sound, like a puritanical alter ego.

– Thursday my pension comes, Jack Linden said, so I do my shopping and what have you. Otherwise I'm here nearly every day helping Derek out.

Derek had put the boys to bed and was upstairs getting shaved. The rest of the family were in the sitting room, Ellen, Drew and their father drinking a mid-evening cup of tea, Tina plonked on a pouffe before the soundless television, homework spread on her knees.

– Oh, we'd be lost without him, Ellen said, watching tea dribble down the side of her father's cup into the saucer poised beneath his chin.

The truth of the matter was (and Ellen knew it) that it was all Derek could do most days to find something to keep her father occupied while he got on with the real work. Things were different a couple of years back when the arrangement first started. They had a regular production line going for a while, Derek turning and working the metal, his father-in-law rustproofing the finished items, ready for glossing. Through time, though, Jack's work deteriorated, until it reached the stage where Derek was having to go over everything he did each evening after he left. And quite apart from the time, the paint was just too expensive to waste. Nowadays he fretted about the garage, making his little cluck sound with his teeth, until Derek handed him a yard brush and asked him to sweep up the swarf or called him over to put his thumb on a tape measure. And when Derek could bear to watch his humiliation no longer he sent him out of the garage altogether to make coffee. Countless cups of it.

His life seemed to be taking on a grotesque symmetry: he

had grown up, left school, worked and retired (early, there was no option), then worked again before degenerating into this current grim parody of apprenticeship. At a quarter past two each weekday he went and stood at the gate of the primary school and waited for his grandsons getting out. Derek silently rejoiced at having the garage to himself while Grandpa kept an eye on the kids and the kids kept an eye on Grandpa. And it was very much a two-way arrangement. Derek was freed from the worry of there being no one there for the boys if he was called out on a job and at the same time Ellen was spared the contemplation of her father stuck in his empty house, alone with his thoughts. He had sagged badly when first his wife, then his mother died in the space of fifteen months and he had never been a man who made many friends.

Derek was downstairs again, changed into a sweatshirt and tracksuit bottoms so close-fitting that, by reason of their very antithesis, they reminded Drew for an absurd instant of the skinners his brother-in-law used to wear back in the seventies.

– God bless us, is there anybody in those trousers at all? their father asked one windy night, watching the jeans snapping at half-mast about Derek's legs as he stood in his usual place opposite their house, hoping Ellen would come out.

Ellen hadn't a lot of time for Derek in those days.

– He's only a wee fella, she said.

In fact, there were just seven months between them, but those seven months meant that when she left school, Derek had to stay on another year. Some nights, though, if she'd nothing better to do Ellen called him over to the porch for a chat and even let him walk her to the chippy the odd time, when she could be bothered.

– That's a sin, stringing him along like that, her father told her.

But their mother, speaking, as she so often did, as though goaded into speech, took Ellen's part.

– If Derek Hastings wants to let her that's nobody's lookout but his own, she said, and her husband pulled in his breath, as though caught by a low blow, extinguishing whatever it was he had begun to say.

25

Derek sat on the arm of Ellen's chair and laced up a pair of imitation brand-name running shoes.

– You going . . . – *jogging*, Drew was about to say, but at the last moment thought better of it – . . . *out*, Derek?

– Did I not tell you? Ellen said. He's doing the taxis now a couple of nights a week.

Derek crossed the room to the TV and kissed the top of Tina's head.

– Bed, now, as soon as you're finished your homework.

– OK, she said, evidently to his reflection.

– Will I drop you round, Jack? he asked his father-in-law, but even as he spoke he was fetching his hat and coat from under the stairs.

– Aye, well if you're going that road.

Drew stood up with his father and took his cup.

– All right, then, Dad?

His father was gripping his cuffs while he put on his anorak, the way he had taught Drew as a child to keep his sleeves from riding up.

– We'll have to get a run down to see this . . . this *bachelor pad* of yours, he said. And maybe you'll come round some night soon – (his dentures clacked furiously, disapprovingly, in anticipation of his joke) – to see me in mine.

– I'll be up through the week, Drew promised.

There was a moment's indecision as his father took a step towards him. But they looked down together and saw Drew was holding a teacup in each hand and his father's own hands fell to buckling his anorak belt.

When they had gone, Ellen produced a half-bottle of brandy and two tumblers from the kitchen. Tina looked round from the TV for the first time since dinner and Ellen pointed the base of the bottle at her.

– Homework finished?

Tina nodded.

– OK, you can have an extra hour, but – (Tina had already dumped her books on the floor and turned the television full blast) – not too loud. And, Tina . . .

Her daughter looked over her shoulder at her.

– Don't you be letting on.

Tina grinned. Ellen noticed Drew's puzzled expression.

– Don't worry, she said. I'm not an alkie or anything. Derek's just a bit funny about the drink. All right in its place; you know, pubs and dances. This – (she poured brandy into the tumblers as though it was wine) – is left over from the Christmas puddings.

And she laughed.

– Thank God, she said, for Christmas.

Drew took a tumbler and drank. His first drink since returning to Belfast. Melanie would never believe him. He had finally got hold of her on Monday evening, but he'd hardly said two words before she'd launched into some story about having packed his things away in the cellar, seeing as how he wouldn't be coming back again.

– Oh, will I not? he asked her, playing along.

– No, she said flatly, you won't.

And then he thought she might not be joking after all.

– You didn't really put everything away, did you?

She sighed.

– Of course I didn't.

– And you do believe this is only for a year at most?

– Of course I do.

– Derek's taking a lot out of himself, Ellen said.

The mirth had drained from her voice, leaving it dry and brittle.

– People think nothing affects him, but I notice it in him, he's terribly failed.

She ran her fingers through her hair, the old habit, pushing it behind her ear, and as she did Drew glimpsed streaks of grey, as though the years of rubbing had worn the colour away. *Look at yourself*, he wanted to tell her, but said only:

– Is he out much, then?

– Five nights a week, sometimes. But what can you do? she said. The railings don't bring in the money they used to, there's not the same demand any more. You take these new Georgian houses they're building everywhere, it's all wee fancy chains they go in for.

Drew's head bobbed up and down, in distraction more than agreement. The image that had been smouldering at the back of his mind since earlier that evening in the kitchen – the sneak preview of his sister middle-aged – was once more fanned into life. Only seven months between her and Derek, but while Derek wore his thirty-two years like an outsize borrowed coat, with Ellen age was revealed for what it was: something you grew into and never grew out of.

He left Ellen's on the last bus, unenthused by the prospect of returning to the flat. Two drinks is always the worst, he thought. Neither one thing nor the other. Better not to start at all as stop at two, even with the measures Ellen poured. He slid down in his seat, listening to the Country & Western music yeehawing from a transistor in the driver's cab. Something alien rattled in his right-hand pocket and he fished out from the detritus of Kleenex and paperclips a transparent plastic envelope, no bigger than a Swan Vesta matchbox, containing four thin cards of thread (navy, brown, black, white), half a dozen needles on a strip of black paper, and a tiny pair of scissors. Ellen must have slipped it in his pocket while she was getting his jacket.

Drew turned the envelope over in his hand and read the inscription on the back: *Stitch-in-Time Travellers' Sewing Kit*. White paint flaked off the letters on to his fingers. It had never been opened. How long had Ellen been saving this? She hadn't been anywhere since she was married.

He pictured her alone in the sitting room, swirling the dregs of the Christmas-pudding brandy around her tumbler, and for a moment when he focused again on his paint-speckled fingers he imagined himself contaminated by a jinx.

He watched his stop approach and let it pass. Two drinks was always the worst. He was going to find a late bar and do the job properly.

3

ONE DAY, WHEN Ellen was still only five and had not long
ago been brought here to live, she was sitting on her
Granny's front step, frowning, when the rentman passed along
the street and stopped to speak to her.

– What's wrong, poppet? he asked, crouching down beside
her.

He had a kind smell so Ellen told him.

– Everything, she said.

The man considered her very seriously.

– Everything?

Ellen nodded. *Everything*.

The rentman looked at her another moment then sat back
on his bottom on the dusty pavement and let out a roar of
laughter. Ellen hid her face in her arm, ashamed at having been
taken in by him and being made to feel foolish.

And yet, she told herself today, she had been right all along.
Everything *was* wrong here. Even snow.

The snow did not drift down, as snow was meant to drift
down, white and fluffy into the yard, but was scattered from
the smudged brown clouds like slack shaken from a coal-sack.
Ellen stood by the back door, feet pinched and smarting cold
in last year's wellingtons, listening to the damp, sticky sound
of the flakes as they struck the insides of the mop bucket:
phut, phut, phut, phut. The sound matches made when caught
between wetted fingers. Old Mr Butler next door snuffed matches that way. Old Mr Butler next door balanced Woodbines
on his bottom lip then flicked them, lit, into his gummy mouth,
only to make them reappear a moment later, still smoking, on
the end of his tongue. Old Mr Butler was horrid. His laugh
was thick and liquidy and before he spoke he spat into a hanky
held up to his mouth.

Once, Ellen had seen him come right out on to his doorstep and spit into the street. She looked away at the time, but the spit was still there when she came home from school, a grey clot at the side of the road.

The remembered sight of it had Ellen squirming her hands deeper into her gabardine pockets, more glad than ever of the snug feel of the new mitts her best friend Rosemary had sent her from England. The parcel had arrived just that morning, a day late for Ellen's sixth birthday, and her mummy had helped her unpick the Sellotape so as not to rip the brown paper. Ellen had never had a parcel addressed just to her and she wanted to save every bit of it. The mitts were wrapped round twice with tissue-paper, not covered with bits and pieces left over from Christmas as most of her presents were. They were knitted in green, red and black wool and on the back of each hand a grinning snowman smoked a pipe. There was a card in the parcel too, made from coloured paper and flattened milk bottle tops. Ellen cried when she opened it. The whole inside was filled with Rosemary's big crawly writing, most of it Xs and Os.

Knuckles prap-prapped on glass behind her and looking over her shoulder Ellen saw her father at the kitchen window make a shape with his hands and another with his lips explaining it. Snowman. Ellen pulled her hands from her pockets, but as she turned away her gaze fell on the snow-slimed grille of the kitchen drain and, a foot or so to the right, the grey frozen twist of a wrung-out floorcloth which all through the summer had been crawling with earwigs.

She wasn't putting her good mitts into this snow for anything.

And yet she remembered her father's warning about sulks and long faces. She glanced behind her again and smiled, with the side of her mouth he could see at any rate, pushed her hair behind her ear, then, suddenly inspired, set off down the yard in an improvised hopscotch, never minding that stamping on the icy flagstones made her feet smart more.

By the time she reached the bottom of the yard he was gone. She blew air through her rounded lips in a series of alternating long and short puffs she called whistling (though the notes rarely survived the tricky journey from mind to mouth) and leant against the wall by a big blue-rimmed chipped enamel tub hanging from a nail. This tub was her granny's washing machine. The spin-drier was a mangle, two long rolling pins, turned by a handle, with which Granny Linden could somehow squeeze the dripping clothes till they were no more moist to touch than freshly kneaded dough.

To begin with, Ellen had thought her granny must be very poor, for she had no television either, just an old-fashioned wireless the size of a small chest of drawers. But then she noticed there was always enough money for buns and iced fingers and chocolate teacakes wrapped in foil, even when there was nobody special coming to visit, and she wasn't sure what to think any more. Except that Belfast wasn't Romford and that almost nothing she had grown up believing to be normal in England was guaranteed safe from reversal here.

That a toilet's place, for instance, was upstairs in the bathroom with the bath and wash-hand basin.

In fact, Granny Linden's toilet wasn't in the house at all, but outside, across the yard from where Ellen was now standing, in a sort of shed beside the coal-bunker. And it wasn't just her granny's house either – all the houses in the street had outside toilets, as did the houses in the next street and, Ellen could only suppose, since they looked much the same, in the street next to that, and the street next to that, and so on, all the way down the road into town.

Ellen had never heard of anything like it. Granny Linden, on the other hand, said that, yes, now that she mentioned it, she had *heard* of toilets in the house, but asked Ellen, her forehead furrowing, was she sure it was altogether healthy. Ellen (whose ear for irony was no duller than any other five-year-old's, but then again no keener) didn't know about healthy, but she could think of few things more disgusting than the pots she had discovered upstairs, stashed away beneath the beds. She nearly died when her mummy told her what they were for and refused to use hers, even after she had wet twice in the first few weeks trying to hold on till morning.

In the end she learnt how to find her way down into the

yard, preferring the groans and gurgles of the darkness to the indignity of squatting on a potty like an overgrown baby.

And in any case, in the months since her arrival the summer before, she had grown used to the outside toilet; more than used to, in fact; *fond of* almost. It was her pretend house, her refuge. To enter the toilet – as she did now to get out of the snow – was to retreat into her own thought-world; a world far removed from her granny's house and the distracting long-drawn-out ticking of the big black kitchen clock, whose alien system of Xs, Vs and Is had so confounded her painfully acquired sense of clock-time, where 3 alone was a quarter, 6 was a half and 12 the hour.

Despite being in the yard, the toilet was nearly always cosy inside, even today. There were different bits of carpet on the floor and a woolly bib round the base of the toilet itself. The lid too had a soft cover on it – pink or lemon or (today's) pale, pale green – and the spare toilet roll was hidden in the skirt of a white-bonneted doll. (Being oldendays style, the skirt was meant to puff out, that was the clever part.) Ellen made the doll her special friend in her pretend house. Her name was Rosemary and Ellen's name then was Louise. Ellen hated her own name. It was dull and old. When her daddy talked about names for the baby she asked him could he pick a new one for her.

– Tell you what, her daddy said, we could call you what your granny called her Auntie Ellen. Would that do you? What was it, Mammy?

– Nellie, Granny said, sucking in her cheeks as though eating a sherbet, and that was the last Ellen mentioned it.

There were times when she forgot how she used to envy her friends for having aunts, uncles, and grandparents living so close and longed for a return to the days when there were just the three of them and Granny Linden had turned up on the hall mat every second Saturday in a Basildon Bond envelope.

Thoughts such as that were at the back of the sulks and long faces her daddy had warned her about. She tried not to think them but they kept coming into her head anyway. If she told herself she was happy living in her granny's house, they told her she was miserable; if she told herself Belfast was nice, they told her it was horrid. The thoughts were forever saying horrid. That was something else her daddy had warned her about. The boys and girls at school would laugh at her if they heard her using that word, he said, not knowing that they laughed at her already – hard, forced laughs – because one day she had said *pop* instead of *lemonade*. And when Mr Kennedy had scolded them for braying like donkeys, they just saved up till break-time and teased her more, following her round the playground, calling her Lady Muck because of her posh English voice. Ellen didn't care. She thought they were all horrid too and after that exaggerated her accent by copying the announcers on her granny's wireless.

At least that way, she told Rosemary, she wouldn't be going back to England talking all Belfast:

I seen a *fillum*.
Brown bread and *budder*.

Rosemary stared up at her with a funny look on her face. Ellen had accidentally pressed her nose with her thumb while nursing her, making her cheeks spread out sideways. She pinched them back into shape and smoothed down her dress to stop the toilet-roll petticoats showing. The dolly had thin legs, but nicely thin, rounded at the back, not like Ellen's legs which were all knobbly and knock-kneed. If her daddy came into the room while her mummy was drying her after a bath he would start to sing *Dem Bones*, letting his arms swing loose at the elbows, or else moving his hands so fast from one knee to the other that it looked as though his legs were crossing over. And when he did that her mummy had to pull the two ends of the towel tight together to keep Ellen from laughing herself right out of it.

She had never imagined her daddy being able to sing. There was always a quiet space around him in her memory, except for Saturdays, when her mummy went out to her job in the Co-op and he clattered about in the kitchen making lunch – boiled egg beaten up in a cup, with more butter than Ellen liked, though she never said. After she started school he would talk to her very seriously during these lunchtimes about what

33

she had learnt that week and though he was her own father Ellen would have been less nervous saying her alphabet before the entire school, headmistress and all.

When she was very young and didn't know any better she had assumed that she and her mummy had always been together and had taken him in as an afterthought.

On Thursdays he paid them (thruppence in Ellen's hand and a brown paper packet in her mummy's) and brought them fish and chips for tea. The first payday after he started work in Belfast, however, he did not, as he usually did, give Ellen the tail-half of her mummy's fish but instead set a flat, battered circle on her plate.

– Wait till you taste this, he said.

– Jack, her mummy said, it'll be too spicy.

– Nonsense, he said and cut it open for her.

It was pink inside, steaming hot and oniony.

– That's what you call a proper pasty, he said. Try it, you'll love it.

– Well? he asked when she had finished eating.

Ellen nodded her head.

– What did I tell you? he said and he couldn't have been more pleased than if he'd invented and cooked it himself. Wasn't I right?

Ellen nodded again. The grease had left the top of her mouth and the backs of her teeth too dry to speak.

She made good and sure she found her voice, though, the day he brought her dulse.

– It's *seaweed*, she said.

– It's good for you, he said. Full of iron.

But Ellen, who couldn't see how the two statements went together, still turned her nose up and watched him eat the whole bag himself, half expecting that at any minute he would shout *Joke!* and open his mouth to show he hadn't been swallowing it at all, like the grass stems he spat into the pedal-bin when he came back from his Sunday walks.

Walking, like singing and eating seaweed, was something else her father hadn't shown much interest in before coming here. Whereas in Romford he had seldom been known to walk further than the bus-stop at the end of the road, in Belfast he set out alone every Sunday afternoon to walk his dinner off in the hills which reared up blunt against the roof-lines of the streets beyond Granny Linden's.

– There's no comparison, he said. You know you've been somewhere when you've been walking in the mountains.

But Ellen worried about him up there on his own and when, one Sunday in autumn, he still had not come home long after dark, she petrified herself with gruesome imaginings, fuelled by the names of the mountains themselves: *Cave* Hill, *Wolf* Hill, *Black* Mountain. Her mummy explained that the clocks had gone back, hoping that would calm her; but it only succeeded in terrifying her more. Ellen took this backwardness – the ultimate reversal – to be somehow bound up with the slow ticking of her granny's clock and if it hadn't been for the street door being opened at that precise moment she would have tried to lift the clock herself and shake it with all her might to make it go faster. Instead she ran into the hall, swallowing sobs, and clung to her father as he struggled out of his coat and shoes, the smell of his hot feet mingling with the smell of chewed grass and the sooty smell of evening let in when he opened the door.

Later, curled against him in the armchair by the fire, she forgot for a while that Belfast was horrid and that her best friend Rosemary lived miles and miles away in Romford, Essex, and fell asleep soothed by the rise and fall of his chest and by the soft regular clucking of his teeth as the breath passed in and out of his mouth.

The dirty clouds had passed on, trailing their snow behind them. Rosemary the doll had gone home to her shelf where she was having tea with her next-door neighbour, Captain Domestos – gallant and upright as ever in his blue uniform and red cap. Ellen stood in the doorway watching runnels of meltwater zigzag across the flagstones and under the gate to the back alley. She was just wondering were they strong enough yet to race matchsticks on when, suddenly, as if yanked up by an invisible rope, an enormous ginger tomcat landed with a snow-sticky *phut* on the yard wall. The cat crouched low, seeing Ellen, who, seeing it, shrank down inside her gabardine.

– Shoo, pussy! she whispered through her teeth.

The pussy opened his mouth, showing his; said nothing. Stared.

They both moved at the same time, the cat down into the Butlers' yard, Ellen round the other side of the toilet door, nailing it shut with her shoulders. She squeezed her eyes together hard, trying to blot out the sight of the cat's baggy fur-belly swishing ice off the wall as it bolted. She knew if she let the image take root in her mind she would lose her nerve coming down to the toilet at nights. After the last time she encountered the cat there, sides sagging over the narrow ledge of the wall, she had had a nightmare that it found its way into her room while she slept and covered her face, stifling her breathing. Then, it had taken another bed-wetting and talk of enforced potty-training to persuade her to risk the yard again.

Granny Linden was afraid of the cat getting into the house too, but not for the reason Ellen was. Granny Linden had a goldfish and was sure the cat was stalking it.

– I never saw a cat round here before we had it, she said and when Ellen's daddy said he doubted the cat even knew the fish was there added:

– You'd be surprised the noses cats have, they can sniff anything out.

Ellen, though, wasn't the least bit surprised. She didn't think your nose needed to be all that special to sniff out her granny's goldfish. It was stinking and, what's more, it looked as bad as it smelt, coiled round its bowl like a you-know-what. But much as she loathed the goldfish, Ellen was always careful not to say anything that might hurt her granny's feelings. Grandpa had given it to her as a present, after all, and now Grandpa was dead and in heaven. A picture on the wireless, next to the goldfish bowl, showed him smiling, slightly out of focus, beside another man whose shirt, teeth and sprouting hair were all a uniform radiant white. Nowadays, Ellen understood that this second man was her Great-uncle Geordie from Melbourne, but originally she had taken him for God himself. He looked old enough.

Grandpa Linden was the first person Ellen had ever known to die, though since her memories of him alive were drawn entirely from a single week he and Granny had spent in Essex when Ellen was three and a half, and were, therefore, as hazy as the photo on the wireless, his death appeared to her not as a sudden departure, but a gradual fading away. And though her grandpa himself was eight weeks buried by the time she came to Belfast, traces of him remained everywhere she looked about the house: the coarse socks, raggedly holed, spilling from the mending basket; the wodge of boxing stories torn from newspapers and stuffed under cushions awaiting a scrapbook; the quartet of pipes in their rack on the hearth, whitening at the mouths. She quickly realised that the chair to the right of the fireplace would always be *his* seat, no matter who else sat in it; and even now, all these months on, nobody drank from the china mug with the gold leaf worn away at the lip without first turning it left-handed, out of respect.

— Ellen?

Her mother's voice called out from the top of the yard and footsteps splattered down the flagstones to the toilet.

— Ellen? Are you in there?

Ellen stood aside to clear the door. Her mummy burst in, wearing one of Granny's old shawls about her shoulders and the short fleecy-lined boots with the zip up the front which Ellen had seen her make a face at on Christmas morning. They were the only shoes that weren't tight on her ankles now.

— Quick, out of the way, she said.

When Mummy had to go, Mummy had to go. The baby did that to her. It was what Granny called *low*. Daddy said that proved what he'd told them from the start (though exactly why he didn't say), that the baby was going to be a boy.

— Are you going or staying? Ellen's mummy asked her, flashing a half-moon of distended abdomen as she eased herself down on to the wooden seat. Shut that door whatever you're doing, I'm freezing.

Ellen chose the outside of the door. Even though she had been told it would be weeks yet before the baby came, she was still afraid every time her mummy went to the toilet that it would simply fall out like a huge plop. She held her breath waiting for the splash, but the only sound was the sound of weeing, then paper being pulled from the roll.

The chain creaked, releasing the water and Ellen released her breath, making a visible *pah!* in front of her mouth. Anticipation, as always, gave way to disappointment and frustration. Why couldn't her mummy just have the baby and be done with it? Why, for that matter, the bad thoughts chipped in, did she have to have a baby in the first place? It didn't seem to make her very happy. For her shape wasn't the only thing to have altered lately; even when the bump was still only small (so small Ellen herself could imitate it by pushing her tummy out hard) her moods, once so reliable and easily understood, had undergone a transformation, becoming as impenetrable to Ellen as the dial of her granny's clock. She would have given anything in the world at that moment to have had her mummy back the way she used to be, before the baby, before Belfast.

But here she came out of the toilet, catching the shawl about her undiminished girth.

– What are you up to? she asked Ellen.

– Nothing, Ellen said.

Nothing comes of nothing, the old mummy would have said, half banter, half scold. *There's plenty you can help me with if you're stuck for something to do.* Ellen knew there would be no rebuke, even in play, this time. Her mummy simply continued up the yard, using the wall for support.

She had one swollen foot already in the scullery when she suddenly threw back her head.

– Damn it to hell! she shouted (startling the ginger tomcat who was just that moment venturing back on to the wall) and, turning, splashed down the yard again to the toilet.

4

ONE WEEK BEFORE Easter, six days before Drew was due to fly to England for the long weekend, his first trip back since returning to Belfast, Melanie phoned him at the shop and told him she'd landed a fortnight's film work in New York, leaving Thursday.

– New York? Drew said. What about our holiday?

– I know, I'm sorry, Melanie said. But this is *film*, this is important. We'll have to make it another week.

– But I've already booked my ticket.

– Can't you ask them to change it?

– No, he said, I can't. It's a special saver.

– Oh.

He heard her think about it.

– Well I can send you the money, she said.

– Oh, that's fucking great.

An old woman, got up in what appeared to be an assortment of hearth rugs, peered at him through the book-token spinner. Not a regular customer, thank God. Hardly a customer in the true sense of the word at all. *Do yous not do men's longjohns no more?* she'd asked him a minute before. *Yous always used to do men's longjohns.* Drew turned his back, facing the window.

– The money's not the thing, he whispered, digging the receiver tight against his ear. I want to see you.

A hole appeared where Melanie was supposed to have spoken.

– Melanie?

– I know, she whispered back at length, her voice unexpectedly close and blurred. I know.

For a moment then everything fell away but the phone against his face. His breath came back at him hot from the handset, confusing his mind already awash with the sound of her breath in his ear. He closed his eyes and the slats of the mouthpiece brushed his lips, light as muslin. If I were to swallow, he thought, if both of us were to swallow and swallow again, the phones would dissolve entirely and we would be devouring each other's faces.

– But we can hold on for another fortnight, Melanie said.

A loud horn blaring from the docks – the berthing pangs of an incoming ship – reduced her voice to a distant tinniness. Drew opened his eyes again, looking out on to Castle Place.

– The next few weeks are no good for me, he said, his own voice finding volume.

– No? she said.

– No.

– Oh, well.

– Oh, well, he said.

Drew stood just inside the shop door, reassessing his plans now that Melanie was going to New York instead of spending Easter with him and now that, to top it all, it had come on to rain in his lunch-hour. A steady, smoky-smelling drizzle, nullifying the outline of the Antrim hills, so that the city looked to have been unmoored from its surroundings and set adrift.

When you can't see Black Mountain, it means it's raining; when you can, it means it's going to rain.

A Belfast proverb. Bum-bumping philosophy. Not so much spoken and heard as transmitted direct from bone to bone, ground into him as he lurched, half asleep, down the Whiterock Road on Sunday afternoons, an outcrop of his father's head, with its hair tufted into tiny, fist-sized handles where Drew, waking in a whiplash panic, clung from time to time to keep from jolting off his shoulders.

Strong daddy. Strong daddy's hands closing reassuringly round his shins and calves.

– Fuck it, Drew said and pulling his jacket to him set off, head lowered against the rain, jogging up High Street and out through the security gate towards the Albert Clock.

He sprinted across the Victoria Street crossing on flashing amber, drawing a blare of protest from the front-line cars, and, still at a run, cut across Prince's Street carpark, only coming to a halt finally on the Donegall Quay side because his specs were streaming so much he was effectively running blind. He shook the water off the lenses and pocketed them, then wiped his face with his cuff, wiped his cuff on the opposite sleeve and the sleeve, in turn, on the back of his trousers.

The river was at that stagnant point of high tide that signified the turn had already begun far below. Drew imagined the irresistible suck of it – the saggin, draggin, Lagan, emptying like dirty, communal bathwater into the lough.

Something moved on the face of one of the mountains of scrap metal on the far side of the river and as Drew looked on, specless spectator, the figure of a man, his clothes, face and hair of a colour with the heap (as though he and it both had spent too long exposed to wind and rain), gradually detached itself and stood for a moment at the summit, shouldering the skeleton of a wheel, silhouetted in a raised fist against the name-plate of John Kelly's coal yard. Then the figure began to descend the opposite side, merging by degrees with the rusting mound, so that in the end the fist's rise and fall might have been no more than the molecular flexing of an enormous listless organism.

Wiping his face, cuff and sleeve once more, Drew hurried on a further fifty yards till he came to a porticoed doorway driven between the ship-chandlers and goods yards. He frisked himself then dug into his right-hand jacket pocket. Somewhere in the snarl of Kleenex and thread he trailed out was an address card which, when he had extricated it, he checked against the brass plate set in one of the pillars: *Quayside Design*. He stuffed the bundle back into his pocket and, taking a stiff shot of damp air, pushed down on the tubular steel door handle and went inside.

The open-plan office in which he found himself was all brightness and space after the lowering clouds out front, as though the glass extension he could see at the rear of the building was designed not merely to *at*tract light but to *ex*tract it, bleeding the surrounding sky of brilliance; as though, in fact, it was the cause of the clouds out front being lowered in the first place. The approach to this extension was flanked by two pairs of angled, and currently abandoned, drawing boards and at its centre was a paper-strewn slab of a desk, behind which, when Drew entered, a small dark-haired woman of about thirty – a chrome Toblerone gave her name as Kay Morris – was talking glumly into a large black telephone of a similar age.

– Yes, she was saying. Of course, yes. Yes, of course.

Then, catching sight of Drew over by the drawing boards, her small frame contracted still further in what at first sight appeared to be a silent sneeze but was meant to convey pleasured surprise. She flashed him an exaggerated teeth-clenched smile, then let her jaw go slack and slumped forward over the desk, eyes crossed in a dumb-show of brain-deadening boredom.

– *Yes*, Mr McAlpine, she said snapping upright again and nodding extravagantly. Monday? Of *course*, Mr McAlpine. Thank *you*, Mr McAlpine.

She replaced the receiver with a flourish, then, levelling her index finger at it, went through the motions of casual execration: bend it, stretch it, double it and send it.

– Old fool.

Drew watched her push the chair back from the desk with her foot, marvelling at the economy of effort with which ham and calf met and parted, the body's efficient transmission of power; a physics lesson in tartan tights.

– What's the matter? the woman said, addressing him at last. She pack you in?

– Hardy-har-har, Drew said as sourly as he was able, though in truth he had a job keeping a straight face.

Kay Morris, he recalled, was nothing if not direct.

– I just thought you might like a drink.

– Now? she said, her eyes drawing his to the paperwork on her desk.

– Or later.

– Later, she said. What time do you finish?

– Quarter past five, but I've plenty to keep me going if that's too early.

– Not at all, a quarter past suits me fine. I'll call for you, will I?

The words themselves sounded innocent enough, but they were accompanied by such a knowing look that Drew, who

had in fact, as Kay rightly guessed, been on the point of propos-
ing the opposite arrangement, felt it incumbent on his dignity
to go along with them.

— All right, he said, offering as further evidence of his equa-
nimity: Ask at the till if I'm not on the shop floor.

There was, of course, nothing to feel guilty about in any
case. All up and down the country on a Friday night people
met other people for drinks after work without implications.
True, such meetings were more easily justified (always supposing you needed to justify them which Drew, in this case, certainly didn't) if they happened to be with people you actually
worked *with*, but that was not an option that was currently
open to Drew. The fact of the matter was that the settling-in
period at work had gone on rather longer than he had anticipated. The office side of things he had well under control:
common sense and routine for the most part. But he still
detected an unease now and then when he was on the shop
floor. Talk was either very small or very strained and any
attempt at familiarity was awkwardly refused. Even Sian, with
whom he had seemed to be making such good headway in the
early days, had not opened up as he had hoped, as though in
cracking the shell of her reserve he had succeeded only in
uncovering another, tougher layer underneath.

At one stage he had tried to put into operation a plan, much
favoured, he knew, by management in branches across the
water, to have everyone round to his flat for dinner: three at a
time, since three was a manageable number for conversation
and since, besides, he only had place settings for four. But the
first week two of the three guests phoned him with last-minute
excuses and he dined alone that night with Pamela Magill.

— Bosses are still bosses here, Pamela said. Staff don't mind
working for you, but they don't expect to have to like you as
well.

Drew wasn't about to argue with his only guest, but deep
down he was convinced that Pamela had got it wrong. The
dinner party idea, though, was quietly dropped and, one month
on, the purity of his conviction remained unsullied by anything
so grubby as active corroboration. The shop-floor reticence was
undiminished. To the best of his knowledge, no one at Book-

store was even aware of Melanie's existence, with the possible exception of Pamela herself and Pamela would be on the five o'clock Dublin train this evening, as she was most Friday evenings.

Indeed, far from Kay's appearance exciting comment, Drew began to suspect he could have been fucking half of Belfast and his colleagues would neither have known nor cared.

He had met Kay the Thursday of the first week he was back, the night he had been to Ellen and Derek's for dinner. The bus from the New Houses had deposited him in Bradbury Place, already gloomy from a combination of his own musings, the driver's Country & Western and the fast-fading effects of his sister's brandy, and finding himself plunged into a still deeper gloom as he realised that — the much-vaunted one o'clock licences notwithstanding — getting another drink in Belfast was not going to be as easy as he had expected. There were queues everywhere, it seemed, the longest of them for a students-only night (and therefore including, presumably, at least some Catholics) outside a bar cum nightclub in Sandy Row, a matter of yards from the Rangers Supporters Club — seat of the local chapter of the Romophobic Society — and a matter of feet from the spot where every July the famous Twelfth arch was raised.

Drew trudged up the road from Bradbury Place past the university, being refused at one packed bar after another, and was just on the verge of calling it a night when he remembered Finney's and doubled back.

Drinking after eleven o'clock had been an established fact of life in Finney's bar long before anyone had thought of enshrining the practice in law. This was all the more remarkable, or else all the less, Drew himself could never quite decide, when you considered that one of its near neighbours was a heavily fortified police station. Drew drank there most weekends in the spring and summer of his last year at school after the bar was taken up, in that mysterious way that bars such as Finney's were taken up in those pre-Belfast-is-buzzing days, as though telepathically agreed upon, by bikers, mods, punks, skins, new romantics and old hippies, by art students, Queen's students, schoolkids, dolekids, apprentices, junior bank clerks and musicians: aspiring, despairing and just plain desperate. Taken up, moreover, by teenage girls as well as teenage boys, the former stimulating, like an overdose of oestrogen, a sudden growth of female toilets in hitherto resolutely male bars. Though in the case of Finney's perhaps *toilets* is overstating it somewhat, the convenience (if that is the word) there consisting as it did of a single porcelain bowl, unencumbered by a seat, in a hastily vacated, inadequately plumbed broom cupboard, without wash-hand basin, bin, or even, on occasion, functioning light.

To begin with, the Finney's old guard, adepts of no little repute in the use of those venerable barroom weapons the banter and the slag, had met this incursion with spirited resistance. But the invaders were armour-plated with the indifference of youth and, eventually, seeing their insults bounce off, ineffectual, and seeing too the broom cupboard become a toilet for girls with starched and scarified hair, or girls with next to no hair at all, the old men lost heart. Taking their half'uns and bottles of stout they regrouped around the totem of the television in the opposite corner and there offered up Saturday prayers to their septicipital deity, the ITV7, smiting their brows and strewing its altar with pink and yellow petals, the rent receipts of their oblations.

I was going to fucking back that.

With their backs to the well of the bar they pretended all was as it had been, continuing to converse below the racket of the newly installed jukebox in their arcane language of yankees, quads, tricasts, and ten-bob doubles. Indeed, listening to them talk, you would hardly have known they were in the same bar as the young people at all. They even called it by a different name. For despite the iron sign above the front window, they never referred to it as Finney's, preferring instead the name on the side of the ship whose black and white photograph hung in an oak frame behind the bar: the Titanic. Over the years other Titanic souvenirs – key-rings, thimbles, commemorative matchboxes, cups and plates – had attached themselves in barnacle-like clusters around the bottom of this picture and, when last Drew saw it, a sizeable flotilla of postcards and yellowed newspaper photographs of itself had steamed, four-funnelled, in its wake.

Drew's Grandpa Linden, then a boy of sixteen and just started into his time, had worked on the building of the liner and its name was spoken with reverence in the house long after his death; by Drew himself before that last summer in Belfast, when a freak army Saracen wheel bounced, one, two, *crunch*, and he sat at the counter of Finney's bar, downing Pernod and blackcurrants hand over fist, seeing the name multiply kaleidoscopically on the wall in front of him – carved, engraved, printed, painted – then finally shatter into seven inconsequential upper-case letters, leaving him contemplating, as though for the first time, a single, incontrovertible fact: *the fucking thing sank.* Where else, he had thought, but here could failure be so revered? And the next moment he was spluttering liquorice-sharp Pernod down his nostrils as an image flashed into his mind, the inchoate but vivid emblem of a unified and independent Ireland: a Dublin-born schoolteacher delivering the Proclamation of the Republic from the deck of a foundering Belfast-built ship.

Irishglug and Irishgurgle: In the glug of Glug and the gurgle gurgle gurgle.

(Four months later, barefooted, trousers rolled, he had waded into a fountain on an English university campus and acted out this vision; an impersonation which had mortified his first lover, Kelly Thorpe, whose great-grandparents on her mother's side etc., etc., and delighted the effusive drunk standing on the sidelines, applauding as enthusiastically as his voluminous vinyl shopper would allow.)

Never again, he had sworn that summer's night, as he puked, pure purple, into the trough of the urinals; meaning not, for once, the drink but the place itself, Finney's bar, the Titanic, that shrine to imperfection and ruin. Never again.

So what on earth was he doing going back there now?

Doubt crashed down in his mind with the force of a cartoon safe, pulverising the last eight years of his life, melding Drew-18 and Drew-26 together to teeter in a wide, Loony Tune circle before finally pegging out on the spot where they started, and the awful thought occurred to him again that going away had been after all nothing more than the prelude to coming back. *For every leaving a returning,* as his Granny Linden had said, with all the conviction with which other people say the sun rises in the east and sets in the west; refusing to kiss him goodbye the day he left for university, not even bothering to look at him, but speaking, as was her habit, with her eyes turned upwards, as though reading off the lines scrolled across her forehead: *I've never seen one leave yet that didn't come back.*

Except Uncle Michael, Drew might have said, but held off, suddenly unsure whether even Uncle Michael disproved her rule. For Uncle Michael didn't go willingly and Uncle Michael would have come back too if he'd had any say in it; if he hadn't fallen face-down, wounded, and drowned (Irishglug and Irishgurgle) twenty feet from the Normandy shore, as much as to say, the only way you'll get me out is in a box.

In fact, could his granny not just as easily have seized on Uncle Michael to argue her point with still greater force, that all that were *able* came back in the end? As meek, Drew thought, as schoolchildren who are so terrified of the playground bully they don't even wait for him to seek them out, but run to him instead, turning out their own pockets.

All came back and submitted themselves to the bully's remorseless and reductive interrogation, his *what are you? what are you?* – the metaphysical mugging. Helping to rob themselves of themselves.

– Watch it there, fella, you're blocking the footpath.

– Sorry.

Drew stepped aside to let a man and woman by. He had been standing, lost in thought, at the bottom of Botanic Avenue, gazing across Shaftesbury Square. The couple glanced over their shoulders as they passed, following the direction of his stare: traffic islands, public toilets, Ulster Bank House, with its cast-aluminium sculptures, like two mutilated angels spiralling from the sky.

The woman was the first to laugh. The man shushed her then sniggered too. Drew closed his eyes. What was he playing at? Getting himself into such a state over an old woman's ramblings, the sour fruits of a lifetime misspent reading the *Sunday Post* and the *People's Friend*. It was all really very straightforward. He was in Northern Ireland working for a year, at most, and now he was going to a bar he once frequented but then grew out of to see could he get a drink before bed. He turned into Donegall Pass, his shoulders straightening and his face settling into an expression of reasonableness the more he repeated this to himself. Indeed so completely did he recover his composure that when he rounded the police station's cement fortifications to discover the Finney's name-plate gone and the old brick frontage replaced by a full-length frosted-glass window, he did not even break stride but marched straight up to the matching frosted-glass door as though this was what he had expected all along.

In the centre of the door was a circle of clear glass twelve inches in diameter with the name *jazzbo brown's* written across it in frosted italics. To the right was a black button underwritten with a single word: *push*.

Drew pushed. A blip of red light pulsed in a corner of the lintel. Stopped, pulsed again. A piano trilled coolly deep inside the building. Drew waited.

The door opened at length with a diffident buzz, admitting him to an enclosed hallway where a young woman sat at a desk, with a money box and a pad of violet ink, practising stamping the bar's logo on a sheet of foolscap. Behind her, his face half in shadow to maximise the sense of menace (though he could have managed all right without it), stood an immaculately dressed bouncer. Drew paid the woman £2 for the privilege of having her perform her practised stamp on the back of his hand (it smudged) and tried to ignore the bouncer's stare, which he felt covering every inch of him, as though searching for some foolhardy infringement of his own very stringent dress code. He could see the headlines already: *Killer confesses – Oxfam suit made me snap*. Despite the suit's lowly origins, though, despite even the missing button, Drew was allowed to progress inside. He sat on the first free seat he saw, an American-style bar stool at the near end of the new-old, black marbled counter, and ordered a bourbon (of which there were as many varieties on display as there were Irish whiskeys) and a Czech lager chaser.

The Titanic picture and all its attendant clutter had, of course, gone the way of the Finney's name-plate. The back wall of the bar between the optics and the chrome knobs of the beer engines was now a seamless expanse of mirror in which the customers at the counter could watch themselves to see they didn't drink too much and at the same time, without turning round, keep an eye on what was happening behind them. Looking in this mirror, Drew now located the trilling piano he had heard from outside, completing a trio with double-bass and drums in a distant, atmospherically cramped corner of the room — where the broom cupboard-toilet used to be, though even as he sat there the memory of that was fading. In the same way, he had no sooner reflected on the unlikelihood of any of the former customers, old or young, surviving the compound hostility of the camera's remote appraisal and the bouncer's fastidious glare, than they too were driven from his mind by the applause which at that moment greeted the end of one of the trio's numbers.

He finished off his drinks and had just ordered another lager when he became aware that the reflection of the woman on the stool next to his was watching him from the mirror; and, when she saw his reflection register the fact, the woman herself turned to him.

– You don't know me, do you? she said and smiled.

She was right. Even with his specs on Drew couldn't place her. He searched her face for hidden clues, fleshing out her cheeks a bit, growing out her high-cut bob, hennaing it, bleaching it and finally cropping it off altogether, in the hope that somewhere along the line he could match her up with some lingering ghost of Finney's past. But it was no use.

– I'm sorry, he said. Should I?

– *Moby-Dick*, she said, not the least put out, indeed, if anything, glad to have confirmed to herself that he had in fact forgotten her.

– The day before yesterday. You had to climb up a ladder to find it for me.

Drew remembered the ladder well enough: middle of the lunch-hour rush, short of staff on the shop floor. But he'd been so busy composing an acerbic memo for the heads of all departments to keep abreast of shelf stock levels he'd barely noticed the customer he was serving at the time.

– Of course, *Moby-Dick*, he said and nodded.

– On you go, she said, you don't remember at all.

– I will the next time though.

– Don't hold your breath. Have you seen the size of that book?

She laughed, so he did too. And that appeared to be that. The woman leaned over the counter to hail a barman and Drew watched himself sip his lager and watched too the trio behind him. They had become engrossed in an extended improvisation, of which Drew could only grasp stray phrases, as if listening to a debate in a language he was still struggling to learn, and he made yet another mental note, though in capitals this time and heavily underlined, to BUY SOME JAZZ.

– You're new there, aren't you?

The woman beside him had her drink but seemed in no hurry to move.

– Yes, just this week, Drew said, then, not wanting her to think he spent his whole day running up and down ladders, felt compelled to add: Did you know Simon who used to work there – the assistant manager? I've taken over from him.

– And you are?

The woman held out her right hand.

– Sorry, Drew said, swapping his glass over to free his. Drew Linden.

– Kay Morris, the woman said.

Their hands met and exchanged formal credentials in the space between them.

– I bet you it's a great place to work, Kay said and while Drew was still formulating an *Oh, I don't know*, went on: And such a beautiful shop too. Belfast would be lost without you.

Drew received the compliment on the shop's behalf.

– I'm glad you think so.

– Though I don't know what I'm being so nice about you for, Kay said now, you turned me down.

– You're kidding, you applied for a job there too?

– Oh, not selling books, Kay gave a light disparaging laugh which rather detracted from her praise of a minute before. Away at the beginning, I mean, when you were refurbishing the shop.

Kay, it turned out, ran a design company – part of the prestige Laganside development – somewhere around the docks. Very small, she said, like her (and it was true, she couldn't have been more than five feet one or two). But, unlike her, still growing. She owned a flat in one of the new town houses just round the corner from *jazzbo brown's* and often came in here for a drink if she'd been working late.

Drew's glass was empty and Kay insisted on refilling it and of course Drew, when the time came, would hear nothing but he would buy her one back.

They sat at the bar drinking and talking. The jazz band played in the distant, astmospherically cramped corner. They ordered another bottle each. Kay paid. The band played. They drank and talked on and on.

By the time last orders was called, each had begun to construct a past of sorts for the other.

Kay, so Drew's version of her went, had studied design in Glasgow (which of course wasn't half the city then that it was now), though throughout her four years there she came back to Belfast as often as once a month due to some Big Thing she had going then, implying by the ironic emphasis she gave it that the Thing in question had not turned out to be as Big as she had thought at the time.

Kay, for her part, learnt that Drew had left Northern Ireland in 1981, the year she had returned, and was only back for a short time filling in until he went to Paris. His movements around England in the years between finishing university and arriving here in *jazzbo brown's*, however, made no sense and therefore were not, she decided, being fully explained. She decided further that the mysterious, indeterminately sexed *person I was sharing with in such and such a place* was, in fact, (a) the same person in every place (b) a woman at that, and (c) sharing more than just the bills. From what she could gather, though, he was living here on his own. She gave him a couple of opportunities to confirm or deny this but he passed them all up and in the end she broached the subject herself.

– Do you not find it funny on your own again after all that time sharing with *people*.

She loaded the last word as heavily as she could. It caught him off guard; he looked up, shrugged, mumbled something.

Now, Kay, she told herself, if you don't ask you don't get.

– So did your girlfriend not want to come over with you?

Drew tried to laugh it off.

– What makes you so sure there is one?

– There usually is.

– Does that mean there's usually a boyfriend too?

– Usually, but not always.

She smiled.

The question and answer slalom had been so rapid that Drew did not realise the distance they had travelled until that final smile. He wondered now why he had not just spelt everything out from the start instead of having the information teased out of him this way.

– Well, said Kay, did she not want to come?

– Melanie?

Drew felt better now that he had at least said her name; a real person was a stiffer deterrent than an abstract construct.

– Melanie has her own career. Anyway, I'll not be here that long.

They were standing at the door of the bar together. Kay took a card from her purse.

– This is where I work. And this – (she scribbled on the back) – is where I live.

Drew was glad they had come outside. The temperature had dropped. All he wanted was to get home.

– Give us a call if you fancy a drink some night.

Drew looked at the card then abandoned it to the depths of his jacket pocket.

– I will, he said, but really, he thought, I won't at all.

Yet here he was, six weeks on, standing, drunk, before Kay Morris's bookshelves while Kay in the kitchen made coffee and Melanie in England packed for New York.

A funny thing happened this evening when Kay and Drew returned together to *jazzbo brown's*. The shadowy bouncer had let Kay past but stopped Drew with a hand on his sleeve.

– Excuse me, he said. Don't I remember you?

– I wouldn't think so, Drew said, wanting to distance himself from any imagined slight. I was only ever here the once. Ages ago. Oh, weeks and weeks now.

– That's what I thought, the bouncer said and Drew inwardly yelped. I was looking at you then. You're Drew Linden, aren't you?

He took a step into the light.

– *Ralph*?

Eight years previously, Ralph Tibbs was a great beanpole of a skinhead, with twelve-hole Docs and knee-length combat trousers, tolerated rather than accepted by the other skins in Finney's who thought him too soft and too ridiculous to be the genuine article. I mean to say, who ever heard of a skinhead called Ralph? The name he had managed to carry off in time, by learning to say it in a burp, but he was still a skinny-looking big glipe. Until now, that was. Ralph had gained, Drew guessed, five or six stone since last they met. Not flab either, but muscle, spread evenly over his wattly frame and baked solid.

He mangled Drew's fingers in his grip and grinned.

– Drew Linden. Haven't seen you in years.

– Been away, Drew said.

– What *away* away or just away?

– Just away.

Ralph was still mangling his fingers.

– That what brought you back? he asked, winking at the door Kay had just passed through.

Drew didn't want to go into it, didn't want to say he was only here marking time. He snuff-laughed and gestured with his free hand: Men . . . Women . . . Life.

– What about you, Ralph?

– Married, Ralph said. Wee lad of three. Living out in Bangor.

– Do you see anything of – Drew had to cast around for the names of Ralph's old skinhead pals – Bradso, Tommy and that crowd?

Ralph let go of his hand.

– Those boys? he said and shook his head. Bad news those boys. Now they have been *away* away.

He skewed the next word out of earshot of the cashier – *Involved* – then continued in his normal voice.

– Nah, this is as close as I get to the pubs these days. Couple of hours in the gym's more my line.

And with that he leaned across and opened the door for Drew, as proudly as if he was opening the door to his own front room.

– Quer changes, eh? he said.

They drank a lot that night, Kay and Drew. Drank methodically; drank, sometimes, without tasting. Drank to fill the hours between a quarter past five and one in the morning, so that when one o'clock did come round they would have an excuse for the impulsive doing of what they had been planning on doing in any case since a quarter past five.

There were times, though, in the middle of the evening when it looked touch and go whether they'd be able to stand each other that long.

They hadn't exactly got off on the right foot. Kay's eyes had darkened when she called at the shop to pick Drew up and found him waiting for her in the street outside.

– That was lucky, he said. I got finished bang on quarter past.

The rain hadn't let up since lunchtime. Kay gave him a look.

– Would you not have been better waiting inside?

– I'm only out this minute, he said.

He was already several yards down the street. Kay had to scurry to keep up and so was otherwise occupied when Pamela Magill, getting a lift this evening from a southern sales rep, left Bookstore half an hour later than she usually did on a Friday.

– Anyway, Drew stopped at the corner, what difference does it make?

– No difference to me.

Kay kept walking, pounding the pavement as though wanting to leave a hole in it.

– Get wet, for all I care.

They both rallied and made more of an effort when they reached the bar. Too much of an effort perhaps. Conversation after conversation foundered on the rocks of over-politeness and even the *jazzbo's* house band couldn't fill the ensuing silences. It was during one of these that Kay asked the barman for a packet of cigarettes. Drew's brow buckled.

– I didn't know you smoked, he said.

– You don't know much, Kay snapped back.

Bitch, she thought and lit up.

– I've cut down loads, she said, trying to make some amends. My mother swears I only do it now to annoy her.

She flapped the smoke away from her eyes and nose, lost her balance and banged her elbow on the new-old, black-marbled counter.

– Annoy myself, more like, she said crossly, righting herself and rubbing her funny-bone.

The whole routine was so comical that Drew smiled despite himself. Kay stopped rubbing and looked at him narrowly. Then her stern face collapsed into an answering smile.

They knew after that they would probably be able to stick it out till one.

In due course, coffee was offered by Kay, accepted by Drew, and acknowledged by both as prop and prompter combined.

Well, it seemed to say, *here we are then*.

Kay played her part by boiling the kettle and filling the cups, and while she was out of the room Drew played his by taking up position (albeit a little unsteadily), stage left, at her bookshelves.

– Do you not find, he said when Kay returned with the coffee, other people's books absolutely fascinating.

– Oh, *ab-so-lute-ly fasc-in-at-ing*, Kay parodied the inebriate's overcareful enunciation, wobbling across the syllables – a verbal tightrope walked on stilts – and grinning at her own drunken devilment.

She handed him a mug. The coffee was too hot, they slurped when they meant to sip. Drew wished Kay would offer to put a record on, but instead she made a sudden lunge across him and pulled a glossy-backed picture book from the shelves.

– Wait till I show you, she said flipping back the pages between her middle finger and thumb, as though telling banknotes.

Such handling of books would normally have appalled Drew.

– What? he said, too far gone even to notice.

55

Kay was jabbing her finger at the figure of a woman in a long white dress, with a white hat and white parasol, crossing a tram-filled street.

— Who is she?

— Who?

— The woman you're pointing at.

Kay looked under her finger.

— Not her: all of it. Look. She raised the book closer to his face.

— What do you see?

An Edwardian cityscape. The first thing that struck him was that everyone was wearing a hat. The second thing that struck him was the distinctive building in the middle distance to the right of the picture, with its elaborately curving bracket of an upper storey. It stood, as he had never before seen it stand, in its immaculate wholeness. But still he could not prevent his foreseeing eyes imposing on it the lines of future divisions, and soon they were drawn to one section in particular, most familiar and least changed.

— Well? Notice anything?

— Our shop, Drew said.

— Hallelujah, Kay said. My arm's breaking holding this.

The book began to flop over. Drew put a hand at the back to help support it. The coffee drifted out of the orbit of their thoughts.

— See the old trams? Kay said.

Drew saw them.

— See the gunmaker's? he said, joining in. See the gas lamps?

There were two index fingers crawling over the page now, while underneath the glossy cover two hands made furtive contact.

See this? See this?

Their legs were touching. Drew's knee came to halfway up the thigh of Kay's tartan tights.

See this? See this?

And then all at once they ran out of things to point at. The book was abandoned, its usefulness spent. They stood side by side, legs touching, staring dead ahead at the bookshelves. So very nearly there. Another little boost was all they needed. Kay pinned her hopes on one more book and stretched to reach it down from a shelf above her head.

– Remember . . . she started to say, but got no further. She came down heavily off her tiptoes, falling against his chest, forcing an *oof* from him.

– Oh, God, I'm sorry. She rubbed his breastbone. Fucking fairy-feet, me.

– No, don't be. It's OK.

He put his hand on her hand, then suddenly, dramatically, gripped it to his shoulder.

Here we go, she thought.

They jabbed kisses at each other for a time, finding their range, before finally connecting in a voracious complication of lips, tongues and teeth. Their heads woozed when they came out of the clinch, their necks hurt from stretching. They half carried each other, half shuffled to a plum-coloured leather chesterfield, where they stopped just long enough for Drew to run his hands vaguely but suggestively up and down the outside of Kay's clothes and for Kay to twig that before she could reciprocate she had to let go of the book she was holding: *Moby-Dick*. This accomplished they helped each other up again and headed, still kissing, Kay, drunk, in charge, for the bedroom.

As soon as the door was open Kay realised she'd forgotten to set the radiator to auto before she left for work. The room was freezing. She retrieved her tongue from his mouth.

– Let's get into bed, she said.

– Un-huh, Drew said, covering her mouth again.

Once they had got over their shivering, they felt around blindly beneath the quilt, every so often flourishing items of each other's clothing, like prizes fished from a bran tub. When the last prize – Marks & Spencer's cotton knickers, white with trim – had been hooked from Kay's ankles by Drew's big toe, she reached over the edge of the bed and pulled open a drawer.

– Drew, she said, groping for the box, you'd better use one of these.

But he, meanwhile, had moved across to the other side of the bed, searching on the floor for his trousers, and as Kay faced round she felt the rubbery drag of him already on her thigh.

— Smart bastard, she said, at the same time crooking her leg around his buttocks drawing him towards her.

He was trying hard not to think how cold her feet were when she took him inside her. She was doing her level best to stifle a burp. Failing.

— Oh, God.

She pushed him away and sat up with a start.

— I'm going to boke.

By the time she came back from the bathroom his erection had gone into serious decline. She made several dexterous (and sinister and bimanal) attempts to revive it, but it was beyond saving. Drew, feeling he ought to be doing something, slid down on her under the quilt. Kay moved her legs apart resignedly, but her sighs grew more and more wearied and eventually she suggested they watch the portable TV. Sweltered and embarrassed, Drew was glad of the excuse to surface. He rolled on to his hip, hearing his stomach slosh in delayed reaction. His shrunken cock stuck from his abdomen like a cork from a bloated goatskin. He wished he hadn't drunk quite so much. He wished it was morning.

Kay wished she had been on her own so that she could at least have had a smoke. This was not at all what she had in mind when he walked into Quayside Design today. *Moby-fucking-Dick* indeed. She wished she had a satellite dish. Using the remote, she flicked up then down the four channels on offer, thought about settling on a film, got bored and went back to channel-hopping. She heard his stomach slop again as he shifted position and she thanked God she'd offloaded her own. She'd be kicking him out if he kept that up.

Shite, she really needed that smoke to calm herself.

But what about him?

What about him. She was past caring. It was her house. She crossed the room to the dressing table, her nakedness feeling about as sensual as a full-length flannel nightgown, and returned with a mother-of-pearl inlaid box.

— What are you doing? Drew asked, watching as she got back into bed and produced a packet of Rizlas from one of the box's green baize compartments and a large amount of cellophane twisted about a small pellet of cannabis resin from another.

– It's my house, Kay said.

– Thank fuck, Drew told her, for there's no blow in mine.

Kay left off licking a Rizla.

– What happened to the man who was so down on smoking?

– You can't imagine, Drew said, shaking his head sadly, the moral torment this will cause me. (*Moral* he could tolerate, but not *professional*; he knew of no central office directives explicitly discouraging the recreational use of cannabis.)

Kay crumbled half the resin on to the tobacco, considered it, crumbled another bit, considered it again, crumbled some more, then decided it was hardly worth saving what was left and crumbled that on too. She stoked the joint up with three or four quick blasts then placed it between Drew's lips. Drew felt it hit immediately. He rolled his eyes behind the lids, tracking the inward plunge. His toes tingled and he heard Kay's laugh as though it were reaching him through a medium denser than air. She had a beautiful laugh, he decided. When she leaned over to give him the spliff again their nipples met and rubbed together. His cock puffed up like a toadstool filmed in time-lapse, the stalk slender and slightly curved, the cap an exotic mauve. Kay held it in the flat of her hand while she toked and, when she'd passed the joint back to him a final time, tried to roll a Durex down it.

– It keeps jumping, she said; her words were mirth-flecked, light as sea spray.

He stubbed the roach and took over from her, fascinated by his fingers' nimbleness. An adult *Interlude*; the potter relaxes from his wheel. Lying on his back, he pulled her on to him.

– Uh, uh, she said, pointing to her head, and rolled him over until he was on top.

They got a rhythm going for a time (a long, long time, it seemed), stoned in unison, then lost it abruptly. Sense and sequence were shuffled in Drew's mind and soon even the parts of his own body appeared not to be moving in harmony. His orgasm broke from him, hare-swift, when he was least expecting it. His hips hounded after it and caught up just as it ended.

He collapsed forward on to Kay's chest, his face buried in the pillow beside her cheek.

Only now that it had stopped did he realise that the moaning he had heard for the final however-long-it-was was all his own and hard upon this realisation a new sound reached him through the fuzz of his hearing. Kay was snoring deeply.

He withdrew, breaking the circuit of their bodies, and lay back against the headboard, eyes closed, brain jagged with disconnected thoughts. And then there was Melanie, standing in front of him, plain as anything.

– Drew Linden, she said. What are you like?

She carried a scrapbook under her arm of all their good times together.

– Do these mean nothing to you? she asked him and began ripping pages out one by one. Nothing at all?

Drew squeezed his eyelids together and Melanie and the fluttering leaves were whited out. But the knowledge remained: he had been a fool. Work was work. It wasn't Melanie's fault she had to go to New York, any more than it was his fault he had had to come here. He couldn't think how he had lost sight of that.

Kay was dead to the world. There was going to be a lot of explaining to do in the morning. His throat was parched and his stomach groaned with hunger. He swung out of bed and putting on his T-shirt went into the kitchen in search of food and drink. He poured himself a glass of orange juice from a carton in the door of the fridge and dolloped three tablespoons of leftover macaroni into a salmon-pink sundae dish.

The living room was littered with the relics of the recent seduction, their significance already hard to recall. The bygone-Belfast book lay open on the shelf, an intricate and seemingly pointless dance of fingerprints on the main photograph uncovered by the bookcase's concealed light. Drew brought the book over to the chesterfield with him. By concentrating again on that familiar tooth-slim slice of the old drapery emporium, he found he was able to reconstruct the modern street: capping a building here and there, extracting and replacing a good many others. He diverted himself with this game for a few minutes while he ate his macaroni, then, all at once sitting forward, he peered more closely at the picture.

Above the window of what had since become the Bookstore sports section, to the right of the proprietor's name, the words *Castle Buildings*, now erased, were clearly visible. Drew tried them over in his head a few times, on their own and in combination with other words, and was pleased enough with the effects to attempt them at last out loud.

So it was that at three o'clock in the morning of the Saturday before Easter, five days before he had been meant to fly out to England for the long weekend, his first trip back since returning to Belfast, Drew Linden, at once stoned and seedless, secured his footing on a leather chesterfield in a flat in a town house, not five minutes from *jazzbo brown's* (née Finney's), and, with a bowl of leftover leftovers in his right hand and a glossy-backed picture book in his left, and with his inglorious bollocks askant below his T-shirt, delivered himself of an address (James! Karen! Phoebe-Moon!) as solid as it was symmetrical, as economical as it was extravagant in its expropriation of tradition:

Bookstore, Castle Buildings, Castle Place, Belfast.

5

SOMEONE MUST HAVE been snitching on Wilbur Worrell, for, without so much as a word of warning, the blue-eyed boy was hauled off to stand in the dunce's corner one fine morning, accused of not doing his homework.

Karen said,

– Really, with the money we paid, you'd think *somebody* might have pointed this out at the very start.

James said,

– Still, at least we know there's one person over there with his wits about him.

(Something – the central heating pipes, perhaps – made a distinct *fink!* sound just then in a corner of the room.)

– And, of course, the way things are shaping up there, he's tipped us off just in time.

They discussed the matter with Phoebe, recently returned from Aberdeen, at lunch the following day, weighing projected costs against potential benefits and future plans.

Phoebe said,

– Go for it.

Lunch over, Karen flew off somewhere known only to the other two, for something kept even from Zena, her PA-and-then-some; James phoned printers and contractors for quotations, and Phoebe counted her second hand round to two o'clock precisely then dialled Belfast. A flustered boy connected her with Pamela Magill.

Pamela wheezed,

– Hello?

– Pamela? Phoebe. How *are* you?

The reply, which seemed to be to the effect that she couldn't complain, only just managed to keep its head above the rising tide of a cough.

– Goo-ood. Phoebe put the phone to her ear again. Listen, this idea of Drew's; Karen, James and I have been talking it over. We think it's wonderful. We want to go all the way with it: revamped stationery, carrier bags, bookmarks, *everything*; full-page ads in all the local press, maybe even a slot on radio and TV. Not that you'd want the advertising to draw too much attention to the new addition, of course. Quite the opposite, I'd've said. The important thing is to make people believe it's always been there. It's like baked beans.

Karen having already been the subject of a *Life in the day of . . .* feature, it seemed highly likely that Phoebe's name would some day suggest itself for the *Independent on Sunday*'s *A Book That Changed Me* column; and if it ever did Phoebe would have no hesitation in nominating Vance Packard's *The Hidden Persuaders*, bought in August 1973 on her first, never-to-be-forgotten visit to a second-hand book shop, an experience which, in setting her on the road that was to lead, via Camden Lock, to her current position as co-owner of the twenty-five branches of Bookstore, could be said to have changed not only Phoebe, but also in no small part the face of British retailing. But *The Hidden Persuaders* had also, the feature would reveal, engendered in Phoebe a lifelong interest in theories of advertising and design, even though she now considered the book itself rather quaint (the psychological equivalent of necking, she would term it) and herself then as delightfully naive.

– Ask Heinz and they'd tell you the only way their cans have stayed looking the same all these years is by constantly changing. The trick is learning to anticipate tastes and adapting in advance. Or take Coke.

Pamela preferred to stick with baked beans. Her topknot sagged to the left as she made a rough calculation on the back of a condemned bookmark of the number of tins she'd got through in the course of her married life. An average of, say, six a week when the children were at home (call it twenty-five years for the sake of argument) and – two? yes – two a week for the last twelve, though one a fortnight was probably nearer the mark since she'd come up here. . . . Ach, she was making a pig's ear of it now. Even so, getting on for 10,000, must be.

Ten thousand! She saw the first crude labels emerge from the

Palaeolithic mists of her early marriage, then enact for her an abridged version of their evolution (a sort of *Ascent of Can*) into the computer-enhanced designs of today.

– Besides, Phoebe returned at length to Belfast and Pamela rejoined her, if even half of what these rumours are saying is true, anything that roots us more firmly in the public's mind at this stage can only be to the good.

She looked at her watch. Two and a quarter minutes! Though not one for self-congratulation, Phoebe was nevertheless quietly pleased at this further proof of her finely tuned sense of phone-time. Years of experience had taught her that two and a half minutes was the ideal length for a conversation of this nature, neither so short as to appear unsociable nor so long as to admit of undue familiarity.

– So, she said (*two minutes eighteen, nineteen, twenty*), what do you think?

– I think, said Pamela, it's as well it was just two words he suggested and not a sentence.

And at that the catarrh finally did swamp her voice.

Phoebe found a laugh of sorts.

– Very good, she said over the hacking. Yes, I like that. Well, speak to you again soon (*twenty-eight, twenty-nine*). Bye, Pamela.

Thirty!

Phoebe shook the receiver free of her fingers like a used swab over an incinerator.

The woman, she had to remind herself, not for the first time, *knows her books bloody well*. And not for the first time that still was not excuse enough.

Drew, of course, never intended dropping Wilbur in the shit. He simply looked, saw, and, in one of those unfathomable flashes of stoned inspiration, connected. Castles, you might say (and Drew did in fact, several times, much, once, to James's particular delight), were very much in the Belfast air that spring, with Royal Avenue now resurfaced as far as North Street in readiness for the grand opening of the Castlecourt shopping centre. Rumours were rife in the book trade of English aristocrats, with Oxford and Cambridge pedigrees and City of

London clout, poised to move into shop units of staggering, palatial proportions. Though last into Belfast, Bookstore, whose own arrival had not so long ago been the subject of just such speculation, was determined not to be first out. So when Drew stood that Friday night and declaimed from Kay's leather chesterfield he was impelled not only by drink and drugs, but also by the intuition that he had stumbled on the ideal way to consolidate the company's position in the city at the same time as stealing a little of their threatened rivals' thunder.

Bookstore would out-castle all comers.

Such were the thoughts left beached in his brain the following morning by the retreating tide of sleep, and so busy was he turning them over and examining them that he completely forgot to feel, as he had sworn he would feel the night before, contrite for betraying Melanie. On the contrary, his renegade prick had decamped while he slept and was now firmly lodged in the cleft of Kay's buttocks. He became aware of this at the very moment Kay herself woke and stretched. He felt her buttocks tense, relax, then tense once more, just to be sure, before she looked at him over her shoulder. For a moment her eyes widened, as though if she had been expecting to see a man in her bed at all that morning it certainly wasn't Drew Linden. But only for a moment.

– Oh, boy, she said, turning away and stretching a second time, was I out of it.

She didn't seem to object to the presence of Drew's erection so he let it stay where it was. Kay asked him the time. He said nine. She asked him what about the shop. He said he was on lates today and didn't have to be in till half-ten.

– Thank Christ, said Kay, it's Saturday. I've some awful client to see first thing on Monday. I'd never have made it in this state.

– Don't worry, you'd've woken all right if you'd had to work, Drew told her, thinking before he was even halfway through: *listen to yourself, don't be absurd*; but thinking too he couldn't very well stop now.

– I'd've seen to that.

– Yeah?

The rank challenge in her voice, accompanied as it was by

renewed and less than respectful cock-clenching with her buttocks (*tweaking* was probably nearer the mark), brought back the shock of last night's snore and Drew wondered did Kay remember at what stage she had passed out. But if she did, she wasn't letting on. Her hand was already curling round the nape of his neck, drawing his mouth down on to hers.

Their leathery tongues entwined, like ancient turtles rubbing necks.

It was only later, when he was hurrying through Cornmarket, with the bandstand clock already chiming the half-hour, that fatigue and guilt hit him, the one immobilising his limbs, the other paralysing that battleground of cerebrum and viscera which he was accustomed to thinking of as his heart. It took everything he had to drag his legs round the corner into the shop, where he got no further than the bestsellers' display, just inside the door, before he had to stop and rest.

Seeing him enter, two Saturday workers who had been standing with their arms folded at the front till, talking, looked about frantically for something to do. Drew stayed them with a weary hand.

– It's all right, he said, your jobs are safe. I won't tell if you don't.

Their smiles were so uncomfortable even Drew's face ached. He gave up on them, became a bastard boss.

– There's a delivery of maps in Travel to be priced and put out. One of you do that – don't forget VAT – and when he's finished the other one can do something about . . . (he made a quick mental tour of the shop, searching not for the messiest section but for the one whose upkeep he knew caused the most belly-aching) . . . Computing. It's an absolute shambles.

The forced smiles faded immediately, replaced by expressions of the purest relief. He was glad Pamela wasn't there to witness them; though surely even Pamela would have to allow that Saturday workers were exceptional cases. Saturday workers were always potentially surplus and as such were almost duty bound to look ill at ease with management.

He dragged himself across the much-praised mosaic of the ground floor to the lift and from the lift dragged himself across the less-praised, indeed barely commented on, parquet of the second floor, to the door, between Religion and New Age, marked Staff Only.

Saturday morning was, as a rule, his favourite time of the week. With Pamela gone, he had the run of both offices and for a few hours before the insanity of Saturday afternoon he could organise himself for the coming week. This morning, however, he went through to his own annexe and sat staring at the windowless wall, as at a private cinema screen. So private that no one else looking in could ever have guessed what it was he saw there. Two Disprin and a carton of Ribena alleviated the most pressing symptoms of his fatigue, but he knew of only one remedy for the guilt which continued to grip his innards. He picked up the phone and called Melanie at the house. It rang and rang. He hung up, tried her at work, got her there.

– This is a surprise, she said.

– I'm sorry, he said, about yesterday. I didn't want to leave things that way.

– No, she said, neither did I. I was ringing you last night.

– I was out till late.

– That's what I thought. Anywhere nice?

– Just a bar. Jazz and stuff. It was all right.

– With the ones from work?

– Mm.

– I'm glad, she said. Listen I'm up to my eyes, what do you say I call you later when we've a bit more time?

– OK, Drew said. I just needed to hear you, that's all.

He wasn't lying either. The sound of her voice put everything instantly into perspective, dispelling the lingering ambiguities of last night's excesses, and he imagined then that he understood something of what actors filming love scenes felt when the director bellowed *Cut!*, their intimacy fading with the studio lights.

The external line was buzzing and he answered on his extension, his voice, like his resolve, firm and steady.

– Good morning, Belfast Bookstore, can I help you?

– Drew Linden, please.

– Speaking.

– Oh, hi. It's me, Kay. Well, is this keen or what?

You could have run a motorway through the gap Drew left. Kay's tone changed abruptly.

– Don't flatter yourself, she said, writing in the words he left unspoken. I was actually ringing to say I don't want to make a big deal of this. I'm not going to be moping around waiting on you calling and I hope for your sake you won't be sitting in waiting on me. I'll see you when I see you: a week, two weeks. Whenever.

Drew watched the office wall a long moment.

– What about Tuesday night? he heard himself ask.

– I'll let you know.

Kay, as it happened, couldn't make Tuesday, or Thursday, and Wednesday, being Melanie's last night in England before going to the States, Drew spent on the phone. So it was Good Friday when they next met. Drew was in the mood for celebrating. James had rung him earlier in the day full of triune praise for his initiative in laying claim to the Castle Buildings title. It was then that Drew said, self-deprecatingly, what he said about castles being in the Belfast air and then that James, impressed now by his assistant manager's modesty and felicitous turn of phrase as well as his initiative, confided in him that he and Karen and Phoebe were all agreed he was in tune with the company ethos. They were, in short, very pleased. *Very pleased indeed, mate.* So was Drew. Only a matter of time now, he thought.

This evening, rather than push their luck a second time, he and Kay cut out the jazz-bar preliminaries and went straight to Kay's flat with a couple of bottles of wine. Kay had managed to score some more dope in the interim, a tablet of Moroccan black, smooth as a stick of sealing wax. It was a slow, mellow, high, all the cooler for being rolled this time with Golden Virginia, new-bought and moist, not tinder from an eviscerated Silk Cut. The evening was already well advanced when they finally got round to undressing each other on the leather chesterfield. Something went bang, somewhere far away.

– Blast bomb, Kay said. Andytown, sounds like.

They gave each other Moroccan black blow-backs while they fucked and took wine warm from each other's mouths.

Late on Sunday afternoon there was a phone-call for Kay. Drew took one look at her darkening face and, without waiting to be asked, withdrew to the bedroom where he lay watching Cartoon Time on mute while she talked – or rather listened, since most of the talking appeared to be at the other end of the line. Elmer Fudd was blamming away noiselessly and ineffectually with his shotgun when she came in and sat, as oddly silent as Daffy Duck, on the edge of the bed.

– Trouble? Drew asked.

– Not what you're thinking, Kay said. I should've been at my mum and dad's today for dinner. It went right out of my head.

It was not altogether surprising. Since arriving at the flat on Friday evening their only other human contact had been with the delivery man from a pizzeria in Shaftesbury Square and nowhere in the myriad words with which they had surrounded themselves in the intervening hours would you have found any reference to families.

– Are they after your hide? Drew asked and felt for it himself under her shirt.

Kay let herself be coaxed further into the middle of the bed.

– I'm fucking thirty next birthday, she said. I'm a respected professional, a partner in a company half my friends would kill just to work in; I refuse to share my life with any man or woman – for God's sake, I won't even keep a cat on principle. But tell that to my bloody parents. It's always *poor Kay* this and *poor Kay* that, but I know rightly it's *poor us* they really mean. Poor us pushing sixty and no grandchildren to visit us. Sometimes I think treating me as if I'm still a child's their way of getting back at me for not being fecund. Holidays are the worst. Do you know, they turned up here to watch the Twelfth last year, *with a picnic!*

The memory of it left her speechless again. Drew was kissing the plain of her stomach below her ribcage.

– What about you, she said at length, nobody keeping your dinner hot wondering where you are?

– No, he said, and kept kissing.

– You don't know how lucky you are.

In fact, the only reason why Drew wasn't expected at Ellen's today (the reason too why he hadn't suggested to Kay spending at least part of the weekend at his place; not that it would have occurred to Kay to notice) was that he wasn't expected *anywhere* in Belfast until some time in the middle of the week. He had decided against telling the family that he had cancelled his trip across the water. Quite apart from the accusations of wasting money (which he was, he knew, but didn't care, preferring to waste money than waste five nights on his own in England), he did not want to give them a pretext for involving themselves any more than they were already involved in his private life. The last time he saw Ellen, however, she had warned him that his father was making noises about getting a spare key cut before he went away. And though Drew had managed to avoid this, by the simple expedient of avoiding all but telephone contact (and that through Ellen), for the past two weeks, he knew that nothing so trivial as the lack of a key would deter his father. At some stage over the Easter holiday he would prevail upon Ellen or Derek to drive him down to Drew's flat and then, belted into his turquoise anorak for added ridiculousness, would walk round the outside of the building looking up at his son's curtained windows.

Housewatching, he called it.

Never mind the state-of-the-art security system. Never mind the round-the-clock Special Branch protection for the judge across the street.

– He only wants to help, Ellen said.

What he wanted, Drew knew, was to think of himself as a normal father with a father's normal concern for the well-being of his son. What he wanted was the creeping absolution of the everyday. Drew was damned if he was going to let him have it.

With an effort Kay might have appreciated if only he had told her, if only, that is, he had not been as averse to involving her in his family affairs as he was to involving his family in his personal ones, Drew had succeeded in keeping contact with his father down to three meetings in the eight weeks since his return from England – the last exactly a fortnight before, his mother's birthday, when Derek drove them out to Dundonald to visit her grave. It was Drew's first visit in nearly six years, since the funeral itself in fact, a day which stood out now in his mind mainly for its obstinate refusal to be in any way remarkable at the time. The cortège was not too big and not too small, the weather, everyone agreed, neither too warm nor too cold for August – pleasant, almost. The funeral-home service was comforting enough for those who found such things a comfort and unhypocritical enough for those who normally found them the ultimate in hypocrisy, the minister, having never, to his knowledge, met the woman whose body he was preaching over, nor heard a single word said in her lifetime for or against her, playing safe and speaking briefly and generally about Christ's victory over the grave while being careful not to make any too-specific promises in regard to the dear departed herself. Even the interment, a version of which Drew, newly BA-ed in Eng. Lit., had sampled together beforehand from the Brontës and Poe, contained, when it came, nothing out of the way, allowing his mind to wander from the ceremony's creaking symbolism to its mundane actuality.

He saw a hole that might elsewhere have given access to water mains or telephone cables. He saw men paid to dig holes, as men had been paid – or made – to dig holes the world over since time immemorial.

When his mother's box had been lowered in, the onlookers (mourners was too active a word for that not-too-big, not-too-small crowd, on that neither-too-hot-nor-too-cold-for-August day) walked silently away. Drew looked back only once. The workmen were gone and a frame of artificial grass had been laid across the mouth of the hole, with the wreaths heaped on top, as though the coffin were some super-concentrate malignant earth-food capsule, stimulating an instant profusion of the fake and dying.

Six years on, the hole had become a monument, though to what exactly was not immediately apparent. A white marble surround enclosing a pool of green gravel (like sea-water petrified) and culminating in a headstone at the centre of which, as though not wishing to draw attention to their shabby selves, huddled the details of a life as skeletal as the remains they referred to: ELIZABETH (LILY) LINDEN, BORN 1 APRIL 1934, DEPARTED THIS LIFE 16 AUGUST 1984, AGED 50 YRS AND 3 MTHS.

Ellen and Derek hunkered by the headstone and worked their way to the foot of the grave, pulling weeds, grass, anything living, from between the sea-green stones, and Jack followed behind them with a rake. Drew meantime was dispatched to the standpipe with the flower-urn's metal flask and when he returned he stood with his sister to one side while Derek held out the daffodils they had brought and their father trimmed the stems with secateurs.

– She hated daffodils, Ellen said in an undertone. He brings them every birthday.

Drew looked at her a moment or two, then turned his attention again to Derek and his father at their silent flower arranging.

Kay went, penitent, to her parents' house on Monday for a belated Easter tea and returned in the evening with a Roses chocolate egg. She made breast cups with the two halves of the shell and came almost imperceptibly when Drew, licking and licking at one of them, wore a hole right through to her nipple.

Next morning Kay, already showered and dressed, woke him with coffee in bed.

– Holiday's over, she said. I'm going into work.

– I've another day yet, Drew said, pulling the covers up over his head to stop the light getting in and spoiling his sleep utterly.

– Yes, and I've people coming for dinner tonight.

– So?

– So the cleaner will be here at eleven and you won't be.

Drew lowered the quilt, relinquishing his last hold on sleep. Kay was at the dressing table putting in earrings.

– Aren't you even going to invite me to eat? he asked.

Kay laughed.

– After the things I've seen you do with your food the past couple of days? You must be joking.

– Well, what about the rest of the week?

Kay half turned.

– Wednesday so-so, Thursday not sure yet. Weekend . . .

Her mouth tightened and she faced the mirror again, jabbing the tine of a silver hoop into her lobe.

– Weekend's out altogether, I'm afraid.

Before leaving, she relented and granted him another half-hour in bed. He took three-quarters, the extra fifteen minutes being exactly the time required for his sense of affront to modulate into the certainty that he hadn't known, till then, he was living. He was having an affair with a woman who was not particularly bothered if she never saw him from one week's end to the next. This was not something you stumbled upon every day. This was sex without complexity. Nor did it really, if he thought about it, impinge on him and Melanie to any significant degree. Eight or nine months from now (much sooner, he had every reason to hope after his recent triumphs at work, and always supposing one or other of them hadn't got fed up in the meantime, which was by no means unlikely), he and Kay would have one last fuck, stoned, for old times' sake, thank each other for everything and say goodbye. They would write occasionally. In a year or two's time they would, perhaps, exchange visits and get along famously with one another's partners.

By Friday evening he was glad Kay wasn't free. Even if she had been, he told himself, he wouldn't have seen her. He had forgotten how much he enjoyed staying home and cooking on Friday nights. It seemed an age since he had last done it. He had spent his lunch break in Marks and Spencer's food hall, sounding aubergines and selecting courgettes for his speciality ratatouille, and, back home, he had just arrived at the messy, buttering stage of making garlic bread when the phone rang.

He bet himself a million pounds he knew who it was.

Are you all right? You should have phoned when you got back from England. You know what Daddy's like.

Why had he not rung after all? One call wouldn't have hurt.

Don't kid yourself, he thought, though in a voice only half his own. McManus the pedagogue – apostatic priest-protector – was prowling the aisles of his mind.

– Right, class, who can remember my first law of family relations? You there, Linden.

– Please sir: *Family expands to fill twice the space you allow it.*

– Very good. And how do we counteract it, everyone?

CLASS (in unison):
Twice nothing is nothing.

The phone was still ringing and, in the way of unanswered phones, sounding more unhinged with every ring. Prof. McManus covered his ears and faded gratefully into insubstantiality once more.

– Frig you, Ellen, I'm coming! Drew shouted, still slapping garlic butter into the clefts in the half baguette. I'm coming!

He grabbed the kitchen roll on his way into the hall and held the phone between his ear and shoulder as he tore off a sheet to wipe his hands.

– Hello?

– Uncle Drew?

Steward's enquiry. Bookies of Britain hold their breath. A million pounds riding on the outcome: Can daughter, in these poll-taxing times, stand for mother?

– Tina, now isn't that a coincidence, I was just thinking about you all.

– Uncle Drew, she said, my daddy's on his way down to pick you up. Grandpa's in the hospital. He's had a stroke.

6

J ACK STOOD ON the hillside, unsure at first what he was doing
there or where he had been until that instant. The only
memory he had brought with him was of an unbearably full
sensation in his head, a pain so great it could not in the end be
contained within him, but had spilt out on to the ground,
solidifying into a huge dead weight, blocking his path. His
world then was pain outside and in. The pain was crushing
him. He struggled with it, trying to clear the blockage. He
strained and he strained and he strained and then in a moment
of exquisite release, he felt the weight give and felt himself
being sucked down into a long wailing tunnel. Sucked down,
spun round, unhitched from time, and forced up and out again
on to this cold and barren mountain lane high above the city.
The most peculiar thing was Michael being there. He was sitting
on his hands on a rusted gate at the turn of the lane when
Jack came upon him (his uniform the colour and grain of dried
cowpats), flicking a Woodbine in and out of his mouth with
his lip and tongue, the way, when he was young, he had loved
to watch Mr Butler next door do. All through one summer,
the year he was thirteen, Michael's lower face was transformed
into a flesh and blood record of this admiration by a shifting
pattern of burns and scabs, which tended ever inwards towards
his mouth as the summer progressed, until – Bullseye! – the
first Sunday morning in September, the Sunday the war began,
the last scab flaked off the underside of his top lip and deadle-
ated to the ground. This morning – five years on, must be, if
he was in uniform (the hazy boundaries of Jack's own history
contracted accordingly and he felt himself twenty-one again) –
Michael was drilling the Woodbine and chewing gum at the
same time. He winked when he saw his brother coming along
the lane, but all he got in return was a frown. Jack stopped by

a hawthorn facing the gate, snapping off the brown spikes and pressing them against the thumb of his right hand, though it was too numb with cold to feel anything. It was not fair of Michael to do this to him. The orders had been quite explicit, Jack, and Jack alone, was to patrol the mountains for the duration. But Michael simply winked again and continued juggling the fag, tongue as rubberly nimble as a circus seal balancing a cylinder on its nose. His cap was tugged through his left epaulette, silver badge up, and his big black turned-up-toed boots beat a rust-swirling march on the crossbar of the gate. Jack scowled down at his own mutton dummies. The right one had a hole in the bottom. Cold spread into his sole from the ice-bound brick of the earth. He stamped his foot to keep himself from freezing to the spot. It must still have been very early, for he couldn't see further than twenty yards beyond Michael's shoulder, where the camber of the hillside plunged the fields into shadow. There seemed to be no good reason for his being here at this time, unless it was to caution his brother for trespassing on his territory. As he opened his mouth to speak, however, a wind whipped in from the shadows, peeling back the pomaded strands of Michael's hair, like a flap of scalp, and shooting – Ow! – needle-sharp into the bared nerves of his own teeth. He shut his mouth tight. Bloody teeth had his head near turned. (The build-up of decay had been going on for many years, but so long as it had kept its more flagrant eruptions to a minimum he had been content to turn a diplomatically blind eye, avoiding anything that might inflame it further. Now, though, there was no ignoring it. Now it was total war. Jack's mouth was a mess.) He pulled the scarf to his nose, filtering the air through its coarse wool. That was better. Had to watch, though, he didn't get any slabbers on it. His father'd have his life if he found out he'd taken it. That four feet of tartan was his father's pride and joy: *There's craftsmanship for you. Ten years I've had this scarf and it's still like new.* Jack's mother had sneaked him it on his way out the door. He'd need a good warm scarf that morning, she said, with the walk he had to get to his appointment. . . . Of course! *That* was why he was here. He'd got an appointment at last. He was going to be late if he stood around much longer at the turn of the lane, and he knew he'd never have another minute's peace until he got there. The family were at their wits' end with him. His sisters were working all the hours God sent in Mackie's, on munitions, and, they complained, with Jack moaning and groaning night after night, they were getting up in the mornings tireder than they went to bed. Dinah, the youngest, had a girlfriend in Mackie's, Della (*Dinah and Della on the hunt for the fellas*, the fellas used to shout after them as they walked, linking arms, up the Springfield Road), who had come down from Co. Londonderry for the war work. Della had digs up the Oldpark and Dinah let it be known that if things kept up the way they were at home . . . well, she didn't say anything outright, but it was pretty clear what she meant. It was pretty clear too what their father, who had heard tell what the fellas were shouting and had had words with her before this, meant by the look he gave her from behind his *Daily Herald: over my dead body you will.* And Jack all this time was twenty-one and feeling twelve before his younger sister, yet feeling too that only her diversionary front stood between him, bronchitic and decaying, unfit for service, and the full force of his father's contempt. The wind blew again and he held the scarf closer to his mouth. He had to be getting on. With a nod of his muffled head he made a move to leave, then stopped, seeing sudden terror in his brother's eyes, and some future self whispered in his brain: *he is eighteen years old and they are sending him away, and you will not see him again but see only a photograph of a white, numbered stone in a numbered row of white stones (their shadows cast at a black angle on the ground before them), with directions on the back which you will none of you ever put to the test, making do instead with a weekly glance at the name chiselled, between Johnston, A. M., and Lowry, Capt. S., on a granite slab in the church vestry; a name known, because heard read aloud every November, to more people than will remember the name of his brother who didn't go, though (something else they won't remember) he was the first to try, in the days when France meant Dunkirk and Normandy was still the birthplace, learnt at school, of a Conquering Duke, whose knights and their descendants spread across England, centuries before, then took to boats again and, where they next encountered land, established a pale, which they immediately went beyond, northwards, building coastal castles, still standing, at Carrickfergus and Dundrum, and another, long gone, at the approach to a ford between the counties of Antrim and Down* . . . But other people's forgetfulness was not Michael's fault. Looking into his brother's imploring eyes, Jack was ashamed of his earlier harshness and ignoring the pain he lowered the scarf to explain the urgency of his appointment. But the numbness in his hand and foot seemed to have spread into his mouth, for he literally could not get his tongue round even the simplest of words and had to resort in the end to a pointing finger – *you, here; me, up there* – then, locking the pointing finger with a numbed one for emphasis – *you-me here together*. And as suddenly as he had panicked, Michael was smiling again, sitting on his hands on the gate the way Jack had come upon him, winking, chewing gum and juggling a Woodbine. Jack hurried on up the lane, telling himself the sooner he got there the sooner he would be back, though with every step forward he was less and less certain where, or when, exactly *back* was, and whereas, a moment before, he had thought he saw a row of headstones he now understood that what he had seen was a row of straight white teeth. Ah, now. Those were the jobs you wanted. The girls went for straight white teeth, all right. Jack had heard them talking in the office. *Oh, see when* – take your pick: Clark Gable, Errol Flynn, Tyrone Power, Randolph Scott, Cary Grant, Gary Cooper, Jackie Linden, I-don't-think – *smiles, don't you just go all* (blubbing their lips and forcing shivers that snaked from the tops of their heads right down beneath their desks to the soles of their feet) *blahahahrr*. Man mad, they were, the lot of them, getting all excited when they heard the Yanks were coming, as if, Jack chaffed them, they were likely to see Jimmy Stewart or whoever coming out of Robb's department store, though it was obvious they thought the joke was on him the day he returned from lunch to find them in a knot at the office window and there below, walking down the middle of High Street was Joe Louis, smiling up to the right and the left of him at the staring faces. And, *oh*, they said, *did you see how white his teeth were?* And straight, Jack thought now, running a fingertip along the newly even edge of his own. . . . He was trying to remember something on the far side of that reminiscence. Something that had happened to him while he was out walking. But not today, surely? He looked back the way he had come. After only a short distance the path faded into mist. No, not today. A long time ago. He faced forward again and adjusted his scarf, crossing it over his chest so that each end was parallel with a diagonal of his sweater's V-neck. The scarf was a Christmas present from Peggy and Walter. One-hundred-per-cent cashmere, the label said. From Henderson's in Castle Place. The sweater, which was sleeveless with a diamond pattern, was out of the same shop, a special treat to himself one payday. Well why not? They'd lived long enough with scarcity while the war was on. Besides, Lily Mooney always said she liked it the best of all his pullovers, which was obviously why he was wearing it today, because he could see Lily waiting for him a little way up the lane, looking over a stile into a fallow field. They exchanged no word of greeting. Didn't need to. They had an *understanding*. Jack simply leaned beside her and looked over the stile to see what she could see. A cow, a donkey and a goat. The cow's udder hung almost to the earth, criss-crossed by swollen veins. The donkey ate very slowly and both it and the cow kept a watchful eye on the goat, which was tethered by one horn to a wooden peg in the middle of the field and which every now and then walked to the rope's full extent and performed a little slant-headed dance before walking back along the slackening rope to the peg. Jack turned, laughing, to Lily, who had once told him, laughing herself, though more from embarrassment, how the first time she saw a goat – she was seven and it was staring at her across a wall as she descended the steps of an evacuee bus – she went into hysterics, because the boy on the step above her bent his head over her shoulder and, stroking his chin to suggest the goat's beard, whispered that that was what you got when a countryman stuck his thingy in a sheep's you-know-what. And even taking into account the *thingying* and the you-know-whats, this was a far cry from the Lily Mooney who had barely said a word of any description to anyone for the first three weeks she was in the office, by which time, it was true, the staff was mostly all men, the girls who had crowded at the window watching Joe Louis walk down High Street having become women and left one by one after the war to marry and have families (apart from Agnes, who had baffled everyone – until they decided she had always been a bit stuck-up – by going instead to study at Queen's). And, of course, it being mostly men now, they had been talking on for weeks about the new woman coming, so their faces fell a mile when they saw how young and (they mouthed the word to each other behind her back) *scraggy* Lily Mooney was, though, in fact, scraggy, as they called it, she may have been (nobody got fat on rations), but she was no younger than the other women were when they started, and the truth was that it was the *men* who were now that bit older. Jack himself, as his father would never let him forget, wasn't getting any younger. When *he* was twenty-seven he already had, let's see – Peggy, Alice, Jack – three children and a fourth, wee Dinah, on the way. Yet there was Jack, not even courting that anyone could see, though God knows, it wasn't for want of trying on Jack's part to make them think they could, acting mysterious about his comings and goings every so often (Saturday nights in particular), hoping they'd suspect him at home of doing a line somewhere in secret. But not even after he'd been four nights in the one week to the same picture house on the far side of town and accidentally-on-purpose left his ticket stubs beside the clock on the mantelpiece did his father let the subject drop: *When are you going to find yourself a girlfriend? Can't blame it on those teeth of yours now.* Then along came Lily Mooney with her funny lank-looking hair that wasn't lank at all when you touched it, which Jack did, and kissed her too, within a month of her starting in the office – a week of her starting to speak to him; and within two months he had asked her to marry him and within three she had said *yes*, but added before he could hug her, *if we can go away from here* and he thought at first she meant the office, but Lily, looking at the floor, said *no, not just the office*, and Jack asked her in succession *Belfast? Northern Ireland?* and she nodded, twice; and Jack was twenty-seven, looking at twenty-eight, and Lily (who had no family but a crabbed aunt, who she hated and who Jack had met only the once – though once was once too often – in the wee room they had shared together since Lily was no age at all, in a falling-down house in Sailortown), Lily was seventeen and had never in three months asked him for anything but that one thing, but asked for it in such a way, her hands all the while twisting a Festival of Britain brochure (borrowed from a friend of a friend who had a cousin who'd been), that he thought *if not me then perhaps someone else.* . . . So they started saving at once and now, four years later, they were meeting here, he seemed to recall, to finalise boats and trains and, before all that, a wedding. Man and wife: Jackie Linden and Little Lily, love of his life. The words succeeded one another as gently and rhythmically as an oar clipping through placid water, but when he leaned closer to murmur them in her ear his tongue caught a crab and where she ought to have heard endearments Lily heard only a wet cluck as his upper denture slurped away from the roof of his mouth. Jack slapped himself on the back of the neck, barking the plate clear of his windpipe and at the same time jolting to the forefront of his mind the real, pressing reason for his being here this afternoon. Because this was not the first time it had happened, as though, having fulfilled their fairy-tale purpose in helping him to find a wife, his teeth were reverting (like Cinderella's pumpkin turned coach, turned pumpkin again) to their former, troublesome selves, and he was terrified that the next time, or the time after that, his reactions would not be so swift and the teeth would lodge in his throat, choking him. He pushed the denture back into place with his fingers. Lily watched the cow and the donkey watching the goat walk to the end of its tether and perform its slant-headed dance. There were tears now on her cheek. Jack reached out a hand to comfort her (taking care to wipe it first), but she shied away from his touch, resting her head on a wooden post and weeping. And as she wept so she was transformed, though inside, not out, as if all that had been Lily Mooney was being wrung from her in the mucusy gouts of her tears, and he had a forememory then of a hospital bed on which a truly lank-haired Lily Linden lay, while a nurse bent over the bedside cot and cooed at the ruddy scrap of baby protruding from the vast white nappy, fighting its smudge of a nose with soft walnut-wrinkled fists. *Isn't she just grand?* the nurse asked (her Derry accent reviving memories of Dinah's wartime friend, Della, and conferring on her, to Jack's yearning mind at least, the status of honorary family representative at the birth of this, his first child, here in England); turning then from cot to bed and rearranging the pillows: *Sure it's worth every minute when you see them lying there in their cots.* But Lily, water-broken, drained of words, said nothing. Unable to quiet her now and with the shock of nearly choking on his own teeth still vivid, Jack began to creep away up the lane, promising himself that he would have all the time in the world with her, after his appointment. Dusk, in any case, had begun to descend and he was anxious to reach his destination before its insidious indistinctness infected him and blurred his sense of purpose again. He was slowed, though, by a cramp in his right leg and despite his resolve he was soon wandering lost in the gloom. So when, at length, he saw a light fending off the darkness at the end of a narrow track away to his left, he made towards it without another thought. Nor was he in the least put off by the shadowy figures of men he saw as he approached the light – a bare bulb bracketed to a free-standing gable wall. For even before they had achieved complete solidity he recognised them (in fact, it was his recognition which finally confirmed their substance) as the same lamplit men who had stood talking at the end of his street late into Saturday nights throughout his childhood, and beyond: had stood there, his mother's letters had informed him, every Saturday night of the seven years he was in England, though by the end of that time (the years passed fast as thought) they were all without exception retired and their continuing to congregate on that evening and no other could only have been dictated by tradition. The same tradition, doubtless, which in the old days dictated that although any man who wanted to could (and did) stop there for a yarn or a smoke, that particular spot at that particular time was, by rights, the special meeting place of the Islandmen, though even among the Islandmen themselves distinctions were made – by age, by trade, by the ships they had worked on. Jack had noticed while still a child that his own father, who seemed to know everyone there was to know, and who would be whistling and hailing all round him when they were out walking, had a certain greeting he used much more sparingly: a half-wink and a respectful *Alec* or *Sam* or whatever the name was. *Who was that?* Jack's mother might ask. *Alec Russell?* he would say, or *Sam Trainor?* (And Jack got so that he could anticipate him): *Alec (or Sam)'s a Titanic man.* The Belfast Jack grew up in was a city of Titanic Men and Special Powers. Mr Butler next door, he soon discovered, was a Titanic Man, so was Mr Cooke across the way and Mr McMurtry next door to him again. Mr Semple, though he had collected the rent from ever Jack could remember the rent being collected, was nevertheless a Titanic Man, likewise Uncle Jim, Great-auntie Nellie's son, therefore strictly speaking Jack's second cousin, but claimed as uncle anyway, not least because, as Sonny McIlhenny, he had fought for the British middleweight title the year Jack was born and led on points until the penultimate round when a scar in the centre of his forehead (carried, it was said, from an accident in his Queen's Island days), opened up and bled his face scarlet, every last inch of it. A rematch was requested but never fought, for the cut healed all wrong, leaving a lump the size of a conker beneath the skin, which, in time, sprouted a crest of thick hair, so that Uncle Jim used to joke (and Jack being small didn't know any better than to believe him) that he kept his spare eye under there, an idea taken up, coincidentally, in later years by wee bucks too young to have heard of Sonny McIlhenny, who would sneak up behind him in the street, yell *Cyclops!*, then run like the clappers when he turned and stamped his foot, though if they had dared to stand their ground they'd have seen him smiling beneath his three-browed frown. As Jack drew near the wall this evening he saw his uncle's surplus eyebrow, grown white now in advance of the other two, raised to its full height – a facial exclamation mark which lent him an air of such startling frankness that even the tallest of his tall tales could never be dismissed out of hand. Half the men listening to him now shook their heads, the other half nodded theirs, then they swapped so that the shakers nodded and the nodders shook, and finally both shaker-nodders and nodder-shakers looked down for respite at their feet – still in reinforced boots never mind that the heaviest thing they were likely to get on their toes these days was their own sparse spit. Then at a *Boul*

Ernie from Uncle Jim all raised their eyes again, Jack included, and there was his father in the big tweed overcoat Jack and his sisters had clubbed together to buy him the birthday before last, his sixty-fifth. *Boul Ernie.* Uncle Jim's greeting was taken up by the other men, and Jack, nearly forty though he was, felt the same thrill of transgression as he always felt hearing his father's Christian name uttered so casually, for even to Jack's mother he was *Father*; even, Jack had once suspected long ago, when (as the men in the office had used to put it, imitating the movements with undulating hands) they *made the beast.* Jack hadn't expected to see his father out of the house, but he should have known that he would have had to have been a lot sicker than the doctors said he was already before he missed a Saturday night at the top of the street. The collar of his overcoat was turned felt side up and at his throat was knotted the tartan scarf he prided himself on having kept as good as the day he bought it, thirty years before. Uncle Jim, MC to his star-turn, made way for him graciously beneath the bare bulb and as he pulled an unsealed envelope from his overcoat pocket, unfurling three sheets of lined paper, the rest of the men resumed listening positions, contemplating their steel-capped toes. Jack listened too, uncomprehending to begin with, but drawn in by degrees by the cadences of the old songs: of bags being packed, lips being kissed, mud cabins left for evermore; of wanderings through cities near and far, but hearts still at home, across yonder sea, where the girls are so gay and so pretty, and where the green Glens of Antrim are calling . . . with a no, nay, never . . . calling, calling, calling. And by the time these rhythms subsided he was perfectly attuned to the pared-down logic of the plainer speech that replaced them: family, name, grandson; Michael, gone; time, tick, gone; time, tick, *time. . . .* Signalling the end by relaxing his town crier's pose, his father carefully sealed the folded pages into the envelope, then scrunched it into a ball in his fists. He shook his cupped hands beside first one ear, then the other, then opened them again, showing them front and back. The letter had vanished. Uncle Jim led the men in an enthusiastic round of applause which Jack had every intention of joining in till he discovered that one of his arms had gone to sleep where he had been leaning against the wall and was refusing to obey his instruction to clap. The man directly in front turned a dirty look on him, seeming in that scything motion of his head to cut himself off from the rest of the group, taking Jack with him, impaled on his withering stare. That stare put years on Jack: three, six, nine, twelve. . . . He rubbed and punched his mutinous right hand, trying to get the circulation going, and trying at the same time, without staring back too insolently, to work out who's this your man was, for he recognised him from somewhere but couldn't think where, couldn't think of anything suddenly but Pandas and Wombles, and God alone only knew what *they* were. All Jack knew was that it was time he wasn't there and he was feverishly concocting a story about an appointment he had to keep when he remembered that he *did* have an appointment of some sort (though its precise nature, like everything else just now, escaped him), and he *would* have to be going, this minute, if he didn't want to miss it altogether. But the look in the man's eyes said he wasn't going anywhere and when Jack, summoning defiance, turned to leave despite him, another man was standing in his path. This second man looked familiar too, even if it did take Jack a few moments adjusting to the black jaw-length sideburns, the drooping black moustache, and the plastic shades, (so green they were as good as black), clipped on to his gilt-framed glasses. He wore a uniform of khaki bush hat (pinned up at one side by an Orange Widows' badge), olive-drab doughboy jacket, and navy pin-stripe trousers, terminating, above the ankle, in tan elasticated Oxford boots; and alarmed though he was at his predicament, Jack still found time to be relieved that among the many things he had forgotten recently he was at least able to identify beneath this motley disguise the Pink Paraffin man who drove round their estate every Thursday night through the autumn and winter in his Pink Paraffin van. Just then, though, a match was struck behind Jack's back. Cigarette smoke drifted over his shoulder. He turned again, remembering as he did that Pandas were what you called collars like the one on the man's shirt. (And Wombles? Wombles were red herrings; TV puppets dragged in by the Pandas under the catch-all catchphrase *Cuddly Toy! Cuddly Toy!*) A striplight shone down from a wall to the right of the smoker's head, illuminating the thrust of a kung fu fighter's foot across a Coming Soon poster and falling obliquely on five human forms stretched, star-shaped, from fingertips to tiptoes, between the wall and the ground before it. Jack understood, of course, that to all outward appearances he was as guilty as these other five. The new orders had been quite explicit, the hills were out of bounds for the duration of the crisis. But Jack was here on Important Business and had a letter to prove it. He felt the reassuring lump against his ribs of its three folded pages, got off by heart twelve years before and buried deep in his inside pocket ever since. The letter would absolve him. He reached confidently into his jacket and withdrew the envelope. But to his horror, the instant it met the night air the paper began to crumble and his heavy-handed attempts to hold it together only hastened the disinte-gration, leaving him, in the end, clutching at nothing. Stammer-ing, he tried to reconstruct the letter's content, but there was to be no second leave of appeal. A fist crunched into his jaw, verdict and sentence combined. He didn't see it coming, only sniffed its inrushing toxic smell, and didn't feel it hit, as though the smoking knuckles had cauterised that entire side of his face they connected with. He reeled backwards, spitting teeth, then waited, eyes closed, for further blows. But none came. When at last he ventured to look again his assailant and his (every-colour-but-) Pink Paraffin henchman, the figures angled against the wall – the wall itself – were all reduced to a tiny point of dimming light far below and he was alone once more on the mountain path. It occurred to him that he was too high up now for anyone else to bother him and though the night had grown very dark, and though he seemed to have been out there for a lifetime already, this thought relaxed him, so that for the first time in longer than he could remember his body knew what it was to move without stiffness. His feet glided where before they had plodded and soon he had forgotten he was walking at all and was conscious only of going forward finally to the place he had been trying for so long to reach. His mouth felt free of a great burden; his tongue, unravelling itself, obliged him with a whistle. He warbled a snatch of this and a snatch of that, till he found a tune magnificent enough to do justice to his newly exalted mood. The words bloomed in his brain and their fragrance was distilled into heart-lifting melody in his mouth. These were his mountains. He trilled it and frilled it, lips and tongue duetting with Woodbinal virtuosity. Then, sensing he was almost there and feeling it would be irreverent to walk in whistling, he was building up to one final ornate *and now I am home*, when he spotted him, roosting on a tree stump at the side of the lane, head hidden in the crook of his arm, and the music was sucked from his breath.

Drew.

His initial instinct was to sneak past before his son woke. But then he wondered how the boy could have failed to hear him approach and he began to doubt whether he was sleeping at all. In that same instant shame shackled his feet. There would be no moving them until son acknowledged father and freed him from reproach. What Jack needed now was recognition, not blind eyes. It was time Drew was made to understand, young as he was, that this was not the way things were meant to have turned out, to understand the ghosts he was supposed to have laid, and the years of frustration before he was born: all the trying and waiting and praying (if he only knew how fervently he had been prayed for) and nothing happening. Again and again nothing, until a certain night when the heavens opened and rain overflowed the gurgling gutters, forming a streaming curtain beyond the brittle, yellowed blinds, while in the narrow bed Jack had shared with his brother Michael till he was past twenty, Lily had bitten and scrabbed him, frightening yet exciting the life out of him, drumming her fists on his buttocks, and, as the wind and rain tactfully turned up the volume to muffle his yowl from his still-grieving mother and sound-asleep daughter, demanded his semen inside her: *Come on, Jack Linden, damn you. Come on!* Weeks later, when they broke the news to the family, Jack, calculating back to that night (floods of tears when it was all over), stole a sly glance at Lily, who kept her face as straight as his – straighter even – and, in riposte to the hoots of *dark horses* and *after all this time*, said it must be something in the Irish water. Jack the Joker. Changed days. *Sure you wouldn't think it was the same fella at all from he came home that time*, he overheard Peggy

87

telling Dinah, long after the baby was born. *If you could see him with that Drew, the yarns he tells him.* (Just think, son, if we hadn't come back here when we did . . .) *And wee mansie in his high-chair, God love him, nodding back at him* (. . . you might never have been . . .) *all serious, as if he understood every word.* But if he understood then, he had forgotten now and it was vital that he remembered. *You must remember, Drew,* he longed to say, but his tongue could find no purchase and slithered and flailed wordlessly on the smooth surfaces of his gums. Then all at once the boy's head sprang up and his eyes lit on the shattered dentures in his father's hand. Disgust spilt like acid across his face. Jack smiled a foolish, gummy smile. There was no explaining now.

The bell might have been ringing only a matter of moments or else many minutes before Jack became aware of it; certainly another few precious seconds slipped by before he realised what its tolling signified and hobbled towards it. A door was closing somewhere very near at hand. He could hear the scrape of it quite distinctly, but could see nothing remotely resembling a door anywhere he looked about the dark hillside. *No,* he prayed, *no, don't shut it yet, I have an appointment.* But, as though in callous answer to his prayer, his right leg chose that moment to give out completely, pitching him, scrabbling, on to the ground. He cursed himself for having stopped when he was so close. *Please wait, it was all his fault.* He was going in circles by this time, as disoriented as a wing-plucked bluebottle, then the bell fell silent and the unmistakable clatter of a bolt engaging reverberated across the hills and he was shut out. Rage erupted in him. Still prostrate, he battled his way round to face his son again, drawing on all his reserves; and with his lungs pumping, fluttering the ragged standard of his larynx, he urged one last effort from his exhausted tongue. Of course it resisted. Of course it did no more at first than twitch half-heartedly. That was only to be expected. It was a ridiculous tongue; the lowest of low tongues: a licked tongue. But Jack wasn't giving in. His chest pounded and before long the twitch had been cajoled into a fitful thrashing and the thrashing in turn had been harnessed by the toiling muscles of his throat and mouth. And still the bellows pumped, firing ever hotter the furnace of his frustration, till eventually, against all the odds, two words were forged, fragile artefacts of his bitter determination. He held them, cooling, hardening, in his mouth a moment longer, knowing that his timing had to be exact, for there might be no more after these. Then all at once he spotted an opening, and, roared on from the cavity of his chest, stormed it with his do-or-die tongue, forcing the words out, a split-second before the inevitable upsurge of remorse could claw them back . . .

L ILTHI.

The alien airway was coughed clear of his mouth with a miasmic guff of breath, pursued by a single definite, though indistinct, exclamation before his tongue veered right, protruding from the corner of his lips, and utterance gave way to mere salivation.

Drew, his hand brushed by slabbery plastic, started so violently he upset his seat and staggered for balance over its tilting back, striking his hip-bone on the windowsill.

Aunt Peggy leapt to her feet.

– Did you hear him? she said. He spoke. Did you hear him?

Ellen, who had just that moment stepped out to the toilet, came running back into the room.

– What happened? she asked.

Her father's right arm strained to break free of its invisible strait-jacket.

– He said something, Aunt Peggy told her. Plain as day.

Ellen tried to replace the airway, but her father was having none of it. His head thrashed on the mattress and his left hand plucked at his mouth, though there was nothing there now but his own tongue.

– Get a nurse, Ellen said and Aunt Peggy fumbled with the call button hooked to the bedside cabinet.

The staff nurse, already alerted by the commotion, was there in seconds.

– Jack, you're all right, he said, talking him through this as he had talked him through everything else in the night now ended.

An auxiliary entered and the staff nurse motioned her towards the bed.

– Rosemary and I are just going to get you over on to your

other side. I know you're fed up with it, but it's not for much longer.

The eyes darted from side to side beneath the gummed flap of the eyelids, but the rest of the body grew calmer and gave what could only be described as a grunt of consent.

– We're well on our way back now, the staff nurse said when they had finished manoeuvring him as much for the relatives' benefit this time as the patient's.

– My aunt here thinks he might have said something, Ellen said.

The staff nurse, who was pressing the flat of a pen on one of Jack's cuticles and getting no response, looked sceptical.

– Are you sure it was actual words you heard? Are you sure it wasn't just a groan or a sigh?

– Definite, Aunt Peggy said and called on her nephew to back her up. Isn't that right, Drew?

But when she turned round Drew was nowhere to be seen.

– If it's the man with the glasses you want, the auxiliary said, he was going out as I was coming in.

Going out? Peggy's mouth stayed shut, but her expression spoke volumes. Well, no matter, she was sure in her own mind she had heard something, and something more than just a groan or a sigh. There were *l* sounds in it, she remembered that.

Then all at once it came to her, its retrospective clarity greatly enhanced by its poignancy.

– I think, God love him, he was calling for Lily.

And as if in response to the name, the seal was finally broken at that moment on one of her brother's eyelids. It rose only a fraction of an inch for a fraction of a second before closing. But the important thing was – and everyone saw it – that it rose at all.

Alice, of course, had to be told at once. You couldn't have her worrying unnecessarily. As soon as Jack was settled again, Peggy went out into the central hallway between the North and South wards and summoned a lift down to the telephones. Breakfast was being served. The smell of it increased in intensity on a scale of G to 8 while Peggy waited. The stainless steel trolleys were being hauled from the service lift behind her as her own lift arrived.

She was glad that she had given in to her heart's prompting and come to hospital when she did. Though she had been retired for going on ten years now, she was still an early riser at the best of times (which was more than could be said for Walter, who would lie quite happily till midday every day if you let him); and today of course was hardly the best of times. She was washed and downstairs as usual for half-past six, but this morning she found it impossible to settle to anything. She had a feeling. Like the feeling she'd had yesterday evening during the Ulster Television news.

– Walter, she'd said, standing up and rubbing her temple. Something terrible's happened.

And hadn't she been right then?

At seven o'clock precisely by the TV-am clock she switched off the television and left the house. She was at the City and in the lift up to Ward 8 North in under twenty minutes, though she'd seen the days, and not that long ago either, when she could have done the journey in a fraction of the time. In those days she would have thought nothing of visiting at both the City and the Royal on the one night. Her house, on the Donegall Road side of Roden Street (separated now from its Grosvenor Road side by the four-lane peaceline of the Westlink), was almost exactly halfway between the two hospitals and even before she'd had the telephone put in there was precious little went on in either that she could have wanted to know and didn't, as if the wail of every relevant ambulance or the slap of every pertinent baby's bum was carried by infinitesimal vibrations through the web of streets to her door.

Her most uncanny hospital experience, though, occurred one Saturday afternoon in October, thirty years ago now. Mildred McAteer from Empire Drive was in the Royal with an ovarian cyst. (More than a cyst, as it turned out – Mildred was dead within the week.) As Peggy and Betty Turnbull, Mildred's sister-in-law, were leaving at the end of visiting hour a stretcher, with doctors and nurses already in attendance, was being rushed – *slip-slap* – through the flapping plastic doors into Casualty. The two women stood back against the wall to let it pass.

Traffic accident, they heard someone say. Peggy nearly didn't look, because, contrary to appearances, she was not of a morbid disposition at all and her regular dealings with pathology and traumatology were but the unavoidable by-products of her real, overriding interest which was for people, for life. (If there had been no need for such things as hospitals in this world there would have been nobody happier than Peggy Simpson, and in fact the true connoisseur of death in the marriage was Walter, who, as soon as the last of the children had left home, had usurped the spare bedroom for his hobbies, turning it, over the years, into a library of mass murder, militarism, and spontaneous human combustion, subjects on which, incidentally, he had tried Bookstore and found them sadly wanting long before his nephew arrived.) But, as she stood there in Casualty that Saturday afternoon in October thirty years ago, it seemed to Peggy more of an affront to that broken man's dignity to shrink from him in his time of crisis than to look on him with compassion. Oh, it was heartbreaking. Black blood matted his beautiful white hair, cuts and scratches scored his face, and a lump the size of a conker sat up in the centre of his forehead . . .

– Hey, wait a minute, Peggy shouted and took off down the corridor after the stretcher. That's my Uncle Jim you have there.

He had been hit by a lorry on the York Road, on his way, it seems, to Seaview to watch Crusaders play. All by himself and with nothing in his pockets to tell him from Adam. And though he passed away without once regaining consciousness the whole family agreed that Peggy's being there at the moment he was brought in had spared him the even worse fate of dying alone, with maybe an appeal having to be put out in the blue-inked Late News column at the back of the paper to establish his identity.

It was, perhaps, more the knack she demonstrated that day of finding things out even when she hadn't gone looking for them, than her position as eldest of the five brothers and sisters which ensured that it was Peggy who, when the time came, inherited from their mother the unspoken title of keeper of the family records, and inherited from her too the habit of rolling her pupils under her eyelids to aid recall, as though dispatching them to rummage in the attic of her memory for the right shoe-box. For comprehensive the records may have been, but organised they were not. Still, if ever you forgot the date of Michael's birthday – 22 July – or if you wanted to know the exact day of the week Dinah died – a Monday, shortly after lunch – just ask Peggy.

Though there, in passing, was a thing even Peggy couldn't have told you: why it was that their generation seemed to be withering from the bottom up instead of the top down as might have been expected. First Michael, then Dinah, then this business with Jack. She had been afraid last night when she came off the phone to Alice that the next call would be to announce another death. Now instead she was bringing news of their brother's first word on the road to recovery. Lily, God love him.

The lift door slid aside and Peggy stepped out into the ground-floor hall where the keystone of the original workhouse building was kept on permanent display.

The Workhouse was built on a green and sloping meadow, when plague and disease were an accepted way of life . . . When anaesthetics were unknown and the patient bit on the bullet. When a nurse was paid ten pence a week. When a man was old at forty, if he survived that long.

Peggy settled her bosom (when had it got so *big*?) with a jerk of her forearm. She never read that legend without a silent thank-you to God and the National Health Service for modern hospitals. Nostalgia? Don't even mention the word.

One of the most pleasing aspects of modern hospitals for Peggy was their activity, even at eight o'clock on a Saturday morning. Here in the City, the hospital shop was already open and great plastic buckets of chrysanthemums were being delivered to the Interflora stand. Orderlies in overalls appeared and disappeared guiding more stainless steel trolleys from the kitchens. Caped nurses changing shifts squeaked by and yawned. People totally unconnected with the hospital passed this way and that, diverted through the Tower by the construction works which had temporarily blocked the normal shortcut between the Lisburn and Donegall Roads.

– Hello, there, Peggy said to each and every one of them,

her words disappearing back into the rich chuckle from which they came.

The replies, from passers-through and staff alike, were studded with Peggys. You didn't live forty-five years in a place as publicly as she did and not get to know people.

She was walking towards Out-Patients, looking for a phone, when she saw her nephew, sitting on the seats facing the travel shop, hands stuffed down into the pockets of that awful old suit of his, feet shot out in front of him. He looked a sight.

– So this is where you got to, she said, lowering herself into the seat beside him. You had us wondering.

A doctor strode down the corridor from Accident and Emergency, cleaving the air before him with an almost fleshless hook-nose. His white coat barely covered his behind. Peggy, at five foot nothing in her stocking soles (and falling, she could have sworn), wasn't the world's greatest judge of height, but she would have put him at easily seven foot tall. She gave him the same chuckle-greeting she gave everyone else.

– Hello, there.

– Good morning, he said.

He had a big gubby grin beneath the bony blade of his nose. Seven foot tall or not, she thought, they're still only children the half of them. She glanced round at the heavy frown on the face beside her. Such a contrast. If he died with a face like that nobody'd wash it, though she checked herself from saying so. It had been a long night, after all.

– Isn't it great, she said instead, your daddy's nearly his eyes open.

Her nephew nodded his head two or three times and his glasses slipped off the bridge of his nose. They were tiny round-framed glasses with a tortoiseshell casing, probably all the rage with the young ones now, though to Peggy they didn't look very different from the first pair he had . . . how long ago? Oh, twenty-odd years, now. Yes, for Jack and Lily were still living off the Donegall Road themselves then, in the house they'd bought on the edge of the Village just in time for his nibs here being born. Twenty-fifth of March, it was. A Monday night. She remembered walking back from the Jubilee with Jack in the dark and the rain. Walter was sitting by the radio when they got home. *Old Brookeborough's resigned*, he said. *Terence O'Neill's prime minister*. And Jack, who was happier that night than she had ever seen him, because he had gained a son without, as had seemed likely at one stage, losing a wife, decided he'd give the baby Terence as a middle name, to celebrate new beginnings.

But the howls of that wee boy the day he got those glasses! You'd have thought he was being murdered. Jack was in an awful state too. It upset him as much to see his son distraught as it upset Drew to have to wear the blasted things. Upset him so much, in fact, that he called in sick to work the next morning and went across to their mother's house and hunted through the chest of drawers where their father's belongings were kept till he found what he was after; so that when Drew came trudging out the school gate that afternoon, speccy face tripping him, who should be waiting for him but his daddy in a pair of glasses of his own. And little by little, just as Jack had planned, the wee fella forgot to be self-conscious about his glasses, though it was many weeks before Jack felt able to start leaving his off about the house, weeks more before he stopped carrying them in his shirt pocket, and months before he got out of the habit (and never totally convincingly at that) of peering to see without them.

But that was Jack all over. There never was a father prouder, though if you'd seen Drew then yourself you'd have understood why, for there was something about him you couldn't help but love. He was that serious when you talked to him, yet comical with it. Like the year some of the kids went round the doors dressed up, singing *Hallowe'en is coming*, and there Drew was in an old grocer's sack that his daddy had cut arm- and leg-holes in then stuffed with newspapers, a sign pinned to his front saying *4st. Best Irish Spuds*. He'd the whole street in hysterics.

You wouldn't have dreamt to look at him then the trouble he would be when he was older, having to be brought home by the police on one occasion, roaring drunk (and the things he was coming off with apparently were nothing ordinary, the very policemen were disgusted and you can imagine how hardened they'd had to become down the years); none of which, needless to say, Peggy ever heard direct from Jack or Lily, but which all got back to her anyway – within forty-eight hours of its happening in the case just mentioned, even though by that stage the family was long gone from the Donegall Road and living three miles away to the quieter south.

And talk about a scruff! For it wasn't just mornings after all-night vigils in the hospital he looked this bad. He'd been walking round for years with his clothes in a million wrinkles. Peggy hated to think how the rest of the staff in that bookshop dressed if this was what the assistant manager got away with. But then she scolded herself for being a complaining old biddy. And anyway, she thought, her hand to her cheek, who are you to be lecturing other people about wrinkles?

– Well, she said. We'd better not leave Ellen up there too long on her own.

Her nephew gave her a most peculiar sideways glance.

God, he was a shifty one.

– If you don't mind, I'll sit here another minute or two, he said. I'm not feeling the best.

– No, Peggy said, nor you don't look it.

She heaved herself out of her seat. Age was cruel and only the means of its cruelty varied from person to person. Its joke on Peggy was to increase the amount of herself she had to drag about in proportion as her strength to drag it decreased.

– Why don't you get yourself a cup of tea or something? she said.

She was in the lift up to 8 North again before she remembered that she had been going to phone Alice.

*

Derek had been working late in the garage that night. Normally on a Friday he tried to be finished for the kids getting out of school to give himself a few hours with them before taking the cab out. He needed the break. Friday nights were fierce in Belfast. But this particular Friday he also had an order to complete. He'd had a call out of the blue a few weeks before, some guy wanting to know did he do garden furniture. Derek had never made anything other than railings and gates in his self-employed life. He said of course, certainly he did. The way things had been going the last while he'd have said yes to a suspension bridge and thought later. As it was all he'd said yes to was four chairs and a round table. He spent a couple of afternoons in the library, starting off clueless in Gardening and ending up knowledgeable in History of Art, shamelessly cribbing ideas and ornamental lines from English aesthetes, German *Jugendstil*ists, and Parisian Metros. He had the designs ready in three days and drove them up to the address he'd been given, a bungalow on the nearby Georgian estate, where he was so pleased to hear the customer accept them and accept too without question the asking price, inflated by 25 per cent at the last minute to guard against haggling, that he rashly promised the finished order for the Saturday after Easter.

Now it was twenty past six on the Friday of that week, he was due in at the depot at seven, and he still had two whole chairs to gloss. And to make matters worse he'd had to put up with Ellen's father clucking around in the background all day: *will I wash this brush out, Derek? these rags any use to you now, Derek? are you ready for another coffee yet, Derek?*

Today it must have been obvious even to someone as obtuse as Jack was capable of being that he was being kept away from all but the most menial tasks. God knows, Derek would have loved to have been able to trust him, but pushed for time as he was now he would be in a far tighter spot if he had to spend another four or five hours undoing all Jack's mistakes. This order was important to him, not least because it was the only order of any sort he'd had for nearly two months. But despite this, Derek, being Derek, still felt rotten. *Give up, Jack, for both our sakes*, he wanted to scream. *Get in the house with the children and watch the TV.*

There was no getting rid of him, though. Not even when he started to complain of a headache (paint fumes! Derek insisted: paint fumes were notorious for giving you headaches) would he heed Derek's advice and take himself off for a while.

– I'll be fine, he said. I wouldn't want to see you stuck.
STUCK!
But even Derek's patience had a limit and, though neither of them was to know, at twenty past six Jack was only a matter of seconds away from finding it. The yard brush was the clin-

cher. Derek had warned him off it twice already, but after a quarter of an hour sitting idle, trying desperately, perhaps, not to ask himself what he was doing there at all, he evidently could resist it no longer.

Just a wee sweep'll do no harm. Over in the corner, out of the way.

He couldn't have anticipated such a gentle motion raising such a cloud of dust.

– Jack!

Derek shielded the still-tacky chairs with his body.

– Are you going out of your mind? Put that bloody thing down before I belt you with it.

Jack ditched the brush and blushed. Derek blushed too, then to hide his embarrassment bent over to inspect the back of a chair. But that only made matters worse. His face when he stood up again was pure beetroot. Jack, luckily, wasn't looking, but was sitting on a step-stool to the rear of the garage wiping an already clean paintbrush with a garment snatched from the rag pile.

– Coffee? was all Derek could think to say. Must be my turn to make it.

His father-in-law, still intent on his cleaning (Derek couldn't wait to see the beamer he was burning), told him not to go making it on his account. Derek said he wouldn't dream of it. He paused on the way out to check the table.

– That's dry, he said. Maybe you'd give me a hand moving it when we've had our coffee?

Jack mumbled something Derek chose to believe was yes. Please, God, he prayed, don't let him get all humpy with me now, and he felt his own irritation return. Halfway across the garden, though, a thought occurred to him which made him smile and by the time he reached the house he was having to bite on the back of his hand to keep from laughing out loud.

– What's up with you? Ellen asked him.

– We've had a tiff out there, Derek whispered. And now your daddy's trying to be all dignified while he sits cleaning brushes with his hands in a pair of my old Y-fronts.

He switched the kettle on, went to lift two mugs from the mug-tree, thought better of it, and switched the kettle off again.

Suddenly, fretting about getting the job finished this evening seemed pointless. Sunday would be time enough for delivering. What's more, he wasn't going to break his neck taking that car out tonight either. He'd have a good wash first. Better still, a bath. He called Tina away from the TV and sent her out to the garage for her grandpa while he rang the depot to tell them he'd be late.

He half expected to see his daughter already back in front of the television when he came off the phone, but there were only the two boys in the living room. (*Ah!* Derek said and they took their thumbs from their mouths.) The cold tap was on full in the empty kitchen. He looked at it a moment, as if waiting for it to explain itself.

Who left you on? Where's Ellen? Where's Tina? Where's Jack?

The tap continued gushing into the sink. And then, of course, he knew. He charged out the back door to the garage.

The table was standing a yard from the spread newspapers where it had been drying, partly obscuring Jack's body. One whole yard, the final measure of his declining powers. His false teeth sat on the table's latticework top. Tina had taken them out first thing when she found him, even before she ran into the house for Ellen. She'd seen it done in an Australian soap. Tina it was too who told them her grandfather should be on his side and Tina who, without waiting to be sent, now returned to the house a second time and phoned the ambulance.

Ellen meantime draped the rug from the back seat of the car over her father's midriff. His face was still red, as though the blush had become trapped there, and his breathing grumbled in the garage like a faulty exhaust. Derek, desperate to do something to help, rolled rags together into a pillow (checking first for more ex-Y-fronts) to raise his head off the cold concrete. Ellen flapped his hands out of the way just in time. They must be careful of his head, she said. Like a baby, Derek thought, and indeed the symmetrical pattern of the old man's life which he had noted before looked to have been taken one stage nearer to completion. He was as helpless and toothless as a newly born, and as close to nothingness, though sadly for him travelling in the opposite direction.

Ellen went with her father in the ambulance. Derek, following in the car, made a detour round by Drew's. His brother-in-law was waiting for him at the front gate. Tina again. It was no surprise to either of them that almost the first people they saw on arriving at the hospital were Aunt Peggy and Uncle Walter. The doctors were still carrying out their tests, but the results when they came only confirmed what Tina had already diagnosed: her grandfather had suffered a massive stroke and was now in deep coma. There was nothing to do but wait and hope that he could find his way out the other side. By midnight he was stable enough for the nurses to reduce their CNS observations from half-hourly to hourly and at Ellen's insistence Derek reluctantly agreed to drop Peggy and Walter off before going home himself.

Ellen and Drew stayed with their father all through the night in room H8. They watched as the periodic checks were made on his blood pressure and respiratory rate, looked the other way when his urine output was being monitored, and left the room altogether on one occasion while he was being cleaned. In between times they were alone and for the most part silent.

Somewhere around four in the morning it occurred to Drew that, at approaching nine hours, this was the longest uninterrupted spell he had spent in his sister's company since she was married. Since before that, even, because for the three years of her engagement Ellen was at Derek's house every night, the Hastings, unlike the Lindens, having a small front room kept for good, where Derek and Ellen were permitted to sit and play records, though not much else, Drew shouldn't have imagined.

In fact, he would have had to go back almost fifteen years, to the summer of 1975, and the day before Ellen left for Canada, to find a precedent for tonight.

Sylvia Rogers, who worked beside Ellen in the Post Office, had an aunt living not far from Toronto and had invited Ellen out with her for a three-week holiday. But what Ellen didn't let on to anyone till that last night, and then only to Drew, was that Sylvia was planning on emigrating if she took to the life there and that Sylvia's aunt, a divorcee with a huge bungalow, had already said there was room for two in the house permanently if Ellen liked it well enough to try for a work permit herself.

Drew's transistor, strapped to his wrist by a thin, skin-denting plastic loop and nestling in the palm of his right hand, was playing I Can't Give You Anything when Ellen told him. They were in the back bedroom – Ellen's room, so-called, though the purple carpet here was the same purple carpet as in the other two bedrooms, and the slubbed wallpaper in all three was an identical petrol-blue. There were no posters on the walls, no gonks, or ornaments, or clutter of make-up on the chest of drawers to suggest an eighteen-year-old girl in general or Ellen in particular. It could have been anyone's room and indeed had been, until recently, their parents', and before that, briefly, Drew's.

Ellen's case, the white one with the scarlet quilted lining, lay open in a silent scream on the floor. She had set aside the whole day to pack and in the end it had only taken her an hour. She'd unpacked and repacked three times since then and was now unpacking for a fourth. Her bras, doubled-up one-cupped then stacked, towered unsteadily above the pastel mosaic of knickers, folded into insubstantial puff-pastry triangles on the coverlet. Cheesecloth and candy stripes abounded. She made her brother swear not to breathe a word of what she'd just told him to their parents, though she might have saved herself the bother; Drew, at twelve, was already a past master in the art of non-communication where they were concerned and on a previous occasion, when the insurance company where Ellen worked before the Post Office sent her on a residential training course, he had gone a full two days without a word to either of them, immuning himself to embarrassment at the table by inwardly conjugating newly learnt French verbs.

But in the end neither Ellen's insistence on secrecy nor Drew's studied silence counted for anything. The first night Ellen was away their mother and father discussed the possibility of her wanting to go back to Canada to live after her holiday. It was July. There had been a massacre that morning in South Down.

– Would you blame her at all? their mother said.

Their father's teeth tut-tutted as he cleared his mouth.

– She'd have my blessing if she wanted to go, he said, as if,

Drew thought, his blessing or disapproval still had any bearing on things.

But at the end of three weeks when Ellen returned and they asked her how she liked Canada she just shrugged and said *all right*, and of course it was not long after that she started going steady with Derek Hastings and no more was said about emigration, not even to Drew.

Drew must have slept. When he woke, the night sky was cut to red ribbons and Ellen was shaking him by the wrist.

– Quick, she said, look at my daddy.

The nurse who had been in a few minutes before had removed the airway from their father's mouth and a peculiarly calm expression had settled on his face. Too calm, as though he had withdrawn somewhere far inside and was getting ready to leave by the back door while his children were watching the front.

– He's stopped breathing, Ellen said.

– No, he hasn't, Drew told her, but at the same time held his hand close to his father's face.

– I'm calling the nurse, she said.

– Use the bell . . .

But Ellen was already gone. Drew looked again at that serene, emptying face and he remembered his mother's body – *the remains of the deceased* – tucked down in the satiny lining of her coffin like used tissue at the bottom of a pocket.

– Oh, Jesus, don't let him die with just me here.

But the breaths he could feel on the palm of his hand, though slow, were regular, and he began to wonder whether, rather than actually dying, his father was only letting on to die, the way he used to, years ago, on the beach at Tyrella and Ballywalter, while Drew, sitting astride his chest, studied the mask of his face for a subcutaneous smile. Drew had a clown's face badge back then too that smiled and frowned depending on how you tilted it, but in such a way that whichever expression was showing the outline of the other was always visible underneath. Sometimes he would try to coax the smile to the surface of his father's face by twiddling a stalk of dune grass in his nostrils. The chest beneath him, though, would continue to rise and fall so slowly that Drew could not be sure for whole minutes at a time if it was moving at all, and the longer this went on the more he tensed himself for the inevitable moment when his father would leap up with a roar and chase him, so helpless from giggling he could hardly run, along the collapsing sand. Yet no matter how prepared he thought he was, his father always managed to catch him off his guard.

If there had been a stalk of dune grass anywhere in room H8 at that moment he would have twiddled it in his father's nose and given him the chance to catch him out again.

– Come on, he said. I know you're in there.

Ellen returned with the staff nurse and another nurse, then retreated with Drew to the foot of the bed, as if by standing too close they risked breathing some of their father's precious air. The two nurses ran a series of checks, but found nothing amiss, and it was true that their father's expression had lost the unnatural stillness of a few minutes before. As a precautionary measure, though, the staff nurse inserted another airway into his larynx and stood over him for a time before leaving.

The first train of the morning slipped through the City Hospital halt without stopping, bound for Finaghy and Derriaghy on request, Lisburn, Lurgan and Portadown. The sky glowed, ruddy and well scrubbed, all traces of the night rinsed clear. Suddenly the world seemed to Drew way beyond his comprehension and he was weak with an unfamiliar longing. Half a mile and two decades from here, on spring mornings such as this, he had heard the trains' rhythmic rattle as he walked to school, breathing air disinfected by the chemical smells from the Monarch Laundry, escorted by his big sister.

She was very grand, his big sister. He thought the other boys and girls were a little in awe of her. At school Drew wrote a story about her.

His sister was called Ellen.

His sister had green eyes.

His sister always wore bits of plastic and elastic in her hair: bobbles, combs, clasps, slides.

His sister was nice.

His sister could easy do a cartwheel if she wanted.

His sister kept brown paper folded in her chest of drawers.

His sister said it was very very old.

His sister was born in Romford Essex.

His sister was going to be English again when she grew up.

His sister in those days was full of stories of the big houses she had seen before she came to Northern Ireland, houses which Drew, of course, could not begin to imagine, because he was only a twinkle then, as his daddy used to say (so that for a long time he thought of the stars as wee babies waiting to be born). When she went back to England to stay, Ellen told him, she was going to live in the biggest house of all, with lawns, and fountains, and verandahs, and a servants' bell in every room. Drew listened to her, enthralled, though he wasn't so sure he would want to live there himself, for who knows, another thing his daddy sometimes said, if the family hadn't come home from England when they did he might never have been born and he felt that in some way he couldn't yet understand his very life depended on his remaining here. And because of this there were other times when his sister made him angry with the things she said – things about Belfast – or even just the way she said them: the *b* she put where no *b* should be, for instance, in the middle of *Crumlin* Road, or the stink-bomb grimace with which she pronounced the name of the Bog Meadow at the bottom of their street. And often then there would be fights (where fight equalled Drew, in loyal tears, flailing, while Ellen, with six years' head start on her brother, held him at arm's length, her hand on his forehead); fights so irrational that Drew could end up arguing black was white, and knowing it was black all along, or even, as he did on one occasion, find himself denying what was obvious to anyone who cared to look, that his granny's enormous goldfish, with its jutting bottom lip, its boggly eyes, and blotchy brown and white markings, was a freak.

Ellen had settled that particular argument by bringing him a picture in one of his own books of a small neat fish, coloured an all-over orangey-gold.

– See! she said. See! That's what a proper goldfish looks like.

It was the same, Drew noticed, looking then at other pictures in other books, with proper policemen, who wore hard pointed hats, instead of the soft flat hats you saw here, and proper milkmen in their white coats and striped aprons, instead of the Co-op's tatty overalls. And yet, Drew couldn't have imagined one of the book-policemen stopping traffic in his street, or his milk being delivered by a milkman in an apron, jingling a crate on his arm. It was clear from the books that you needed a front garden with a gate for that sort of milkman, or at the very least, a path for him to jingle his crate along; rose-bushes too, preferably, and a metal semicircle saying *Please Leave* then an arrow indicating 0, 1, 2, 3 or 4 *Pints Today Thank You*; not a scribbled-on scrap of paper stuffed in the neck of an empty bottle . . .

There was a light tapping at the door.

– It's only me, Aunt Peggy whispered. I asked the wee nurse fella if it was all right.

– There's no need to whisper, Drew said, though louder even than he had intended.

His father stirred in the shallows of his coma, body chugging then falling still. An engine failing to catch.

– How's he doing?

Ellen crossed all eight fingers for quadruple luck.

– A lot better, thanks.

Drew gave up his seat to his aunt and sat on the windowsill on Ellen's right. Aunt Peggy pulled a quarter of sweets from her pocket and offered them round. Drew's heart staggered under the increased burden of remembrance, of how as a boy he had eyed his aunt's raincoat when she called at the house, trying to guess from the lumps which pocket the sweets were in today. Same raincoat, his sensitised gaze now observed, though become indecipherably lumpy all over since then. Same sweets too. Toffee bonbons. He sucked the sherbet tuber smooth between his tongue and the roof of his mouth, transferred it to his left cheek, wearing down the sugared outer shell till the sweet was soft enough to chew, then gnashed the toffee into a dark golden leaf which gradually dissolved on the ridge of his bottom teeth, flooding his mouth with viscous spit.

Ellen was still sucking, eyebrows arcing with the unaccustomed effort, eyes focused on a point six inches from the ground, midway between her knees and the bed, where her own particular version of the past had bled into the present.

She remained transfixed by it for a while after swallowing, then slowly disengaged her stare, letting her head roll back into a luxurious yawn. Her arms scarecrowed outwards and the worry lines which had settled on her face during the night lifted and scattered. The first yawn triggered a second, bigger one, then a third, bigger still, which lifted her right out of her chair, fingers fluttering towards the ceiling.

— Blimey, she said when she landed, as though her mind had transported the word back as a souvenir of its wandering, an anachronism odd as moon rock.

— Will yous be OK here a minute, she said, while I nip down to the loo?

— Take your time, Aunt Peggy told her. Have a bit of a walk. Get some breakfast.

— I'll see.

— Yes, do, said Drew, moving into the empty seat at the bedside as his sister left the room.

And that was how he came to be sitting in direct line of fire when a few seconds later his father extruded the suction tube and airway, and those two malodorous syllables:

Lilthi.

The shock sent him clattering over the back of his chair. He ricocheted off the windowsill and careered on down the room as Ellen dashed in from the hallway and told Aunt Peggy to ring for help. He had got within a yard or two of the door when the staff nurse entered and raised his father's right arm against the wall's calm beige backdrop. *Lay-deez an' Gen'le-men, I give you.* . . . Sick. He felt sick. The unity of the morning was shattered. An alarm bell he hadn't noticed till then was ringing itself hoarse somewhere out across the roofs of Sandy Row. He bolted from the room before the staff nurse withdrew his support and his father's arm flopped back, powerless, to his side.

Ellen found him where Aunt Peggy had told her she would find him, by the travel agent's, drinking coffee.

— You all right?

— I'm sorry, he said. I just felt really odd all of a sudden.

– It's OK, she said, rubbing her eyes with the backs of her wrists and displacing her jaw sideways to stifle another yawn, I know how you feel.

You don't at all, Drew thought.

– The doctor's with him now. They're doing more tests to see what movement he has.

She pushed her hair behind her ears, slashing it grey. Another microscopic layer of colour gone. (Drew imagined it staining her fingers brown.) The worry lines too were beginning to settle again, on her brow and around her eyes, and it was obvious now, as it should have been obvious, Drew realised, from the start, that they had merely been hovering somewhere or other about her head all this time, waiting for the opportunity to descend.

So their father wasn't going to die; the question now was, what sort of life would he have to look forward to?

Drew bought her a coffee from the vending machine in Accident and Emergency. Handbills in the travel agent's window offered 14 NGTS S/C CORFU £199, 07 NGTS B/B LARNACA (X2) £656, BATTLEFIELD TOURS OF N. FRANCE: 07 NGTS ½-BRD £330 (WAR GRAVES ITINERARY BY REQUEST).

– You know, don't you, Ellen said, enormously interested all of a sudden in her styrofoam coffee cup, that Aunt Peggy swears she heard him call Mum just before you left. The nurses think she's imagining things, of course. They don't think Daddy's, well, *able*.

She turned the cup 360 degrees in one direction then 360 back.

– What about you? She addressed the question to the top of the corridor. Did you hear anything?

Drew considered the back of her head.

– Not Mum's name, that's for sure, he said. Not anything, really, you could call words.

The expression his sister turned to him was dragged down one moment by distress at what the nurses' doubts, thus confirmed, seemed to imply, then hauled up the next by relief that on top of all the other agonies and indignities her father had been made to suffer in the last fifteen hours he had not been tormented by visions of his dead wife.

– That's what I thought, she said.

Drew took off his specs and wipe-wipe-wiped them on the sleeve of his shirt, very gradually, and without at first realising he was doing it, increasing the pressure of forefinger and thumb, counting rapidly under his breath as he rubbed. Onetwothree-fofisiseneighninetenlevntwelve. . . . A childhood whimsy: if he could reach a hundred without the lenses breaking the world he would see through them would be utterly transformed.

But then as now the glass didn't break and now as then the wiped-lens world was unchanged, for when he hooked the legs behind his ears again he was still sitting in the foyer of the City Hospital Tower with his sister; and, despite what he had told her, he was still convinced that his father, emerging from a stroke-induced coma a hundred feet above their heads, had just called him a little shit.

8

– Little shit.

He caught him just behind the ear with the side of his open palm: only a glancing blow, but Drew, who had been on his guard since Ellen and his mother left for the supermarket half an hour before, went down in a heap anyway, hiding his head in his arms, knowing that what the eye couldn't see the hand couldn't hit. Drew had plenty more strategies where that came from: If there's no room to fall, at least keep your face turned towards him, because as a rule he doesn't like to hit you there; cry if you can, but not too much; on no account yell or scream. He had understood early on the need to strike a balance between resistance and acquiescence. Extremes of either only provoked him more.

A hand swiped the air where Drew's head had just been.

– Stinking little bastard shit.

The voice was his father's, but squeezed out unrecognisably thin through taut lips, like clothes wrung from his granny's mangle. Drew pressed his face into the carpet. Tiny pieces of tarmac, walked in from the street, were trod down into the intricately coloured fibres. This close up the pattern was impossible to make out.

Another slap scudded off the back of his locked hands, with the wet *pock* sound of an egg being cracked on the lip of a baking bowl.

– Ow! he said, just loud enough to remind his father who was on the end of those hands.

Sometimes if you said nothing he would simply forget to stop; and since Drew was responsible for him getting into this forgetful state of mind, it seemed only right that it should be up to Drew to do something every now and then to help get him out of it. The effect this time was instant. His father's joints made two quick clicks as he straightened up and started back across the floor. One step, two steps, three steps . . . Four?

Drew strained his ears listening. The stop-start of an electric drill outside. *Newsroom* inside. But no fourth step.

The armchair's leatherette cushion farted under his father's lowered weight. The clack of his teeth, keeping pace with his breathing, told off the seconds in bundles of two or three. Outside, the drill whined and stopped, whined and stopped. Time was taking for ever to pass. Time, like everything else today, had gone haywire.

Drew was already familiar with the great timeless holes that opened up in the aftermath of bomb-blasts (as if at first the world itself had no more idea than the people in it what to do next), but this afternoon there had been twenty-two bombs in Belfast, one after the other. Drew knew. He and Charlie Russell had looked out from the wooden crow's nest at the top of the playground slide counting them off on their fingers.

– Where was that one? Charlie asked once or twice when they were still in single figures.

– How do you expect me to know? Drew said.

They were only wee lads, they didn't know anything much. Then a bomb went off somewhere very near at hand. The crow's nest shuddered as the time-sucking sound ripped past, reducing it in its agitation to a precarious arrangement of like-painted planks. The two boys dived for cover, clutching handfuls of each other's jerseys. Their mouths formed mirror-image Os, as though they were silently singing to each other of their surprise.

A toddler screeching over on the baby swings set the world ticking again. Black smoke, rippled with flame, bloomed fantastically beyond the ridged rooftops to their left.

– Fuck a duck, Charlie said. That was close.

Oh, oh, chongo, Drew thought.

Oh, oh, chongo, he thought now, hearing a second leatherette fart as his father rose from his seat. Drew inched his head into the angled gap between the sofa and the other armchair, but in doing so lost track of his father's movements. His ears made a frantic radar sweep of the room, but any signals his father might have been giving off were lost in the drill's whine and the TV's solemn commentary. *Newsroom* had returned to the day's main story. Belfast. Latest reports said up to ten dead, scores more badly injured. Parents were advised that children might find the pictures that were about to be shown distur . . .

The last syllable was displaced from Drew's hearing by an exclamation of his own – half word, half gasp – as his father grabbed him by the ankles and tried to trail him into the middle of the floor. He jabbed his elbows out just in time, wedging them against the sides of the suite. His father tugged twice more, then, in sheer frustration, let go of his ankles and slapped him on the back of the legs. The slap stung like mad, but Drew took advantage of it to pull his knees to his chest and his whole body further into the gap in the furniture. His father's breath came in snorts as he stood over him, looking, Drew imagined (though how the image managed to surface through his anxiety at that moment, he had no idea), as bemused as the big cat he had once seen on *The World About Us*, puzzling over a porcupine. Rolled into his tight ball, in that inaccessible niche, he even thought he felt a fit of the giggles coming on, but the sudden urge to laugh was quelled by the equally sudden fear of what might happen if his father were to begin hauling the furniture around to get at him. Ellen and his mother could land back in on them at any minute and Drew had grasped well enough by now the absolute necessity of keeping the details of what went on in their absence a secret. Instead of laughing, he decided the moment had come to start to cry. It wasn't difficult, the last slap really had hurt him, and after forcing a few sobs to get going (the way he sometimes had to prompt his dick to piss, even when he was bursting), he was soon in full flow.

– Shut up, for God's sake, his father said. There's nothing wrong with you.

The voice was less compressed than it had been, the anger in it more mundane, even a little embarrassed.

They were just about through.

Drew mopped up the half-cried tears with a couple of super-absorbent sniffs while his father adjusted the Venetian blinds, tilted earlier *to keep the sun out*. Heavy bars of light tumbled into the room, like eavesdroppers surprised, spanning the divide between chair and settee, their middles sagging down on to the carpet at Drew's nose. Drew, however, barely noticed them. He was too busy counting footsteps again: One, two, three . . . (*Go on!* he urged *Go on!*) . . . four!

The hall door opened, then the front door. The whine of the electric drill stopped and didn't start again. Drew walked on his knees to the window. Only his knuckles and the top of his head, all skew-whiff hair and National Health specs, showed above the sill – a 3D version of the cartoons that had begun to appear on walls all over Belfast lately with the warning *Touts beware! Informers will be shot.*

– Norman, his father said.

Drew had to rest his head against the glass and twist his neck painfully to the left to see the person his father was addressing. The figure of Mr Norman Russell, Charlie's father, naked from the waist up, tattooed on one shoulder and red in the face from exertion, grew out of the rafters of an unfinished living-room extension of roughly hewn quarry stone. Mr Russell was never done working on his house. He had added or taken away so many bits over the years that Ronnie, Charlie's elder brother, claimed theirs was the first family in history to have changed house completely without moving an inch.

– Jack, Mr Russell said.

In keeping with the rest of that disjointed day a period of silence ensued before either spoke again.

– Desperate business that this afternoon, Mr Russell said at last.

Drew's father shook his head slowly, his features contracting into a pained huddle in the centre of his face, just as they had earlier in the evening when the full effects of the twenty-two explosions Drew and Charlie had counted from the top of the playground slide first became apparent.

Drew's heart went out to him all over again.

– Don't talk to me about it, he said.

Mr Russell didn't need much persuading. The two men contemplated their matching crazy-paved front gardens (Mr Russell had done them both the year before the Lindens moved in) and the matching rose-bushes which grew on oases of soil in the centre of them.

– That's a gorgeous evening now, Charlie's father said.

– Oh, gorgeous, said Drew's.

They looked at it through the breaks in the terraces opposite, stretching ahead of them for what seemed miles and miles (though it was little more than two) until it ran up against the sullen bull's-back humps of the mountains, stuck by the very television mast which at that precise moment was relaying the *Newsroom* closing titles into Drew's front room.

*

Drew was six when the walks in the mountains stopped. One week he and his father went out as usual after Sunday dinner, the next week they didn't. In between times the soldiers came. There was hymn-singing in the streets the day they arrived.

Drew's mother had taken him and his sister into town that afternoon, to get one shoes and the other a blazer for the return to school in a fortnight's time. They were in a cafe in Castle Lane when the shooting started. A year or two on the customers would have calculated in an instant where the shots were coming from (Cupar Street/Clonard, a mile and a quarter due west), shaken their heads sadly and carried on taking their tea and iced diamonds. But this was still the 1960s, people's ears, and nerves, weren't yet attuned to the sound of gunfire. They did what everyone else in town was doing at that moment. They panicked. Teas were left untouched, bills unpaid, tips uncollected. Outside the buses were in chaos with people trying to get home. Mrs Linden decided to walk it. Drew hung on to her hand. Each time there was a burst of gunfire he gave a little start as if hit and, though she knew he couldn't have been, the trembling passed through his hand, up her arm and into her heart. To calm them both, she sang the only hymn she was confident she knew the words to:

> Jesus bids us shine with a pure clear light
> Like a little candle burning in the night
> In this world of darkness, so-o we must shine . . .

– You in your small corner, Drew sang between sobs and

even Ellen, walking a couple of feet behind them, looking in the shop windows, joined in, very quietly, absentmindedly, almost:

– And I in mine.

They met Aunt Peggy, waiting for Uncle Walter, at the top of Roden Street. The workers had to be let out early from Mackie's for fear of trouble. A woman Aunt Peggy knew on the Springfield Road had had her windows put in by stones thrown by one side and a big Shankill man she worked with had been hit on the head with a rock (*the size of a turnip*) thrown by the other. It was the beginning of a protracted period of nightly hospital visits for Aunt Peggy and she wasn't too well pleased.

– I thought I'd lived to see the end of all that carry-on, she said.

(Aunt Peggy's first job had been as a carder in York Street Mill. After the last big riots, in 1935, some of her Protestant carder friends refused to work beside some of her Catholic carder friends, forcing the factory to close for four days. By the time it reopened, Peggy Linden had found herself another job. She was too disgusted to work in that mill a minute longer.)

– If you'd seen the hate on the people's faces this afternoon, she said, it would have broke your heart. It's worse than the thirties.

This time the current of Linden trembling passed from mother to son, rattling the latter's teeth.

(Lily Linden had no memories of her own of 1935 – she was barely fifteen months old that July – but she had any number of her aunt's hand-me-downs, principal among them being the story of how her sister, Lily's mother, just out of mourning after the death of her husband the year before, had met a British soldier, who swore blind he loved her, seduced her on a stairwell under cover of the curfew, then disappeared with the Emergency, his only legacy a remembered smell of bay rum in her nostrils and a dizzyingly subdividing cluster of cells in her uterus. Disowned by her family, save for her sister, Lily's aunt, and too proud to go chasing after her soldier seducer, she half starved herself and the curfew-conceived foetus to feed her existing child, Lily herself.

– I warned her time and again. Even at nine months she was like that, Lily's aunt said, holding up her index finger.

The baby, a boy, was dead before it was born and three days after she'd been delivered of it the mother herself died, leaving little orphan Lily living with her tale-telling aunt in a single room in Sailortown, till a man as desperate in his way as she was in hers – the one to belong, the other to escape – and as much at a loss to envisage any solution besides marriage, clucked and bumbled his way into her life and, yes, her affection, and she bartered her lifelong repugnance of sex for a passage to England.)

– Jesus bids us shine first of all for him.

Lily Linden took up her hymn again and marched on down the Donegall Road, son to the right of her, daughter to the rear, towards the sound of intermittent gunfire.

Drew cried.

– *Jesus bids us shine first of all for him*, his mother repeated and this time jiggled the rhyming line out of him:

– Well he sees and knows it when our light grows dim . . .

A crowd had gathered at the junction of Donegall Road and Broadway, gazing, almost respectfully, across the grounds of the Royal Victoria Hospital and the Falls Road beyond, to where thick smoke, interrupted occasionally by the dull woof of exploding gas mains (associated ever after in Drew's mind with the phrase *eruption of violence*), was beginning to drift eastwards from the vicinity of Clonard monastery.

– See that stupid fucker O'Neill, one man said and ground a knuckle, tattooed with a blue *L*, into the corner of his eye: He ought to have been strung up.

Lily Linden, hymn-singing no longer, plunged unerringly into the midst of the crowd and plucked out her husband.

– Well, she said, I hope you're happy.

He looked far from it.

He *looked* as if he'd seen a ghost. He *felt* as if he'd just seen half his world being swallowed by an earthquake.

Curlicues of ash danced above the reopened fault, taunting him.

– Well? His wife practically screamed it. Are you, happy?

Drew had somehow become detached from her in all of this

and when she stalked off he was left behind with his father. His father's lips were moving, small, silent movements to begin with, like bubbles in thick soup, but growing bigger, louder, till each movement was a word, the same word repeated over and over:

– Well? Well? Well? Well?

It took Drew a moment or two before he realised this question was now being directed at him. He was as stumped for an answer as his father had been.

Another gas main exploded.

– Pardon *me*, the O'Neill hater said, suddenly finding the whole thing very funny.

By the time the next summer came round the Lindens were well away from the smoke and the ash of the Donegall Road. There was a space called the Green in the centre of the estate where they lived now (though the only green in it was a clump of hydrangeas at the end nearest the shops), with a seating area, a playground of sorts, and two gravel tennis courts. The courts could be booked for a shilling an hour from a little maroon shed, raised fastidiously off the ground on breeze blocks, and people came from all over the district to play on them. It was 1970, Drew collected Esso World Cup coins. He had four Paul Reaneys when nobody else had any. He gave away the spares and made three friends. His friends asked him was he not scared living in his old house.

– Scared of what? Drew said.

One night when Drew was at the Green with his friends he saw his parents come away from the ticket shed carrying hired rackets. They laughed at themselves as they batted their solitary gravel-greyed ball underarm to each other, trotting over every two or three strokes to retrieve it from the net. A large man with a florid complexion and wire-wool hair was looking on from the perimeter fence, hands in pockets. The human end of a lead was looped round his right wrist, the dog end attached to the collar of an elderly labrador (its body the misshape of a badly rolled blanket), which was squatting, blinking, over a tapering Mister-Whippee spiral of dog's dirt. The man stood on the same spot most evenings and considered himself something of an authority where tennis was concerned. Drew was mortified for his parents. There was something not quite decorous about them running around in public in their matching tan Moses sandals, and the thought occurred to him that these were not young people. His mother crossed the court and turned the handle at the side of the net a fraction, reducing the tension. His father, meantime, suddenly resolute, had taken up position on the baseline opposite and was rocking from one Moses sandal to the other, holding the ball to the face of the racket. Drew prayed for a big hole for them both. None appeared. His father tossed the ball in the air and met it on the down with the centre of his racket.

– Oh, good shot there, said the man with the squatting labrador.

Drew's father had served an ace.

– Sure, said Ellen, when Drew told her, did you not know? They used to play loads.

Loads, she meant, before they returned to live in Northern Ireland. Drew added this nugget of information to his small store of impressions of their life *across the water*. He decided it fitted perfectly with striped-aproned milkmen and Ellen's fabulous houses and began to appreciate just how much his parents had left behind so that he could be born.

When the weather was good that summer they lay on bath towels in the crazy-paved front garden. Butterflies flew erratic flight paths in and out of the rose-bush. Drew borrowed a spotter's guide from the library to help him identify them. For once the general and the particular tallied. He imagined other boys, his age and height exactly, looking up from identical books at identical butterflies in their identically crazy-paved gardens, and on still August afternoons he daydreamed that the house had been picked up, like Dorothy's house in *The Wizard of Oz*, and deposited in one of those summer-sounding, cricket-playing English counties: Surrey, or Hampshire, or Kent – or Essex, even.

Winter, though, was punctuated by reports of bomb-blasts and there was no mistaking where he was.

A soldier died, then another, then another, then three more all together. His father's hands developed a tic, or rather a whole range of tics, tumbling over one another with the sudden flittering sound of a sparrow dust-bathing one moment, scratching each other's palms the next, and, when they were doing neither of these, rotating very slowly and deliberately about the pivot of touching thumb pads, as though trying to gauge the dimensions of an invisible, constantly evolving object.

The winter nights were long and sombre. The front door was shut when his father came home each evening and stayed shut till he left for work again the following day. In between times no one called. Just the four of them and the TV. There was an advert on then that Ellen was always singing.

Ulster '71, come and join in the fun!

Mornings were small blessings. Drew prayed for summer, but summer when it came brought more constraint, not less. Bombs exploded in the city centre. Drew's parents took to doing their shopping locally. His father volunteered for the vigilantes that were being formed in case things got right out of hand. Wooden barricades were stored at the entrance of the estate to seal it off at a moment's notice.

But there were some things even wooden barricades couldn't keep out.

In the early hours of the morning of the second Saturday in August 1971, a sniper operating from the darkened window of a terraced house in an estate on the foothills of the Antrim Plateau discharged a rifle for the second and last time in his life, sending a single high-velocity bullet flashing down into the Lagan valley, evading the soft exposed parts of a platoon of soldiers pinned down behind a hedge a block away, evading chimney-pots, treetops, road signs, traffic lights, advertising hoardings, lampposts, church spires, flagpoles (an inordinate number of church spires and flagpoles), and all make and manner of buildings besides, till, closing in on the darkened window of another house on another estate two miles to the south-east, it drilled a perfect hot-poker hole in the glass, puncturing with ease the roll blind, the drapes, the kitchen's boast door, and the chipboard wall of the larder, where it entered and exited in turn a box of Kellogg's cornflakes, a packet of Polson's cornflour, a packet of Atora suet, a box each of Whitworth's sultanas and raisins, a tin of Campbell's cream of tomato soup; entered, finally, a full bag of Tate & Lyle sugar (annihilating the craggy sugar-cube gladiator), but, encountering solid brick on the far side, did not exit and came instead to a stunned halt deep in the granular belly of the bag.

The bag teetered for an instant, then collapsed forward, spilling the guts of two pounds of sugar across the larder shelf.

Not a sinner in the house stirred.

The carnage in the cupboard was not discovered till four hours later when the householder, Mr Norman Russell (the same), came downstairs to fix breakfast. Picking the bullet out of the sugar, he very calmly called the police, then called up to his wife, then dropped to the floor in a dead faint. His wife, seeing the bullet and seeing her husband stretched out on the floor beside it (and forgetting in her panic that he had been fit enough a moment before to call her) called on God to help her and got the Lindens from next door. Mr Russell came to in time to stop the Lindens calling an ambulance. More neighbours arrived. The bullet – an inch and a half long with a dented nose – was passed from person to person in the recently decorated mustard and brown living room.

The police response to Mr Russell's call wasn't exactly swift, but then even bullets must be prioritised, and a bullet in a larder in south Belfast wasn't exactly top of the list that Saturday morning. After months of clamour on one side and months of rumour on the other, internment had finally been introduced the previous Monday. Gun battles had been raging uninterrupted ever since. Hundreds of homes had been burnt, thousands of refugees had fled across the border, and more than twenty people had been killed, among them the eighteen-year-old sniper who had fired the bullet which struck the Russells' house – betrayed by his first muzzle flash, pinpointed by the second, and claimed as a hit the very next instant by an eighteen-year-old sniper from Hunslet, Leeds, a private in the self-same regiment that Michael Linden was serving with when he fell, face-down, wounded, and drowned (Irishglug and Irishgurgle) twenty feet short of the Normandy shore in June 1944. Funny old war.

To the children of the street at least, though, the police were well worth waiting for, because, when they did finally arrive, there were *two* army land-rovers in attendance. What's more, the soldiers in these land-rovers wore not the normal berets, but black envelope caps with ribbons at the back and a border of red and white check.

– Scotchies! the children shouted to each other. Scotchies!

Only Drew Linden, looking on from the tilted blinds of his own front room, was unmoved. He had crept over home under cover of the policemen's entrance into the Russells' crowded living room, though not before he had overheard them saying where they thought the bullet had come from. He could see the place they meant through the break in the houses opposite: a beige blur on the side of the mountain.

But what the policemen hadn't said was why anyone would want to shoot up the top shelf of Charlie Russell's larder, though it could only be a matter of time before they worked that one out too. The bullet was a warning: Drew Linden was a dangerous person to have for a neighbour. He attracted trouble. It had driven his family out of one house already and now it had followed them here. A couple of feet higher, one of the grown-ups had said, and there could have been a tragedy. Drew had caught his father's eye just then. He knew what he was thinking: a couple of feet higher *to the left* . . .

Drew took off his specs and bunching his cuff between his forefinger and thumb began to wipe the lenses. *Onetwotheefofisiseneightninetenlevntwelthirteenfourt* . . .

The front door opened and closed. Drew gave up counting, put his specs back on. He didn't even bother to look round. His father entered and stood beside him at the window, his hands, under the influence of their slow tic, turning this way and that about the pivot of his touching thumbs. Beyond the tilted blind, children clambered over the army land-rovers and tried on the soldiers' black envelope caps. The soldiers themselves lounged at the kerbside, smoking cigarettes, chatting up two girls in hairdresser's overalls, keeping them late for work.

Suddenly his father's right hand broke out of the orbit of the left and slammed into the back of his head and the next thing Drew knew he was on his backside on the floor. Little noises were flaring like match-heads in his ears. His father kept his eyes fixed firmly on the window, his hands for the moment quite still, as though Drew was a fly that had been annoying him for a long time and that he had at last succeeded in swatting. Drew remained on the floor while his brain composed itself. He didn't think since his father had put him there he ought to stand just yet unbidden, but a moment or two later his father knelt and picked him up, in that over-careful way in which people will pick up a cherished ornament they have accidentally upset, as though it was the picking up and not the knocking over in the first place that caused the damage.

There was no apology. He just smoothed the hair at the back of his son's head (with the same hand that had ruffled it) and disappeared upstairs. No sooner was he out of the room than the front door opened again.

Drew was sitting on the settee with his hands folded in his lap when Ellen and his mother came into the living room.

– What have you been up to you're so quiet? his mother asked.

He didn't tell her. Not that time, nor the next time, nor the time after that again. Not ever, in fact. He accepted it as part of his disgrace to have to bear his punishment in silence. Because Drew was in no doubt that he had brought this on himself, for if the family had to come back here in order for him to be born, then, balancing the scales, it stood to reason that had it not been for him they would never have come back at all and exposed themselves to such repeated danger.

Every subsequent explosion compounded his guilt, every Friday night drinker and Saturday shopper atomised, every limb lost, every face disfigured, every soldier and policeman shot, every last body found hooded and dumped in verges and entries, playgrounds and burnt-out cars.

At one stage he had thought that if he were to run away it would all stop. The beatings, the bombings, everything. But he didn't see how he could just walk on to a boat or a plane, and he knew that as long as he remained anywhere within the border (which he had never seen, but imagined as a high wall topped with barbed wire and gun-towers) the violence would not abate, so that in the end there seemed to be nothing for it but to stay where he was. Instead, he made himself as quiet and unobtrusive as he could about the house and tried to avoid being alone with his father, though that was not always possible and then more than ever he was convinced that what was happening to him was somehow just.

This evening, for instance, his sense of guilt and foreboding multiplied by a factor of twenty-two, he had trailed round the kitchen after his mother as she made out her shopping list, asking *please* could he go with her to the supermarket. But his mother told him to for crying out loud quit *bothering* her (if there was one thing Drew's mother hated it was being bothered), and then, of course, as she and Ellen were on their way out the door his father was adjusting the living-room blinds.

To keep the sun out, he said.

To keep the secret in, he meant.

Drew switched over to *The Virginian*. He had missed the start so couldn't tell who Trampas was fighting with or why. (He hoped it wasn't because of something he'd done.) His father came back in from talking to Mr Russell, laughing, relaxed, more like his old self. He unfolded the evening paper, snapping the spine straight and holding it up in front of his face. The headlines were bulging with *b*s:

Best Banned for Two Weeks

on the left side, and on the right (its casualty estimate already way out of date):

Bomb-a-Minute Blitz in Belfast – Many Injured

The inside pages read back to front in the mirror over his shoulder.

— Do you see what's on at the pictures? he said to Drew. *Chitty Chitty Bang Bang*. What do you think, will we all go tomorrow night?

Much more like his old self. Drew smiled.

— Yes.

9

— No!

Derek was pacing the corridor when Drew and Ellen emerged from their interview with the doctor looking after their father the morning after his stroke.

— Well? he'd asked them. What did he say?

Ellen gave it to him in two words. Derek turned each portentous syllable over in his mouth — *hem-i-ple-gi-a, a-pha-si-a* — as if searching for a flaw. Finding none, he broke down and wept. Ellen held him and wept too.

— It would have happened anyway, she whispered. These things don't come from nowhere. You know how he's been lately.

The doctor had warned Ellen and Drew that their father was likely to be very confused for a time when he finally regained consciousness. One moment, it would seem to him, he was lifting a wrought-iron table in his son-in-law's garage, the next he was lying in a hospital bed, unable to move one whole side of his body, unable even to talk. As distressing as it was for them, he was going to need their support.

Ellen and Derek composed themselves at the door before entering his room. But Drew, arriving behind them, still could not bring himself to cross the threshold again. He had come too close earlier to forgetting how long it had taken him to fight free from the sentence of self-reproach which that old man in there had handed down on him as a boy of eight; a sentence from which he might never have succeeded in exculpating himself at all had he not chanced to be passing the picture house on the edge of their estate one mid-May afternoon in 1974 (Richard Nixon, Kevin Keegan, kung fu fighting, Kojak, streaking) at the very moment that his father and five other bewil-

dered men were dragged from the back of a Pink Paraffin van
and spread eagled against the picture-house wall.

There were barricades on the streets again that May – the
old vigilante barricades, though, unlike the old vigilante times,
their purpose now was to keep people in by day rather than
out by night. Indeed, there was at least one old vigilante among
the six men who had fallen foul of their resurrection on Drew's
estate, while those of his captors who had vigilanteed with him
(back when *protection* implied nothing more sinister than an
anorak and warm gloves) had since extended the scope of their
activities beyond mere street patrolling, to the point where they
could contemplate taking on governments and even, if it came
to it, armies, having thrown in their lot with vigilante remnants
from scores of other areas and created something more potent
than the sum of its parts could ever suggest, something hinted
at in the Touts Beware graffiti on one side of the picture-house
porch (*Remember you're a Womble!*) and spelt out in the crest
and *Quis Separabit* motto painted on the other: UDA, the
muscle behind the mouths that for the past six days had been
calling on Protestants to stay away from work and bring down
the treacherous power-sharing Executive.

Wee lads on choppers and five-speed racers buzzed about the
picture-house forecourt behind the six faceless Xs angled
against the wall. A man with wire-wool hair and a shapeless
labrador stopped to watch. Drew's transistor played.

Yes all lovers make, make the same mistakes, as me and you.

Every time one of the men at the wall bent an arm or a leg
he had it bashed rigid again with a pick-axe handle, so that
when at last they were told they were free to go all six collapsed
in a heap on the ground, as though the steady accumulation of
knocks had finally shattered their entire insides.

The strike was solid on their estate from there on in.

A week later the Ulster Workers' Council ordered a massive
reduction in the electricity supply, demonstrating symbolically
and actually that the power-sharing Executive had no power
worth sharing, and by the end of the day the Executive had
bowed to logic and resigned. With it went the barricades, the
tilley lamps, and all the other local ephemera of the shutdown:
the volunteer binmen, the commandeered bread vans, the scab

parades at the picture-house wall. The picture house itself soon followed, blown inside out later that year (seconds after the last patron was evacuated and with the film, a Carry On, still running) by a holdall stuffed with gelignite and abandoned in the foyer. But, close and all as that bomb was, Drew's father kept his fidgeting hands to himself. Perhaps because he was not altogether sorry to see the picture house go. Perhaps because he knew better by now than to try anything else. For it must have been as clear to him as it was to Drew that he had lost more than just face that May afternoon at the picture-house wall. Then, Drew had thought sure he was in for a hiding when his father got home, but, in the event, his father's hands trembled so much it was all he could do to unbutton his own coat and he went to his room without a word, leaving Drew time to ponder on his friend Charlie's admission – almost overlooked earlier in his anxiety – that *his* father had been to work that day as well.

– It was pure luck, Charlie said, the UDA lifted your dad instead of mine.

Luck was not a factor that had previously figured in Drew's calculations of responsibility. Introducing it now had the transforming power of the final tenth clocked up on a milometer brimming with nines: simple but profound, nullifying the mine, mine, mine, mine, mine, mine of the previous three years' assumed guilt and translating the bullet that had started it all, by ripping through the Russells' downstairs window, into a chance in a million stray. He must have been thick not to have seen it for what it was at the time. As thick as champ, as thick as two short planks. As thick, in fact, as an Irishman. The whole world knew the Irish were thick. Irish comedians went on TV and told everyone how thick they were; how an Irishman trying to blow up a ship burnt his lips on the funnel; how an Irish woodworm starved to death in a brick and an Irish goldfish drowned. Irish people themselves sat at home and laughed (though that last joke at least was not considered in good taste in the Linden household, not since the previous April when Drew pushed open the bathroom door and found Ellen kneeling on the oval mat with her arms plunged into the bathwater and an empty bowl on the lino beside her). So they would have loved the one about the eleven-year-old Irish boy who blamed himself for his father beating him up (becoming, in effect, an accessory to his own abuse), blamed himself, moreover, for the deaths of upwards of one thousand people in indiscriminate bombings and random shootings in all corners of the country, few of which, needless to say, he had ever visited; and all because, long ago, he had learnt to blame himself for having been born in the first place.

Funny ha ha.

From that moment forward Drew began to dissociate himself, compiling a mental list of his compatriots' crimes, till one day, seven years on (unlucky for one), a bouncing wheel descended like a freakish full stop at the end of this litany of calamity and contingency, and he puked pure purple, then departed, vowing never to return.

So perhaps, Melanie was right all along; perhaps coming back, even for a short while, was a complete mistake, and whatever befell him hereafter he would have no one to blame for it but himself.

He was sitting on the triangular window-ledge in the corridor outside his father's hospital room, looking out across the slobby inner city, across the Lagan and the progressively less congested suburbs of east Belfast to Dundonald, where the city disappeared through a gap between the Castlereagh and Holywood Hills into County Down. That way, on past Scrabo, lay the seaside towns of the Ards Peninsula: Portavogie, Ballywalter, Millisle, and, his mother's unaccountable favourite for a time when he was young, Donaghadee – only six miles from Bangor, as the song said, though it might as well have been six hundred for all the comfort that was to Drew and Ellen, whose dislike of the place was as fierce as their mother's attachment. Donaghadee was *dead*, as Ellen pronounced it during one particularly dreary visit. It had come on to rain that day the second they lit the primus to boil their kettle, so that they were having to eat their picnic lunch in the car, with the windows steaming up as fast as they were wiped and with the sky, in any case, rung down like a curtain between them and any prospect of note beyond the mouth of the harbour.

– Let me hear no more of your moaning. We're here and that's that, their father said, ominously, or so it sounded to Drew, who, guilt-ridden as ever, convinced that the weather, and consequently the dark mood he could sense his mother slipping into in the passenger seat, were, at least indirectly, his doing, was opening his mouth only to eat.

Rain strafed the windscreen and Ellen's complaint fizzled out unsupported. A greaseproof-paper ball unravelled itself in the dashboard ashtray. Drew crunched a silverskin onion embedded in his meat-paste sandwich. The vinegary charge exploded in his mouth; tears lashed his eyes. Then, quite unexpectedly, even by her desultory standards, Granny Linden, seated in the back between her grandchildren, said:

– Just here's where your grandpa helped bring the guns ashore.

– What guns, granny? Ellen asked.

– The UVF guns.

– *The UVF?*

– Not that UVF, her father said. The real UVF. The men of 1914, Lord Carson's UVF.

– I suppose that makes it all right then, Ellen sarked.

Her father rounded on her.

– The guns that were landed that night, he said, his false teeth clacking in advance of his words (so that he seemed to be deciphering a telegraph message rather than speaking for himself), were what kept Ulster British.

Ellen looked out her rain-slurred window at the dismal little seaside town.

– I'm sure the British were delighted, she said.

(– I'm sure, Hugh McManus once said, echoing her, Nial was delighted with his deal.

The windows were again streaked with rain, though these were on the opposite side of the curtain from Donaghadee. Nine years had passed since that claustrophobic picnic lunch, two hours since Drew, envenomed by four pints of snakebite and eight weeks of playing the Paddy into a cathartic douching, had stepped from the campus fountain, de-Irished, if not completely detoxified, and accepted Hugh's invitation back to his room. They were drinking tea brewed from scrapings filched from other people's lockers. Kelly Thorpe, turning in her sleep on the room's only armchair, had kicked her cup across the nylon carpet which was now giving off a fetid milk and dust steam, though neither Hugh nor Drew was paying any heed to it. They had just discovered they had something in common: they had both been named, one overtly, the other discreetly, after O'Neills.

Terence and Hugh, the tergiversating two, Unionist turncoat and fleeing earl; a reluctant reformer and a grudging Gael.

– Both, you feel, would just as soon have been Englishmen, Hugh said, but both were cursed by name and a sense of destiny.

The O'Neills, at one time, *were* Ulster, descendants of the fabled *ur*-Nial who, in a two-boat, winner-takes-all race for the Ulster shore, laid claim to the prize by lopping off his right hand and hurling it on to the beach, and who, said Hugh, in preferring to mutilate himself rather than concede what he coveted to his rival, set the tone for all the Province's subsequent history.

– I'd give my right arm to be ambidextrous, Drew said, his tongue thick with damp tea dust.

– Precisely, said Hugh.

Kelly Thorpe turned again in the armchair trying to get comfortable. Christmas and her postal gaffe were still a month away, Melanie Bishop slightly more. Down the landing someone opened a window and expectorated hugely into the night.

– The most poignant aspect of Nial's story, though, Hugh went on, is that by the very nature of his triumph he doomed himself to a future of doubt about his ability to defend what he had won. Bloodshed in pursuit of land is only half his legacy, insecurity in possession is the other.)

Across the railway tracks directly below Drew's window, on the waste ground bordering the crossroads of Sandy Row and Donegall Road, wood was already being collected for the July bonfire. The working-class Protestants' annual burnt offering to the great dead hand of Ulster loyalism which had kept them, as much as their Catholic neighbours, in their slummy places for half a century while erecting the vast, mausolean pile of Stormont – long home of Unionist Northern Ireland, secured in part, as Drew's father had once said, by the arms brought ashore at Donaghadee, and visible even from this distance, even to myopic Drew, on the rising ground to the Holywood side of the Dundonald gap, almost opposite the cemetery where his mother lay sunk in a green gravelled tomb.

Drew could not recall having given the graveyard more than a passing glance all the many times they drove by it in his childhood. No doubt because, more often than not, he was trying to glimpse the castle where the prime minister lived in the trees surrounding the parliament buildings. (He was decidedly unimpressed the first time he saw 10 Downing Street on TV: an ordinary terraced house, not even a front garden.) Right up till the day his mother died he had not known of the plot's existence. He often wondered whether she herself had, for that matter, and thought how odd it was to have a piece of ground lying in wait for you all those years, like a well-laid trap.

The final resting place.

Irish earth to Irish earth.

He shivered. He was going to make damned sure his didn't end up in it.

– Drew?

Derek.

– Is there anything the matter?

He turned from the window to the hospital corridor. An empty bed was being wheeled across it from left to right.

– Only it looks a wee bit bad you standing out here all on your own.

It looks a wee bit bad. The ultimate rebuke of a reasonable man.

– The doctor did warn us not to crowd him, Drew said.

A look stole over Derek's face, as close to sceptical as any Drew had ever seen there.

– You're in luck, then, Aunt Peggy's just leaving. That's why I came looking you, she wants to say a prayer before she goes.

Drew didn't move.

– Fine.

– She wants all the family in, Derek said, at the same time easing open the door behind him.

Drew had an oblique view past his brother-in-law's shoulder into the room. Aunt Peggy sat hunched forward, hands already clasped, over a section of blanket on which another, unpaired hand lay stranded.

Oh, no, this was too much.

– I'm sorry, he said, I can't.

Derek shut the door again, bringing his face close to Drew's.

– What's so special about you that you can't pretend like the rest of us? Do you think Ellen and I walk around singing hymns all day long? One prayer can't do any harm, can it? And who's to say, it might actually do some good.

Drew had forgotten how intimidating his brother-in-law could be when he put his mind to it, suddenly exercising muscles that in the normal, easy-going course of things were kept in decorative reserve. He had a dim memory of seeing him fight once in his skinners days, sitting on the other fella's stomach, pummelling his chest and head. Unspectacular but methodical. He could have buried Drew.

– Though I'm wondering, Derek said, whether even if I could prove to you that it did you'd join in then.

– Meaning? Drew said.

The back of his head was touching the wall.

– Meaning if you don't know there's no use me telling you. All I'm saying is, stop and ask yourself some time what it is has been making your daddy so uptight this last lot of weeks.

The instant he said this, the spell of his physical presence was broken. He appeared to Drew to shrink before his eyes, while, behind them, he saw (as though it had been crowded out till then by Derek's bluster) the outcome of that long-ago fight: just at the point where you would have staked your life on him winning, Derek seemed to lose all self-belief; his opponent, finding his, threw him off and kicked his lights in.

Drew pushed past him, glad to have found a focus for his anger, and began walking along the corridor towards the exit sign.

– Drew! Derek shouted after him, but a nurse came out of one of the offices and upbraided him.

– Please! This is a hospital.

Derek walked till he was safely past her, then opened up and ran. Drew was at the lifts, pushing every button in sight. Up and down, passenger and service.

– I'm sorry, Derek said.

– I don't want to hear.

A lift arrived two along from the one Drew was waiting at. Marching down to it he got in and pressed Ground, but Derek pursued him and held the doors, preventing them closing.

– I'm fucking warning you, Derek, let go.

The angrier he got the better Drew felt. An Asian doctor crouched to see under Derek's arm.

– Going down?

Drew nodded, pressed Ground again, bending his thumb back, striping the nail purple and white. Derek stood aside reluctantly, watching the doors merge.

– Drew, listen.

– NO!

All the way down he told himself just to keep walking when the lift stopped: past the hospital shop and the Interflora stand, through the foyer and out the automatic doors; past the Jubilee wing where he was born, across the front of the university block and on up the road to his flat, stopping there only to pack a bag, ring Melanie to tell her of his decision, and ring a cab to take him to the airport. He'd post his resignation from England. They were hardly going to arrest him for not working out his notice. Besides, he was determined, he would not be trapped by guilt again.

The most direct route home though was blocked by building works. He came to a standstill on the pavement before the Tower, momentarily confounded by the shocking elemental reek of bulldozed clay, then turned sharply and gratefully left along a landscaped walkway which brought him out 250 yards further down the Lisburn Road than he'd originally intended, into a mini-dependency of medical suppliers, dentists, health laboratories and dieticians. The Cool FM news jingle sounded from the wound-down window of a glazier's van waiting to turn right into Claremont Street. Drew looked at his watch.

Eleven o'clock. That was, let's see, five, no, *six* o'clock in New York. (Nine days into her assignment, Melanie's fortnight in the States had already become a month and might yet, she suspected, become two months.) Perhaps he should wait another hour anyway before he rang. He might as well quit work first, then he'd really have something to tell her. Yes, that's what he'd do, seeing he was this close. Get it over with. And anyway, he hadn't called in yet to explain why he was late this morning.

He crossed the mouth of Sandy Row into Bradbury Place and had begun island-hopping across Shaftesbury Square towards Dublin Road before he thought to ask himself who exactly he was planning on handing his resignation in to. It was Saturday morning: no Pamela. Damn. Now what did he do? Traffic swirled around him, centrifugal, centripetal. The sky was big and blue and empty. A helicopter hung like a mobile over the Lower Falls, half a mile to the north-west, its drone drowned by the clanging and drilling from the building sites hidden behind green netting all the way down Great Victoria Street to the Europa Hotel.

Well do *something*.

There was no point going into work, that was for sure. He dashed across to the east side of the square and phoned the shop from a box outside the post office. Sian answered. He told her his father had been taken ill.

– Oh, she said. I *am* sorry.

– But I'll be in this afternoon, he found himself saying.

– Don't hurry yourself on our account, we've plenty of staff in, Sian said, a little too quickly, it seemed to Drew, and, despite his decision to leave, this reminder of his failure with her and the rest of the staff still rankled.

Stepping out from the phone-box he was confronted again by the massive grey and yellow slab of the City Hospital Tower. In there, at this very moment his father was lying, little more than semi-conscious, with one side of his mouth downturned in a sour carp grimace and one hand limp as a lame dog's paw. He wondered what sort of person he had become that that thought could leave him completely unmoved. But then he wondered too whether, with the remembrance of all that he had put him through so recently revivified, he could submit himself to sit docilely at his father's bedside and he didn't wait for the answer. He walked the few yards to the corner of the block, then, making a snap decision, turned left into Donegall Pass and was immediately caught in the sequence of cameras and mirrors which supplemented the eyes watching him from the pillbox in front of the police station. He offered himself to them boldly, imagining his reflection being pulled apart and decoded somewhere deep inside the station. *Justifiable anger*, the monitor would say, then project him, reconstructed, back on to the footpath and allow him to continue on his way.

Beyond the fortifications, *jazzbo brown's* was opening for the day. Ralph the bouncer, jacket off, sleeves carefully folded back, was wiping down the chrome crescents of the door handles with a chamois.

— Ach, Drew, he said. What's wrong you haven't been in lately?

— Been too busy, Drew said.

— What, Ralph leered, *busy* busy, or just busy?

— Bit of one, Drew said, bit of the other.

— Oh, you're a fly man. Ralph was delighted. But, here, you were as well out of it last night.

— Trouble? Drew asked.

Ralph scanned the handles for blemishes.

— There's this whole pile of hoods lands in from Sandy Row, see, beating at the doors, looking late drinks. Here's me: *Smart dress only, lads*. Trouble? There was near a fucking riot.

He opened out the chamois to show Drew a fist-sized blot of mopped-up blood.

— All that for a drink.

He folded the cloth again and went back to wiping.

— Too many of them for just me, like. Had to get the Feds in from down the street in the end to give me a hand.

The night the Titanic sank in his estimation, the Feds from down the street had come for Drew as well. He'd been turfed out finally for boking on a barman, who was trying to make him clean up the purple mess he'd made of the bogs, and had proceeded to boke again all over the footpath and once more, for good measure, out the rear doors of the police land-rover as it sped him, against the better judgement of five-sixths of the crew, southwards out of the city centre. If it hadn't been for them finding out what school he'd gone to – the same school as the son of the oldest policeman, the one who held his head for him while he lashed up over the yawing asphalt – and the fact that he was leaving soon for university, they'd have taken him in for sure. As it was, by the time they got him home, there wasn't a single officer didn't wish they had, for when he wasn't retching out the back of the vehicle he was lolling on the floor, snorting obscenely,

– What's this, what's this: *Clunk, click, crunch?* A car driving through north Belfast. Get it? Clunk, click, crunch!

Under cover of dark, one of the policemen stuck a boot up his arse while a colleague dragged his head up by the hair and yelled – salmon and onion breath – into his face:

– That's not fucking funny, you. Do you hear?

But it didn't matter what they breathed on him, or where they stuck their policemen's boots, Drew still thought it was all a scream. Clunk, click, crunch!

The policeman whose son went to Drew's school shook his head sadly when he delivered him to his parents' front door.

– That's one sick wee boy you have there, he said.

The day before, a man had starved himself to death in a jail ten miles to the south of where they stood. That same night, four miles to the north, another man, caught up in the obligatory obsequial riot, was crushed to death in his car by the shed wheel of a crashed army Saracen.

Fucking right their wee boy was sick.

– Ah, well, Ralph said. No rest for the wicked, what?

He hung the chamois on the rim of a bucket and hoisted it into the hallway of *jazzbo brown's.*

– Come down and see us some night in Bangor, he said at the door. Bring your girl with you.

– I might just do that, Drew said, feeling as always with Ralph there was no point explaining; in this case that, in so far as she could ever have been said to be *his* at all, Kay Morris was soon to be his girl no longer; that he was returning to Melanie and to England at the earliest possible opportunity and fervently hoped never to see Ralph, or Bangor, again in his life.

Round the corner, Kay's curtains were still drawn. Drew hesitated before deciding to knock. He gave the door two or three light taps, then waited. No Kay. He knocked again, less tentatively, and put his ear to the Yale lock. Still nothing. It had suddenly become very important to him that he see Kay Morris and he was just reaching for the knocker a third time when it unexpectedly evaded his grasp and there in the open doorway stood a woman in an ivory silk dressing gown.

Drew, already thrown off-balance, took an involuntary step back and glanced at the front of the house. Definitely Kay's, as, to the best of his knowledge, was the ivory silk dressing gown. But the woman inside them both was most definitely not Kay herself. She was a good four or five inches taller for one thing and a good four or five years older besides. Despite her undress, her face was carefully made up. Her hair too showed signs of meticulous grooming, wound round and round into an enormous fringeless turban which unravelled here and there in twisted sashes – chestnut rippled with darker brown – about her shoulders. Yet, for all its spectacular volume, Drew got the impression (not least from the woman's peculiarly rigid posture) that a sudden jolt might scatter it, like a dandelion clock. It was at once the most wonderful and the most ludicrous hairstyle he had ever seen. Or perhaps *ever* was going too far; and, in fact, the next instant he was convinced that he had had cause to remark on one very like it at some stage in the past. The Titanic bar reared up in his mind, but he dismissed it out of hand. The woman before him was too old to have drunk there when he did.

Something to do with the TV then?

Hardly. Unless it was *Dallas* or *Dynasty* he was thinking of. Or Sindy, even.

– Who is it, Anna?

Kay's voice. The woman bounced the question on to him with a raised right eyebrow, at the same time pulling the left down into a frown.

– Drew Linden, Drew said.

– Drew Linden, the woman called over her shoulder, never for a moment taking her eyes off him.

– *Drew!* Kay's voice was shrill. Why's he not at work?

The frown peeled away from the woman's face.

– Why are you not at work? she asked.

Kay appeared, crouching, at the end of the hall, trailing the hem of a dilapidated mohair jumper down over her thighs.

– Well come in if you're coming in, she snapped.

Drew decided he was and the strange woman shut the front door behind him. Kay let go of her jumper. The hem sprang back then settled again but higher up than previously so that when she turned and walked into the kitchen two segments of pale buttock were plainly visible beneath it. She filled a glass with cold water at the kitchen sink, drank it off, filled another, swallowed half of that.

– Anna, she said facing Drew but looking past him, this is Drew Linden, a *friend*.

Drew half turned. The woman in Kay's dressing gown by the fridge was all hair and stillness.

– How do you do.

– Drew, this is my . . . sister, Anna.

He did not go into work at all in the end, but, at Kay's insistence, slept through the afternoon and into the evening in her bed. She brought him fresh orange juice when he woke.

– I'd no idea you had a sister, he said.

– *Half*-sister, really, Kay said. My father was married before.

– Even so, you never mentioned her.

– No? She's been living in Dublin, I hardly see her. Anyway, listen who's talking. I thought you'd sprung from the earth fully formed.

Drew had told Kay all about his father and the hospital while she was putting him to bed. When he was dressed again, she handed him a cordless telephone and stood over him while he rang through to Ward 8 North. His father had been conscious since lunchtime but was now sleeping comfortably. Ellen and Derek had gone home. Drew phoned them there.

– Thank God you called, Ellen said. Derek's been everywhere looking for you.

Drew spoke to him, apologised for the scene, blamed exhaustion. Derek said they were all under a lot of stress. Drew accepted his invitation to go to them tomorrow for Sunday lunch after visiting at the hospital.

Kay had held Saturday dinner back for him waking. Three candles burned in the centre of the table at which Anna was already seated eating black olives. Her make-up was again flawless, though more exotic than this morning's – a palette of reds, blues and purples – and there was a real flower in her hair. Drew's own hair was all over the place. He licked his fingertips and dragged them through it a few times in a vain attempt to tame it. He needed a shave and a change of clothes. His shirt had been dirty even yesterday. Anna, on the other hand, wore a formal-looking blue dress with chiffon sleeves. In the light of this, Kay's keeping her apron on over her own rather chic dress throughout the meal seemed to him less an oversight than a declaration of allegiance, and indeed as the dinner progressed he sensed all was not right between the sisters. Kay reserved most of her conversation for him. Anna spoke little. She smoked a single cigarette between each course and when, at the coffee stage, she got a spot of ash on her bodice, she said a quiet *feck it*, the Southerner's euphemism, which, far from seeming mealy-mouthed, like *fudge*, Drew had always thought, made the Anglo-Saxon word sound like a clumsy Ulsterism. Kay, though, took exception.

– *Uh*, she said. You're in the north now, you say *fuck* it.

Anna glared across the table with that almost stick-insect stillness which Drew had noted earlier and which combined with her ludicrous pile of hair, flower and all, to make him feel suddenly very sorry for her.

– Oh, sister, take a joke, Kay said.

Anna's smile had all the joy of a facial exercise. Her near-perfect front teeth were the porcelain-grey of crowns, and the ragged regression on either side ran the spectrum of off-whites into yellow.

– More coffee? Kay said, jumping to her feet and stacking the plates noisily. Whiskey? Brandy?

– Nothing for me, Drew said. Can I give you a hand?

– Sit where you are, Kay told him. I'm just leaving them on the sideboard.

She went through to the kitchen. Anna stubbed out her cigarette half-smoked and straight away lit another. Drew stirred his coffee.

– Have you been living in Dublin long? he asked, unimaginatively, he knew, but conscious that he ought to say something.

– Wicklow.

The word fumed from her lips.

– I only work in Dublin.

– Wicklow, Drew corrected himself, though feeling that she might have been a little more gracious. Have you been living there long?

– Four years, she said and offered nothing further.

It was clear she was going to make him work for every word he got out of her. He doubted very much whether in the normal run of things he could have been bothered with the effort, but she was Kay's sister – *half*-sister – and he was her (*half*-)lover and for this evening at least, let's face it, they were stuck with each other.

– Listen, I don't know what's going on here . . .

He stopped. Kay returned with the coffee pot, picked up the remaining dishes, left again.

– I don't know what's going on between the two of you, he said, and I'd rather not get involved.

– Lucky for you that's got the choice.

This was spoken very quickly, half into her coffee cup, but as Drew was leaning forward to beg her pardon she faced him squarely.

– We haven't seen each other much lately, you know, Kay and I.

– Kay said.

– What did Kay say? Kay asked, coming through from the kitchen a second time and flopping into her chair. Something dreadful I hope.

– I was just telling Drew that you never come and visit me, Anna said.

– Are you wise? Down there with the bogtrotters?

But this time, unexpectedly, they both laughed.

*

Kay lifted the quilt to let him in beside her and nuzzled against

139

him sleepily. Drew lay in the smoke-thick darkness listening to her stoned breathing. She had pushed a towel into the gap at the bottom of the door to stop the smell of the dope escaping on to the landing. Likewise, later, when they were making love, she had stifled his groans with the heel of her hand (her own orgasms were ultrasonic affairs: open-mouthed, bomb-shocked silences), thus ensuring that even as he was coming with one sister Drew was conscious of the other, stretched out, perhaps, in all her unknown nakedness in the next-door guest-room. It was Anna alone who had occupied his thoughts ever since. He had got little of sense or value out of his whispered exchanges with Kay before she drifted off beyond the reach of speech. There was mention of a boutique, a fashionable quarter of Dublin, and a con of some sort. Titbits only, nowhere near enough to satisfy his suddenly ravenous curiosity. He wanted to know *everything* about her sister. Starting with what she did with all that hair when she went to bed. He had found a flossy ball of it in the bathroom pedal-bin just now when he was sluicing his mouth out (for it was a hang-up of his that, despite all their recent intimate kisses and licks, he could not bring himself to use Kay's toothbrush). He had found too the damp cotton-wool pads, stained red, purple and blue, with which Anna had erased the careful composition of her face. A bag of these pads hung by its drawstring from the wicker chair which was normally piled with Kay's magazines, but which had been cleared to accommodate a small tray of Anna's bottles and jars. He had taken off a couple of the lids and looked inside, had seen in one the slowly filling channel worn by the pressure of her index finger. Cold smell – he broadened the track with a finger of his own – deliciously cold touch ... His whole body shuddered as he fumbled to replace the lid.

Someone, his Granny Linden would have said, was walking across his grave.

10

GRANNY LINDEN KEPT a lucky penny tucked away in the purse she always carried in her apron pocket. The penny was black with age and the old woman on the front seemed about to fall asleep. Her name was Victoria and she had been the queen for a very long time, which was probably what had made her so tired. There had been four kings since then – two called Edward and two called George – and another queen, the present one, Queen Elizabeth.

Granny Linden had memories of them all.

She told Ellen that the blackened penny had been shiny and new the year she was born (she was called Greta Parks then instead of Granny Linden) and the date on the back said 1899. Ellen, at six and a quarter, understanding as yet only imperfectly the principles of addition and subtraction, worked out that that made her granny 164 years old. Her granny told her, further, that she had lived in two different countries without ever moving more than three doors from the house where she was born, but Ellen had no idea what *that* made her, except, maybe, magic. Certainly such an explanation would have been consistent not only with her phenomenal age, but also with the peculiar trances Ellen had seen her go into sometimes when asked a question, during which the lines on her forehead grew tight-packed and rigid and her pupils vanished up behind her eyelids for what seemed, to Ellen, an age. And, what was almost as strange, whenever she did at last give her opinion, she rarely began it with *I think* or *I'll tell you*, but, more usually, with *My father would never have stood for* whatever it was, or *If your Auntie Mary was alive she'd not have done* this or that; or, again: *Wee Mrs Smart always used to swear by* something, and *The doctor in the Sunday Post recommends* something else.

You could have talked to Ellen till you were blue in the face in those days, but you would have had a hard job convincing her that there was anything in the world more remarkable than a grandmother who was able to remember the thoughts and sayings of so many people on so many subjects, and who had lived in two different countries without leaving the street where she was born, over 160 years before.

To do her justice, Ellen was not long in realising the mistake she had made calculating her granny's age, though she need not have persisted in it even for the short time that she did (and thank goodness she had not told her teacher, as she had intended doing at one stage) had her granny herself thought to correct her the first night she made it. Then, though, Granny Linden had just nodded vaguely and continued watching the television. She'd only had the set a month and still seemed to be half expecting the contents to run out at any moment, like a seaside slot-machine. Ellen's daddy had hired it for her when they moved out into their own house. To bring her up to date, he told Ellen; for c-o-m-p-a-n-y, he told everybody else.

Ellen had been working away quietly on the rug in front of the kitchen fire since her granny had shown her the lucky penny. Her school jotter was open before her, its pages dotted with ragged grey circles where she had traced the coin by placing it under the paper and shading over it with the side of her pencil-lead, the way her granny had taught her, so that the date stood out magically clear. It was the first time since she arrived that afternoon that she had stopped running about and chittering. She couldn't help it, she was just glad to be back. She had even summoned a friendly smile for her granny's enormous goldfish. The goldfish's bowl now sat on top of the television, together with the photograph of Grandpa and his brother, and Granny Linden had acquired the disconcerting habit, every time something on the screen below struck her as particularly funny or exciting, of shouting out to one or other of them:

– Oh, you should see this!

Probably to the goldfish, Ellen decided. She had heard her granny talking to it on more than one occasion in the past when she put it into the pudding basin to change its water. *Poor fella*, she'd say. *Nearly done. Soon be all nice and clean again. Poor fella.* Ellen kept well out of the way while this was going on, sitting in the next room holding her nose, when she could bear to remain in the house at all.

The time by the big black kitchen clock, which Ellen had at last learnt to read shortly before moving to the new house, was eighteen minutes past seven when she closed the jotter on her startling discovery and got up on to the sofa beside her ancient granny. A chilly drizzle had set in for the night, though there was still a little daylight in the yard, because (something else Ellen had now grasped the meaning of) the clocks had gone forward again just the day before. Soon it would be Easter, then summer, and she would be finished school; and before any of that her mummy would be getting out of hospital, without that horrid old bump, and Ellen would have a new baby brother. *Or sister*, her mummy kept insisting right to the last, though her daddy had talked about a boy so often by now that Ellen couldn't really imagine the baby being anything else.

And some day later, maybe, when the baby was a bit bigger they would go back to England, taking Granny Linden with them.

That, at least, was what coming here to stay again this afternoon, with all the memories it stirred of the first time she set foot in the house, had encouraged Ellen to hope. It was, though, a quieter, more distant hope than previously, for she had not yet forgotten the pain of past disappointments. Her expectations had soared the day her daddy sat her down in Granny's kitchen and began to tell her about the new house he had found for them, but then she cottoned on it was still Belfast he was talking about and she cried her eyes out. Her daddy slapped the arm of the chair as he stood up.

– Now what's the matter? he asked.

Ellen's mummy, slouched on the settee, big belly swelling, snorted. Ellen herself, fearing a shouting match, cried harder.

– Belt up before I give you something to really cry about, her daddy yelled, but Ellen didn't hang around to see what the something might be and raced from the house, pursued by his hurt and angry shouts.

She dodged into one entry, then another, then another entry off that and another off that again, till finally she stopped hearing him altogether. The running had dried her tears as well as clearing her ears. After a quiet while, she walked back along the entry in which she had been hiding and turned into the one below, but at the bottom of this second entry she couldn't remember which way she was meant to go next. Both sides looked the same: yard walls and gates, skirted here and there with thistles. Powdered ash swirled about the flagstones. Ellen didn't panic. She stood facing the entry she had just come down, making scales of her open palms, trying to work out whether she had taken a right- or a left-hand turn into it. Right, she decided, then changed her mind to left and back again, straight away, to right. She skipped a few steps for confidence. Yes, right was right. A pale silver sun was half sunk behind the rim of the mountain, like a sixpence jammed in a black piggy-bank. Dark muscular skies were massing around it, as if to press it down all the way. Ellen skipped faster, then froze, one foot raised. Through a collapsed gate on the left of the alleyway she had caught sight of the ginger tomcat that mooched around her granny's yard, flopping now all over another, littler cat and biting the back of its neck. The poor wee mite was all twisted beneath it, its tail and tilted jaw pointing straight up in the air, and, in between, its belly arcing downwards into the ground, as though it was trying to squirm free.

Ellen felt instinctively she ought to help. She spied a chunk of brick in amongst the weeds and, snatching it up, advanced on the broken gate. The ginger tom watched her approach without flinching. Ellen had not really expected to have to throw the brick and wondered now how she was to do it without hitting both cats.

And then the little one hissed. Not at the tomcat, but at Ellen herself.

Confounded, she let go of the brick and began to retreat down the entry, at first only dimly aware of the tickling sensation on the back of her hand. With every step she took from the source of her confusion, however, the tickle became more insistent; but when at last she could hold off scratching no longer it eluded her fingertips and ran further up her arm. Ellen not only felt this movement, but saw it too: black, shiny and six-legged.

A huge clock, fallen from the brick, was clambering over her elbow. Ellen shrieked and shrieked, stiff with fear. The clock scuttled in circles on her skin.

Then suddenly her arm was being shaken and the petrifying tickle was wiped away at the same time as a foot-stamp echoed off the entry walls. Her daddy's face loomed over her.

– Don't smack me, don't smack me, she pleaded, but he couldn't have lifted a hand to her now even if he'd wanted to.

– Never you run away like that again, he said, hugging her. Do you hear?

– Oh! you should see this, Granny Linden said as peals of laughter broke from the television. But Ellen, by then, was fast asleep. The kitchen clock chimed half-past seven. Grandpa smiled, slightly out of focus, grey beside Great-uncle Geordie's bright white shirt and radiant God-hair. The goldfish gave the settee a magnified sideways glance, then followed its tail on round the bowl.

Meanwhile, in the Jubilee wing of the Belfast City Hospital, Ellen's mummy, Lily, in the ninth month of pregnancy, torn, as she had been for the previous eight, between holding out and giving up, was finally induced into doing the latter and her second child, a son, a brother, saw the world the wrong way up and shrieked.

The baby was born with masses of dark hair which fell out after less than a month then grew again, a shade lighter, but twice as thick. They called him Andrew Terence, which seemed such big names for such a tiny thing that from the very beginning he got plain Drew for short. Ellen's mummy was sick for a long time after he was born and for a long time after that again she was weak and easily tired. Ellen spent many more nights at her granny's house, so many, in fact, that even after her mummy was completely better, she kept on going at weekends out of habit. For several years the pattern of these weekends varied little. Her daddy dropped her off after dinner on Friday and collected her again in time for dinner on Sunday. For the dinner in between her granny made stewed steak, carrot and onion and for afters she and Ellen split a cold custard bun or, as a special treat, an eclair.

At ten-thirty precisely each Saturday morning Victor Butler's maroon Ford Zephyr pulled up at the kerb outside his grandparents' front door and at ten-thirty precisely each Saturday morning Ellen just happened to be sitting on the step outside her granny's front door as he got out of the car.

– How's tricks, kiddo? Victor would say and cock a pair of finger-thumb guns at her.

There was a ruby set in gold on his left pinky.

Victor was a salesman for a confectionary wholesaler and travelled the length and breadth of the country in his Ford Zephyr car. But no matter how far away he was on Friday night, he never failed to make it back to Belfast the following morning to take his grandparents shopping and then drive them over to his house in Glengormley for their lunch. Old Mr and Mrs Butler had become very feeble, very quickly in the months since Ellen first met them (Ellen was sorry now she had once called them names) and apart from Saturdays they hardly ever went out over the doorstep any more. Not even to spit.

Saturday was also the day the van came round with the Butlers' laundry (Victor it was – *who else?* Granny asked – who paid the account) and the boy would leave it with Granny Linden if they were still not home. Ellen watched all afternoon for the Ford Zephyr's return then sprinted next door with the crinkly parcels the second she saw it turning into the street. Victor kept his grandparents well supplied with sweets and old Mrs Butler always brought the tin in from the sideboard and let Ellen pick something for running the message. Grown-up sweets: clove rock and army and navy gums, raspberry ruffles, butter balls and brandy balls. Ellen's favourites, though, were the glacé fruit drops. She thought these were very elegant sweets, especially the reds and the purples which looked semi-precious and tasted as deep and rich as they looked. She knew for a fact that a quarter of them cost more than she got each week for her pay and she was sure Victor must be very well-off if he could afford to give so many away.

Her granny had told her it was impolite just to take the sweet and run and so she sat on the very edge of the settee, sucking as quietly as possible, her face pinched and long (though gracefully so, she thought), while Victor and his grandfather watched wrestling or muddy rugby. Whenever she stood up to leave, old Mr Butler would rouse himself and sit forward in his chair.

– Rrrrsn. . . . Rrrrsn. . . . (a fumble for his hanky then a cough) Isn't she a quer girl, Victor?

– She is, aye.

And Ellen would blush like mad and look at the carpet. She was nine when she learnt the word crush and realised she'd had one on Victor for the past two years. For a long time afterwards she equated true love with the jaw-aching sweetness of glacé fruit drops. When her first boyfriend kissed her and his tongue found the inside of her cheek she felt her mouth turn liquid, until he, misreading the sign, began to flick his tongue everywhere and nowhere and the feeling subsided.

Victor, though, already had a wife. Her name was Mandy and she was an ex-model. She came with him occasionally, but always stayed in the car while he went in to get his grandparents. Her hair was a vibrant orange and she wore it parted at the side, curving round in two sharp points below her cheekbones. Ellen was in complete awe of this woman. Whenever she spotted her in the passenger's seat she did not sit forward, as she usually did, to receive Victor's greeting but tried instead to make herself very small in the doorway. She was evidently not always fast enough, though, for on one such Saturday she heard a window being wound down after Victor's door banged shut and the woman's voice calling:

– Hey, you there, behind the door.

Ellen sat where she was.

– I can see your legs.

Ellen pulled them into her chest, then, feeling foolish, stood up on them and walked out on to the footpath.

– I don't bite, you know, the woman said to make her smile. Ellen managed half a one.

– Is that your house? she asked.

Ellen was still too overcome by shyness to go into details. She nodded.

– A rose among the thorns, the woman said. She had the tiniest nose Ellen had ever seen.

– Have you heard that before?

Ellen shook her head. The woman asked to see her tongue. After a moment's hesitation Ellen showed her the tip of it.

– Just checking, she said.

A colour magazine lay open on her lap. She caught Ellen looking at it.

– Do you know where this is?

She held up the folded magazine. Ellen saw a ceremony of some sort. Indians in head-dresses; Mounties.

– Canada, she said, very quietly.

– Canada, Mandy said back. That's where I'm for. As soon as we get the papers sorted . . .

She whistled through her teeth and made a looping motion with her hand. Up and away.

The Christmas before her eleventh birthday, Ellen heard that Victor and his wife had emigrated to Vancouver. As it was, neither of them had been seen around Granny Linden's way for some time past. One Thursday the previous summer Victor's grandfather woke up and, still in bed, lit a Woodbine then waited for his morning cough; but when it came, instead of spit, he coughed up blood and once it had started to flow nothing anyone could do could stop it and by the time it had stopped of its own accord he was dead. A fortnight later his wife, who was almost completely blind by this stage but who refused point blank to be moved from her home, put the chip pan on to boil thinking it was a pot of water and set the kitchen on fire. She was taken away in an ambulance and never brought back again. Granny and Aunt Peggy visited her two or three times before she died.

– Such a sight, Aunt Peggy said bitterly. God forgive me, but she's better off dead.

By the following autumn Ellen had all but stopped sleeping over at her granny's. Drew was five and a half now and pestering to be allowed to go as well and their daddy said it was too much to expect Granny to look after them both.

– A lot of nonsense, Granny said.

But, in any case, on the couple of occasions that the two of them had stayed together it hadn't seemed the same to Ellen somehow. It wasn't that she disliked having her little brother around, on the contrary, she was normally very fond of him; but Drew had been back and forth to his granny's house almost from the day he was born and looked on it merely as an extension of his own. He had grown up with both houses the way he had grown up with hands and feet: they were different, yes, but perfectly in keeping with one another. To Ellen, however, her granny's house was a hole she had fallen through to another world and though most of its enigmas had long since been rationally explained, it had nevertheless retained a magical quality for her, a sense of possibility she felt nowhere else. If the fall could be reversed, she had always persuaded herself, it was more likely to be reversed while she was there.

Such fragile fancies could not survive long with Drew hurtling about the place.

Besides, since she started secondary school that September her weekends had become increasingly dominated by home-work and – even more frustrating – the tedious task of deciphering the notes she had amassed, without regard to sense or legibility, throughout the previous week. Looking back, indeed, Ellen's chief impression of that first term was of a succession of forty-minute monologues, punctuated by herd-like migrations between buildings and differentiated less by subject than by the degree of difficulty posed by the various teachers' idiosyncrasies of dictation. One (Geography) stood at the black-board for the entire period, back to the class, a stump of chalk in her left hand and a textbook in her right. She spoke the words aloud as she wrote them, wiping the top half of the board clean whenever it was full and starting again, forcing her pupils to write so fast to keep from falling behind that their pens wore grooves in their numbed fingertips. Another (RE) sat with her head bent over her book and spoke in such a mumble that the whole class would end up with their heads on the desks level with their scribbling pens, ears cocked like funnels to catch her words. Still another spurned his desk for a lectern and delivered his lessons in an uncompromising har-angue pitched, literally, above the children's heads at a spot two-thirds the way up the back wall of the classroom.

This was Mr Craig, charged with teaching Ellen's set history, though woe betide anyone who interrupted his rampage through the ancient world to ask him to repeat himself or explain a point. Pupils with older brothers or sisters at the school spoke darkly of eight or nine exercise books full of notes to revise for the exams.

So it was with some relief, not to say surprise, when one Monday afternoon in the bleak mid-term, he pulled up short somewhere in the Fertile Crescent and instructed the class to lay down their pens and attend to what he was about to say. For the remainder of the period the Tigris and Euphrates were deserted in favour of the river Foyle, on whose banks the weekend before policemen had fought with Civil Rights demonstrators. *Mis-ter Wilson's friends*, as Mr Craig styled them. The aim of these demonstrators, he told the class, was quite simple: to force Northern Ireland into Eire (*Error*, he said it) against the wishes of the majority of its subjects. He switched on the overhead projector by the blackboard and laid a transparency over the light-source. A free-hand outline of Northern Ireland wobbled on to the screen, coupled to the west coast of Scotland by a string of wide-spaced letters that together spelt the word DALRIADA.

– The island of Ireland has never contained a single, unified people, Mr Craig said, any more than the island of Britain has. The 1920 border only reconfirmed what this diagram of sixth-century alliances shows to be true, that there have always been two Irelands.

And that, odd as it might seem at that late stage of 1968, was the first Ellen Linden had given any thought to the meaning of Partition.

The border was represented on Mr Craig's diagram by a broken red line, as improbable, when you saw it like that, as the archaic letter-link across the water to Scotland. But while the latter had long since dissolved, the former had taken on the insoluble character of the simple mathematical fact which Mr Craig was in the process of writing on the history room blackboard:

Six into twenty-six won't go.

– One million Protestants, he said, dusting his fingertips, is a very awkward statistic to ignore.

And summoning the class to their feet he led twenty-nine of the most awkward-looking statistics you ever clapped eyes on in singing the national anthem. Both verses.

It was then too that Ellen finally understood (though the riddle had been submerged for years) how her granny could claim to have lived in two different countries without ever moving more than three doors from the house where she was born.

Neat.

11

ERNIE LINDEN DREW the line – *absolutely* drew the line – at shaving his moustache off for her.

Ernie Linden was the first man ever Greta kissed. He said he loved her and all, but he drew the line at that.

Ernie Linden was always drawing the line at something or other when Greta met him. He had a great big moustache then that he was forever preening. Oh, he thought he was gorgeous. Only thing was, her face would be all out in a rash mornings after she'd been with him, so of course everyone started getting ideas about what they'd been up to the night before. Greta said to him:

– Make up your mind, either that moustache goes or I go, I'm not having people talking.

– Away and chase yourself, he said, stroking it, as if it was a wee dog and she'd hurt its feelings, but then one night she left him standing three hours waiting on her at Gibson's Corner, with all his pals walking past with their girls, keeping him going, and off it came.

He was twenty-four. He'd built ships, run guns and fought in a world war. He never missed an evening shaving from then till the day he died.

Greta was twenty when she married him and still twenty when Peggy was born. Minnie Butler next door came in to her. Minnie already had three of her own and another one expected. She drank tea while they waited for Greta's and when it was over she sent her youngest down to the end of the street to where the men stood with word that it was a wee girl. The men followed Ernie up to the door of the house, yelling and carrying on, shouting they weren't going home till they'd seen the new arrival. Ernie held her up to the window and they all gave three cheers. Lying in her bed, Greta watched one of their caps sail past the window and drop out of sight again.

Poor Alice, though, had to make do with just Minnie and Peggy for company when she was born. Everyone else (Ernie included) was away into town that day to see the King and Queen open the new parliament.

– Never mind, wee love, Greta told her, at least they've put the flags out for you.

There were flags and bunting in every street, of course (well, every Protestant street anyway), and in all of them the kerbs had been painted red white and blue on account of the royal visit. Ernie was longer recovering from that day than she was, though Greta didn't begrudge him his bit of fun for a minute, for those were desperate times, the Troubles that there were – the *war*, you might as well call it – and he'd little enough chance to enjoy himself. He joined the Specials just after that, saying it was every loyal man's duty to hold the line against the Sinn Feiners and defend what had been so hard won. And it did seem a fragile thing in those days, their queer-looking new country. Even so, Greta wished he could have stayed at home and she was heart-scared every night he was out on patrol of a knock at the door to tell her her two wee ones had been left with no daddy to mind them.

Oh, they were desperate times altogether.

Jack was the first child she had born into peace, though a rare kind of peace it must have looked to anyone who hadn't lived there through the couple of years before it. The curfew was still on, Ernie still went out on duty at nights, people were still on edge. The men especially seemed to do nothing else but talk and worry about the number of Catholics there were, looking over their shoulders all the time to see were they catching up. Numbers, numbers, numbers, they'd've put your head away listening to them. It was simple arithmetic, they said: if the Catholics kept breeding faster than the Protestants, then sooner or later the Protestants were bound to be outnumbered, and when they were the border would be rubbed out and they'd be lost for ever in a United Ireland.

For all Greta knew, the Catholic men were at it too, worrying that the Protestants were getting too far ahead. It was as if the war had never stopped at all, only now, instead of guns and bombs, women's bodies were the weapons. No sooner had you dropped one brood than you were loaded up again with another. From the day and hour she was married Greta was either getting pregnant, being pregnant, or she was getting over being pregnant and there seemed to be no likelihood of a let-up. He wasn't a bad man, her Ernie, better than most. Dozens of times he made sure and pulled out of her before there was any damage done, so to speak. But, when it came down to it, she couldn't always depend on him controlling himself at the vital moment, and there she'd be, trapped again. She'd had five children by the time she was twenty-seven, she was wearing out. Something had to be done.

She'd tried it before, bringing herself on when she was late. Sometimes it worked, sometimes it didn't, and sometimes she didn't know whether she hadn't just miscounted and would have come on anyway. Looking about her now, though, she saw no end of women like her, women coming down with children, old before their time. Surely to God, she said to herself, I'm not the only one wondering what's going on here? So she asked around a few of her neighbours, very discreetly, of course, and, sure enough, it turned out all any of them ever thought about, like her, was how to avoid getting caught and, if they couldn't, how to keep themselves from going the full term. One woman had tried one way, another woman had tried another. They swapped stories, howling with laughter at some of the things they'd got up to shut away in their bedrooms and outhouses – the accidental tumbles down the stairs they'd all had that took three or four times to get right – crying their hearts out at the memory of some of the others.

From then on they looked out for each other. They agreed no woman need have a child that didn't want to, and any new wives moving into the neighbourhood they made sure and put them wise, the young ones in particular. Some of them, if you'd seen them, were hardly more than children themselves. One wee girl arrived there already six or seven months gone. She didn't seem to understand properly what had happened to her, how this baby of hers had got inside her. She certainly had no idea where it was going to come out. She cried herself sick when they told her. *But I'll break*, she kept saying. *I'll break.*

Like another wee girl Greta knew, years later.

The men of course weren't long in getting suspicious. The women would catch them looking at them, trying to work out what was wrong none of them were getting fat any more. Not that they would have dreamt of asking, like; not their women-folk anyway. At nights, though, they'd stand at the top of the street, smoking and talking it over amongst themselves. There was a phrase they used then, being crude, to tease a man that had been married a while and hadn't got his wife pregnant yet: they said he was shooting blanks. Now they all seemed to be shooting them, old and young alike, and they couldn't fathom it.

Some of them must have gone to their churches in the end, for the next thing was the ministers had started paying the women wee visits when their men weren't around and finding some way of bringing up the sanctity of life over a cup of tea and a currant scone. Well now, Greta hadn't had much of an education, but she'd read enough of her Bible to know that the sanctity of life had its limits and that God himself wasn't above going beyond them when he saw fit. So the day her minister came calling she was prepared, with the Bible open on the kitchen table and Michael, who would have been about four then, yes, for Dinah was just started school, Michael shepher-ded to her in the crook of her arm.

– Ah, what a picture, the minister said and framed it with his hands. It's heartening to know that in this day and age there are still some homes where the Bible isn't only kept for Sundays.

– I was reading to the child.

– Please, don't let me interrupt, he said and sat down by the hearth, with his hands folded now a little way beneath his chin.

– Reading from the book of Exodus, Greta said to Michael (though she could have recited the passage by heart), the twelfth chapter, beginning at the twenty-ninth verse:

And it came to pass, that at midnight the LORD smote all the firstborn in the land of Egypt, from the firstborn of

Pharaoh that sat on his throne unto the firstborn of the captive that *was* in the dungeon; and all the firstborn of cattle. And Pharaoh rose up in the night, he, and all his servants, and all the Egyptians; and there was a great cry in Egypt; for *there was* not a house where *there was* not one dead.

(*Real* people, mind. What was so wicked, Greta wanted to know, about women stopping being born those tiny wee things, not yet quickening inside them, when set against the slaughter of real living and breathing people? Besides, all that sanctity claptrap seemed to take it for granted that life itself was a good thing, a blessing to be wished on children. But you would've had to have been blind not to see that life for children then was as awful as it was for everyone else, curving their bones through lack of vitamins, making them cough and retch their lungs out with its soot and filth. As soon as your children were born the very men who preached about what a wonderful blessing life was were telling them to shut their mouths, endure its hardships and pray for the release of death.)

– Here ends the reading from God's Word, she said and gave Michael a squeeze with her elbow.

– Amen, he piped up.

It was a good job the minister had kept his hands folded beneath his chin, otherwise he might have done himself an injury, the speed his jaw dropped. The Reverend Harbison, you called him. He became some sort of Grand Panjandrum in the Orange after he left their church. For years you'd see him walking at the head of the Twelfth parade, saluting the crowd with his rolled umbrella, as if he was royalty, and when the war with Germany broke out again there was barely a day went by when he wasn't giving forth in one paper or another, telling the young men to join up and fight.

Greta's oldest boy, Jack, volunteered on his seventeenth birthday and was passed unfit for service. He was mortified, though he must have been the only one who hadn't seen it coming. Just running up the stairs left him gasping. The doctor who examined him recommended plenty of walking to build him up.

– You're surrounded by mountains, he said. A couple of good long hikes up there each week would make all the difference in the world to you.

Jack, his mother thought, was glad of the excuse to get away from the men at the end of the street. Some of them, notwithstanding Ernie was their friend and neighbour, had vicious tongues on them and had already had a few digs at him about pen-pushers only being good for pushing pens.

Michael, now, was a different matter altogether. Michael, from he was a wee boy, was more the active type. Michael was used to physical work. The men loved Michael. The army couldn't take him quick enough when he went to enlist. He was sent to a camp somewhere in England – a scout camp, you'd have thought from his letters, for all he talked about was the games they played. He was allowed home only once before he shipped out. That was when Greta began to worry. He looked so grown-up in his uniform.

– You could take him for a man, she said to Peggy. How are the Germans to know any different?

As it turned out, they never even let him get close enough to doubt. A friend of his from the same regiment told them after the war that he had been shot running to get out of the sea.

– No, Greta said, before she remembered herself. He never liked the water.

His equipment was that heavy, he was dragged under and drowned before anyone could haul him out.

D for Dead Day, Greta called it.

Ernie near collapsed when he saw the postman standing at the door with the telegram. He had visions of Michael already heading for Paris by that time, entering the city like the Americans on the newsreels liberating Rome.

The entire street called in to pay their respects, even though there was no body to pay them to, just a big hole where Michael wasn't. Ernie was like a caged tiger stalking about the house. *If he ever got his hands on the German that shot his son. . . .* He mangled the air in his fists and his whole body shook with frustration.

Greta was sure it was frustration, more than anything else – for, with all his faults (and who doesn't have them?), he really *wasn't* a bad man – that made him say what he said, when the last of the neighbours had gone, about God always taking the best.

– You only have to look at our house tonight to see the truth of that.

And you only had to follow his glare across the room to see what (or who, more like) he was getting at. Jack, sitting facing him, blushed.

– Father, Greta said, thinking of nothing else at that stage but stopping him from saying anything more hurtful, it seems to me God takes whatever he can get whenever he can get it. He'd have taken the lot of us by now given half the chance – good, bad, and indifferent.

Her voice started to shake as she heard what it was saying.

– That's blasphemy.

Ernie was more frightened than she was.

– That's as may be, she managed to say, but it's the truth.

She was remembering all those Egyptians he had smote in the Bible, all the Midianite women and children he told Moses to massacre out of sheer spite, and all the thousands upon millions of other men, women and children he had let be butchered in his name right down to today.

– He's a blinking . . . *gannet*.

The silence in that room was awful. They had their share of rows, Ernie and her, but never in the forty-three years they were married did she recall another silence like it between them. They might have been sitting there yet, staring at each other, like fossils, if Jack hadn't stood up and left the room. Greta sent Ernie out after him.

– He's as much your son as Michael was, she said. Every bit as good in his own way.

He went straight away and did as she bid him, give him his due. But it was Ernie himself who once told her that you can unsay a thing all you like, you can never guarantee that the other person will unhear it completely, and there were times, many years later, when she got the impression that Jack was still trying to earn his father's forgiveness for being the son who lived.

Staying at home as long as he did didn't help matters, of

course. He was past thirty before he was married and once or twice, she knew, as the years slipped by, Ernie despaired of his ever leaving them. She was concerned herself. They wouldn't have been natural if they hadn't wanted to see him settled down, though settling down, she had to admit, was the last thing either of them hoped he would do with Lily Mooney when he brought her home. Ernie didn't sleep a wink that night for worrying.

– We've reared a cradle-snatcher for a son, he said. The fella hasn't the sense he was born with.

– If he loves her, that's his choice, Greta said, though without much conviction.

Lily was a nice enough wee girl, but Ernie was right, she looked seventeen going on twelve. Still, there you are, as every parent knows, you can't live their lives for them. Jack was happy and so was she, from what you could tell, for Greta didn't believe she ever heard much more than a please and thank you out of her before the day she stood in front of the minister and repeated her marriage vows in that big echoey church of theirs. Lily had no church of her own, you see, and no close family either, except that crotchety aunt. (Her grandfather who gave her away had to have her pointed out to him at the wedding rehearsal.) No nothing really. Not even a friend she could, you know, *talk to*, Greta remembered thinking.

One of the nurses at the maternity hospital across the water, a Derry girl, told her when she visited that Lily cried for her mammy the whole way through her first labour.

– If you'd heard her, the nurse said. It would've broke your heart.

Lily opened up more in the forty minutes Greta spent with her that afternoon than she had in all the years she had known her previously. It was Jack started her off, not knowing he was doing it. He had come to the hospital in his lunch-hour, full of himself and the baby, of course, and when he kissed Lily good-bye before going back to work, he turned to his mother and said that all it would take to make his happiness complete was for Lily and him to have a wee boy next time.

– Next time, nothing, Lily said when he was gone. That's

me done, and I don't care if we have to sleep in separate rooms from now till doomsday.

– Well, Greta told her, there's no sense cutting off your nose to spite your face. There's ways and ways.

And there were far more ways then than when Greta was her age – there were even special clinics, for dear sake, where you could go to find out about them. But whatever it was she did in the end, there were no more babies for a long time after that, till, just when Jack seemed to have resigned himself to there never being any, all Lily's years of work were undone by a single Irish letter.

Greta's blood froze the day she came through from the scullery and found Ernie sitting at the kitchen table with the writing pad and fountain pen out.

– What are you doing? she asked him.

– What does it look like? he said, all affronted, him that had never written a letter in his life.

– I know what it looks like, she said, that's why I'm asking, I can't believe my eyes.

She tried to read the upside-down scrawl, but *Dear Jack* was as much as she saw before he covered the page with his arm.

– You're in my light.

– Don't you be filling that wee boy's head with any of your nonsense, now, she said.

– What nonsense?

– *What nonsense?* As if you didn't know.

From he took bad that previous winter he had been acting odder and odder. One day she was the world's worst and he couldn't think why he ever married her, just because she was home five minutes later than she'd said she'd be from the shops, the next day he was coming to her all lovey-dovey, bringing her some sort of a peace offering, like a couple of bits of steak for their dinner, or like that poor cratur of a goldfish he landed in with one time.

– What's that for? she asked him. To keep a watch on me when you go?

He had been *going* two or three times a week since Christmas. She had to try and joke him out of that sort of talk, even though she knew (for she'd warned the doctors she wanted nothing kept from her) he really was getting no better. That's what chilled her most seeing him at the kitchen table, writing, it looked too much like he was settling his accounts.

That and the nonsense, of course. She knew rightly what he was up to writing to Jack. All that stuff about The Name that he'd woken her in the middle of the night a week or two before fretting over.

– Michael's dead, he said, I'm dying, and if our Jack dies without a son, then that's it, the name dies with him.

– Catch yourself on, she said. There's Lindens the world over. It'd take a lot more than our Jack to kill the whole name off.

– Ah, but you don't see, he said, deadly serious, here's the only place the names count.

It was as if the last forty years had never happened for him. He was still back in the 1920s fighting the numbers wars.

She found Jack's reply to that letter months later, when she finally got round to clearing out the newspaper clippings stuffed under the cushion of his father's armchair. It was full of talk of all sorts of things she never remembered them doing together, promises about The Name carrying on and hopes of coming home again, though *one day*, he was careful to say, *God willing*.

But Jack was stranded in Heysham by rough seas the night his father died, raging with himself that he hadn't got back sooner.

– It's no way to live, a blinking sea between you and your family, he said.

Within weeks of the funeral he had fetched Lily and the wee girl over home with him and when Lily fell pregnant almost immediately after they returned (thinking, Greta always suspected, that if that's what it took to turn him right back round again, then that's what it took), he read it as a sign that he had made the right decision coming back. He was so sure from the start the baby was going to be a boy that he refused even to think about girls' names, and Lily herself, though she did her best to keep him from getting too carried away, seemed to be daily more persuaded that she was fated to have a son.

There was a nightmare she told Greta about that she had on and off throughout her pregnancy, where she grew and grew till she split clean in two – like a pea-pod, was what she said – and a full-grown man walked out smoking a pipe. The nearer it got to her time, the more agitated she became. Then one afternoon halfway through her ninth month she had a sort of fit in the kitchen. She was rushed to the hospital and induced before the convulsions could get any worse and though Jack had had his heart so set on a son, he couldn't have cared in the end whether the baby was a boy or not, just as long as he didn't lose it or Lily, that was the main thing. And at first it seemed as if all his prayers were answered. You never saw a healthier looking baby, and Lily, though she was sick, was soon out of danger. But Jack wasn't to know then how much the birth had taken out of her and, if he didn't lose her altogether, Greta didn't think he ever did get her back again properly. She remembered the day Lily was buried, her son coming to her in tears, telling her that when he'd taken his wife's hand one last time before they screwed the coffin lid down the wedding ring had slipped off her finger.

– Just like that, he said. No tugging or anything. And do you know what else, Mammy? When I looked at her finger there wasn't even a mark. After all these years, there wasn't even a mark.

What could she possibly say? She held his head to her. The way she'd held his daddy's head to her in the dark hours. The way she'd held all their heads to her at one time or another.

*

Greta Linden died on a Monday morning in early December 1985, with the sun slanting in across the foot of her bed, just beyond reach of her own feet, and the clock-radio tuned to Radio 2. She had been quite resigned to dying, asking only of death that it give her a few minutes' warning in which to prepare herself. Instead, death, when it came (and she felt it enter the room damply), caught her, just as she had hoped it would not, completely unawares. She had wanted to be sitting up to meet it, but found when she tried to raise herself that all her strength had gone. She had wanted to have the family gathered round her bed, but she was quite alone.

– Oh, dear, she said, disappointed.

She need not have been on her own at all if only she had shown some special sign that she was about to die when her breakfast tray was taken away an hour before. But she had shown none. On the contrary, she had eaten all her Readybrek and drunk her Complan and had even said she might try sitting downstairs for a while later on, something she hadn't managed in more than a week.

Her mind at rest (on that score at least), her granddaughter, Ellen, who had taken the tray from her, had left Laurence at playschool and, at the precise moment her grandmother died, was sipping a cup of coffee in the sitting room below while sorting through a bumper box of Oxfam Christmas cards. (She had not bought charity cards in the past because of a notion Derek had that the charity was being conferred on the buyers, trumpeting to the world that they were too broke to be able to afford anything else. But this Christmas, as it happened, she and Derek really were broke, and, like it or not, they really couldn't afford anything else.) Nathaniel, who was two and a half, was sprawled on the carpet at his mother's feet, playing animal dominoes, which he did by taking an unmatching cardboard tile in each hand and rubbing the picture faces together, snarling. For a change, though, all was quiet out the back. Derek had put the roof-rack on the car when Ellen brought it home and had driven out to Dundonald for a new consignment of wrought iron. Ellen's father should have been with him, but when he rang first thing that morning to ask what sort of night his mother had had (as he had rung first thing every morning for the last month) he told Ellen he was waiting in on a glazier coming. His next-door neighbours, the Russells, had had their windows smashed the night before by a crowd of hoods throwing stones. The family had been getting threats ever since the summer when their youngest son, Charlie, a policeman, was identified on TV breaking *Orangemen's* heads in a right-to-march riot in Portadown. One of Jack's upstairs windows had been smashed by a stray stone in last night's attack. Ellen had swung round by his house on her way back from dropping Laurence off. The hoods had sprayed *All Cops Are Bastards* and *SS RUC* in red paint on the Russells' crazy-paving. The single rose-bush had been trailed from its island of soil and hurled up on to the porch.

Worries about the decline of the old estate kept cutting into Ellen's thoughts as she sorted through her Oxfam Christmas cards, picking out the best ones – or at any rate, the least cheap-looking – to send to their best friends first.

– Oh, dear, Greta said, out loud, though not loud enough to be heard over the clock-radio and Nathaniel's animal dominoes.

Three miles away, Peggy Simpson, oblivious for the moment of her bulk and the cruelty of age, leapt from the settee to the foot of the stairs and shouted to her husband who was still in bed.

– Walter! It's a quarter to eleven!

– So what? he said.

Peggy rubbed her temple and crossed the room to the settee again. Right enough, she thought, so what?

The second hand of the sitting room wall-clock moved once and she had a mother, moved again and she had none.

*

That final illness had shrivelled her grandmother, like a crisp bag tossed on the fire, into a tiny crinkled replica of herself, turning her skin violet and yellow. Her voice shrank in proportion to her body, but her control of it never wavered and she remained lucid right to the last.

– Close the door and sit here a minute till I tell you, she'd say and Ellen would pull her legs up beneath her on the edge of the bed, pushing the hair behind her ear the better to hear, though with a little coaxing and a lot of luck Nathaniel might stop roaring about the room and nap beside her, one thumb hooked wetly in his slack cheek, while his great-granny very gradually talked herself to death.

Her talk was of firsts and lasts, beginnings and endings, bearings and buryings. It was a story she had been retelling and revising all her adult life.

One evening, three weeks before the end, when she was still able to spend some part of every day downstairs, the whole family had congregated in front of the television and watched as Prime Minister Thatcher and Taoiseach Garret FitzGerald, seated at a table in Hillsborough Castle, put their signatures to the Anglo-Irish Agreement, triggering a crackle of camera shutters and a pyrotechny of flashes, like a parodic presentiment of the ructions that were to follow in the towns and cities across Northern Ireland.

From her already habitual position on the pouffe, two feet from the screen, Tina, a news and current affairs veteran at six and a half (operating on her great-granny's one-time principle of if it's in the box, watch it, though, unlike her great-granny she could not conceive of the box ever running out and was, in consequence, less, not more, likely to tire of it), turned to her parents and, worried by the dire prognoses of dissenting politicians, asked:

– Does that mean we're something else now?

Her parents were none too sure themselves. Her grandpa's head said one thing and his teeth another. Only her great-granny seemed not to be in any doubt.

– What we are is what we've always been, wee love. Doesn't matter how much they tinker. The ordinary people had nothing before Stormont, they'd nothing under Stormont, and they've had no more since.

Later, however, when Ellen brought her grandmother a bedtime drink, she found her sitting up in bed, dabbing at her eyes with a corner of the sheet, laughing.

– Poor Ernie, she said. All those years he spent worrying about keeping ahead and in the end all's it took to beat him was two pens.

The funeral was a sodden affair. Belfast was brown-shrouded in rainclouds from dawn to premature December dusk. Holly wreaths dripped from the lintels of fruit shops and florists as the four-car cortège stop-started through the centre of town. Outside the City Hall, in a grotto mounted on the back of a trailer, on the spot where, a fortnight before, Unionist politicians had denounced the Thatcher sell-out before upwards of 100,000 people, a choir of schoolchildren, singing Once in Royal David's City to an audience of none, tracked the hearse's progress with a certain detached horror. Standing together, shoulders touching, warm inside their duffelcoats and anoraks, they felt themselves at an eternal remove from the cold, old body lying in its coffin. (Because death, for all that this was Northern Ireland, was still to them the monopoly of the old.) The conductor fanned their attention in towards him again with feathery fingers then placed one fingertip on his lips and immediately the sound from the loudspeakers diminished to an exaggerated, tuneless whisper.

. . . Lived on earth our Say-ay-ay-viour ho-ly . . .

Ellen turned, smiling, from her window to find Drew scowling, tight-mouthed, out his at the fleeting front of a sports shop looted during last month's rally. Despondently she reviewed in her mind's eye the news footage of demonstrators in ski goggles pelting police with golf balls. She wished she could have offered him an explanation – drink, youth, *the crowd*, the confusion of the times – or, at the very least, have let him know she understood and shared his disgust. But not for the first time that day her tongue balked at the gulf it was being asked to leap, and she said nothing.

He had rung at half-eleven the night before to say he was booked on a flight arriving first thing in the morning at the Harbour Airport. Ellen, who had not had cause to go there before, drove down alone to collect him. She was ashamed when she saw the poky wee terminal where she was to meet him. Drew shrugged it off. It was pretty much what he'd been expecting. He looked crumpled and disgruntled after the flight, though he'd been in the air less than an hour. Ellen put her arms around him. There was a moment's hesitation, then he rested his chin on her shoulder briefly and patted her, twice, on the back.

His only baggage was a workman's lunch sack, dyed a coincidental black, which he wore over his right shoulder and which, judging from its contours, contained little more than books.

– When do you fly back? Ellen asked when they were in the car.

– Tomorrow morning, he said, then was silent a moment or two while she tried to nose out of the airport gates on to the Sydenham Bypass.

– Has Derek a spare black tie I can borrow? he asked. I couldn't find mine.

They had to drive out along the dual carriageway towards Holywood for a mile, then turn through 180 degrees at the Knocknagoney roundabout to get back on course for the city. The illogicality of the detour, effectively doubling the journey, infuriated Ellen, the more so since she was convinced she had detected the beginnings of a smile on her brother's lips when she checked in the rear-view mirror before completing the turn. She shifted into top gear and gunned along the swooshing road hoping to burn off some of her annoyance. She did not speak again till they were repassing the airport entrance.

– So how are things over there?

– All right, Drew said, distracted. Yeah, good.

The tide was down, turning the moat surrounding Victoria Park into an offensive-smelling, greeny-brown glaur. To their left, across the Belfast to Bangor railway line, wizened pigeons scavenged in the refuse behind The Oval football ground. Needless to say, it was raining. The city could hardly have looked less appealing. The windscreen wipers toiled on regardless, shaving broad clear arcs on the stippled glass:

Phu-hum-mip, phu-hum-mip, phu-hum-mip.

– What about you? Drew said.

– Oh, God. Ellen laughed. Same as ever.

This was not at all the conversation she had intended having. Yesterday evening it had seemed imperative that she drive down to collect him on her own, even though most of the day's other arrangements had already fallen to her and even though the children were quite capable of screaming the house down to get going with her to see the planes. They needed time to talk freely, sister to brother, before submitting themselves to the constraining formalities of the family gathering. There were things to be said. Important things. Things that had only recently begun to make sense to her. She had imagined looks of recognition passing between them. Hugs, perhaps.

But the closest they had got to a hug was that frigid embrace back there at the airport and, instead of the momentous phrases she had scripted for herself, her brother's sullen aloofness had reduced her to mouthing mere commonplaces. Yet again.

Underneath the nothing chat she finally surrendered to the truth that they had become completely separate people and admitted to herself how little she could honestly say she knew of her brother, this *man* slumped in the seat beside her, peering down queasily into the sludge of the Lagan as they crossed the Queen's Bridge to the city centre.

He had a job, she knew that, with one of those bookshop chains that didn't have branches in Northern Ireland and whose bags students returning from university across the water always carried, as if to signify that the very knowledge that had come in them was of a different calibre to any that could be acquired here. Ellen had actually come across a photograph of the shop where he worked, in a feature one of the English papers ran on the company, and had tried without success to conjure her brother's face from the white blobs dimly discernible through the fuzzy newsphoto-greys of the shop window.

And there was a girlfriend too, Melanie, though Ellen had not even seen so much as a photograph of her. She had spoken to her any number of times when phoning for Drew, without once having really *talked* to her, though if she was being truthful, she would have to say that was in large part her own fault. Try as she might, she couldn't help being intimidated by the younger woman's self-assured south London accent; an accent which for some reason was associated in Ellen's mind with the knack of picking up perfect-fitting fifties' summer dresses for next to nothing off street-market stalls.

But that was as far as her knowledge extended: a job, a girlfriend, and nothing more. She could not visualise his daily journey to the one, or the flat he shared with the other; she could not construct a satisfactory image of his evenings in or his nights out, populate his life with friends and acquaintances, nor trust herself any more, were she put to it, to provide even the most trivial list of his likes and dislikes. He used to like watching the football results on BBC rather than ITV, because BBC had the teleprinter. (Did he even follow football at all now?) He used to like the top of the milk and the fat between the bacon rind and the fried-purple meat, eating hers as well when, as often happened, she couldn't face it herself. He used to like autumn better than spring, summer better than autumn, and winter better than all the rest put together. He used to hate Tuesdays and love Thursdays. He used to spot butterflies.

He used to think Norman Wisdom the funniest man alive and James Cagney the world's greatest actor. The first time he saw *Yankee Doodle Dandy* his eyes had all filled up at the part in the final scene where the soldier asks George M. Cohan (Cagney), not recognising him, does he not remember the words to his own song. Drew, aged seven, remembered every one of them and had marched round the house for days afterwards singing it:

> The Yanks are coming, the Yanks are coming,
> The drums rumtumming everywhere. . .
> Over there. Over there.

It was anybody's guess how he felt about the Yanks being over there today with their cruise missiles and air force bases, or about what they were doing in Central America and the Middle East, or about what any other nation was doing, for that matter, anywhere else in the world. Her map of his own inner world, she realised, had scarcely been updated since he was a boy of eleven or twelve. Only in one area of it did she feel she was still able to read the references correctly: he hated coming back here. Nor did that require any special sisterly insight. Last year, for instance, the day after their mother's funeral (a day, Ellen remembered, as flat and empty feeling as a Boxing Day), he had, for reasons best known to himself, decided to take issue with Granny Linden when she started in with her bound-to-return routine. He ought to have known she couldn't help it, that certain sayings had by then become reflex with her. But, no, he was never coming back, he said and, when their father suggested that never was a long time, added that it wasn't half long enough so far as he was concerned.

– Well, you'll have to come over once more anyway, Granny said, to bury me.

This year, back to fulfil at least that part of her prophecy (Ellen was careful not to mention it), his loathing amounted almost to a presence in the car with them. But a presence, on second thoughts, suggested something vital and this was a dead thing. An *absence*, then. Yes, that was it. It was a chasm that had opened up between them into which their trite words disappeared like so many loose pebbles into a canyon. If she could just say one thing in defiance of it – it didn't have to be important now – any little thing would do to get them started, so long as it wasn't about the weather or flight times or how work was.

She said the first words that came into her head.

– Did Granny ever tell you about the time she made Grandpa Linden shave off his moustache?

As she spoke she spotted a familiar congestion at the junction of Oxford Street and East Bridge Street. A Belfast congestion, unrelated to traffic signals. She indicated right, cutting down between the Law Courts and St George's Market into May Street, but here too the traffic was backed up.

Road blocks.

She braked.

Damn it.

She reached across her brother and felt around in the glove compartment, keeping her eyes on the car in front all the while, easing forward a few yards each time it did as another car further ahead was checked and let through.

– Have you not got your licence? Drew asked her.

– Don't worry. I know where it is.

She banged the glove compartment shut and twisted in her seat reaching for the shoulder-bag lying in the back. She was still searching this when the lead soldier beckoned her forward then raised his hand for her to halt outside Dan Magennis's bar. Ellen wound down the window. The soldier crouched beside it and looked into both their faces.

(They had pictures of suspects – *players*, they called them – all over the barracks. Or so Ellen had been told. Taped to the dining tables and the walls of their sleeping quarters, even to the back of the toilet doors.)

– Morning, madam. This your car?

– Yes, Ellen said and reeled off the number plate.

The soldier nodded, unimpressed. His wrist was resting on the rubber sill and his palm hung down expectantly into the car. Ellen rooted in her bag some more.

– I don't seem, she said and made a show of looking in the glove compartment again, to have my licence with me.

She gave an apologetic smile. The soldier raised himself off his haunches so that his head and shoulders filled the window-frame. His uniform smelt damp. He had been smoking recently. A second soldier, sheltering from the rain at the back of a land-rover at the corner of Verner Street, had already begun relaying the car's details into a radio handset.

– Orange Opel Ascona, registration number . . .

– Where was it you said you were going? their soldier asked.

Ellen, of course, hadn't said at all. She did now. District first, full postal address second.

– And where are you coming from, Mrs . . . ?

– Hastings, Ellen said. The Harbour Airport. Picking up my brother here, from England.

Ellen laid hopeful stress on the last two words, which the soldier chose to ignore. It was Drew's turn to be scrutinised.

– You're brother and sister, then?

– Yes, he said.

The soldier nodded. Looked from one to another for a family resemblance.

– England?

– Yes.

– Holiday?

– I live there.

The soldier stood up, nodding, and walked round the car. Ellen could feel the suspension was low at the back. God knows what all Derek had in the boot. She'd asked him to clear it out weeks ago. The soldier returned and crouched by the window again.

– I don't suppose you'd mind just pulling in over there, madam?

He pointed her to another two soldiers then set about clear-ing the backlog of traffic. The people looking at Ellen from the car windows made no attempt to hide their reproach. *Well,* she could just hear them saying to each other as she opened the boot, *they don't pull you over for nothing.*

It was nothing, though, the soldiers decided when they'd taken out and inspected every last hammer, hacksaw, tin of paint, railing offcut, old shirt, overall and work-shoe that Derek had stored in there. The biggest weight was a rusted wrought-iron balustrade which he had rescued from a council skip and was planning to restore, when he found the time. Ellen felt like Harold Steptoe's sister. The soldiers, however, passed no comment. They found all sorts, she supposed, in people's cars. The chattier of the two, a youth of seventeen or eighteen, told her he was on his first tour of duty and complained in a friendly way about the weather. Three days he'd been here and the rain hadn't stopped once.

– Don't tell me this is normal?

– I'm afraid so, Ellen said.

They were clear of the city centre entirely when Drew asked his sister what she had been saying about Grandpa Linden. But Ellen was fuming. Not at the soldiers – they had been decent enough, and it was stupid of her to have come out without her licence – but at the thought of the effect such a rigorous check so soon after his arrival would undoubtedly have on her brother's impressions of home.

– It's gone out of my head, she said. I'll tell you another time.

Back at the house, Derek had the children washed and dressed, but there were a million and one things still to be done. *Another time* didn't present itself till they were in the funeral car, diverted through town by a security alert on the road they should have taken. (It was that sort of day in Belfast, Ellen was sure her granny would have appreciated the final irony: even her funeral route was disputed territory.) But the scowl on Drew's face as they passed the looted sports shop beyond the grotto of carol-whispering schoolchildren signalled that that moment too had been lost.

The following morning when Ellen drove him to the Harbour Estate they had four little ears in the car with them.

– Aw, Laurence said, seeing the airport, where's all le big planes?

His Uncle Drew boarded a small one and that was the last they saw of him for four years.

12

THE CASTLECOURT Centre – a vast, crystal palace of consumption, which had itself, in the course of its erection, consumed the former Head Post Office, the Avenue picturehouse, the *whole* of Garfield Street, and the sundry, tawdry shops to which the Grand Central Hotel had been reduced in the wake of its personal military occupation – opened for business the Thursday after Easter, the day before Jack Linden removed his hands from his son-in-law's Y-fronts and tempted fate in the shape of a wrought-iron garden table. But though the bookshop contained within the new complex was every bit as huge as rumoured, it had inexplicably opted to stock newspapers and magazines, even a limited range of American confectionery at point of sale, and what floor-space was devoted to books was badly under-utilised: heavy on lead titles, light on the rest of publishers' lists. In the days immediately after its opening, relieved Bookstore staff took delight in phoning to ask for some of the more obscure titles they themselves kept in their respective sections. Their calls were directed to a general enquiries desk, where, they were told, their query would be checked against the computerised stocklist, something which might have impressed the lay person but which was a sure sign to *real* booksellers that their opposite numbers were expected to be little more than button pressers and cashiers. It came as no surprise to anyone at Bookstore that in almost every case the outcome of the computer search was the same.

– I'm sorry, sir/madam, we don't appear to have that particular book in stock at the moment, but if you'd like to place an order through our computerised ordering system . . .

– No. Thanks all the same. I think I'd be quicker trying Bookstore first.

Some of their regular customers confessed to having been

tempted into the new shop, purely out of interest, you understand, but said they had found its sparse modernity alienating and were glad to be back in the intimate clutter of Bookstore.

Artie Mateer, as always, was more forthright. Artie, who had left school at fifteen with no qualifications and prospects to suit, was one of Belfast's leading bookies, a self-made man (*which accounts*, he'd say, poking ribs, *for the few rough edges*), though by his own lights only a semi-self-educated one, having long ago set himself the task of reading the entire Penguin Classics list, in alphabetical order, and having arrived, at the age of forty-two (and after three gruelling years of Ms), at the letter N.

– See that other place? he announced to a Saturday-crowded Bookstore, while Drew rang up his Nietzsche and Norse Myths. See their classics? Jane Austen, the Brontës and Dickens and that's about the heap. They've more types of jelly beans than they have Penguins. I said to them, call yourselves a bookshop? Sweetie shop's more like it.

And the Sweetie Shop was how the staff at Bookstore referred to their rival from then on.

Other customers, of course, notably those who could be seen to flinch whenever Artie Mateer was holding forth (for that Saturday was no one-off), let it be known that they had never had any intention of giving their custom to the newcomers, no matter how well stocked they had proved to be, while others doubted they would be around for long in any case, citing in their support the hubris of the Castlecourt developers in building a complex fronted entirely with glass in the centre of Belfast. (Though *fronted* was all: the sprawl of streets to the north and west were offered only the baboon's arse of a redbrick rear.)

Still others wanted to know what the *castle* in Castlecourt referred to anyway.

– Unless they meant to say *cattle*.

This, again, from Artie Mateer, whose wife's family, so he claimed, had carried on a butcher's trade in the vicinity for generations, when Royal Avenue was still plain Hercules Street and Smithfield Market at the rear sold livestock instead of Made-in-Taiwan ornaments and second-hand Patsy Cline records.

– A castle in Royal Avenue? he said. Was there what! The nearest thing there ever was to a castle on Royal Avenue was the bloody shambles.

The following advert had recently appeared in all the Northern Ireland daily papers:

For centuries the history of Belfast was the history of its castle. Today there is one bookshop uniquely positioned to provide you with that history. Your Bookstore, Castle Buildings, Castle Place, Belfast.

This time, however, the simple exterior shot of the shop which was the hallmark of Bookstore ads was accompanied by an artist's impression, copied from a seventeenth-century original, of the old castle – a many-chimneyed Jacobean manor house, with cupola and ensign (left, for the purposes of the advertisement, a non-partisan blank). A procession of books and pamphlets (histories of the city – social, economic, photographic – biographies of eminent citizens, collections of street songs, government reports) fluttered out through the arched gateway of the former and in the front door of the latter, linking them together.

The Bookstore sales figures actually rose in each of the four weeks after their rival opened, to such an extent that the Belfast shop featured for the first time in the top ten of the company's sales-per-square-foot league table. Phoebe herself faxed them the good news with a message of congratulations.

Well Done All at Castle Buildings!

– They'll have you canonised for that little suggestion before the year's out, Pamela Magill said, bringing the fax through to Drew's annexe.

Drew very discreetly turned his notebook face down on the desk as he took the paper from her.

– I hardly think so.

– I don't know. You nearly fulfil the most basic requirement as it is.

– What's that?

– You look half dead, that's what.

A fan to one side of the desk blew a hole in Drew's hair

through to his scalp and chased Pamela's smoke over her shoulder back into the main body of the office.

– Thanks, he said.

– You're welcome.

She scanned the room for an ashtray, remembered where she was and cracked the ash-shell delicately into her palm.

– How's your father keeping? she asked.

– A lot better, thanks.

Pamela had sent a basket of fruit up to the hospital the Monday after Mr Linden's stroke, but Drew suspected something more than an employer's legitimate concern in these occasional questions (*what does all of this reveal about you?* they seemed to be asking) and was careful what he said in reply. So he didn't mention that his father was still unable to speak, that his paralysed limbs were responding only very slowly to physiotherapy; didn't describe to her the anguished stares of a man sentenced to silent confinement within himself and his own inability to bear them for more than a few minutes at a time.

– It's a strain on everyone, Pamela said, talking to the spines of the ring-binders on his shelf. I remember even when Pascal had his wee thing, I was afraid to leave the house for weeks after.

Pascal was Pamela's husband. His *wee thing* was a transient cerebral ischaemia which had hurled him to the floor of a Cork supermarket three Christmases back, but which had left him completely unscathed, if a little wary and, even now, more than a little superstitious.

– Now, wouldn't you think that would have to be some kind of Christmas miracle? he asked friends. Passing right through like that without damaging anything?

– Wouldn't you wonder, instead, Pamela would say, lighting another Carrolls, whether there was anything there to damage?

And Pascal would grin, content to let her have her joke, because he'd felt the tremor inside him and he knew.

– What I mean is if you need time off or anything, Pamela said, you just have to ask.

– I'm all right, Drew said. Really.

– Oh, I know you are. Pamela waved away any suggestion that she was fussing. I'm only saying *if*.

– Thanks, he said.

But she waved away his gratitude too, walking through the archway to her own desk, the downtrodden backs of the Chinese slippers she wore about the shop slapping against the soles of her feet.

Drew waited for sounds of her settling before turning his notebook over again. The open pages were crammed with columns of tiny handwriting, as were (the fan peeled the leaves back one at a time) the pages before that and the pages before that and (the fan grew increasingly random in its selection) the pages a quarter, a third, a half the Black n' Red notebook back. And each page had exactly the same number of columns, and each column was exactly the same length and width, because each was composed of exactly the same word written over and over, the end of each taking him back time and again to where he had begun – perpetually insoluble, perplexing and palindromic; the indefinite article whichever way you looked at it:

anna anna anna anna anna anna anna anna anna anna
anna anna anna anna anna anna anna anna anna anna
anna anna anna anna anna anna anna anna anna anna
anna anna anna anna anna anna anna anna anna anna
anna anna anna anna anna anna anna anna anna anna

....

He had woken, without preliminaries, at the dry, rasping end of a snore, staring up at the ceiling, his sense of who he was lodged somewhere dark and not immediately accessible within him. He looked to his surroundings for a clue with which to winkle it out. The bed had an enormous scalloped headboard, upholstered in a material he took to be satin, and above it hung a picture, lumpy with oils, which someone had once told him was worth less than its frame, but which, this same elusive someone had said, they would not be parted from for the world.

And?

Nothing.

He didn't panic.

Standing out from the wall on his right was a wardrobe, huge and heavy and old, bowed at the front, its door panels, lacquered alternately light and dark, fanning out in a sunbeam pattern reminiscent of the cutaway front of an old-fashioned wireless set. His name came in that instant, dragging with it a ragbag of memories and associations, simultaneously apprehended, flesh to the bare bones of *Drew Linden*. His Granny Linden's wireless set, Kay Morris's wardrobe. Kay Morris's headboard and worthless-priceless painting. Kay Morris's the sleeping form whose warmth was leaking out across the mattress towards him.

They were lovers, Kay and he, on the Q.T., here in Belfast. His other lover, his *partner*, Melanie, was halfway across the world in New York. His Granny Linden was in her grave beside her husband. His mother was in her grave, alone, under sea-green stones, and his father was in the hospital, robbed of a voice and the use of the hand with which he had once knocked his son down and picked him up again like a fragile ornament.

All facts at this hour carried equal weight. He felt neither anger nor sadness nor remorse. This was his life.

And this was his throat. It appeared to have been shrinkwrapped. He worked his tongue this way and that till moisture rose from its roots and his gums relaxed their too-tight hold on his teeth.

He became aware of the movement at the foot of the bed at the same moment as it occurred to him to wonder why he had wakened when he did, for the light through the blinds was still a crepuscular blue. More curious than afraid, he felt for his specs and raised himself, blinking, on one elbow.

Kay's sister was sitting before the dressing-table mirror, brushing her hair, her head inclining with each downward stroke of the brush, tipping one side of her reflection into deep shadow, offering the other up to the blue half-light. She had on again the silk dressing gown in which she had answered the door to him yesterday morning and which at the time he had taken for Kay's – *mis*taken, he now saw, because Kay's dressing gown was at that moment draped, like a flow of skimmed-blue milk suspended, over a screen in one corner of the room. (She had *just gone off it*, she told him the following day when he asked her why she'd stopped wearing it.)

– Anna? he said, or thought he did, for nothing registered on her face, apart from a slight frown as she teased out a tat.

– Should you not have the light on?

He was certain he spoke this time because he felt instantly the stupidity of the question. Anna had all the light she needed in her own head. Anna was sound asleep.

When she had inclined her head to the other side, then forwards, then back; when she had cleaned the brush with a comb and sent the dead hair skittering down the tin insides of the waste-paper bin, she rose from her seat and began walking towards the bedroom door. There was a looseness about her movement absent when he had seen her awake, an unburdening too complete to be comprehended, even jokingly, by the phrase *letting her hair down*. She passed within a yard of the bed, smelling richly of a cream which Drew was quick to recognise as belonging to the tub in which their fingerprints had commingled beside the bathroom sink.

The door on to the landing already stood ajar, but when Anna pulled the handle to open it wider it moved only an inch or two towards her then twanged to a stop. The towel with which Kay had sealed the gap at the bottom of the door at bedtime and which had evidently yielded enough for her sister to squeeze into the room in the first place, had now become very definitely jammed, preventing her from getting out again. Anna, however, continued to tug, with the blind persistence of an infant bashing a broken toy to make it go. The door shuddered so that Drew feared it might crack. He slipped out of bed and crept round behind her to clear the blockage, taking care as he did so to hold the door off with his other hand to keep her from pulling it on to his fingers or, more likely, into her own face the second it was freed. But Anna in any case had already ceased tugging and was standing instead with her left arm held out to the side in an elegant swan-neck spout.

This was getting too weird for Drew. Still crouching, he tried to move towards the bed, but, though Anna's face remained impassive, the tight beak of her fingers wagged her impatience and it became clear that Drew, or whoever Drew's sleep-sensed presence had been transmuted into, was meant to take hold of them. He stood awkwardly, covering himself with the towel. Her fingers were slender and ringless, folding as compactly under the light pressure of his hand as the spokes of a collapsible umbrella. Elbowing the door wide open, he stepped out on to the blue-lit landing with her. There was a moment during their short walk when he thought he might have heard her speak, but leaning closer he caught only a whisper from her lips — something less than a whisper, the faintest echo of the swish of the brush through her hair. She was shushing herself, was all.

As they approached the guest-room Drew disengaged his hand one finger at a time, so that when he led her over the threshold only his thumb remained in position, and this too he now withdrew. Anna carried on without him, untying her robe, shaking it off her shoulders as she reached the edge of the bed. But Drew was out of the room long before it hit the floor.

– Who's that? Kay asked as he got back into bed beside her.

– Me, he said and kissed the nape of her neck. Drew.

Day was breaking. A crow woke and cawed. *Whaaat?* it said.

Next morning when they surfaced for breakfast Anna was gone. There was a note beside the kettle which Kay read and binned without comment. Drew for his part said nothing whatever about Anna's sleepwalking. A secret for a secret was his reasoning and it is a measure of the distance he had travelled between going to bed and getting up again that he did not find this in the least bit strange.

With secrecy came subterfuge. Loath now to ask Kay anything outright about her sister, he offered her, by way of enticement, select confidences about his own family, beginning, inevitably, with his father, but moving on as soon as seemed decent to his sister, whom he was to visit later for Sunday lunch. He sketched her house, its rise and (relative) fall, précised her marriage, enumerated her children, evoked her adolescent wanderlust (in ironic counterpoint to her present job with the stationery firm) and dwelt especially on the awkwardness that had grown up between the two of them after he moved away. But Kay could not be tempted. Indeed, though she had appeared interested in his revelations to begin with she grew noticably more impatient, irritable even, with them – or him, or something else – and was soon making it quite plain, with her questions about visiting hours and Sunday buses, that she wanted him to go. A date was made for the middle of the week: a lot of ifs and maybes stuck together by an afterthought kiss just inside the front door. Drew thanked her rather formally for yesterday. Kay hoped, equally formally, his father was going to be all right.

– Look after yourself, she told him.

– You too, he said.

He had not gone more than a few yards when a blue Alfa Romeo with Southern number plates turned into the street and manoeuvred into the closest available parking space to Kay's house. A thin drizzle was falling and before getting out of the car the woman driving undid the scarf knotted at her breastbone and cast it like a net over her soaring hair.

Anna.

Drew felt a shrinking inside. It seemed obvious to him (so obvious he couldn't imagine why he hadn't thought of it till then) that her sleepwalking the night before had been a practical joke hatched between the sisters. Kay was probably watching at this very minute from behind the blinds. She and Anna would have a big laugh about it later.

– Did you see the hack of him trying to get the towel out from under the door?

– His *face* when you started flapping your hand at him . . .

But he knew from the look that Anna gave him across the roof of the car that this was nonsense and that the previous night's encounter was a complete blank to her. She was the Anna of dinnertime again, distant, self-contained. Her hello was composed of all the mechanics of speech and almost none of its known emotions.

– I thought you were away, Drew said.

– No, not yet awhile.

She wore a black woollen turtle-neck, pearled now with drops of drizzle, and black pedal-pushers with tiny Vs let into the outside of each calf. But her exaggerated poise could make even casualwear appear constricting. Drew was at a loss to understand why just a few minutes before there were no lengths he wouldn't have gone to to find out any little detail of this woman's life. She was, as he had first thought, quite ridiculous.

They had both taken a few steps towards the front of the car, Drew on the footpath, Anna on the road.

– Well, I'll see you again, no doubt.

Drew's hand went out automatically. Anna had to step up on to the kerb to accept it. Her shoes, black loafers, were caked red with clay.

– No doubt you will, she said, doubtfully.

But no sooner were the words out than her whole demeanour changed. She prolonged the contact with his hand, trying to pump some unaccountable touch-memory to the surface. Confusion ruptured her mask of self-possession then recast it in a look of even more intense concentration, and as it did so, Drew felt return with redoubled force the belief that he had seen her somewhere before, somewhere moreover that instinct now told him he might do well not to try to remember. He let his hand go limp, though it was a moment or two before Anna detected his slackening grip and relaxed hers. Their hands slipped apart and dangled foolishly at their thighs. Drew covered for his by using it to wipe his specs. Anna raised hers to her head and patted her scarf. Then, shrugging, mumbling goodbyes, they turned in opposite directions and fled.

A dog, it is said, passing that spot three hours later sat down on the footpath and howled its bafflement. Howled and howled until its owner whipped it, kicked it, and finally dragged it, whining and yelping, out from under the ghostly X of their clasped hands.

*

The second floor of the Belfast Library and Society for Promoting Knowledge (founded 1788, second librarian Thomas Russell, hanged for high treason, 1803 – a lot of learning was ever a lethal thing in the north of Ireland, a person can know too much for their own good); a sunny Monday lunchtime in May.

The GCSE and A-level students have abandoned their revision stations to join the shop assistants, building workers and office clerks eating Wimpys and Marks and Spencer sandwiches in the grounds of the City Hall. They sit on coats and jumpers (for appearances are deceptive and, despite the May sunshine, deep in the earth it has just turned March), or cluster about the plinths of the statues and monuments which face out on to three of the four sides of Donegall Square: Queen Victoria, Empress of India, the Marquis of Dufferin, Viceroy of the same, annexor of Burma, ambassador to Turkey; Sir Edward Harland, shipbuilder to the world, left hand resting on the model of an unknown ship, back turned on the memorials to the fallen of the Boer war and the drowned (Irishglug) of his own yard's (Irishgurgle) Titanic.

A helicopter thwack-a-thwacks into earshot every once in a while above the city sounds on its interminable circuit of west Belfast.

Back in the library sun-shunners pursue their private obsessions from page to page of age-charred newspapers, encyclopaedias, dictionaries of this and companions to that, glossaries, almanacs, atlases, gazetteers, contemporary archives, and thick slabs dislodged from the wall of Belfast street directories, extending from the deep dusty crimson past by the librarian's desk to the vermilion of the present hard by the window, beneath which Drew Linden sits leafing through the Telecom Eireann Dublin and District Golden Pages.

This was his second visit to the library in under a month. On the previous occasion, the lunchtime of the day after he parted from Anna in Kay's street, he'd searched the Dublin community directory making a note of all the A. Morrises, and, just to be on the safe side, all the B.A.s, C.A.s, D.A.s etc. he came across as well. Even then there were only a handful. He rang round them that night when he got home, but none of them was Anna.

A good thing too, he'd told himself afterwards. What excuse could he possibly have made for phoning if he had found her? Why, for that matter *had* he been phoning? It scared him to think he had gone so far without asking himself that simple question. His shirt was sticking to him. He wondered if he was right in the head. But, then, it had been a traumatic couple of days. Perhaps his sudden fascination was only a function of that. The vigil at his father's bedside the night before they met had left him drained, oversensitised.

He buried the memory of the whole sorry episode beneath a flurry of digits. There was a transatlantic pause, two discrete burrs, a click, then Melanie said *I'm sorry I can't take your call right now, but if you leave your name and number I'll get back to you just as soon as I can.*

Drew waited for the beep, told her he missed her, asked her when she was coming back.

He made no mention now of quitting his own job and leaving Belfast.

The next day he threw himself into his work again. He even left off seeing Kay for a time (though Kay, as ever, wasn't exactly breaking her neck to get in touch with him). He bought an answering machine of his own so as not to miss any of Melanie's calls. He had taken to staying late at the shop most nights, then stopping off at the hospital, walking home in May dusk infiltrated, on a level below conscious hearing, by the strains of B-flat flutes from band huts and Orange Halls the length and breadth of Protestant Belfast.

– Change the record! Pamela shouted to him through the archway one afternoon during this period.

It was a Friday, she was packing up ready for the train.

– What?

– That tune you're never done whistling.

She demonstrated the burden. Lillibullero. The Protestant Boys.

– Are you kidding? he said. Me whistling that?

– Only for the past week.

Her doughy topknot slipped right as she stuck her head round the partition.

– So it's true, is it, what they say?

She pulled a werewolf face.

– Once the marching season starts yous just turn?

Then clearing his desk one evening he turned up a memo covered from top to bottom with Anna's name. He assumed it had been lying there for some time and was shocked to discover on looking closer that it bore the previous day's date. He couldn't remember a thing about it.

That same night he dreamt Anna somnambulated into his room, naked under the curtain of hair falling to the tops of her thighs.

– See enough? she asked and, before Drew even had a chance to speak, was answered by a fusillade of negatives.

– No, no, no, nonononono.

Drew discovered, or discovered that he had known all along, that he was surrounded by row upon row of men in dirty-looking surgical gowns. He sensed his father was somewhere among them, though his face eluded him. Anna meantime was mounting a dais, swinging her hips from side to side in time to some sleazeball slide-trombone.

– Stop! Stop! Drew called out, suddenly realising what she was about, but his objection was lost in the roars of approval.

– Come on ahead!

– Show us it!

She bunched the hair into tassels, twirling them and flipping them provocatively.

– Go on you girl, you!

– That's the stuff!

Drew looked away. He would not be a party to this. The walls of the auditorium, though, were screens from floor to ceiling and every one of them showed Anna in lurid close-up. The tassels flipped and twirled.

– Higher, higher!

– Wider, wider!

A drum roll began. The walls were closing in. She was near enough now for Drew to feel her hair on his face.

– Yahoo, the men shouted. Ya-*hoo!*

He covered his eyes with his hands, crying, but his fingers corroded in the salt of his tears. There was no escaping her. The drum roll spilt over into a mess of cymbals. The hair curtain parted.

An outsize beermat revolved on the fulcrum of her pubis.

Free the Spirit, it read, always upright whichever way it span.

The man in the stall next to Drew slid off his seat, helpless with laughter.

– I mean to say, he said from down the fag-ends and crackling juice cartons. Like, it has to be said.

Clever ads these Pernod ads was what he meant to say had to be said, Drew knew, though he couldn't get it out for laughing. The man had somehow acquired a suit by this time, as had all the other men in the audience. Drew alone wore a gown now, gaping obscenely at the back. Ralph the immaculate bouncer patrolled the aisles with the Feds from down the street. Anna was gathering armfuls of the long-stemmed roses that were landing at her feet. She curtseyed and smiled (her teeth greyish running to yellow), but reserved eye contact for Drew alone. *I know you*, the eyes said, *and you know me*, and so here he was, lunchtime of the very next working day, back on the second floor of the library, changing tack, but nevertheless searching for Anna again.

He had been stupid not to look for her work number on his previous visit, as the phone book itself never tired of telling him.

A Minute Spent Pre-shopping These Pages May Save Hours.

If he was interpreting Kay's weeks-old mumblings correctly, her sister worked in a boutique in central Dublin. *Con* something, or something *-con*, maybe, though he was quite prepared to ring every boutique in Dublin 1 and 2 if need be.

Waste No Time – Don't Spend Ages, Find it Fast in The Golden Pages.

Arriving in next to No Time at a page headed *Bou* for Boutiques, he flipped open his notebook and cracked the top off his fountain pen, prepared for some detective work.

The third entry in the list was a shop called Anna's.

Don't Get Overlooked. Advertise in Golden Pages.

It hadn't occurred to him that she might actually own the place. But then again – he recalled the blue Alfa Romeo – why not? He checked the address against a map of Dublin city centre: a shopping precinct off Grafton Street. Yes, why not? He scribbled the number into his book and ran down the two flights of stairs to the street.

Be Courteous on the Phone, the directory exhorted him in parting, *Hang Up Gently*.

There was a phone across the road from the library, but Citybuses revved and hissed in their bays right next to it and he turned instead through the Fountain Street gates into the traffic-free tranquillity of the city centre control zone. Towards the far end of the street two call-boxes stood in the lee of a cafe wall. (French name. Good mouth. No, wait, an idiom: pleasant taste.) A child with violently orange hair sat in a pushchair outside the right-hand half of the pair, sucking something even more violently orange from a teated bottle, dribbling down its caked chin and bib each time the pushchair was rocked by the hand which reached out to it from inside the kiosk. The young woman on the end of this hand was oblivious of the effects of her rocking, but was concentrating on the man with her, who had propped a form against the telephone's punched metal backboard.

– It was *next week* last week, the man was saying as Drew approached. If it's *next week* next week again that'll be a month.

Drew dived into the left-hand box and turned his back. He had expected there to be time for last-minute scruples before he was connected, but hardly had he jabbed in the final digit when the call was through. It was answered on the first ring by a girl with a light Dublin accent.

– Hello, Anna's, can I help you?

Much too young to be an *Anna* herself.

– Is Anna there? he asked, thinking this was absurd, there was no such person, it was just a shop name same as any other.

– I'm sorry, the girl said (*See*, he told himself, *I knew it*), she'll not be back till later this afternoon. Can I tell her you called?

– No. He punched the air. That's fine, I'll ring then.

Outside, the child in the pushchair had fallen asleep with the teat still gripped between its teeth. The woman's hand jiggled it sporadically. Juice stain was added to juice stain, becoming indelible.

– I'll swear if I bloody like, the man was saying. You'd be swearing too if you had to live in it.

Drew had no intention of ringing Dublin again, at least not immediately. He had succeeded in breaking the circle of secrecy Kay had drawn around her sister and for the time being that was enough. Now that he knew how to reach her, in fact, the urge to do so rapidly decreased. As the afternoon progressed, though, he began to wonder if this might not all be a huge coincidence, if the Anna at Anna's in the precinct off Dublin's Grafton Street might not be a different Anna altogether from the Anna with whom he had promenaded down a blue-lit landing in a house off Belfast's Dublin Road.

He called back just after five; got through to the same girl as before, asked her the same question he'd asked her then.

– Is Anna there?

One moment, though, was what she answered now, then another, older voice took over.

– Hello?

Oh, God. He panicked and put down the phone. That was her. That was Anna.

Wasn't it?

He replayed the voice in his head: a long-drawn-out *ha* and a crisp, clean *lo*. But two syllables wasn't a lot to go on, not when you took into account possible long-distance distortion. He started dialling again. He would apologise and say they must have had a bad connection last time. Yes, and if it was the Anna he knew he could tell her he wanted a surprise present for Kay – clothes – and was looking for advice. All the while the numbers were pittering between him and Dublin. The ear-piece cheeped as the receiver was picked up at the southern end.

– Yes? Hello?

The voice was tenser now. It was definitely hers. But the Kay story withered into implausibility and nothing else took its place.

– What do you want?

– He had a Belfast accent. The girl's voice in the background sounded worried.

– Surprise, surprise, Anna said, away from the mouthpiece, then spoke directly into it. I know who you are and you don't scare me.

She'd guessed then. He had nothing to gain now by maintaining his silence, indeed he had much to lose by it, for it had never been his intention to frighten her. At the same time, though, there was a firmness in her voice belying the fragile poise which he had associated with her till that moment and he was more cowed than ever. He whispered a *sorry* so feeble that it was mistaken in Dublin for a mocking sigh, then (belatedly acknowledging the Golden Pages maxim) he hung up as gently as his shaking hands would allow.

All that night he expected a call from Kay, certain that Anna would have phoned her the second he'd rung off. But no call came. Not that night nor the next day, though that didn't stop him worrying. Even if Anna didn't breathe a word of it to anyone, ever, he still had to contend with the fact that he had become a man capable of making that kind of phone-call.

He had Friday off that week and by Thursday evening he had convinced himself that the only way to clear his conscience was to go down to Dublin and explain everything to Anna's face, from start to finish. Never mind that he still had difficulty explaining most of it to himself.

It was mid-morning, and the temperature was already in the low seventies, when the train pulled into Connolly Station. Drew stood for a moment on the sliproad down to Amiens Street, twiddling a button of his jacket, trying to get his bearings. Two Dart trains crossed at speed on a bridge to his right, shivering the silver and blue scales of an advertising hoarding appended to the bridge's side. *Brighter futures begin with*, Drew read, but the rest of the advert was defaced by missing scales and without them the solution was just an indeterminate ripple. He continued down the incline, above and beyond the courtyard of the City Morgue, still not one hundred per cent certain where he was in relation to the rest of the city. Dublin (so called, Hugh McManus had used to insist, because all the streets had been named twice, once in English, once in Irish) was not a city he visited often.

The button he had been fiddling with came off in his hand. He dropped it into his pocket with the long-neglected sewing kit, as if in the vague hope that their pairing might prove in some way productive.

The sun belted down.

Fuck, Dublin was warm.

A stray breeze struggled by, trailing with it a whiff of the
Liffey's mouth: sea-sour, but welcome, for, the river located,
all else at last fell into place. He set off in the direction the
breeze had come, crossing the river below the Custom House,
passing under the railway again at George's Quay and along
Burgh Quay, turning into Westmoreland Street at the southern
foot of O'Connell Street bridge. In a bank facing Trinity he
exchanged half his sterling for violet and lavender Irish tenners
and big exotic pound notes from which the head of mythical
Medb looked out: cowled, tousled, languid-lidded, and, in her
enigmatic self-possession, uncannily reminiscent of the woman
he had come here to see.

He was spooked a little, not so much by the resemblance,
which, when he did a double-take, he admitted was fanciful in
the extreme, but by the very fact that he had seen such an
unlikely likeness in the first place. He wondered again if he
was quite well and decided as he entered her precinct from the
Grafton Street end that he was in no state to call on Anna just
yet. On his first pass through, therefore, he succeeded so well
in giving the impression of not looking for anywhere in particular that he found himself out the other side unable to remember
anything at all beyond the granite pavement and the blue and
gold clock above the tunnel of shops leading to the exit. He
bought a *Hot Press* from a newsagent's across the road and,
folding his suit jacket over his arm (his annual concession to
summer), strolled, calmer now, to the top of Dawson Street,
along the north side of St Stephen's Green and back down
Grafton Street as far as the precinct again.

He took it more slowly this time, even pausing to look in
the occasional shop window, though his attention was always
fixed at least a couple ahead of the one he was stopped at. In
this way, he first spotted Anna's while ostensibly contemplating
a stripped-pine rocking chair – going so far as to mime his
interest to one of the assistants. (She showed him the price tag;
he showed her his palms: *I'll see*, they said.) The boutique's
name hung from the arm of a lamp bracketed to the granite
frieze above the door. Capital *A*s, small *n*s, the tail of the *s*

the barge on which the rest rode across a surprisingly tacky aquamarine perspex background. Surprisingly, because the clothes adorning the featureless metallic mannequins (he noticed them from the side window of the gents' exclusive grooming shop two doors down across the way) were far from cheap. A vision of summer composed of May Balls, garden parties, and race courses. Even the beachwear looked formal. Anna's shop without a doubt. He had seen enough before he reached it to be able to pass by taking in the cafe-cum-juice-bar opposite. Four customers at three circular tables; a girl in culottes being served at the counter.

Emerging on to Dawson Street once more, he acted out a debate with himself concerning time. He consulted his watch, frowned, shook his head doubtfully, then he shrugged, raised his eyebrows whattheheck?, slapped his thigh with the *Hot Press* and, turning on his heel, returned to the juice-bar.

The colours of the various juices were approximated in the chalks they were written up in on the blackboard over the kitchen: yellow for pineapple, red for cherry, purple and green for red and white grape, and so forth. Drew ordered the yellow. Hearing him speak, the girl who had been walking towards the door when he entered glanced over her shoulder, startled, and exchanged a look with the woman behind the till.

Him? the woman's eyes asked her.

Drew, studying the cold counter, saw none of this.

– And a slice of your banana cake, he said, straightening.

The woman managed to see past him as she bent to reach it. The girl in the doorway moved her head. More a tremble than a nod. She was nowhere to be seen when Drew carried his order across to a table set back from the window (though still with a clear view of the shop opposite) and opened his paper.

– And anyone less like a man sitting casually reading a *Hot Press* you never saw, the woman who had served him whispered into the kitchen phone a few minutes later. Hasn't so much as turned a page from he came in, and his eyes all over the front of your place.

She arched her back to see round the door frame into the seating area.

– He's at it even as I'm talking to you, she said, then ducked back into the kitchen, cupping her hand over the mouthpiece. Wait a minute, he looks like he's getting ready to leave.

Drew collapsed the paper and pushed his plate into the middle of the table. The roof of his mouth was coated with a film of pulped banana cake. All of a sudden his whole inside felt clogged and slimy. He had deluded himself in thinking his coming here could solve anything. It was more likely to compound the fault, causing Anna, perhaps, even greater distress. A letter would have served the purpose so much better. He looked at his watch for real now. He had been in Dublin a little under forty minutes; there was a train back to Belfast within the hour. He'd make sure and be on it.

But at that moment Anna opened the door of her shop and started across the arcade towards him.

His heart beat up into his throat. Too late to snatch up his paper again, he hunched over the table, clamping his hands on his head. He heard her enter and pass by without hesitation on her way to the counter. *She hadn't noticed him*. Now did he make a run for it while she was being served or sit tight and risk being recognised as she left?

Make a run for it.

He slipped his jacket off the back of the chair and waited for the signal of her voice placing her order. He waited. And waited. Someone left. A heavier tread, he thought, but perhaps not. Perhaps she just didn't see anything she fancied and had gone elsewhere. Perhaps perhaps. He waited a few seconds more then chanced a glance out. Across the granite passageway, in the window of the boutique, a girl in culottes stood between two featureless metallic mannequins and nodded once: *that one*. Instinctively, Drew tilted his head to see behind him and there was Anna, hair swelling forward like a tidal wave about to break over him.

Her eyes turned to grey pebbles dropped in the determined set of her face. Wrinkles of surprise rippled out from them and when they had dispersed they left behind little eddies at the corners of her mouth.

– Oh, God, it's you, she said and sank down, laughing, into the seat beside him.

– It's all right, it's all right, she called out, he's a friend.

An *ah!* of dawning realisation lit up the face of the woman behind the counter. A brawny youth who had come out to stand by the till, wielding a mallet, returned to the kitchen.

– It's OK, Anna mouthed to the girl in the shop window. I know him.

The girl appeared unconvinced but moved none the less.

– You'll have to excuse all that, Anna said. You're not quite who I was expecting.

That much he had already guessed. She seemed genuinely surprised – he'd go so far as to say pleased – to see him.

– No?

Anna lit a cigarette.

– *No*, she said and with her bottom lip diverted the smoke away from the space between them.

No Medb, maybe, but very Kay, he thought, and thought too how previously it had been their differences, not their similarities, which he had focused on.

– So, what brings you down here with the *bogtrotters*?

She gave the word just the inflection Kay had given it that night at dinner. Now he was being admitted to their private jokes, as though she was cementing a friendship already well begun at Kay's and untroubled by any telephonic unpleasantness since. (*He's a friend*, she'd said.) Drew saw nothing to be gained from challenging this interpretation just now and, remembering the address of a Dublin publishing house he sometimes dealt with, invented a business appointment earlier that morning.

– Right.

Anna nodded, half-inhaling, then breathed out. Smoke and doubt clouded her eyes.

– But why didn't you call in, instead of sitting over here?

– I was starving, Drew said, thinking on his feet, or rather arse. I hadn't eaten since I left Belfast.

Anna looked at the unfinished cake.

– Banana, he said. Too sickly on an empty stomach.

She banished both clouds with a bright wave of her hand.

– Well come on, then, till we get you some proper food, I've had no lunch yet myself.

She rose part-way out of her seat.

– Unless, of course, you've a train to catch or something.

– Not at all, Drew said. I've stacks of time.

They stopped in at the shop while Anna got her bag then plunged into the lunch-hour crowds. He noted her ease of movement through the busy thoroughfares, her knack of side-stepping collisions, even while turned towards him talking, as though sixth-sensed, or as though she trusted her body to look after itself here. (He, on the other hand, seemed to be forever bumping into people then having to skip to catch her up.) As they passed the Dail she told him that he wasn't to mind Tara. Tara was Anna's assistant, the girl in the culottes, who had kept well in the background the short time that they were in the shop. Not that Drew had been particularly put out.

– I had a couple of funny phone-calls the other day, Anna said. Tara thought you were the phantom caller. I'm afraid a Belfast accent's a Belfast accent to Tara.

Any remaining worries he might have had that Anna had somehow known it was him making the calls were now dispelled. But the relief he felt on his own account was instantly outweighed by the concomitant realisation that Anna must still be anxious that whoever it was she thought *had* been responsible might ring again. Even so, he did not see how he could own up now without declaring himself a coward (for not confessing earlier) as well as a phone freak. Dilemma sharpened its horns and dulled his appetite and once arrived at their destination – a bar in Baggot Street whose menu-board said simply *Dublin Bay Prawns* – he ate only to keep up the pretence of hunger. Anna, however, ate and talked with gusto, chatting above the snap of prawn-heads, chatting as she shucked the shells with deft thumb movements, pausing perfunctorily before each pink-marbled comma and then picking up where she left off two bites back.

Her conversation for the most part centred on Kay.

How nice her flat was.

How nice her office was.

How well she was doing for herself.

How much better she would do too.

How she always knew exactly what she wanted.

How more often than not she got it.

– Of course (prawn-pause) I'm telling you this, you probably know her better than I do now.

– I wouldn't go that far, Drew said. We only met a couple of months back.

– Is that all?

Anna switched a bitten prawn through a blob of mayonnaise.

– Still, how long do you need to get to know someone?

– No, Drew said, you're right, and they both chewed this over a while in silence.

In fact, Drew was perplexed to discover later, reviewing the day, that he knew as little about Anna at the end of it as he had known at the beginning. Yet she had seemed to be saying rather a lot. It was as if her words on that particular subject had been infected with a virus which caused them to corrupt – like the descaled hoarding by Connolly Station – at the very moment when he thought they were safely stored away in his memory.

From time to time as lunch progressed they each thought they detected a slight puzzlement in the other's eyes and once or twice they each cut short sentences to let the other say whatever it was that seemed to have leapt so urgently to his or her lips. But always on the point of utterance the anticipated words vanished with an apologetic shake of the head and a lame *I'm sorry, what were you saying?*

Each, in fact, was, unknown to the other, experiencing a recurrence of that inexplicable sensation they had felt shaking hands in Kay's street a month before, namely that they had more cause to remember the person facing them than could be accounted for by a single dinner at their half-sister/half-lover's house. Of course, if they had only taken the trouble to say what was on their minds and had compared in detail their particular versions of this sensation, the chances are that they could quickly have satisfied each other that there was nothing inexplicable about it at all; Drew by telling Anna of their dawn walk, hand-in-hand, down Kay's hall, Anna by telling him that, yes, she had been on television once, years before. But, in the absence of any direct questioning, Drew thought it wiser not to mention her sleepwalking, in case it embarrassed her (*was I dressed? did I say or do anything awful?*), or worse (*did **he** do* *anything awful?*), frightened her, while Anna had never seen her brief TV appearance – indeed, was only dimly aware at the time that she was being filmed – and consequently rarely remembered that anyone else might have been tuned in watching.

It was well after three when Anna looked at the clock above the bar.

– Oh, Christ, poor Tara, she said and drained her Ballygowan. I'd better be getting back. What about you?

Drew was twenty minutes late for one train and three hours early for another.

– I'm all right yet a while. I'll walk that way with you.

They had turned off Kildare Street into Molesworth Street when Anna again sensed that her companion was on the verge of saying something important and adopted what she hoped was an encouraging silence. Drew bit his bottom lip bloodless – like someone, she was tempted to tell him, she had known in another life, before he asked her, stammering, ears blushing, if she would, perhaps, consider going out with him, though he would understand, of course, if she said no ... But *yes, yes, yes, YES* was what she'd said when he eventually got to the end of it. And *Tara was right*, was what she heard now.

She mistook it for the beginning of a joke and prepared herself to laugh.

– Right? Right about what? she asked, then reading the answer off his suddenly paper-white face shrank from him.

– Oh, no.

– I'm sorry.

– Oh, no, she said again.

Her mouth was a tiny mobile gash in a carapace of stillness.

He had foreseen this, had understood that her reaction now would be much worse than if he had spoken up three hours earlier, before lunch, before all their chat. But in the end he had realised that he could not in all conscience board the train for Belfast knowing that he was leaving her prey to anxiety every time the phone rang.

– Why didn't you speak to me for heaven's sake?

– I don't know, he said.

Her anger came in a snort down her nose. She strode ahead

of him, growing stiffer and stiffer – more and more her Belfast
self – with every stride, till finally she stopped dead, as though
petrified entirely. As Drew caught up with her, however, her
shoulders sagged.

– I can't think what could have made me do it, he said.

But Anna wasn't listening. Her lips were pursed and her
lower jaw made small lateral movements, like a dinner guest
who has found something alien in her food and is torn between
the horror of her discovery and the embarrassment of spitting
it out.

– I phoned you once, she said, the urge to spit at last proving
irresistible. I got the number from Directory Enquiries, but you
were engaged when I rang and I took that as a sign and didn't
try again.

Her shoulders had drooped further in the course of her confession.

– What were you ringing for? Drew asked her.

– I don't remember.

They walked on in puzzled silence till they reached the
entrance of the shopping precinct.

– Will you tell Kay about this? one of them asked the other.

– I wouldn't know what to tell her.

– No, me neither.

*

Drew met Kay, quite by chance, that night in Belfast. He was
walking, with no firm purpose, citywards from Central Station
and she was coming out of a bar close to the Law Courts. It
was Kay spotted him.

– Hello, stranger.

She had a cardboard crown, sprayed gold, on her head, and
a golden-tanned man on her arm. This was Angus. And this,
she explained to Angus, was Drew. Five or six other people
joined them out on the pavement. Drew recognised a few of
the faces from Kay's work. They were celebrating, she told
him, and pointed to her golden crown.

– By appointment to the governments of Europe and the
Americas.

Quayside Design had had its tender accepted for the conversion of a pair of embassies relocating down by the Liverpool boat.

The city conspired with Kay in her affectation of grandeur. Over her shoulder a glorious, almost *Elyséan*, vista opened up along Chichester Street, Donegall Square, and Wellington Place, coming to a suitably splendid closure half a mile distant, just short of the Lower Falls, in the white-pilastered front of the Royal Belfast Academical Institution, Inst grammar school.

Drew recalled his unexpected elation earlier as the train rattled along the last few miles of the vulnerable cord that was the cross-border rail line and entered Belfast through the southern opening in its surrounding skull of hills – capped this evening with preposterously lovely, red-rinsed bouffant clouds. He was glad then that he had gone to Dublin, but gladder still that he had returned when he did, feeling that, despite his lingering confusion, he had succeeded in pulling himself back from a more tortuous involvement, and forgetting for the moment that the place he had pulled back *to* was the place which formerly he had been trying to pull back *from*.

Leaning on a wall across the broad hump of East Bridge Street from the station, he had watched the river flame into the lough. Downstream from him, cars launched themselves over the sister easter-westerly bridges, every crossing a leap of faith. Directly below him was a twenty- or thirty-foot drop into what had once been May's Market and was now, by all appearances, a carpark, though a carpark currently without cars: bare concrete relieved only by islands of weedy cement and, in the far corner, a bonfire of broken crates stoked by a solitary middle-aged warehouseman. A desolate scene, yet, in Drew's current elevated mood, one that was touched with dignity by the glory of the evening. Everything about it spoke of a duty discharged, a use fulfilled, an order passing. Someone had told him (in all likelihood, Kay) that there was to be a concert hall built on this site. Already on the opposite side of the river the water's edge had been transformed from industrial wilderness into a public walkway, paved in pinky brick: the inexorability of progress.

– You may take this if you wish.

Outside the pub, Kay offered him her free arm with queenly

disdain. The sun drifted deeper into the fabulous cloudbank. Belfast blushed at its own comeliness. Dublin paled further. Drew threaded his arm through Kay's.

– Where to? he asked.

They lost Angus somewhere along the way. In one bar he was still there, in the next he was gone. The others dropped away too. Kay held on to Drew more tightly. By the end of the night they were the only ones left.

– Come home with me, she said.

Her crown had burst its staples and sat on her shoulders like a starched collar.

– I don't know, he said, her Puritan burlesque briefly touching a raw, work-ethical nerve in him: I'm on earlies tomorrow.

– Go on. Just to sleep. I'm too tired for anything else.

He smiled.

– Oh, good, she said, and kissed his ear.

Later, going to bed, she came and stood in the bathroom doorway.

– What are you doing with all this?

Drew looked. Punts. He finished sluicing his mouth.

– Where'd you get that?

– It fell out of your trouser pocket. Well?

Drew reached for a towel.

– Customers send it from the south for books. I was taking it to the bank and I forgot.

– Taking it to the bank? In your pocket?

Kay approached bunching the notes in her fist and shook them in his face.

– If I thought you'd some wee Geraldine stashed away down there in Dundalk, she said and grabbed his dick, I'd pull this off.

– Listen who's talking. What about Angus?

– Angus Bangus, she laughed and kissed him tonguily. His scrotum crawled as he stiffened in her hand.

The clock read ten past two. It was Saturday morning, 26 May. Tomorrow would be his one hundredth day back in Belfast.

13

No one could say with certainty where, or when, it started, but within a matter of days one week at the beginning of June a rumour Wilbured round every Bookstore in the country that Karen, James and Phoebe were negotiating a merger with a mystery European company. In the Belfast version of the rumour (it was there in the staffroom, along with the full complement of local and national dailies, when Drew arrived for work on Wednesday morning), the Bookstore name and upper management structure were to be retained but half the existing branches were to be sold off and the money used to develop the EC English-language market.

Pamela was in Sardinia with Pascal when the rumour broke, leaving Drew (such was his luck) to placate the staff as best he could alone. Of course he refused to give the rumour any credence, of course he advised them not to either. All the same, as soon as they were on the shop floor, he phoned the manager of his old branch for reassurance. Yes, he'd heard the rumour too. *He'd* been told by the manager of the branch *he'd* started in that it was all a lot of malicious gossip put about by an ex-employee at central office who had had a grudge against James, or a crush on Phoebe, or vice versa, or both, or all four even. Anyway, the long and the short of it was that the man was a pathological liar and clearly not to be believed.

Drew passed this on to his staff by way of a jokey aside the following morning, thinking to pre-empt any repetition of the previous day's nonsense. But he realised, too late, that he had miscalculated. They detected in his story a managerial counter-rumour and closed ranks to protect their own.

It grew, quickly and splendiferously.

Should the merger proceed, the word on the shop floor now ran, Belfast was number three, behind Carlisle and Perth, in the list of priority closures. Drew appealed to reason. What about the recent sales figures? Why would any business shut down one of its best performers? Richard, however (Richard who had, from the outset, been the prickliest of the whole prickly bunch and who had now assumed, whether by default or design, the role of spokesperson), thwarted him with an appeal of his own to a more persuasive logic:

– Look at the centre of Europe, he said, then look at us.

Drew wasn't exactly helped by other rumours then current, unconnected with the world of books; like talk of the Liverpool boat being taken off, breaking the last sea link between the north of Ireland and England.

The mood in the shop turned mutinous. Drew gave in to pressure and phoned central office. He got through to Zena, Karen's PA. Karen, James and Phoebe were in a meeting. Could she help? Drew mentioned the merger rumour. Zena sighed.

– You're about the twentieth person this week has asked me that.

– So what did you tell the other nineteen?

– Not a word of truth in it. *At All.*

Drew was holding the phone out to the staffroom as she said this.

– Now are you satisfied? he asked when he had hung up.

But if they were, they kept it well hidden. Richard changed tack, reluctant to relinquish his position of power so soon after acquiring it.

– It's OK for you, he said. You're not the one has to worry if all this turns out to be true.

He chewed the tuft of hair on the underside of his bottom lip. His chin bristled belligerently, the glimpsed skin beneath his beard angry and red.

– I have as much investment in this shop as the rest of you, Drew said. (Remembering the scene later, he thought perhaps he banged the table at this point.) If I have my way this shop will be so successful no one would ever dare close it down.

– Funny, Sian Miles pulled a smile, tight as a bowstring; let it go. That's just what *Simon* used to say.

And *Simon*, as everyone present knew, had stayed all of five months before he moved on. Drew finally had the measure of their dislike for him. He looked around the table at the faces looking at him. Every one was as closed to him as on the first day he saw them.

The atmosphere in the shop degenerated further to one of imminent breakdown. Orders went astray, phone-calls that ought to have been made weren't. A Pan delivery was two-thirds unpacked before anyone noticed it was addressed to the Chichester branch. Customers sensed something was wrong and became snappish. Three wrote letters of complaint to Pamela (which Drew, deputising, answered himself, forging her signature), two stormed out vowing never to return.

On Monday the air conditioning packed in. It was the beginning of one of the hottest summers on record. They boiled. They seethed. They stewed. All semblance of normal practice ceased.

On Tuesday Drew was at Pamela's desk drafting the staff rota for July, projecting order where he feared only chaos, when Matt, the youngest of his booksellers, came to the door of the office and, with an impressive blush, even by his own high standards, and a visible struggle against all he had been brought up to believe right and proper, announced a visitor by his (stammered) Christian name: *Juju* . . .

A tall blond man wearing a jacket of unbleached linen, chinos, and brown plimsolls on sockless feet, strode across the floor and took Drew's hand in both of his.

. . . *James*.

– Drew, mate. How's it going. All right?

He tossed his jacket across the back of a chair. His T-shirt was white with a central design of orange, black and green, which, when viewed from certain angles, resolved itself into a picture of an endangered species and, when viewed from certain others, formed the words *Save It!* Worried by the reports of disaffection pouring into central office from every corner of the Bookstore kingdom, Karen, Phoebe and he had decided the day before to split the country threeways and embark on a whirl-wind, morale-boosting tour. James alone had been to two shops in the Midlands already that day before catching the plane to Belfast and was carrying on tomorrow to Scotland. He asked

Drew if he could find him a hotel for the night, but told him not to worry if he couldn't.

– I can always crash on your settee, can't I?

By closing down all but the till nearest the main entrance and deploying the uniformed security guards upstairs on shoplifter alert, Drew was able to keep the bookselling side of the operation going solo – *and* find time to book a room in the Europa – while James assembled the rest of the staff beyond the door between Religion and New Age and gave them his thirty-minute pep talk.

– You're a star, James told him afterwards. Do you know that?

He called on the staff to give their assistant manager a round of applause, and, whatever he had said to them in there, *they bloody gave him it too.*

Drew knew who the star was all right.

James had been to Belfast on several occasions in the past, for interviews and the like, but always on flying visits, always in winter and always, it seemed, in the rain (*chucked it down, mate, every time*), with the result that he'd never yet managed to get much of a look at the city. So today, he told Drew (they were drinking tea together in the now tranquil staffroom) he intended to take advantage of the free evening and the good weather to see a few of the sights.

A few of the sights. Drew brought the teacup to his mouth, surprised to discover that he still harboured something of the old suspicion of these words; the distaste for tourists, common to those of his background, who knew that all too often seeing a few of the sights involved nothing more than a ghoulish fairground ride up the Shankill and down the Falls, gawping at murals and fortified bars, having the potentially life-saving nuances of the rival black taxi services explained and a murderous significance ascribed to every street corner, public house and patch of waste ground. The *this was where* and the *over there* of twenty years of violence.

You could find anything you wanted if you went looking for it, and you only had to go looking in any direction other than narrowly west in Belfast to find a different city altogether.

Drew lowered his cup.

– I have a friend works round the corner, he said, knows the city as well as anyone. We could always call for her.

– I leave myself in your capable hands.

James opened his own hands magnanimously and Drew was satisfied then that his suspicions had been misplaced.

Kay, though, was just leaving when they arrived at Quayside Design. She had to look in on her embassies for a minute, but only for a minute. They could come with her if they liked.

– As long as you don't mind, James said

– Not at all.

They went Donegall Quay, Queen's Square, Custom House Square, Tomb Street. A rubbly route, but elevated by the Custom House itself and interrupted at intervals by new architectural growth. James commented on the amount of building he'd seen already on his way in from the airport. He had expected to see more . . . well, more destruction, frankly.

The battle between *de*struction and *con*struction, Kay told him, warming to her guide's role, was the oldest battle in Belfast. The congenital predisposition of various of its inhabitants for periodically dismantling the city had been matched at every turn by the efforts of those who, against this and other, even more elemental enemies, had struggled throughout its history to build it up. Men (for men, in the past they invariably were) who had looked at mudflats and seen shipping channels, had looked at water and seen land. Belfast as a city was a triumph over mud and water, the dream of successive generations of merchants, engineers, and entrepreneurs willed into being. They had had to build the land before they could work it. Dredging, scouring, banking, consolidating, they fashioned a city in their own image: dry docks, graving docks, ships, cranes, kilns, silos; industry from their industry, solidity from the morass, leaving an indelible imprint on the unpromising slobland, and their names driven like screwpiles into the city's sense of itself. Dargan, Dunbar, Workman, Wolff, Harland . . .

These were Kay's ancestors. Their struggle was her struggle, and it was a struggle, moreover, which she had internalised and ritualised; a struggle she re-enacted in miniature several times a week in her own life, hurling herself on dissolution in the bar-dark hours, piecing herself together again the next morning (as Drew had seen her do many times), then increasing in vitality as the day progressed, as though energised rather than sapped by prolonged exposure to the city, so that now she set a pounding pace up Tomb Street for the two men to follow.

(Those authors of the city's fortunes might have been horrified by Kay's lifestyle, to say nothing of her sex, but they would undoubtedly have applauded her energy, and her zeal now as she recounted their achievements to James.)

– You'll hear a lot of talk here about stolen land, she said.

James already had.

– Well, it's all true. Where we're standing now . . .

They had arrived in Corporation Square, facing the Liverpool ferry terminal.

– Where we're standing now is stolen land. And all that over there – (Queen's Island, the shipyard) – is stolen land: stolen from the sea.

– I'd never thought of it like that, James said.

– You and fifty million others, she said, in that Kay way that was impossible to take exception to.

Dinner took them to a restaurant by the BBC and afterwards they strolled back towards James's hotel beneath a sky burnt red by the tortuously slow descent of the sun. A curved sheet of clear water poured from a free-standing wall across a square at the bottom of Franklin Street. *Blackstaff* Square, said the letters behind the water, after the river which skulked across the city, eastwards from the Bog Meadow, before debouching into the Lagan at the gasworks.

But surely, Drew said to Kay, that wasn't real Blackstaff water falling from the fountain?

Real Blackstaff water, he told James and you wouldn't have been able to see the wall, never mind read the name.

Real Blackstaff water, Kay chipped in, and it would have seized up before it reached the ground.

Kay, as ever, had got it just right. The Blackstaff was as black as a congested lung. The Blackstaff had once been voted the dirtiest river in Britain – *Europe*, some Belfast people would insist, with the same perverse pride with which they would tell you that the Europa was the most bombed building in the world, though as Drew would have been quick to assure James, those days, like the hotel's perimeter fence and search hut, were long gone.

At the opposite side of the square from the fountain, the history of the city was kept under lock and key in a pair of maroon-trimmed display cases. Prints of megalithic tombs and the ancient, eponymous sandbank ford; maps showing the medieval keep and the early walled town at the head of the untrained river; a portrait of Sir Arthur Chichester, first Lord of Belfast, grandsire of all the Earls and Marquises of Donegall who controlled the city for close on two hundred years, and an impression of the fire which destroyed his castle a century after his death – this last a black and white illustration reminiscent in tone of certain old-fashioned children's comics, so that James, pausing before it, said he half expected to see Black Bob in among the feet of the frantic citizens with a pail of water gripped in his noble collie's jaws.

They cut across the square on to Amelia Street. (*Amelia*, James murmured catching sight of the sign, *Amelia*. He thought it was the loveliest street name he had ever heard.) There were police land-rovers parked in the taxi rank at the bottom of it, their rear doors and side doors open, their engines turning over at a gentle pant. An RUC man in shirtsleeves brought his colleagues drinks in polystyrene cartons from a nearby Indian restaurant. Outside the bar on the left-hand corner, two bouncers, sweltering in tuxes, adjusted one another's wilting bow ties, while winos with sunset complexions worked the overspill of punters from the bar on the other corner, touching them for odds.

– Twenty pence there, fella, one of them said to Drew, with the regretful tone of a bus conductor asking for a fare, as if to say *if it was just up to me, you know, I wouldn't ask.*

– Twenty pence there for a . . . and here he said a word that managed to convey a bed for the night, a cup of tea, something hot to eat, a bath perhaps, maybe a haircut, and the outside chance of a drink if there was anything over.

Drew rooted in his pockets preferring not to take out his wallet in case all he had was notes. He dredged up a ten-bob bit, gave him that.

He was a sport. Dead on. Know what I mean? Him and the wino. Right? Fuck the lot of them. A sport, boss.

James and Kay were waiting for him up ahead on Great Victoria Street. Framed between their profiles, on the far side of the road, was a billboard announcing the construction of the Great Northern Centre. Everything was Great these days, or what wasn't Great was Grand. Like the Opera House just letting out down the street. (*Daisy Pulls It Off a sure-fire summer winner from Theatre Clwyd.*) Coach drivers wound up their smoking-bee and kept an eye out for their provincial parties. Next door the New Vic boasted *Bingo At Its Best* in a loud blend of orange, red and flourescent green hoardings. A pair of buskers under its awning, alive to the passing trade, launched into the Everlys at the drop of their hat, knees pumping (*dream, dream, dream*) like bellows. A customised Morris Minor stopped at the traffic lights, sun-roof down, stereo blasting out some fierce dance track. Heads turned (the doors were stencilled with pink and white flowers; the boot said *Love!*), then turned away again. Suddenly it was as though a thousand windows had been thrown open. The street filled with music. Fifties pop, acid house, a shriek of jazz trumpet from somewhere, a crash of metal from a jukebox somewhere else, Indian restaurant music from the Indian restaurant. Discrete yet oddly harmonious; a symphony for any city, summer 1990.

Then a single discordant note was introduced. A distant percussion, like a heel being brought down smartly on an empty Coke can. *Crumpcrack.* Everyone – punters, bouncers, winos, drivers, Morris Minor customisers, *Daisy*-goers, bingo buskers, shop-chain owners, on-off lovers – seemed to register it simultaneously, and register that everyone else was registering it, yet keep on doing whatever it was they had been doing up till then: adjusting bow ties, admiring street names, asking for odds; all hearing music. The second sound, which in reality was less than a heartbeat after the first, coincided with the tyre-shredding roar of land-rovers bursting out on to Great Victoria

Street, doors flapping, polystyrene cartons yinging back over their shoulders.

It was the land-rovers' urgency as much as the third-fourth-fifth-sixth sounds (and perhaps seventh and eighth, they came in a cluster, it was difficult to tell) that made up the civilians' minds what was going on, all except James's, which, having been on comics such a short time before, was remembering a free gift he had got with one of his once, a contraption akin to a three-cornered brown-paper hat that you held between fore-finger and thumb and flicked in such a way (the mechanics of it escaped him) that it opened out with a bang.

Drew took a step towards Kay and placed a hand on her arm at the same moment as Kay placed a hand on James's, and by means of this chain reaction was James made to understand. People, in any case, were saying it out loud now.

– That's fucking shooting. It fucking is. It's fucking shooting.

And it was fucking echoing off the fucking buildings, making its exact source impossible to pinpoint.

They looked to the diminishing backs of the police land-rovers for guidance. Past Inst and the Tech (the Black Man maintained a stony disregard, the first five flushed-neon letters of the Progressive Building Society sign peeped out, in entirely the wrong direction, from Wellington Place), on to King Street and out of sight. The continuation, though, wasn't hard to guess: left on to Divis Street – Divis Street, Falls. Where expected.

The shooting had stopped. James's face and hands where white.

– It's all right, Kay was saying, it's all right.

Drew caught hold of his employer's other arm, closing the protective circle, and that was how they crossed the road to the hotel.

A helicopter, which had been hovering unheeded somewhere in the vicinity, banked closer, announcing its presence, as a fridge will, suddenly shuddering.

They drank neat whiskey, with no apparent alcoholic effect, in the upstairs lounge bar. Sirens came and went. Journalists left and, at length, returned. The waiter collated snatches of talk and left them at each table with the emptied ashtrays. A

policeman had been shot in Castle Street. The killers had posed
as a courting couple, the woman carrying pink and white carnations which she dropped as she fled. In fact the carnations
belonged to someone else, but it was these flowers – generally
photographed from pavement level – that the papers focused
on the next day (an angle, they call it), elevating routine violent
death in Northern Ireland to one of its rare national top
billings.

– *Castle* Street? James said.

– No, don't worry, Drew said. The shop's on Castle *Place*.

– But it can't be far from here.

– Depends what you mean by far.

– How far exactly?

Drew thought about it.

– Five hundred yards, maybe?

Kay's plumped-out lip said more or less.

– *Five hundred yards*? James said. And all those people just
stood there. *We* just stood there.

– Five hundred yards is a long way in Belfast, Kay said and
that wasn't bravado. Five hundred yards *was* a long way in
Belfast. A world away. Significant distances were measured
rather in tens of yards: the distance between Springmartin and
New Barnsley, Suffolk and Lenadoon, between Percy Street,
Conway Street, Manor Street, and their anitpathetical erstwhile
other halves. Significant distances were the span of a single
borderline street, the thickness of a wall, a wrong turn, a foot
out of place, a whisker, a hair's breadth, the skin of your teeth.

That night Drew and Kay lay in bed, not sleeping, not talking, arms and legs not quite touching.

On Sunday, Melanie rang.

It was a wonderfully clear line, though Drew attributed some
of the clarity to the fact that he'd gone to bed early the past
few nights, sober and alone.

– God, you sound close.

– Closer than you think, Melanie said. I'm here, in England.
I'm back.

And that was only her first surprise.

– I'm in bad need of a break, she said when they had exhausted the circumstances of her return. I was thinking maybe I would come over there and see you.

Drew did something then he thought people only did in films. He looked at the telephone as though it were animate.

Melanie coming to *Belfast*? he asked it.

– Are you serious? he asked her.

– Why wouldn't I be? she asked him, disingenuously.

Pamela Magill wasn't due back to work until the beginning of the following week. Drew suggested to Melanie that if she was to leave it till the weekend after that he'd be able to swing four or five days off. Melanie said, fine, if he thought he could hold on that long, and she whispered something totally obscene down the line.

– I hope you didn't learn *that* in New York, Drew said.

They spoke daily, their conversations forming for Drew an ever more concrete bridge back to his other life. He began to appreciate afresh the satisfying complexities of their relationship. He had been wary of the language of love for too long, considering it too elusive, too susceptible to redefinition. You could no more build a life on love, he had once thought, than you could build a house on water, and he had been so pleased with the formulation he had written it in one of his notebooks – had even aired it one night in the campus bar, during one of those mass pairing-off sessions they had used to style philosophical debates. The first night he could remember speaking to Melanie. She had stuck her tongue out slowly as he finished talking, with an ice cube riding on the meat of it.

– What about this? she asked, when the ice cube had dropped into her palm.

She set it on the table and very carefully fused together a wigwam of matchsticks and tried to balance them on top. They slithered, fell, lost their heads. She discarded those matchsticks and began again, her hands trembling as they withdrew. Again the matches fell. She began a third time. The wigwam stood a moment, unaided, then collapsed. The game caught on all round their corner of the bar, till every table-top was awash with carbon-flecked ice-water. The record was four seconds.

– Told you, Drew said.

– So, Melanie said, wasn't it good fun trying?

(*See that Melanie Bishop one*, Kelly Thorpe said as she and Drew walked back to his room, the break between them ten days away.)

He had all but forgotten till now what had made Melanie stick out her ice-laden tongue that night.

Love, like water, could crystallise, however briefly. Love was the instant of saying you loved and one of these days he would say it to Melanie.

He saw Kay a couple more times, neither of which was the right one to tell her about Melanie's forthcoming visit. Quite independently of that, however, he began to get a sense of ending. The weather was hot and humid. Bodies prickled in close proximity. He and Kay preferred to sleep alone. One evening, it is true, without either of them really intending it, they brought each other off sitting side by side on the leather chesterfield, watching *Brookside*. But even that could not disguise the fact that the bonds between them were becoming unstuck in the largely sterile heat.

Then Kay took off abruptly for a villa in Sardinia with friends from work and Angus Bangus. (It was no coincidence that she and Pamela should chose to go there at the same time. Half the island of Ireland was going. This was *Italia '90*, the crossover World Cup. The unrepresented North was cheering on the South. People who had never watched a football match before in their lives were packing the bars for penalty shoot-outs. Italian opera singers spoke of having *kept the door* in their youth, while England players danced a victory dance like scallies on a rave.) Kay was booked on a morning flight out of Dublin and caught the train down the evening before. She didn't tell Drew where she was staying that night and Drew didn't ask her. The call, though, when it came the next day, wasn't entirely unexpected. Another half an hour and he might have been tempted to pick up the phone himself.

She was nervous as hell, her breath short from too many cigarettes and her continued bewilderment at her part in all of this.

— It's Anna, she said and he said *I know*.

She had business in Belfast next weekend, she said. She wondered if he was going to be around.

It was as though a tape that had been held on pause since he crossed the border returning from Dublin was set running again. He knew exactly what she was asking and exactly what he was going to answer.

– I will be.

He was surprised at his sangfroid.

Cold blood.

Cold as ice-water.

14

I'M AFRAID WE'LL *have to put it off for a couple of days*, he'd
said. *Something's come up.*

Melanie turned the hot tap on full and shut the bathroom
window.

I'll bet something has, she thought. Your fucking dick.

She knew straight away what was going on. Oh, Drew, she
had wanted to say, it's me you're talking to; credit me with
some sense. Remember how *we* got off together, the backs *we*
had to go behind, obliterating scruples and spectres of jilted
partners with eggcupfuls of Hugh's smuggled-in-poteen. (They
had been seeing each other over a fortnight before they risked
a sober fuck. Melanie recalled the trepidation with which she
had approached it, like her first time on a two-wheeler without
stabilisers; her relief, on both occasions, when it was over and
she hadn't come to grief.)

The trouble with Drew, though, was that he never could
remember from one infatuation to the next, and so every time
they had to go through this charade that nothing was amiss.
She would watch him, over a period of days or weeks, once
even months, become more distant and haunted-looking, then
gradually, meekly return, with that dazed expression on his
face: *how could I have done that to you?* He seemed to blush
for days afterwards. His body was hot to the touch and he
made love emphatically, impressing himself upon her, so that
when they rolled apart she was covered in red blotches, on her
thighs, on her stomach, on her breasts, neck and arms. And
always, she knew, he was telling himself, *that's it, that's it,
that's the very last time I hurt her.* And always, she knew, he
meant it at the time, which was enough.

She had come across the following in one of his notebooks:

Duplicity is the Northern Irish vice. We are always (at least) two people and always false to (at least) one of them.

If she tried to picture him when they first moved in together, the summer after they met, it would be with one of these notebooks in his hand at all times. He was going to *write* then, of course, everybody said so; it was, she supposed, part of what had interested her in him, though by the time she realised the unlikelihood of his ever doing anything more than endlessly filling notebooks (far in advance of Drew himself realising it, if he had realised it yet at all) it had ceased to matter to her one way or the other. Almost without her noticing, in the space of a few months, their lives had simply grown together. Everything fitted. Their routines, their tastes, their faces when they kissed, each other's shirts and jeans. . . . Later, in other flats, he would sit reading through his notebooks on certain predictable evenings each week, then just certain evenings, then just the odd evening here and there, then not at all, though he still carried them everywhere he went, and occasionally she would see him toss one – its pages plumped with use – into the bottom drawer in their bedroom. When, at the beginning of this year, he had left for Belfast and she had dragged the bottom drawer down into the living room and tipped the contents on to the floor with the rest of his belongings, she had counted at least thirty such books, ranging from the little rough-cut school jotters in which he had transcribed French words and phrases in an uncertain hand (now childish, now precociously mature, but always showing traces of his present style – a calligraphic snapshot of him at twelve or thirteen), to the more familiar Black n' Red notebooks, each of which, following the example of the jotters was coded with a letter, W or P, and a number on the spine.

In the P books she would read:

In the early days, when they thought this epidemic was much like other epidemics, religion held its ground. But, once these people realised their instant peril, they gave their thoughts to pleasure. And all the hideous fears which stamp their faces in the daytime are transformed in the fiery, dusty nightfall into a sort of hectic exaltation, an unkempt freedom fevering their blood. (Camus, *The Plague*)

and below that:

Promiscuity in face of annihilation. Our little act of creation eclipsed. Metaphor for human condition.

then elsewhere in the same book:

Why did the chicken cross the road?

The *W* books were just words and definitions. English words now: *hyaline, amaranth, diaspora, archimandrite, eclosion, priapic, monad, threnody, noumenon, phenomenon, nemesis, pollyanna, fimicolous* .... From time to time Melanie thought she discerned a pattern of sense or sound struggling to emerge, but inevitably this would be followed by a word so illogical or so discordant that she concluded the only organising principle at work was chance, words plucked from the dictionary as and when they caught the eye, like certain pebbles pocketed from a beach full of pebbles. Many had been entered more than once, *teratogeny* twice within three pages of W13 (begun in October 1984), indicating to Melanie that whatever his original intentions had been in starting these collections they had finally become obscured by sheer force of habit.

The duplicity remark was typical of the *P* books' constant preoccupation with Over There. On page after page his pen nib returned to the subject, scratching away at it, like a fingernail picking at a scab. The tone too was typical and, what's more, deeply familiar to Melanie. She realised that what she was reading was a conversation Drew had kept up with himself over the years, a continuation of the conversations he had once had with Hugh McManus and the rest of that crowd he had hung about with when she met him: the Ex-Pats! the Ultimate Britons! Iconoclasts all, or so they had seemed to begin with, such a welcome change from the ardent republicans and staunch loyalists and their coteries of Irish wannabees

(Kelly my-great-grandparents-on-my-mother's-side Thorpe) who traded blood-threats across the floor of Student Union meetings. In time, though, with Hugh's departure for London, Melanie began to suspect that this pose of ironic detachment only masked an obsession with origins as unsound in its way as anything that the extremists in all their blinkered bigotry could conjure up, and that the Ex-Pats had become just a name to gather under to drink Guinness and feel the tragedy of their birth. To hear them talk about the place now, even to traduce it, you'd have thought it was somewhere, the centre of the significant universe. Not a misshapen little jug of a country teetering on the brink of a continental shelf: one ten-thousandth of the earth's surface. She had got that from an atlas. Not to use against them, but to help her keep a sense of proportion whenever she felt herself in danger of being sucked into their self-important fictions. And yet you could see how they had been encouraged in such grandiose thoughts. They had grown up believing in the intrinsic newsworthiness of every last detail of their lives. Their homes, their schools, their shops, their parents' jobs, or lack of them, their songs, their jokes, their games, their street corners, their wall paintings (above all their bloody wall paintings!), you name it, someone somewhere was sure to have covered it.

Drew told a story about a Swedish film crew turning up at his primary school one morning when he was nine or ten. Three men and a woman with long, pale faces wandering the corridors peeping in through classroom windows. There was an election of some kind on, or a referendum – wait, *the Border Poll*, that was it, Melanie remembered being creased up by that: so civilised sounding, so *proper*; so at odds with fertiliser bombs and cars resting on their heads in ploughed fields. The Swedes, it seems, had mistaken Drew's school for one which was being used as a polling station. So, while the director made reverse-charge calls from the headmaster's office, the crew stood about in the playground, all mustard and maroon anoraks and bru-shed-denim jeans. At some point the bell had rung for morning break and the playground had filled with children. They appeared not to take any notice of the adults in their midst, not even when the cameraman, on a silent signal from his colleagues, switched on his shoulder-camera and the sound engineer moved among them with her boom. They neither shied away from the lens nor tried to hog the show, but carried on as before, as though it was taken for granted that a Swedish camera crew should want to film them at play. If you had looked and listened very carefully, it's true, you might have detected a slight exaggeration in their movements, an unwonted clarity in their diction; but this was less affectation than an appreciation of the language gap, an unconscious concession to the viewers tuning in at teatime in Stockholm and Malmö.

They were just being themselves, as Drew described it, only more so.

The night before the Border Poll opened a woman had thrown herself from a tower block on a nearby housing estate worried, some of her neighbours said, about the vote going whichever way it was (against, very likely) she didn't want it to go. The Swedish director learnt of her death in the course of his phone-calling and the camera crew was dispatched to film the scene before going to the school they should have been at to begin with.

Another time Drew told Melanie that his memories of primary school often took the form of this never-seen ninety-second news item: He is in a scrum of children (most of whom he knows only by nickname), though the camera tracks him alone. He runs, he jumps, he stands still and throws his head back laughing. A heavily accented voice says, *On the day Ulster decides, children play their tigs* – that's the way the voice says it, *tigs – while the tension for some is so great. . . .* And here the camera drifts beyond the black, blunt-headed railings to where (in sight in memory, out of sight in reality) stands a block of council flats with a scrubbed-wet patch on its still-frosty forecourt . . .

Melanie's mother would have switched off this memory of Drew's long before then in much the same way that she could be seen mentally switching off whenever the name of her misguided daughter's boyfriend cropped up in conversation.

– That's quite enough of that, thank you, she would have said, reaching for the remote.

Melanie's mother strongly disapproved of the amount of

media coverage afforded to goings-on in Northern Ireland. Melanie's mother wanted Britain to get the hell out of the place, troops and news crews first. Bans and gags were too little too late; there were one or two of those characters and Melanie's mother would have had their tongues cut out to silence them permanently. (She would also have birched vandals and castrated sex offenders; Melanie's mother was a firm believer in the reformatory powers of mutilation.)

Melanie thought her mother was as bad as the media for going on about it so much (and she *did* go on about it), pointing out that every letter she wrote to the newspapers only added more column inches to the acreage of print she wrote, in part, to condemn. But that didn't deter Melanie's mother.

– If they'd kept the cameras out years ago, it would all have been over in a matter of weeks, she said, knowing, as she did (Melanie's mother had three degrees), that in this day and age what the camera didn't show couldn't exist.

Hugh McManus had thought the cameras were getting out of hand too. He told Melanie, the last time she saw him, that one had been discovered in a derelict building across the road from his parents' Belfast law practice. The local TV companies sent their cameras round to film it. A crowd gathered, as crowds do. Someone said that a car which had passed the scene several times was army undercover, taking pictures. The car sped off when someone else tried to take a picture of it. *What did I tell you*, the first someone said, and someone else altogether said, *It's the cameras you never find you have to worry about*, but nobody was listening to him, for the woman with him had launched into a story about this character the Special Branch turned whose house was fitted out from top to bottom with hidden cameras, and it was ages before the Boys, who used the house for planning ops, could work out why so many volunteers were being arrested all of a sudden, till finally, having ruled out all other possible leaks, they staked out the stake-out and discovered that your man had the *TV rental people* round brave and often, fiddling with his aerial and one thing and another, so they got the hold of him and took him to a place where the only camera was their camera and they videoed his confession for his Special Branch handlers before shooting him dead. But then another woman interrupted her, *Your head's cut, you, I seen that in a film*, she said. *Oh, yeah? Seen what in a film?* the first woman asked her. *That there that you're only after saying: Dirty Den was in it*. But the first man interrupted the both of them. *There's that car back again and it's stopping*. It wasn't the same car at all, though, but one the spitting image of it, and here, when the door opened didn't a pregnant woman get out. *Take a reddener, you*, his mates all shouted, and he got the hump up, saying he wouldn't put it past the Brits to use pregnant women (reckoning, no doubt, that if they could be used to conceal a gun or a bomb, then why not a camera?), but anyway, just then, there was the helicopter circling overhead, getting its angles, and the man looked up and looked down again, dead nonchalant, and said, *Good of God to drop in*, meaning, of course, there was hardly a thing went on around there that the helly-telly didn't pick up, but a fella just arriving at that moment, a known player whose pirated mugshot, it was rumoured, had recently gone on general release in Protestant areas of the city, shot him a dirty look. *Some fucking God*, he said and stamped on his fag, *Remember South Armagh*. And the man who had been speaking when he came along, terrified of being taken up the wrong way, said, all pally, *Remember it? Haven't I got the video?* and one of the women glanced over her shoulder, *What video's that?* she asked. *The time the Boys shot down the helicopter*, the known player said, *they filmed the whole thing*. And another woman, who had been in the conversation earlier then drifted off, came back in again, *Wait a minute*, she said, **that was the film I seen with Dirty Den in it**.

You forgot sometimes till you went back, Hugh said, how bad it was. Somebody was always filming somebody else. You didn't know from one moment to the next if they were filming you too. The temptation was just to act as if they were at all times. Was it any wonder people were walking round asking each other what they were? As the police and politicians were never done telling them, everyone had a part to play, be it ever so humble. Bit parts, tit-for-tat parts:

an unemployed Catholic man
two Protestants drinking in a pub
five workmen heading home on such and such a road
ten workmen heading home on such and such another
a woman out walking her dog near the seat of the
   explosion
a schoolgirl caught in the crossfire
a boy, aged twelve, struck on the head by a plastic bullet
a father of three, from Reading in Berkshire
a boyfriend too distraught to talk to the press
a wife and four children, the youngest only eighteen
   months
forty-seven injured, some seriously . . .

Somebody had to play them.

Melanie had been very worried about Hugh that last time she
saw him. She and Drew had been following his career the past
year or two in the law columns of the daily papers, watching
him gradually making a name for himself. Lately, though, he
had begun turning up well away from where they had come to
expect to find him, often, in fact, in papers (Drew saw them all
in the shop) that carried no law reports at all. Ugly little gossip
pieces, ripe with insinuation: a cousin interned in 1971, a family
holiday cottage across the border in Donegal, *an area long
known to security chiefs in N. Ireland as a haven for republican
terrorists.* Much had been made too of the vinyl shopper he
was invariably seen carrying, even into court – the same vinyl
shopper which he had been carrying since his student days, yet
which he still on occasion seemed amazed to find dangling from
his wrist when he raised his hand to emphasise a point. The
word *bachelor*, pincered between inverted commas, as though
too suspect to touch directly, became his regular tabloid tag.
The papers, it appeared, were intent on making a name for
him too, by subliminal declension: Father Fiacc, Father Fear,
Father's Fear's Fairy Counsel.
   People accused of plotting against cabinet ministers, even (for
the time being at least), the Environment Secretary, were deeply
unpopular with the British press; and though no direct refer-

ences to the case were ever made, people defending them were scarcely less so.

And the trial had not yet begun.

Hugh was still preparing the defence, shuttling backwards and forwards between London, Liverpool and Belfast, in the air, he sometimes felt, more often than he was out of it. And before every flight, without fail, he'd be singled out at the door of the departure lounge and given a wee green card to complete.

Surname (Mr/Mrs/Miss) Maiden Name Christian Names, Date & Place of Birth, Nationality/Citizenship, Home Address, Address Visited/Visiting, Purpose of Visit, Occupation, Employer, Date.

– I'm sure you could fill this in for me by now, he'd once said to one of the Special Branch men.

He'd got so he recognised quite a few of them. They were never discourteous, but they were punctilious. That particular man had detained him the very next time he travelled, looking from the green card to his bank card (Hugh carried no other identification) and back again.

– I'm sorry, sir. He held the green card up to the light.

– This isn't your signature.

– But you just saw me make it.

– Well, it doesn't look like it.

Another detective joined him, compared the signatures, made a doubtful moue.

– Nope, doesn't look like it to me either.

– Let me see, Hugh said, but the first policeman snatched both cards away. He pushed a blank slip of paper towards him.

– Sign that, please.

– What?

– Sign that.

The detectives put their heads together, studying the conflicting signatures and Hugh's slip of paper. Hugh was thrown into confusion. He couldn't remember what the signature on the bank card was like, or how the signature on the green card differed, or which of the two was his usual signature. He couldn't even remember how he held his pen. Each letter was a minefield of possible errors, he approached the *g* as though he'd never met with one in his life.

When eventually he had finished (his hand was racked with cramp), the two detectives examined all three samples. For a few seconds Hugh's authenticity hung in the balance. Then both men nodded, satisfied. He was himself after all.

– But it was a close thing, he told Melanie. If I have to keep on giving them my name at this rate, there'll soon be nothing left of me.

He pulled the corners of his mouth down into an apologetic grimace. Melanie felt herself smile, though in fact throughout the afternoon she had been thinking how little like the Hugh of old he looked. She was facing him across a kitchen table on which stood a brown glazed teapot she had bought once in a sale and instantly regretted, two mugs, a sugar bowl, a carton of milk, sell-by yesterday, and a packet of petticoat-tails, hardly touched. It was early October, prematurely bleak. If Melanie glanced past Hugh's head, which she did every so often, according to their unconsciously negotiated rhythm of engaging and disengaging eye contact, she could see two Yorkshire terriers in tartan body stockings wading through the drifts of dead leaves about the wire divide between her house and the house next door. If Hugh glanced past Melanie's shoulder he could see a Schwartz spice wallchart, and a Madonna postcard, dangling at an angle from a single red tack.

It was nearly a year and a half since they'd last met up together, when Melanie and Drew paid Hugh a fleeting visit in London on their way home from Greece. Then, Hugh had been his familiar, awkward, angular self, his movements quick, bordering on the chaotic, too expansive for the tiny studio flat he received them in. (There had been a brief but memorable affair some years back between Hugh and a visiting Sudanese student, as raw-boned and flailing in conversation as he was. Things *broke* when Hugh was about – which perhaps explained why he had so few possessions of his own – and when Hugh and Fidelma were together everything around them seemed at risk. Their lovemaking, Melanie had always believed, would have been something to behold.) Now, though, seeing him again after a gap of eighteen months, Melanie found herself thinking what friends had said who had met Hugh after hearing her and Drew talking about him:

– He's very nice and everything, but, I don't know, I think I was expecting somebody much *bigger*.

Perhaps it was true, perhaps Hugh did gain in the retelling; Melanie herself was aware, now that she was doing it again, of having had to make a slight downward adjustment to her expectations of him in the past. But she was convinced that there had been a more definite diminution of late, as though something of himself had indeed been lost in all the to-ing and fro-ing between countries. He seemed lesser in every conceivable way. Even his hair had shrunk, from the gargantuan quiff he had sported as a student, to a closely clipped, tight-fitting cap, which drew attention to the surprising daintiness of his skull. His face too was altered, his cheeks become pinched as though acted on by an inner vacuum. Pressure of work, of course. And no doubt, too, overwork was to blame for a less easily definable alteration, a certain constraint, or want of energy, restricting him to one gesture where before nothing less than half a dozen would have sufficed.

He had confessed himself all in when he arrived at the house, unannounced, earlier that afternoon. Drew had left just an hour before – for London, of all places. He had even talked of calling on Hugh while he was down, but then worried he might be too busy and decided against it. This evening he was attending a Bookstore literary dinner-dance, whatever that was (though whatever it was, Melanie had told him from the start, he could count her out of it), and by the time he got back tomorrow morning Hugh would already have left. In all probability their trains would cross halfway.

– I'll give him a wave as he goes by, Hugh said.

Melanie felt herself smile again and wondered whether, even supposing he could see him, Drew would recognise his friend.

Among the other things Hugh had lost in his travels back and forth was his taste for drink (and pity the person who came upon *that* unawares at 12,000 feet on the Belfast Shuttle). Besides, some public houses were becoming a little too public for Hugh's comfort lately. He much preferred the cinema these days and after they had eaten, Melanie looked up the what's on guide and called out the names of the films showing in town for him to choose from. The film he chose was an old Woody Allen, Melanie, who was a big fan, had, by one of those unaccountable quirks of memory, forgotten which. She remembered practically everything else about the evening. She wore Drew's overcoat and her wide-brimmed felt hat, pinned up at the front with the brooch Hugh had given her for her twenty-first. She was having her period and had a blind spot on the underside of her chin. She remembered too that they arrived at the cinema after the film had started and left again before the credits, and wound up walking in a park set into the right angle of two busy main roads not far from her house. The park had four paths criss-crossing it like spokes, or the bars of the union flag, and at the hub stood an old sooty fountain, long defunct and recently sprayed in luminous silver paint with the words *Eat the Rich!* A woman had been attacked in this park the month after Melanie moved to the city and she never set foot in it alone after dark and rarely, if ever now, in the day. She and Hugh sat beside each other on the fountain's stone lip. A skateboarder passed at speed: a rattle of wheels, a splash of music spilling from a Walkman, then a specific silence in the surrounding city hum.

Seconds passed. Forty, fifty. Hugh said he was thinking of buying a place of his own. *Buying?* Melanie asked him. Yes, Hugh said, buying. An actual house. He would paint every room white, except for one, his bedroom, which would be – Melanie recalled he was quite categorical – cornflower blue.

This was Hugh speaking, who had been living in that glorified bedsit they visited him in since arriving in London; who had once cited as the ideal human habitation the university study-bedroom with sink *en suite*, and more than once claimed that what couldn't be carried in his vinyl shopping bag was surplus to his requirements. Now here he was talking about a chest of drawers he'd seen and the bed he had his heart set on (Hugh and his future Fidelmas, clicking like demented knitting needles). He would have a lodger, he said, for the company, rather than the money, and to feed the parrot (for there was to be a parrot too) when he was away. A student, maybe; maybe – Melanie, still trying to take on board his sudden embracing of domesticity didn't pick up on this till much later – someone come across the water looking for work. Another man, certainly.

Melanie picked that up. He'd better watch, she said, the papers didn't get wind of it.

– Oh, you've seen all that?

– Drew brings me home the clippings from work. We're thinking of starting a scrapbook.

Hugh winced flexing his throat muscles.

– I suppose I should be flattered they have gone to so much trouble to discredit me, he said, and it did make you wonder when you saw him sitting on the lip of the sooty fountain what the papers were so afraid of.

In fact, despite what he'd said earlier, Hugh admitted now that he was sometimes glad to get back to Belfast where, with everything else that was going on, few people could work up much indignation about the trial of a man, priest though he was, accused of conspiring with persons unknown to use substances never found to cause an explosion at a time and a place inferred entirely from coded messages pencilled on cigarette papers he professed not to own.

There (unlike here), almost the only comment it had excited was from a soldier on foot patrol in the city centre. He had passed Hugh under the Castle Street gates, clocking him from the notorious bag up, and what he said was:

– I hope they hang the fucker, you Paddy ponce.

At least, that's what Hugh thought he said. When he turned in surprise the soldier who had spoken had turned too, equidistant with Hugh from the intervening gate, rifle levelled, covering his comrades' rears. Both took a step backwards, the soldier one step further into the security zone, Hugh one step further into – what then? The *in*security zone? *Otherness*, certainly, because in that land of excluded middles you were either one thing or the other, one of us or one of them, for or against, inside or out. (On a previous visit Hugh had followed the inquest into the shooting dead of a teenage joyrider from one of the mountainy housing estates above west Belfast. The soldiers who fired the fatal shots – named in court as A and B – claimed that the car had driven straight at their VCP leaving them with only a split second in which to interpret its intent. One way or the other. The coroner, finding the cause of death to be gunshot wounds to the neck and head, noted that at the time of the incident the deceased had been walking with the aid of a stick, the legacy of an IRA kneecapping for previous *anti-social behaviour*. Even Otherness has its Others.)

Back in Castle Street, meantime, the soldier had taken another three or four steps in reverse. Hugh matched him stride for stride in the opposite direction. The channel between them remained eerily clear, their gazes remained locked. All else paled and blurred, wobbling on the brink of dissolution. Perhaps, Hugh thought, if they both walked far enough backwards something definitive would give, like a trapdoor in the here and now, plunging the scene beneath the surface of the particular, past the facilely allegorical (British soldier menaces imputed Irish queen at the gates of planter town) to arrive at a more basic but altogether more complex coincidence of symbols. A gate let into a fence, a person within, a person without, a gun, and a bagful of legal papers.

Their present distribution was only one of several Hugh could envisage: the person without, for example, could have the gun (i.e. might) and the person within, the papers (right); or the person within (or without) could have might and right both; or neither. The only configuration that was not permissible was the two people simultaneously within (or without, it didn't matter which) *with* the gun *and* the papers. For it was in the nature of enclosing that it included one thing and excluded another (*any* other) and to have the two people on the same side of the fence *with* the papers *and* the gun would make a nonsense of the fence, to say nothing of the papers and the gun. A nonsense, in fact, of the mind's attempts to maintain a distinction between them.

But at this point Hugh's soldier performed an abrupt about-turn and another soldier took his place, sighting up the windows and doorways on either side of the street as the patrol pushed on into the throng of midday shoppers. The moment became particular again, vulnerable to more partisan interpretations (for had not the Castle Street gates been raised, like a folk memory reactivated, on almost the exact site of the seventeenth-century rampart between the settlers and the risen Irish?), and Hugh saw the perfect logic in stealing a car and driving straight at a vehicle checkpoint, the enticement of a tilt at the great escape that would take you – Steve McQueen! – accelerating beyond the roadblocks and ramps and folk-memory ramparts and curfews and intermittent internments and peace walls and Derry's walls and no surrendering and no-going here and no-going there and no-going any-fucking-where, not ever; accelerating beyond the segregated schooling and sec-tarianism in the workplace and one door closing while another shut in your face; foot to the board, accelerating and accelerat-ing and accelerating, until *BOOM!*, you broke free altogether . . .

– Bye, bye Fat Lad, Melanie murmured.

Hugh halted in full flow, looking, for a moment, stunned to find himself in this park in the dark with Melanie Bishop. Then he beat his feet on the ground,

– Oh, fuck me, he said. The Fat Lad!

*

Summer, three – God, no, *four* – years before. A party in their flat. Living room dense with foliage, kitchen table swimming with spilt punch. Dusk. Street lights coming on, pinky-blue. Windows all open, *Two Tribes* on the turntable, the Annihil-ation mix. Time after time after time. And in the back bedroom Drew on his knees with a pillow up his front and hands clasped over his heart, singing.

As I was slowly passing an orphans' home one day,
I stopped for just a moment to watch the children play . . .

Hugh conducting with a corkscrew.

– Louder, you fat bastard. Louder!

Just the two of them, Hugh and Drew, like old times. (Hugh had moved south the summer before last and the day after tomorrow Drew and Melanie would make the first of their two moves north.)

I'm nobody's child, no-ho-body's child,

I'm like a flower, just growing wild,
No mammy's kisses, and no daddy's smile,
Nobody wants me, I'm no-bo-dy's child.

A couple of Melanie's work friends looked in at the door, laughing. At or with? At, probably, and at her too for putting up with it, but fuck them. Melanie herself crossed the room and stretched out on the bed. The mirror lay beside her, sprinkled with white crystals. Beneath them the ceiling was a fresh linen tablecloth (a little wrinkled at the sides where roller met brush), the light fitting a long-stemmed vase containing a single tight yellow bud. Melanie looked at the vase for a long, long time till the bud blossomed into a white blur. Drew had stopped singing but Hugh was still berating him.

– Look at the state of you, he said. Can you not do something about that gut?

The pillow was straining at Drew's shirt front. (The shirt was striped, white and blue, gone lavender at the yoke, a number on the inside collar in indelible lavender ink. Second-hand, prison issue.) A button popped.

Drew and bloody buttons.

– I am that I am.

He hung his head. Mister Melodrama.

Later, when everyone who was going home had gone home and everyone who wasn't had found a place to lie; when the mirror had been restored to the wall, and the light-bulb had reverted to a luminous fruit about to drop into darkness, Melanie positioned that same pillow beneath the small of her back and opened herself to him. He cried as she had never heard him cry before when he came and she sat forward, hugging him, kissing his eyes, kissing his nose, licking the tears from the ridge of his chin. *Oh my love, oh my pet.* The walls of her vagina tightened around him, devastating him even as she comforted him. He was twenty-one years old pumping inside her, dragging her into the undertow of his frantic rhythm, half that age – a quarter – no age at all – whimpering on her shoulder, and before her consciousness shrank to a tiny point of almost unbearable intensity she succeeded in imagining her lover as she had failed to imagine him earlier in the evening:

228

four years old, trailing a satchel along a landing to a bedroom where his sister, an English schoolmistress, aged ten, waits for him and orders him to sit down at once, in a voice that hovers between the childish and the adolescent, the real and the put-on, between here and there.

When she was very young, Drew said, pillow-gut bulging, and just come to Northern Ireland from England, his sister Ellen couldn't always remember from one day to the next where it was she lived exactly. The county, that is. And on the days when she could remember she was certain to have forgotten the name of the county to the left of it, or the county below it, or the county to the left of that, or the county to the left of that again, or the county, finally, above that. Once, when asked to recite the names at school, she could manage only three and got *two* black marks on the star-chart. Ellen Linden, who had been the first person in her class – boy or girl – to have the colours of the rainbow off by heart.

Red, orange, yellow, green, blue, indigo, violet: Richard of York Gives Battle In Vain.

Her daddy had taught her that. Her daddy, when he heard about her black marks, thought a long while then taught her something else using the initials of the elusive six counties, scoring them on her wooden ruler with a blue biro to help her memorise it.

By the time Drew was old enough to play school with her, his sister had a swish new plastic ruler. *He* got the old wooden one (it was lying on his desk – a coffee table with screw-on legs – when he entered her room), chewed now at one end, splintered at the other, grubby in between, but with the six letters still clearly visible through the grime, divided into two equal groups – *words*, among the first Drew had ever read, or, rather, felt, his fingertip following the deep, blue, regular grooves made by their father's hand, steady on the biro. Carved there like the name of his sister's favourite pop star, her idol, her crush: FAT LAD.

*

Another skateboarder rattled past the fountain, feet planted firmly apart, leaning back into unseen currents, city-surfing.

– Shall we go, then? Melanie said (big black coat, big black ha).

Hugh nodded, then bent forward for his bag. There was a tiny inlet of hair growing against the grain in the depression at the base of his skull.

– When all this is over ... (*This way*, Melanie said and steered him left) ... When all this is over the two of you will have to come down and stay some weekend.

Melanie pressed his arm.

– Yes.

When all this was over someone would force a gun against that inlet of hair at the base of Hugh's skull and pull the trigger. In the middle of the street – in the middle of *London* – in broad daylight. Witnesses would testify how they had thought at first the whole thing was being staged and how their instinctive reaction was to look round for the cameras, till one man glancing at something glistening on the sleeve of his camel-hair overcoat found there a piece of ... he didn't know what exactly but *scalp*, in fact (perhaps the very piece of scalp Melanie had noted that night in the park), and screamed his horror. Unperturbed, the gunman, or gun*men* – there was even some confusion as to whether there was one or two – fired twice more as the body pitched forward, then walked – sauntered – to a waiting car and drove off.

Drew could not sit still for two minutes together the night the news came through, but roamed from room to room, his hair a clash of dark hand-whipped waves, his eyes behind his glasses wild with anger.

Anger at the manner of his friend's death and anger at his friend for allowing it to happen.

– Why did he have to go and get *involved* again?

The very question Melanie asked *him* twelve months later when he told her he'd applied for a job in Belfast.

– It's not the same thing, Drew said.

– How's it different?

This was day one of forty-two consecutive days of squab-

230

bling. Drew's glasses were already off and being rubbed furiously.

– It just is.

Glasses jammed on again, as if to say: you can't possibly see this as clearly as I can.

– OK?

But there were ways and ways of getting involved and Melanie knew Drew's ways of old.

The sap.

A first seam of sweat trickled the length of her side, from underarm to hip-bone. The hot tap gushed. Steam rolled in waves across the ceiling and down the bathroom walls. Her reflection came and went in the mirror above the sink, each reappearance fainter than the last.

This evening's call had been a disappointment but no real surprise. She was even aware that to the outsider she might appear to be in some way to blame herself, an accessory before the fact. *I put it to you, Ms Bishop, that because in your heart you were convinced the relationship was doomed when Mr Linden left, you made no effort to save it; and because you made no effort to save it – indeed, quite the contrary, deployed all your not-inconsiderable energies against it – it is more definite now than ever that the relationship is, in fact, dead.*

Exhibit A: P.T. Thomas, handsome, thirty-some, thickdicked.

She had embarked upon the affair within days of Drew's departure, partly out of pique at his going and partly to prove to herself that his going, or staying, was all one to her. P.T. was a friend of a friend of a friend at work, a doting father and (in all other respects) loving husband. Which suited Melanie fine. Unlike Drew, she had always been able to keep her affairs at a manageable remove from the rest of her life (actors were strictly out); they might be mildly distracting or they might be intense, one-night stands or year-long passions, but they were always separate. Because Drew, when all was said and done, was always Drew.

Even after he left and she packed his belongings into cardboard boxes to go down into the cellar.

At the end of the first week she had unpacked them again and stashed the collapsed cardboard boxes under the bed.

If he came back, he came back, she thought, and for a time was content to leave it at that.

It was on the flight home from the States that she suddenly decided to go and see him in Belfast. After two months in New York nowhere was so exceptional it *couldn't* be visited. She phoned him from the airport and, riskily, for it was a Sunday, phoned P.T. from the house. P.T. came round as soon as he could get away, looked hurt for a few minutes when she told him they were finished, then, seeing that wasn't going to get him anywhere, accepted defeat and talked amiably for half an hour before leaving.

Melanie watched him go, fighting an urge to call him back and have him, grossly, there and then in the hallway, on the red-rough doormat, against the meter box with its puncture repair kit and piece of junk mail addressed to the occupants before last, *Open this envelope today and WIN £250,000!*

At the bottom of the path he turned and waved.

– You know where I am.

Melanie's lips stayed pressed tight.

The urge passed.

Drew was always Drew.

Until tonight. Tonight he had put himself at a double remove from her. This time there could be no way back.

The bath was three-quarters full when she got in. Water cascaded down the outside on to the floorboards. Water lifted her yellow hair and spread it in an aureole about her head. Water magnified her every movement, rocked her, lapped her, leaked into her and out of her and down the overflow. Water made her sweat. The walls sweated with her. The taps the tiles the toilet the mirror the window the woodwork the paintwork sweated with her. When the water cooled she pulled the plug and rinsed the scum from the sides of the bath then filled it again from the hot tap. She did this three times. When she got out the fourth time there was nothing more to rinse away. Her skin emerged new-pink and wrinkled from the tight wrap of her towel.

She opened the window and let the steam out, then unlocked the door and walked along the landing to the bedroom, knelt naked on the floor and dragged the cardboard boxes out from under the bed.

15

SATURDAY MORNING IT poured. The city was an all-over slate-grey relieved by brown. She picked him up at the Donegall Road roundabout, her mouth a perfect vermilion, her hair loosely covered with a pale green chiffon scarf, her eyes obscured by wing-framed tortoiseshell sunglasses. She was stationary in Belfast for all of fifteen seconds while he got into the car and fixed his seatbelt, then she was off again.

M1 in, Westlink through, M2 out.

They had not bothered to maintain the fiction that she was coming on business beyond Tuesday.

Belfast was *difficult*, she said. She'd prefer to go somewhere out of town. She *had* to be back in Wicklow by Saturday night . . .

There was a twin room booked in Drew's name in a guest-house in Portrush. Just in case. He had clean socks in his outside left pocket, clean pants in his outside right, a stick deodorant and a toothbrush in his one and only inside pocket.

M1 in, Westlink through, M2 out.

She had to dip her chin occasionally to peer at road signs over the top of her sunglasses. Her eyes were hazel running to pink. Tiredness? Tears? Drew wiped his wet specs with his cuff and stared out neutrally into the rain haze veiling the raw hump of the mountains. On the dashboard lay a map folded to show a thick blue vein emerging from a tangle of red vessels. The red vessels were the city centre and the blue vein was the motorway they were driving along. He watched their progress. To their right on the map was the lighter blue of the lough, separated from the motorway by an indeterminately shaded area signifying mudflats. But the map was out of date. This area too was now consolidated. Stolen from the sea, as Kay would have it. Bin lorries trundled over its flat landfill-scape, trailing garbage, tailed by hordes of quisling gulls.

Where the dark blue vein divided, they kept right, on to the M5 and from the M5 they took the A2, veering inland, north-west, at Whitehead, along the sheltered shoreline of Larne Lough and on to the Antrim coast proper at Larne itself. Still it poured. This was more like the summers Drew remembered. The sea was leaden, rained in, barely disturbed by the limp foam fringes of the waves. Puddles formed in the suddenly surfeited fields. He wound his window down an inch or two to let out the fug from her cigarettes, the smell of damp from his clothes, and the New Age Irish crap that had been burbling away in the cassette deck since they left Belfast, the vocals pulsing like sonar through a syrup of synthesised strings and pipes. She appeared to take no notice, of him or anything else but the road, gripping the wheel with both hands till her knuckles whitened, as though this pressure alone was what drove the car forward. She drove it through Carnlough, Cush-endall and over the Glens to Ballycastle, where she got out to stretch her legs. Her legs were clad in expensively ill-fitting jeans, pulled tight at the waist by a brass-buckled belt. Drew bought a poke of chips in Pavlovian response to the smell of salt air. He offered her share. She smiled a narrow smile which broadened when she took a fat yellow chip. The rain had eased a little. They got back in the car. Anna gripped the wheel again, though less grimly than before, and pressed onwards. On the far side of Portballintrae her left hand slid from the wheel on to his right hand, resting on his thigh. She held his hand after that off and on into Portrush. She held it for a moment without speaking when she switched off the engine on the outskirts of town at the porch of a modern pebbledash house with exten-sions of bare red brick jutting into the sandy soil at the back and sides; held it again in the doorway of a pink-papered room, with pink-candlewick-covered beds (separated by a locker with a pink-shaded lamp and pink porcelain ashtray), while the landlord demonstrated the Teasmade sat on a table beneath the bay window. But when the landlord left, she let go and lowered herself on to one of the pink bedspreads, her own two hands pressed flat between her knees.

Drew pulled open an echoing drawer and chucked in the socks and pants from his outside pockets. Anna discarded her headscarf but not her sunglasses. She watched him cross the room to the sink, place his toothbrush and deodorant on the blue-glass shelf below the mirror, unhook and pocket his specs, and scrub his face with the complimentary tablet of buttermilk soap.

– I can't go through with this, she said.

Drew paused patting his face dry and looked out through the net curtain. The sun was trying to break through. Intrepid family groups passed, walking in to the beach from outlying caravan sites.

– I don't suppose you fancy a game of pitch and putt? he said.

Pitch and putt.

She left a long pause.

– OK.

They pitched and they putted, turned in a cumulative score approaching 200, and called it a tie, nine holes all. They ate more chips, drank some Coke, and drove back along the coast road to the cliff-hanging ruins of a castle – Anglo-Norman, overlaid with Ulster-Scots – whose kitchens, they read, had once plunged into the sea; cooks and all.

Late in the day, when the sky had turned a deep velvety blue, cushioning the decline of a blood-orange sun, they stood on adjacent basalt columns, bladderwrack bobbing just out of reach of their toes, gazing across at the Donegal headland and the North Atlantic beyond, while, behind them, a party of Dutch youth hostellers, perched on a crest of prehistoric stone, sang along in stilted English to a Simon and Garfunkel song picked out on a battered acoustic guitar.

I am a rock, I am an island.

Corn-balls.

The tourist centre was shut up for the night when they drove into the Causeway carpark (deserted save for an Avis car and a right-hand-drive VW minibus) and began the descent of the cliff path. Halfway down, two weathered, white-haired Americans, with hiking boots and slack socks on the end of their bare sinewy legs, stopped and asked Drew if he'd take a snap of them against the backdrop of the Antrim coast. They were from Colorado themselves, they said – Rocky Mountain country. But, gee, this Giant's Causeway really was *something*, wasn't it?

From that distance, in fact, the Causeway looked like nothing. Standing now on the visible tip of it, Drew recalled his initial disappointment when he visited here as a child of six or seven, coming round the bend in the cliff path where this evening they had met the Americans, and seeing, a quarter of a mile or so below, the pillars of stone, staggering out higgledy-piggledy into the sea. What it was, he supposed, he had expected the Causeway itself to be gigantic.

The closer he had got to the bottom, however, the more his sense of wonder had increased. Cliffs crumbled into lichen-covered scree on his right, on his left, waves smashed themselves into a million flashing shards against the prow of volcanic rock.

Except of course when he was a child he didn't know it was volcanic. When he was a child, he knew only that Finn Mac-Cool had built the Causeway to walk across the water to Scotland.

When he was a child, he told Anna, he believed in giants who could overcome the sea with pillars of stone; this morning on the shore of Belfast Lough he had seen ordinary men choking it with garbage.

Creating a land in their own image.

Anna opened her mouth, hesitated, closed it, then opened it again and said, quietly but decisively,

– I watched them take my first shop out there on the back of a lorry and scatter its remains.

Drew said. . . . But there was no time for him to say anything once she had begun.

A long slow wave slewed towards him and slopped over the top of his column, squeezing between his feet and the rock.

*

The day after the shop was burnt she picked her way through the blackened interior in a hard hat and wellingtons accompanied by a fire chief and a surveyor. The roof, ceilings and back wall had fallen in and labourers were busy shoring up what remained of the front with roughly planed timbers. For what it was worth. The fire chief's ruddy face was crammed between a high serge collar and a low white hat.

– I'm afraid, he said, it'll have to come down.

– Oh, it's ruined, the surveyor said.

The surveyor's boots had a drawstring at the top. She had watched the mournful precision with which he had secured his trouser bottoms with bicycle clips before tying them on and thought how many times he must have had to walk through devastation like this. He was a man in his early forties, with a heavy gold bracelet and a parti-coloured beard, but trapped in his grave professional demeanour was the look of a boy who has stood by helpless as the tide overtook the sandcastle he spent all morning building. He was close to tears.

– Ruined, he said.

It could be no comfort to him, or to her, for that matter, that it had been a ruin anyway (otherwise she could never have afforded it, even with the compensation); that the plumbing was suspect and the wiring hair-raising, or that the little room at the back where she did her books had floor-to-ceiling fungus. To him it had been a fine example of Low Victorian domestic architecture, built entirely of local brick; to her, on her own, it had been a living, more than a living, a *life*. Either way, there was little to salvage. Plastic had melted, metal had buckled, thousands of pounds worth of cloth had gone up in smoke. Bricks broke underfoot, twice-fired.

Incendiary devices didn't come any cruder than that one: a petrol bomb through the window, trailing flame like a rip in the darkness. There had been dozens of similar attacks elsewhere in the city that night. On the homes of policemen and civil servants, chiefly. Lackeys of the Anglo-Irish diktat, sellers of the Ulster birthright. Turncoats.

And her? She had turned her coat a decade and a half before for a skinny Mod with lobster-red ears she fell in love with at the LP rack of Woolworth's record department. Conor, you called him – Con for short – and, as if that wasn't enough of a giveaway, he told her he came from *the top of the Grosvenor*

Road, i.e., he might as well have come right out and said it, Up The Falls. She was from across the river, the Woodstock Road (East meets West, the Belfast classic), fifteen, with a chunky rope of waist-length brown hair (if she tipped her head back) that the boys at school had used to give her torture over but only pulled now for an excuse to get touching it. Her stepmother said that hair would be the undoing of her, a notion she had apparently got (where she got most of her peculiar notions) from reading the Bible. Her stepmother had religion in those days, though not any that you'd recognise, a sort of free-floating anxiety would be more accurate, a cocktail of mainstream doctrines (mainstream *Protestant* doctrines, she wasn't *that* anxious) with a twist of old-fashioned superstition.

In her stepmother's world pride always came before a fall and a woman ought to have power on her head because of the angels.

And her father listened to all this without demurring. He had contracted religion too by this stage, though a less virulent strain. *Keep yourself out of trouble*, was his basic tenet. *Find the right person, settle down, have a family*. She was already going steady with a boy from round her way by the name of Nelson, *one of the Woodstock Road Nelsons*, no less. This one had only two years of his apprenticeship left to run and wanted them to get engaged on her sixteenth birthday, that 13 August coming, 1970.

It was April when she fell for Con. They played safe for a while, meeting in the no man's land of the Botanic Gardens after school. Just smoking, really, and talking: all sorts of nonsense. But she was mad about him. She started arriving home later and later, giving out any old excuse that came into her head. She packed in her apprentice Nelson. She wasn't ready for a whole big heavy romance, was what she told her parents, but the real reason soon got out. For 36 hours that July the Lower Falls was under curfew. For 36 hours she had no way of contacting Con. The news coming out was of deaths and injuries. After two nights without sleep she heard a name that wasn't his but sounded close enough to make her crack. She screamed the house down for him. Her stepmother shook her trying to quiet her. Her father shook her stepmother to stop her shaking his daughter too hard. Her half-sister, Kay, who was ten, just shook.

Afterwards, when they had all exhausted themselves, her stepmother levelled a finger at her.

– If ever I saw an ill-starred wee girl, she said, you're her.

In her stepmother's world no good could ever befall a child born, as she had been, on Friday the thirteenth.

It was a Friday the thirteenth the following year, August, her seventeenth birthday, when she was grabbed by a crowd of girls as she walked home late along the Woodstock Road after seeing Con. The girls tied her to a bus stop, egged on by their boyfriends and their boyfriends' friends (among whom she might have seen *one of the Woodstock Road* . . . but she never let on, one way or the other). They punched her and kicked her and spat on her. Called her a Taig-loving whore, chalked on the footpath at her feet: FREE RIDE.

Before untying her, they hacked off her hair and made a pile of it in front of her and set it alight.

(Do you know what that smells like? Not just a singed eyebrow, or a stray lock shrivelled by a match, but a whole head of waist-length hair? It fucking stinks.)

Getting the hair to burn properly was harder than they had imagined. They squirted it with lighter fuel, made wastepaper spills, scorched their fingers, cursed her more. But eventually they managed it. Of her thick rope of hair they made a brittle, burnt-sugar shell. One girl brought a stacked heel down and the shell broke scattering little black granules which rode the wind haphazardly across east Belfast.

Her stepmother sat with her all that night, never before so tender.

Next day she dyed her remaining clumps of hair burgundy and covered her bruises with pancake make-up. Her stepmother, tender no longer, threatened to throw her out of the house. She denied her the pleasure by leaving two nights later while everyone else was asleep in bed.

Con left home that same night. A short time before, a man he didn't know from Adam stopped him in the street close to his house and pressed something cold into his hand. A live bullet. It wasn't meant as a souvenir.

These were the days after internment, the city was streamlining its divisions, ironing out the bumps. Or whatever else it took to get rid of them.

They looked for a place in amongst the other bumps and oddments in the streets around the university and found a flat in a forbidding-looking Victorian terrace, from which, if they stood on the bathroom sink, they could see down into the Botanic Gardens where they had used to meet.

Ulster 71, come and join in the fun.

They were seventeen. There was a low-intensity urban war in progress and a pair of mice in the bread bin. They shared a single bed for a week before they went all the way together for the first time. Con ran round the flat afterwards with a blanket draped over his shoulders, puffing his chest out, shouting *Su-u-perman*. Hip-bones you could have hung a hat on. Scaldy glans peeping out from the fuzz of his crotch.

In March Stormont was suspended.

In April two fellas Con knew from the top of the Grosvenor Road were found dead on waste ground near the peaceline. Catholics in the wrong place at the wrong time. Picked up and shot.

In July an old schoolfriend of hers was on a bus out of Belfast when she remembered something she'd forgotten to do in town; got off (that was the type of her, it couldn't have waited till tomorrow), walked back into the city centre, straight into an IRA car bomb. She lost both her legs, her right eye, and three fingers of her left hand.

In September they threw up their jobs and went to Dublin. Stayed there half a year, looked at each other one day. Shrugged. Came north again.

And all the time her hair was growing. Slowly at first, then in great flamboyant spurts, like silk scarves flourished from a magician's hat. She swept them up, caught them with lacquer, complemented them with dramatic mixtures of make-up.

Con adored her.

She was working now in a very *Glam* city centre boutique. Her clothes were the kind that turned heads in the street. Two turned one afternoon when he and she stepped out together on to a pelican crossing in front of the City Hall. Her father's and her sister's. Another – her stepmother's – kept staring resolutely forward, leaving a single word smouldering in its wake. *Brazen.* She herself had stopped, stock-still, looking after them. Con pulled her on to the pavement as the green man flickered out. Cars, trucks, buses, taxis poured into the hole they had left.

– Forget them, Con was saying. Who needs them?

And she did forget them, then and there. Turned, shook her head, and out they went.

He said let's have a baby.
  So they tried
  And tried
  And tried
  And nothing.
  She went to the doctor
  Who sent her to the hospital
  Where they looked her over
  And ran some tests
  Then sent her home, to await results.
  – Are you sure, she asked him, balling the letter,
  You wouldn't settle for a cat?

They bought a house in the north of the city, in a corridor running between one side and the other. Their peculiar niche. *A quiet couple, never bothered much.* They liked to stay in at night. Reading, watching TV, listening to music. Their not so peculiar pleasures. She saved up and bought him a camera their second Christmas in the house. A Nikon, fully automatic. He photographed her waking, sleeping, towelling her hair, lighting two cigarettes with one match, trumpets of smoke bellowing from her nostrils. He photographed them both together using the timer and photographed himself, dozens of times, in the mirror. (Which was asking for it, she thought, much, much later.)

He photographed a toddler wearing a black armband, lost and crying in the crowd at Bobby Sands's funeral.

An Australian journalist offered him £50 for the film. *Done,* said Con, and sauntered into the house, fanning his face with the five tenners. She gave him dog's abuse.

What was he playing at selling photographs to that circus?

What was he *doing* at the funeral anyway.

– Coincidence, he said.

Conor Bradley and Bobby Sands were born in the same hospital on the same day in 1954. March ninth.

– Coincidence your behind, she said.

In the heat of the argument money and camera both ended up on the kitchen floor. Each blamed the other, each refused the other's blame. The notes and the camera lay where they fell, all the next day and the day after that. When she returned from work on the third day though, the kitchen floor was cleared. He was sitting at the table, working at the camera.

– I'll need to leave this in to be fixed, he said, without rancour.

Of course she caved in at once.

– Use that £50.

– I can't, he said. It's gone.

– Gone where?

His ears blushed.

– They came round at work collecting for Barnardo's.

She regretted her anger afterwards. It had been a dreadful couple of weeks waiting for the first hunger striker to die. Eighteen days he had hung on after being given the last rites. There were evacuations, predictions of full-scale civil war, just as there had been ten years before when she and Con left home together. But, though there was mayhem for a day or two, as before, the worst was averted. Even when a second hunger striker died, then a third, then a fourth. Nothing stays unusual for too long, not even voluntary starvation. Hunger strikers five and six followed numbers one to four. It was just another way to die now, proof that the 2,000 deaths to date hadn't exhausted the possibilities. The world kept turning. Charles married Di. The day was marked by street parties in some parts of Belfast, apathy in others. That weekend two more hunger strikers died in quick succession.

It was a Sunday, after half-eleven. We'd only two cigarettes left. I said that would do us till the morning, but he hated the thought of running out. He wouldn't be five minutes. He was

*just after a bath, his hair was still damp. I didn't say you'll
catch your death, or anything like that. I had no premonition.
He just took the keys and left. Kissed my ear, I think. I was
reading a library book at the time, I didn't look up.*

It wasn't much of a riot. A few bottles and stones, the odd,
misdirected petrol bomb. A mark of respect for the last to die,
was all (thinking, perhaps, we turned out for all the others, it
wouldn't be right there being no one out for him). Routine for
the army too. Send a Saracen hurtling up and down the street
now and again to let them know you're there. No real hope of
catching anyone. Spot a couple for later, maybe, haul them out
of bed.

It was a flukey shot that knocked the Saracen out, oddly
transgressive: direct hit, eye-level, driver's side. Not much
danger even then, of course, with all that armour, but in the
instant of the bottle shattering, *flambé*-ing the vehicle from nose
to tail, the soldier lifted his hands from the wheel, then grabbed
again and pulled and pulled to keep from running into a row
of houses.

Like turning a rampaging elephant by the ears, one newspaper said.

Pulled and pulled till the Saracen was clear of the footpath.
All save the lagging back wheel, clipping the lamppost . . .

Drew saw the collision in slow motion, saw the concrete standard snap as easily as a lollipop stick. Saw the wheel come
away from its axle, just as he had imagined it then, and lope
lazily down the years towards him. Saw it as if trapped inside
somebody else's nightmare. *Clunk, click* . . . he closed his eyes
before the *crunch!* and when he opened them again he was at
the counter of Finney's bar, gawping up at the television.

Flashing lights, yellow and blue, falling on a crushed car and
a monstrous wheel.

He ordered a double. Pernod and black. Gulped it down,
ordered another as the crippled Saracen was towed away. A
reporter's head and shoulders shifted on screen. The mouth
moved.

Tragic.

Freak.

Accident.

Drew drank his drink, ordered another, drank that. Felt himself become abstracted.

The picture cut to an unmarked police car drawing up before an unremarkable house, then an astonishing woman was led from the door of one to the door of the other. It was her almost supernatural stillness amid such ordinariness that so unnerved him, every last strand of preposterously teased hair held in check. As though she was afraid that by relaxing her vigilance even for a second she would give herself the slip and fly apart in all directions. She fixed the camera with a painfully intense, quizzical look and for one appalling moment before she released it, Drew, drunk and desperate for detachment, had the impression that she was staring through a window into the Titanic, straight at him . . .

She was staring straight at him.

The Dutch youth hostellers were long gone. Behind him there was only an assault course of rocks and a quarter-mile cliff path leading to a car he couldn't drive, parked miles from anywhere worth driving to. Before him, the sun had dissolved into the horizon, obliterating Donegal, spilling an orange slick back across the water to them.

He averted his eyes from hers.

– I must have been over it a million times, she was saying. What if . . . ? What if . . . ? What if he had been held up somewhere by traffic lights? Or hadn't been? What if he had been going five miles an hour faster? Or slower? What if he'd arrived at that spot even a moment sooner, or a moment later? *Just one moment*. The gap between life and death, between Con and that awful bloody mess they showed me in the mortuary.

– What if, the judge said, I was to suggest to you that it was no coincidence that Mr Bradley was in the vicinity at the time of his death?

– I would deny it.

Her claim for compensation was contested on the grounds, brought to light at the inquest, that a camera had been found in the wreckage of the car. What was Conor Bradley *really* doing out at that time, in a dangerous part of a dangerous city in the most dangerous summer for almost a decade?

A magazine was produced in court with the photograph he had sold to the Australian journalist.

That was a one-off, she said, the journalist asked him for the film; and, anyway, the camera had been broken shortly afterwards. It had been lying in the car for weeks for him to leave it in to be fixed.

– He has a head like a sieve, she told the judge, then corrected herself. *Had*, I mean.

Reports of these messy proceedings did not go unremarked in certain quarters, where an action of that nature against the Northern Ireland Office (especially a successful one) was interpreted as an attack on the validity of the state itself. Not long after she opened the shop, the first of the letters arrived on her doormat. Unsigned, Valentine-coy.

Judas, it said: *What about the Fenian scum that threw the petrol bomb. Did you ever think of suing him?*

He was fourteen. The police asked him why he did it.

'Cause the Brits let your man die.

Your man let himself die.

For the five demands. He was a hero.

He was a pig. He lived in shite.

The Brits made him.

Nobody made him do anything.

They tried to make him wear a uniform.

He was a criminal.

So the Brits say.

He was caught going to plant a bomb.

To get the Brits out.

*The **Brits** are only here because people like your man plant bombs.*

Your man joined the Fianna at fifteen, the IRA at sixteen, was interned in Long Kesh at seventeen, released at twenty, arrested again, still aged twenty, nine months later, held for seventeen months, tried and sentenced, aged twenty-two and redefined a criminal, to twenty-two years in the renamed Maze; rejected the legitimacy of all three terms, went on the blanket, joined the No Wash and Dirty protests, put himself forward for hunger strike, was elected TD for Cavan and Monaghan on the twenty-first day of his fast, and died on the seventy-third, one day short of the Irish record, two months short of his own twenty-sixth birthday.

Towards the end his mother showed him a picture of the republican plot where he would be buried. *Beautiful*, is what he is said to have said.

Her father had come to the house the night before Con's funeral.

— You're ten years too late, she said and shut the door in his face.

(Kay was out of the country at the time. She had been back a fortnight before anyone thought to tell her about Con and by then, she said, she was afraid her visiting might do more harm than good.)

For weeks she saw no one. Alone, she tortured herself with the thought that she had been the involuntary instrument of their misfortune. There were three Friday-the-thirteenths that year, the first time that had happened in all the years she and Con had been together. There was only one the year she was born. Only one and she'd got it. Her rotten luck. *Con's* rotten luck, to be stuck with a scud like her in a year like that.

But then she would remember the sheer numbers of people who had combined in his death and wonder whether chance alone could be credited with such intricately choreographed calamity.

She dug deeper.

She clawed his mirror-portraits to pieces, frustrated by the impenetrable surface of things. She wanted to get to the heart of the matter, to be able to point and say, *there, that's where it all started to go wrong*.

When we moved over to this side of town.

When we came back from Dublin.

The day and hour we met.

Before we met.

Before we were even born.

Before our parents were born.

Before our parents' parents were born.

Before our parents' parents' parents were born.

But it was like trying to hold a pattern in a kaleidoscope, one tiny chip slipped and the whole configuration changed. There was always at least one more factor to be taken into account and the heart of the matter, she came to see, was that there was no heart of the matter; or else (which amounted to the same thing) many millions of hearts.

*

Imagine being dangled over the deepest darkest spot in the ocean. Imagine the soles of your feet skimming the surface of the water. Imagine your terror.

Imagine Drew's, realising who Anna was.

And then just when it had seemed the abyss of past blame and self-hate would open and swallow him completely, she had thrown him a lifeline, a tangled rope of mutuality. A multitude of hands reached down to help pull him clear.

Waves slapped against the stones to the right and the left of him, his shoes were wet through, but beneath his feet was solid rock.

– I'm sorry, he said knowing it had nothing to do with him.

Nothing and everything.

With half a moon to guide them, they helped each other over the ridge of stones and on to the path again. The path the old couple from Colorado had walked up and the Dutch youth hostellers had walked up. The path thousands of visitors walked up, year in, year out. The path up which, aeons and aeons before, a two-headed giant had laboured, the lower head spinning yarns to the upper. Jack Linden, colossal in tan Moses sandals with his son, Drew, hoisted high on his shoulders.

Every step then earth-shaping.

Every step now a small reclamation.

They drove, at no great speed, down hedge-bound A roads, along a main street spanned by an Orange arch and laced with bunting, then followed the coastline, back past the cliff-hanging castle, to the guest-house on the outskirts of Portrush, where in the early hours of the morning, in mutually observed silence and in the sure and certain knowledge that the moment would never be repeated, they very slowly, very deliberately, and, as though recognising what was involved, very carefully, made love to one another.

What was involved was a supporting cast of family, lovers, friends disposed collusively about this island and the next and the continent beyond; a conspiracy of events both local and global. What was involved was generations of groundwork, courtships enacted, marriages contracted, births, deaths, and all that fell in between, small happinesses and big fears, modest achievements and heroic failures, titanic struggles, stacked odds, seismic change, adaptability, elation, boredom, certainty, doubt, resignation, restlessness . . .

Vast movements of peoples were communicated in the silence of a single kiss. Borders were crossed, identities blurred. Land masses rose and fell with their bodies.

Not surprisingly, their lovemaking was long and intricate and when it was over they felt the moment ebb away into the future.

*

After yesterday's deluge Belfast seemed redeemed by colour, unfolding like a flower as they entered it from the north.

Like a flower? A load of brick and glass and tarmacadam and coloured metal and concrete, slabs of water and oceans of mud, flecked with greenery (and here and there whitery and goldery and, it being the first of July, prodigious amounts of red-white-and-bluery)?

Like a flower. Compact and complex.

She dropped him at the bottom of his driveway, leaning across to kiss his cheek as he got out of the car, then drove off, her hair loosely covered with a pale green chiffon scarf, her eyes obscured by wing-framed tortoiseshell sunglasses, her lipstick smudged a little where she'd kissed him.

There were five calls on his answering machine. He put the kettle on for coffee and pressed the playback. The mechanism made three clattering false starts then beeped.

– Drew, mate, it's James, it's Saturday – day off, yeah? – it's, let's see, nine-thirty. What would you say to a trip over here next week? Heh? Call me as soon as you can. All right? Cheers, mate.

The machine beeped a second time.

– Drew? James again. Saturday afternoon. I'll be here till late. Be sure and call.

Beeped a third.

– Drew. James. Ten o'clock. I take it you didn't get the other two calls. It doesn't matter what time you get in: phone me.

The fourth beep broke the sequence.

– Drew? Are you, ah . . . God, I hate these things – are you out? (Laugh) Obviously. Well, ah, maybe, ah . . . maybe you could ring me. It's, ah, it's about Daddy actually, oh, Drew, I have to tell you, they're letting him out tomorrow. Isn't that great . . . ? But ring me, OK? Well, bye. Oh, it's me, by the way, your sister, Ellen.

Drew often thought afterwards of the way she said that. *Your sister, Ellen.*

The fifth beep brought James back.

– Where *are* you? Things have been *happening* here. Haven't you seen the papers yet today? It's Sunday morning, just gone eleven. If I don't hear from you by one I'm going to go ahead and book you on the first flight to London tomorrow. Karen, Phoebe and I are taking you away from there for good.

The Sunday paper lay on the settee, folded in four, ignored. Drew unfurled it now and thumbed through the sections till he found what James was referring to.

He laid the paper down again. A helicopter buzzed backwards and forwards across the sky like an angry insect. Drew sat for a long time watching it, letting his coffee go cold.

The Bookstore chain, one of the retailing success stories of the 1980s, yesterday announced that it was to merge with Swiss sports and leisure giant, Glass-Muller. The announcement, which came after intense negotiations in London and Geneva, puts an end to weeks of speculation in the book trade. Both parties last night declared themselves well satisfied with the deal. William Rodgers, Glass-Muller's UK representative, said the company regarded the move into books as 'a natural progression'.

'There is more to the leisure industry,' he said, 'than inflatable bananas and karaoke.'

Said Karen Urquhart, one of the 'Bookstore Three', who launched the chain at the end of the 1970s, 'This is a historic day, one which guarantees Bookstore's future into the twenty-first century. My co-founders and I are still very much in control, the merger has simply provided us with capital for growth. Looking ahead to 1992, we must expand our base if we are to be competitive in the Single Market economy.'

Plans are believed to be already well advanced for English-language bookshops in mainland Europe, with Paris, Brussels, Milan and Madrid being spoken of as the most likely locations. But, while acknowledging that economic harmonisation would require all businesses to look closely at their margins, Ms Urquhart denied rumours that the Glass-Muller deal would lead to redundancies among Bookstore's 400-strong UK workforce.

'Quite the opposite,' she said. 'With such a major institution now behind us the move will undoubtedly secure existing jobs nationwide.'

Bookstore, she said, would maintain its position in the vanguard of the retail trade. 'We were among the first to detect the British consumer's dissatisfaction with bland uniformity in the High Street, the interchangeability of city centres. Shopping in the 1990s must be a unique experience every time or it is nothing and we intend to export that philosophy to the rest of Europe.'

16

THE HELICOPTER BUZZED backwards and forwards across the sky a while longer then settled down to a steady drone above a street of solid semis arranged in matching rows of six pairs, with a thirteenth, unmatched pair standing apart in a slight recess at the top of the road. From the rear of the right half of this last twosome there rose a twist of whitish smoke. Figures darted in towards its source and away again, others rolled on the ground, then leapt up flapping their arms. One – the figure of a woman – raised her hands to the sky in entreaty.

– Just you stay there now, helicopter, and blow those clouds away till we're done.

A man in shorts flourished an object which glinted viciously in the early evening sun.

– Funny mummy.

– Funny mummy, funny mummy, funny mummy, Laurence and Nathaniel squawked, parroting their father, and continued careering round the garden, making gun noises, dying extravagantly, counting to ten, getting up and running again.

Derek warned them a third time about straying too close to the fire.

– Don't come crying to me if you get yourselves burnt.

He showed them a charcoal-striped circle of meat then flipped it, pink side down, on to the grill. It sizzled ominously, spinning more smoke skywards. Tina trotted from the back door with a stack of raw meat patties separated by sheets of greaseproof paper.

– Auntie Peggy says that's the last of the mince.

Derek counted the hamburgers already cooking and those on the shelf beneath the barbecue waiting to go on.

– I suppose that'll have to do, he said, though you know your grandpa and hamburgers ... (six months ago Tina's grandpa wouldn't have let a hamburger near his mouth. The week before last he'd scoffed two then slipped his son-in-law a note asking were there any more.) He's liable to eat half a dozen. Aren't you, Jack?

But Jack was facing the wrong way and did not reply. There were still times when he seemed not to be aware of anything that went on on his right side. Ellen approached from the left and hunkered down in front of his chair.

– Do you hear what he's saying about you, Daddy?

Derek, having secured his attention, tried again.

– You could too, couldn't you, Jack – eat half a dozen.

– Yes, he said, haltingly, but with a smile, a slanting half-smile like Ellen's own.

He was just returning from another walk, with Derek this time, when Ellen came home from work. He looked worn out. Ellen made him sit down and rest on one of Derek's garden chairs. The chair and the table beside it were black with gold rosettes. The table had, in addition, an emerald green lattice-work top on which her father's stick currently lay, crossways, between an empty glass and a loose-leaf pad (*the edict book*, Derek called it). Ellen lifted the glass.

– Would you like a drop more in this?

– Yes, he said and his left hand went out to retrieve the straw from it.

It was a lavender see-through straw, eighteen inches long and coiled in the middle. The boys would stop whatever they were doing the instant their grandfather started drinking through it, and watch him watch the rising liquid, waiting for him to roll his eyes as it looped the loop on its way to his mouth. Sometimes, at the very last moment, he would whip the straw from between his lips and stopper the top with his thumb. The drink would be caught then in confused suspension until he removed his thumb again and let it slither back down the straw and piddle into the glass. The boys enjoyed this last part especially. Their grandfather was able to regulate the flow of the stream depending on how far and how fast he moved his thumb. Even Ellen had to admit it sounded authentic and though she was still a little taken aback by such ribaldry from her father (though a

253

little was all by now) she was nevertheless encouraged by this agility after only a day and a bit's practice.

Tina had bought him the straw for his birthday, which, strictly speaking, was yesterday, though they were having the party a day late since Derek had rashly promised the boys one last barbecue before they went back to school on Monday and it had rained all yesterday evening, as it had most of that week. Today, though, had started fine and continued finer, save for that one shower, the briefest of skiffs (the drops drying almost as soon as they touched the ground), when Derek was getting the barbecue going. Ellen was still nominally on cloud watch – a Derek-device to get her to take things easy too – but now that the sun had shown its face again behind the hovering helicopter, her mind was beginning to empty pleasantly. Tina popped up at her elbow and took the glass from her.

– Here, let me.

Tina had been a different wee girl since her grandfather had taken ill: resourceful, diligent, supportive. She was eleven now and changing in other ways too, gaining height and losing weight, so that a face recognisably her own could be seen emerging from the contested blur of last year's puppy fat. It was a determined face, a going-places face, not unattractive.

Actually, if she did still favour anyone in the family it was her Uncle Drew.

It was a shame that Drew couldn't have stayed till the end of the week, but Ellen understood how pressed for time he was just now. At least his card had come. That had pleased her father. She knew by the care with which he made room for it on the TV beside Derek's and hers who it was from.

– Drew? she said.

She was stopped at the mirror on her way out to work, blotting her lipstick on a folded Kleenex.

– Yes, he said, slant-smiling.

– *Yes!*

– Mum.

The barbecue sizzled. The helicopter hummed overhead.

– Mum, Grandpa, wants something, Tina said. What is it Grandpa? Can I get you it?

– Yes.

He took the refilled glass from his granddaughter with his left hand and tried to point out the problem with his right. But it was getting late and his arm was stiff and useless. Ellen thought he might have been pointing to his head.

– Have you a sore head? she asked him.

– Yes, he said and shook it.

– His hat! Tina said. He's looking for his hat.

Derek, at the barbecue, angled his back, scouring the grass.

– Your hat, Jack? I saw it earlier.

– It's in here, Aunt Peggy called from the kitchen and Tina ran inside to fetch it.

The hat was a buttercup yellow beanie and don't ask Ellen where it came from. Her father was wearing it the day she and Derek arrived to bring him home from the hospital: brim turned up right the way round, like a coronet. It was so . . . so *unlike* him, and he was so reluctant to remove it (he barely had it off his head the first week he was home), that she concluded one of the other patients must have given it to him. Someone he'd been specially fond of. Someone who'd since died, maybe.

Or maybe he was wearing it for a joke.

They were unsure how to take him then, unsure too what they could and couldn't say without giving offence, so they ended up saying nothing whatever about his singular headgear at the time and now, all these weeks later, it was just *Grandpa's hat*.

The boys, not surprisingly, loved the buttercup beanie as much as they loved the piddling straw, which is to say, as much as they loved the newly acquired conspiratorial droop of their grandfather's right eyelid; as much as they loved his wheelchair (which he needed less and less now and consequently let them play on more and more), as much as they loved the mute dignity with which, this evening, he bowed his head to receive the daisy-chains they had made for him.

To see them playing around him, to see his gentleness with them, it was not always easy to remember that there had been a time when this same man had repeatedly beaten a boy not much older than they were now.

The realisation of what her father was doing to Drew had been a gradual process for Ellen; a sense of rather too much order on coming into rooms they had been closeted in together, a depth of silence between them that all the desperate distractions of background noise only made more apparent. She was aware, however, that for a long time then she had resisted drawing the ever more obvious conclusion from these and other clues and that ultimately the acceptance that her father was capable of violence against one of his children only came when he was violent towards the other one too, that is, Ellen herself, though she was no child by that stage, but turned seventeen, in work, in and out of love.

Her father was past fifty and beside himself with rage.

– *Murderer!* Do you know how much that meant?

Ellen had just killed her Granny Linden's goldfish. She had lifted its bowl down from the unit in the dining room, taking extra care not to let the water slop over the sides and on to her hands (because for *water* read that soup of faeces, food and its own dead, dandruffy scales that the goldfish made of ordinary H_2O within minutes of coming in contact with it); lifted the bowl down from the unit and carried it through the living room, up the stairs, and into the bathroom, where she emptied the goldfish into a bathful of water, covered its gills, and broke its back.

She'd been ranting on about having the smelly animal in the house that lunchtime at work, when Fascinating Freda Thompson came out with one of her infamous did-you-knows.

– Did you know that goldfish only have a three-second memory? That's how they can live in such wee bowls without cracking up.

The rest of the girls pelted her with crisp bags and yoghurt tubs and howled her down for a liar. But the idea was perfectly plausible to Ellen. Indeed, looking more closely at her granny's goldfish later at home, watching the way it picked up speed from time to time, becoming, on occasion, almost frantic, she was convinced that it had no memory of the tail in front of it being its own. She even began to think that it might be chasing itself for a screw, forgetting, of course, every three seconds, that it had never managed to catch itself yet.

Suddenly, and quite unexpectedly, she felt enormous compassion for the stupid thing.

That was when she decided to give the goldfish a proper swim.

It was April, the start of the light nights. Everyone else was out. She went upstairs and ran a tepid bath then came back down into the dining room. The goldfish was going mental, whizzing round and round the bowl in a snowstorm of its own skin, as if it knew exactly what she was up to.

– Poor fella, Ellen said, in the sad, soothing voice she remembered hearing her granny use. Poor, poor fella.

Upstairs again, she set its bowl by the taps and trailed a finger the length of the bath.

– Look at that! Look at all that lovely water!

By now, the water in the bowl was just a stirred blur, streaked with faded orange. The goldfish was practically shaking itself to pieces in its excitement. Ellen sat on the toilet waiting for it to settle.

Mr Russell was hammering away at something next door, as ever. A new bathroom, an attic conversion, dormer windows, patio doors; a patio. Children were skipping out in the street. Ellen listened to their reedy voices rising and falling in time to the turn of the rope. Slap, slap, slap, went the rope on the road. The goldfish resumed its monotonous circling. Head, middle, tail. Head, middle, tail. Slap, slap, slap, went the rope. Head, middle, tail, went the goldfish. Head, middle, tail. Head, middle, tail.

The bath would seem an Atlantic to it after that. Even with a three-second memory it would surely notice the difference. For the first time in its life, maybe, it would feel like a *real* fish in *real* water. Ellen knelt on the floor – The mighty salmon! – dunked her elbow in the water to check the temperature – The dashing pike! – then, lifting the bowl in both hands, she emptied it into the bath.

A cloud of debris spread beneath the water's green-clear surface. She watched the edge for the flash of her granny's grateful goldfish.

And watched.

And, as the murk dispersed, she finally saw it. In the middle of the bath, describing a perfect circle, the exact circumference of its bowl.

Ellen screamed.

– That's disgusting!

She slapped the water with the flat of her hand.

– Swim straight, can't you. Look, like this.

And without another thought she had plunged her hands – wrists – forearms – elbows – into the water, floundering in the goldfish's curved wake. It couldn't elude her for long, though. She realised that she need only keep her hands poised in one place and the goldfish was bound to come round, time and again. It passed and repassed through the tunnel of her fingers. Downstairs the back door opened and closed. Ellen ignored it. The goldfish came and went through her hands, its fins fluttering against the inner rim of the Os she had made of her forefingers and thumbs. Then she narrowed the openings a centimetre more and she had it. Cold and gnarled.

– Swim straight, fishy, she said. See? Like this.

But the goldfish was more stubborn than she had anticipated. She bit her lip.

– Like. This.

There was a sound close by and when she glanced up Drew was standing in the doorway.

Perhaps, on reflection, that was the moment, before her father had even laid a finger on her, when she knew for certain what had been going on. Her brother looked swollen, not in any one particular place, but all over. Pudgy, you might almost say, though *pudgy*, maybe, had a too-comfortable ring for what confronted her. *Forced* was the word she was searching for, like veal.

Under the water her hands continued to oppose the goldfish's unnatural bent until at last it yielded.

– Get out, Drew, she said.

He backed away to the haven of his bedroom. Ellen heard her father's voice in the dining room. Three wet clacks and a querulous cluck.

– Who moved the goldfish. Drew? Ellen? What have you done with your granny's goldfish?

She looked into the water.

Let it out.

Weeks later, when Derek Hastings first undressed her, there were still bruises on her back.

Derek asked her who'd given her them. She said it was none of his business. He guessed her father and said he'd kill him. She said he'd do no such thing. He said he'd go to the police, or, better yet, the Other Lot.

— You dare, Derek Hastings. You dare and I'll never speak to you again.

Just because you bucked a girl once (even if you bucked her well, like Derek had her), it didn't mean you owned her. Besides, she didn't need Derek Hastings, or anybody else, to fight her battles. She had the measure of her father. Her father was a weak and frightened man. She had read the weakness and fear in his eyes when he was hitting her. His eyes were appalled by what his hands were doing. *How have you come to this?* they were asking. (That the prisons of Northern Ireland were full of weak and frightened men then was no excuse. No coincidence perhaps, but no excuse either.) Ellen pitied him. She knew that's what he read in *her* eyes. It must be a terrible thing to be pitied by your children. Ellen's father simply folded in the face of it. She left him sitting on the boxroom floor, sobbing, broken almost.

The Other Lot got him later in the month anyway during the Ulster Workers' strike. Ellen accused Derek of pointing the finger. Derek denied it. What he'd said before was only bluster. Ellen believed him (there were a lot of blustery men then too — the younger, generally, the blusterier). She believed him, but she stopped speaking to him all the same.

He's dead cute, she told her friend Rosemary in England, *but dead clingy.*

Cute was one of Rosemary's fave words. *Fave* was another. She had broken a decade's silence the year before by sending Ellen a birthday card addressed to her Granny Linden's house. The message inside was in lime-green felt tip and heavily punctuated: *Surprise?!?!?!?!*

Ellen sent Rosemary a letter thanking her for her card and

Rosemary sent Ellen a letter thanking her for hers and before long letters were criss-crossing the Irish Sea every three or four days.

They talked of getting a place together in London. Rosemary – Rosie, she signed herself now, with a five-pointed star on top of the *i* instead of a dot – *Rosie* knew people there already, in a rambling house out in Twickenham where there were always lots of rooms going spare and always lots of *parties!?!?!?!?*

Some months ago, Ellen had read in the paper that a Rosemary Jackson (32) of such-and-such-a-street in Deptford, was it?, had been jailed for five years for smuggling cannabis. A small picture accompanied the story, but the woman was shielding her face with her hand and Ellen couldn't be sure it was the same Rosemary Jackson she had known.

– *Ham-burgers!* Lovely hamburgers! Get them while they're hot!

Derek clanged the fish-slice against the barbecue's metal surround. Laurence and Nathaniel processed from the house, carrying bowls of potato salad and coleslaw and crinkle-cut crisps; their sister followed with their Aunt Peggy (barely recognisable without her raincoat), carrying plates of tomato and onion and Kraft cheese slices. The procession halted before another of Derek's tables, to the right of the barbecue, and the plates and bowls were laid out on its protective sheet. This particular table was part of an order for one of the luxury houses which were being built beyond the Georgian bungalows to the south of Ellen and Derek. (If it didn't say luxury in front of it, Derek said, people didn't think it spelt house any more.) Derek was selling his tables, chairs and flower-stands as fast as he could make them. He'd never known a summer like it for work. Or any other season, come to that. Not that he was complaining. He'd had new cards made:

HASTINGS for Railings,
Gates, And
FINE GARDEN FURNITURE

While the rest of the western world slipped deeper into recession, Derek's thoughts were of expansion.

The most important thing, he said, was for him to find a proper workshop, as far away from the house as possible.

The *most* important thing, Ellen said, was for him not to overstretch himself. But she knew he was impatient. He had become increasingly troubled lately by the damage his work was doing to their surroundings. He would come home from clients' houses full of the wonderful things he'd seen done with even the most modest gardens, then stand frowning out the kitchen window at the bald evidence of his own failed husbandry.

– Well, what's to stop us doing something with ours? Ellen finally said to him.

– *That?* he said, poking his finger through the slats of the venetian blind.

– Yes, she said. (It was a bloody tip.) *That.*

And there and then they had set about clearing one end of the garden of scrap metal and other junk: just the two of them, working till after dark, preparing the ground for planting.

Her father had taken an interest from the outset. He turned out to have something of an eye for landscaping and spent hours poring over catalogues and hours more making out lists of bulbs and shrubs for Ellen and Derek to buy. He had taught himself to write again, slow and left-handed, his earliest attempts just sprawling sequences of letters whose aggregate intent was often open to conjecture (and here again the boys, Nathaniel in particular, felt a new affinity with their grandfather). But he had worked at it and worked at it, with a strength of will that Ellen, for one, had never imagined him capable of – revealing, literally, a whole new side of him – until he had succeeded in bringing this unaccustomed hand under control and making himself understood.

A week ago he had returned from his Chest, Heart & Stroke club with an early anniversary card for his daughter and son-in-law. Inside was a left-hand-written promissory note for £10,000; which they refused; which really *did* upset him; which changed their minds, finally.

For the first time since they were married, Ellen and Derek had no immediate money problems.

Yesterday evening they had sat in the dining room together long after everyone else was asleep, drinking coffee, talking about what they could use the windfall for.

The workshop. The mortgage. The children. The future.

– A continental holiday, Derek said. Here's the plan: we dump the kids, jump on the first plane out of here and let it take us where it takes us. It'll be weeks before anyone finds us. Imagine, weeks just lying beside a swimming pool.

He clicked his fingers – *Waiter!* – then clasped his hands behind his head and a blissful expression spread across his face. (His forehead was spotted with red oxide paint, fading into freckles beneath his hairline. A little patch of grey had recently appeared by his left ear, in solidarity, he told Ellen, with her own.)

– Maybe next year, Ellen said.

Sylvia Rogers had sold her Canada, in part, with fantasies of swimming pools. Ellen had pictured them sunken and tiled, replete with springboards and king-size lilos – *lifeguards*, for God's sake, the way Sylvia went on – kidney shaped, guitar shaped. Anything but the great, sagging bags of water suspended from tent poles that she found when she finally got out there.

She was working in the Post Office at the time. Sylvia, who worked alongside her, had an aunt outside Toronto and the offer of a job in a factory making towels: a bit of a comedown, Ellen thought, until she converted the hourly rate from dollars into pounds. It was exactly twice what they were getting in the Post Office. Sylvia *begged* her to come too. Ellen reminded her about the small problem of a sponsor.

– Well, that's easy solved, Sylvia said, blinking.

Sylvia had this way whenever she was about to say something outrageous of blinking her eyes into an artless roundness.

– All you do is get off the plane and snare the first good-looking fella you see into marrying you.

– For God's sake, *Sylvia!*

They decided on a three-week holiday to see did they like it and booked their tickets through the Maple Leaf Club off the

Holywood Road. They shopped together in the lunch-hour for their holiday outfits. They both bought halterneck tops and white crossover sandals with the biggest cork platforms they had ever seen. Over coffee in the Ormo Shop, they made a pact and both went on the pill.

– You never know your luck, Sylvia said.

On their second day there, Sylvia got a double sunburn and refused from then on to set foot outside her aunt's air-conditioned basement. Ellen spent the next nineteen nights by a succession of saggy swimming pools, drinking bottled beer in the company of stotious Irish-Canadians whose voices faltered when they sang Danny Boy and The Sash My Father Wore. On one of these nights, drunk enough herself, for some reason (boredom, maybe), to go skinny-dipping with someone she'd only met a few hours before (but not so drunk that she forgot to check first that she'd taken her pill that day), Ellen let a man with long black hair and a zapata moustache have her in the bushes behind a carport.

When they had finished he told her he was in Canada on a secret mission, buying guns for the UVF. Ellen, still on her back, stared up at him, his head surrounded by a nimbus of white moon, his semen descending her vagina in clots.

– What do you expect me to do? Clap?

The few *Canadian* Canadians she did meet weren't much of a relief. In pizza parlours, bowling alleys and theme parks their ears would prick up whenever she spoke.

– Pardon me, is that an Irish accent I hear?

English, Ellen would say to begin with, or *Not exactly*, or just plain *No*. But it made no difference what she said, because even in denying it she betrayed herself and one way and another it always came out in the end where she lived. She became a connoisseur of expressions of commiseration and incomprehension.

– What's wrong you guys can't sort out your problems and live together?

Which, Ellen sometimes thought, was like asking someone who's just had their legs broken what's wrong they can't dance.

– We have friends visited Ireland once, one woman confided

in her. Said they had a great time in the south, but in the north . . .

She shook her head. Ellen was in a queue at a donut stand. Sylvia's aunt had gone into the K-Mart and was meeting her back at the car. The woman who had spoken couldn't have been that much older than Ellen herself, twenty-one or twenty-two, maybe. Twenty-three at the outside. She wore a Steely Dan T-shirt and a badge saying *I Found Out*.

– They sent us a postcard, though, from, let's see . . . where was it, honey?

Honey, if anything, was younger still. He had a sleeping baby dangling from a harness at his chest and glasses which he kept pushing to the bridge of his nose and which kept slipping back straight away to the tip.

– The Mourne country.

– *The Mourne country*, the woman gave the words their full tragic weight. That's in the north isn't it? Such beautiful scenery. So how come you have to fight all the time?

How come indeed, when you put it like that? And how come the government hadn't seen the possibilities before now and dropped thousands of postcards of the Mournes all over the province? Ellen imagined the hush as the enormity of their pictorial message was digested, the shuffling of hundreds of thousands of feet as, slowly, Protestants and Catholics began to come out from behind their lines, blinking in the blinding light of realisation. *We never knew they were there*, they would tell each other. *We never knew*. Last to emerge would be the gunmen and the bombers, casting aside their armalites and gelignite, clutching only their postcards of the Mournes. *We're sorry*, they would say while happy people brought the pilots flowers and cups of tea. *We never knew*.

But Ellen, as ever, was politeness itself and assured Honey and the woman that she would do her best to pass on their concern when she got back to Northern Ireland.

It seemed there was no getting round having to answer for that place. Even to her friend Rosemary.

What turned out to be Rosemary's last ever letter to her had arrived the week after the Birmingham pub bombings. It was one line long:

How could you? it said.

Ellen wrote her one line back.

How could you not ask until now?

A cloud passed across the face of the sun. The smoke from the barbecue flattened out in the risen breeze, then sent up spindly shoots again as the cloud drifted on.

– I thought you were meant to be watching them, Derek said.

– And I thought the helicopter was.

But when Ellen looked up the helicopter itself was lost in the cloud. Only its sound remained, a reverberation so indistinct she had difficulty telling whether it was in the air or in her head. People noticed helicopters here the way, elsewhere, they noticed the weather. *There's a lot of them about today*, they would say, or, *they're very low this morning, aren't they?* Some days they were turbulent and intrusive, and some days they were subdued and hung limply. But mostly they were just there.

One night towards the end of her holiday in Canada, Ellen had wakened feeling scared and lonely and confused. It was something outside. She listened hard, covers to her chin, heart in her mouth, then realised that what the something was was actually nothing. It sounded as though the world had been switched off. She lifted the corner of her blind. The sky was vast and void. She felt adrift in its empty silence. She missed the helicopters' familiar, nagging chatter.

She missed home.

She had just begun stacking the barbecue dishes when her father's right arm went into spasm. For a moment his eyes widened in panic. Ellen fought down the impulse to run and help him. Then her father caught hold of the spastic limb with his good hand and gently coaxed the stiffness out of it. In the past Ellen had seen him turn this painful wrestling with himself into a pantomime for the boys.

– Are you tired, Jack? Aunt Peggy said and hoisted herself up. He's getting tired.

– Tina, Ellen said, but Tina was already disappearing into the kitchen.

– I know, coats.

Derek tossed Ellen the car keys.

– Do you want to drive?

Ellen tossed them back.

– No, you drive. I'll finish clearing up.

She turned to her father.

– I'll be down tomorrow anyway, see how you're getting on.

Now that the schools were starting back and Derek was on the lookout for a new workshop, her father was going to stay with his sister. Peggy's Walter was at home right now giving the woodwork in the spare room a lick of paint. His ghoulish library had been dismantled and packed away in tea-chests and an old cast-iron bedstead had been reassembled in its place. It would be nice, Peggy said, to have a bit of life in there again after all these years.

Jack's own house was up for sale, hence the promissory note for £10,000. Drew had seen it safely on to the market before he left. It was, he said, the very least he could do. He felt bad about going at such a difficult time. Right to the last he was talking about cancelling his flight and staying. But Ellen wouldn't hear of it.

– My daddy's not going to live for ever, she said. Suppose you do stay and in five years' time or three years' time or *one* year's time, even, something else happens to him? Then where are you? Besides, he's looking forward to going to Aunt Peggy's.

The fact that this was the answer her brother wanted to hear didn't, to Ellen's mind, detract from the sincerity of his offer. She had noticed distinct signs of change in him in the run-up to his departure. He had become more open, for one thing, less anxious to patrol the distances that separated them, though, in truth, she already knew more about him by then than he gave her credit for. She knew, from watching him in the months he was back, that he viewed many of the circumstances of her life with horror: the chaos of kids and a house that seemed, at times, to have acquired a demonic will of its own; the constant preoccupation with keeping their heads above the water – living, it must sometimes have appeared, only in order to go on living.

She knew, because they were in part her own eyes through

266

which he viewed such circumstances. She would never have believed herself at seventeen that she could have ended up here, like this.

There was a photograph of the family posed outside their new house the day they moved in, the summer of 1970: Ellen standing to the right of her mother, holding her hand, her father standing to her mother's left with his arm around Drew's shoulder. The only photograph ever taken of the four of them together, though even then they look more like two and two, instead of four, because the chain is broken in the middle where Ellen's mother has, at the last moment it appears (her husband's fingers are still splayed from the uncoupling), pulled her hand away to straighten her collar.

Somewhere along the line, brother and sister had swapped sides. Now it was Drew and his mother who were, in their very different ways, severed from Ellen and her father.

Ellen had unearthed this photograph again a couple of nights before Drew left. The two of them were going through their father's roof space, deciding what to keep and what to throw out when the time came for him to move. There were boxes there, taped-up boxes, which Ellen and Derek had helped her father store away after Granny Linden died. The boxes had names written on the outside in her father's old hand: Mum, Dad, Michael, Dinah. At the time, she remembered, they had quite a struggle taping some of them shut at all. Full lives reduced with difficulty to more manageable proportions.

Her own mother's life, on the other hand, at least on the evidence of her father's roof space, came down to a scant rack of dresses and a bundle of photographs in a Boots carrier bag.

Arranging these photographs into chronological order, Ellen was alarmed to find herself reconstructing the narrative of her mother's demise. Hers, the photo-story ran, had not been so much a physical deterioration (physically, in fact, she altered remarkably little between the first picture in the sequence, taken when she was in her teens, and the last), but something much more intangible and much more appalling. A complete loss of interest, was the nearest Ellen could come to describing it. Her mother seemed to be there and yet not there, increasingly not there with each passing picture. Or perhaps her interest was not so much lost as withheld. Ellen's memory of her mother was of a woman from whom everything had to be coaxed: smiles for the camera, conversation, enthusiasm, affection. Her kidneys had to be coaxed daily with water tablets, her bowels with periodic doses of salts. In the end, the very breath had to be coaxed in and out of her lungs, though not enough could be and one August afternoon she turned black in the face and died, barely fifty years old.

Lily Linden, it occurred to her daughter, as she replaced the photographs in their bag, had simply willed herself away. She had spent the last twenty-one years of her life in one place wishing she was in another. But if you asked Ellen, everywhere was here once you were there. That was what she had decided on the plane home from Canada when she was eighteen. She decided too that committing yourself to someone, somewhere, having a family, was no small ambition. Back in Belfast she told Derek Hastings what she wanted. The same commitment or nothing. Their marriage-house was a statement of intent. It was big and, when they moved into it, empty of almost everything except possibility. At night Ellen dreamt of silk threads spinning out from it into the darkness, and other threads, from other, unimaginable sources, spinning in towards it until their beginnings and their endings had woven the entire blank space of the house into a block of dazzling colour.

Drew and Ellen stayed up in the roof space for over three hours. It was hot under the eaves. Their necks and shoulders hurt from stooping, their eyes smarted from peering in the poor light and their noses itched from breathing dust. Another couple of minutes, they agreed, and they'd call it a night. In the front left-hand corner, Drew shifted a stack of old biscuit tins and found his 1970 World Cup coins in their souvenir folder. On the other side of the chimney, in the back right-hand corner, Ellen dug her hand into a decrepit linen basket and pulled out her granny's goldfish bowl.

The inside of the bowl was stained green and brown. A hairline crack zigzagged across it from lip to base. Ellen rose slowly to her feet. *Now*, she thought. *Talk*.

– Would you believe that? Drew said, out of sight. Paul

Reaney's lost. I'd so many swaps of him at one time I was giving them away, now he's the only flipping one missing out of the whole set.

For a moment the words had been on the tip of her tongue. But that moment went the way of all such moments before it. Oddly, though, she didn't despair. There would be other moments. One day they would talk it out.

– Ellen?

She turned the cracked bowl in her hands a few seconds longer, then put it in with the rest of the rubbish.

– Finished, she said.

*

Tina guided the sleeves of the raincoat over her Aunt Peggy's blindly feeling hands. The raincoat embraced her, gained definition from her, and she from it. She buttoned it to her throat, becoming more like herself with every button, keeping her brother going now about what he was letting himself in for coming to stay with her. The physiotherapist had told Jack he was to get out walking as often as he could. Peggy would get him out walking, all right. She'd have him up in those blinking mountains again before long. It was no distance from her house, up the Springfield Road.

Derek, taking it all far too seriously, said they'd want to be careful these days on some parts of the Springfield.

– Nonsense, Peggy said. There's people knows me the length and breadth of that road. And, sure, even if there wasn't, who do you think's going to bother us? Look at me, I'm just a fat old biddy, and God love him, but nobody'd ever guess what our Jack is, not being able to say No. Would they, Jack?

Jack smiled awry, seeming to bow a little under the weight of the pendulous daisy-chains as he rose from his black and gold chair, stiff but dignified, lavender straw cradled in the crook of his arm, buttercup-yellow beanie perched, brim up, on his head.

– Yes, he said. Yes.

The rain held off just long enough after they had gone for Ellen and Tina to clear the last of the dishes from out the back of the house. Then the heavens opened.

17

IT WAS RAINING, at that moment, where Drew was too. Real late-summer rain, spiteful darts flung from a tumultuous sky. Beyond his open window the treetops held their dripping green tassels at arm's length, like bedraggled cheerleaders. Drew lay on the bed, staring at the liver-spotted ceiling, listening to the gurgle of the rain in the gutter in the yard below. Beginning again. It was raining when he left here for there and raining the day he left there again for here.

Rain unites us and fills the sea between us.

He wondered should he write that down before he forgot it. Probably. He lay where he was. There was movement out on the landing. Drew counted down the soughing floorboards to the bathroom. The door was scraped shut and bolted. Pipes rattled. The shower coughed, spluttered, then hissed evenly over the sound of the rain. A few moments later, this sound too was drowned by a whistled medley of TV sporting theme tunes. Wesley, you called the owner of the whistle. *Elvis* Wesley, fêted, fleetingly, on his birth, thirty-five years before, as Britain's first rock 'n' roll baby. He had arrived at the guest-house the same day as Drew, on the latest leg of a never-ending fact-finding tour of the country's Football League clubs. Over dinner the previous evening he had quizzed Drew about the recent expansion of the Irish League, about Omagh Town's home form and Ballyclare Comrades' away kit. He asked if there was ever to be such a thing as a Belfast United football team, how well it would do in England. Drew hadn't the faintest notion.

– Pretty well, he guessed.

Elvis Wesley said it was a place he'd always wanted to visit, Northern Ireland, and was just getting round to asking Drew where his family lived in relation to the various football clubs, when the landlady swooped and began clearing the tables. She told Drew later that she wouldn't wish that man on anybody's family. The landlady wasn't one for gossiping, mind, but if you asked her, Elvis Wesley wasn't the full shilling, hanging around football grounds even on non-match days (in fact, he attended very few actual matches), watching fourth division training sessions and youth team practice games, and spending his nights updating the dossiers he kept on every player – apprentice to international – he had ever seen.

The landlady, frankly, blamed his parents. With a name like Elvis Wesley hanging over him, it was no wonder he'd turned out the way he had.

There was a Mrs Elvis Wesley too at one time, she said. She had accompanied her husband on his first couple of trips (for he'd been coming here the same three days of the last week in August every second year for more than a decade), trying to make proper holidays of them; but she was on a hiding to nothing and she had divorced him eventually on grounds of unreasonable conduct. For all the difference it seemed to have made to Elvis Wesley.

– Marriage! the landlady said.

She was a large-built woman in her early sixties with an impressive collection of antique rings and an unlikely penchant for Louis L'Amour westerns.

You saw enough of marriage in her line of business, she said, to put you off the institution for life. She'd give Drew this piece of advice for nothing: *You want to stay sane? Stay single.*

It would have pleased the landlady to learn, then, that Drew's sanity was under no immediate threat.

The guest-house was a little over a mile and a half from the street where he and Melanie had lived together before he left for Belfast, but Drew had not been round there since he got back to England this time. When he came over earlier in the summer he had caught the train up from London, unannounced, hoping to take Melanie by surprise, but had ended being the one who was surprised himself, walking into an empty house to find his belongings packed away in the cellar. Baffled, he sat down to wait for Melanie to come home and explain.

He waited all afternoon and evening. When she still wasn't back by half-past eleven he phoned her best friend.

– You're *what*?

Her best friend sounded more than routinely surprised to hear where she was calling from.

– You mean Melanie didn't tell you?

Melanie had gone on holiday. She'd got a bucket seat just there at the weekend and headed off on her own.

Just there at the weekend, Drew's conscience crowed, *when you were in Portrush with Anna.*

Melanie's best friend asked him had he come to pick up his things. (In a corner of the sitting room the tailor's dummies stood back to back, stuck all over with pins.) That was when he understood it was finished between Melanie and him.

– Yes, he said, I have.

He slept on the settee that night, too wretched to get into their bed. In the morning he arranged for his belongings to go into storage then caught the train down to London again. He passed the journey listening to a French language tape on his Walkman, writing any unfamiliar words and phrases into stiff-spined Black 'n' Red notebooks. He had had a meeting with Karen, James and Phoebe – and Bill of the new parent company – the previous afternoon at which he had been offered the assistant manager's job in the projected Paris branch. He had not said yes right away. He had wanted to talk it over with Melanie first. (There was a lot he had wanted to talk over with Melanie first.) But when the train arrived in London that morning he made straight for the telephones and rang central office. James took his call.

– Great news, mate, he said. You've made the smart decision.

Drew wasn't sure that was quite the way it would be viewed by the staff back in Belfast. Relations there couldn't stand many more reverses and he still had nearly two months to work before moving to France. Pamela Magill, though, handled the situation brilliantly. First, she suggested to Karen, James and Phoebe (and Bill, of course, and Bill) that a successor be appointed at once, so that Drew could show him/her the ropes before he left; then, she convinced them of the need to promote this successor from within the existing Belfast staff, and, lastly, gave Richard her personal recommendation.

And now Drew really did make a smart decision: he seconded him.

Richard was duly appointed and immediately adopted a policy of non-aggression towards Drew. To Richard and the rest of the staff, he was now, at worst, a necessary evil, at best, an impending irrelevance, and as such was capable of being tolerated and even, at a pinch, liked.

There was a more than creditable turnout at the after-hours in-store drinks party the night he finished. All the full-time and part-time staff from their own shop came, along with staff from rival shops, publishers' reps, favoured customers, and an intensity of local poets.

Beneath all the music and hilarity, Pamela told him candidly she didn't think the Belfast shop would last the year.

– No! Drew was vehement with drink. You're wrong there. It was one of the things I insisted on knowing at the interview. They're all committed to it, even Bill.

– They're committed to making money, Pamela said, lighting a Carrolls. And who can blame them? They're running a business, after all. When this squeeze really grips, you'll see, they'll cut and run.

This squeeze was every retailer's worst nightmare that summer. Many had already succumbed to its pressure and many more were expected to follow, though the people of Northern Ireland, having been squeezed, one way and another, so hard for so long (God save us, things were so tight when they were drawing up the border one third of Ulster got squeezed out), were slower than most in realising there was anything exceptional about this latest contraction.

Drew, his vehemence turning momentarily to despondence, asked Pamela what she would do in the unlikely event that the shop did close down.

– Oh, retire, I think, now, Pamela said, then paused. Maybe do just a tiny bit part-time in one of the bookshops down home to keep me from going completely gaga.

Bookselling, Drew was reminded, was something you either had in you or you hadn't. Pamela Magill had it in every fibre of her being. Sian Miles, it turned out, didn't have it in her at all. Sian had handed in her notice at the beginning of July, after emerging, pale-faced and trembling, from a prolonged stint in the stock-room, preparing hundreds of paperbacks for return. It was, she said, like slaughtering animals for their fur: the actual texts were so much dead meat to be discarded, and only the glossy pelts of their jackets were kept as having any value.

She had decided instead to go into teaching, where the inside, not the outside, of books was what mattered.

That was in those schools that still had the money to buy books, Pamela said.

Earlier on the day of the farewell party a bottle of champagne had arrived at the shop from Kay. The card with it said she was sorry she couldn't come and wished him every happiness in the future. Drew had not got round to telling her about the break-up with Melanie. They had seen each other only rarely over the summer, and then, generally, only in passing. Kay was too busy changing the face of Belfast and too busy being in love. Not with Angus Bangus, as Drew had half expected her to say when she told him (they bumped into each other in Cornmarket – unlike certain other things, being out in the street was no bar to confidences so far as Kay was concerned); not with Angus, but with someone she had met through her work at the embassies. Ulf. *Very beautiful; very Scandinavian*, was as much as she was able to say that day before rushing off, pounding up the street in that way she had, determined, as always, to leave her mark.

Besides, whenever he found himself in Kay's company these days, Drew had to bite his tongue to keep from asking her about Anna; or, more specifically, to keep from asking her why she had never once tried to explain to him about her sister. (One stoned mumble in five months hardly constituted a serious attempt at explanation.) In the absence of guidance from Kay, he felt free to entertain any stray speculation that suggested itself to him: she was embarrassed by her parents' conduct, ashamed of her own; she was prevented from speaking by some lingering notion of family honour.

Overriding all of these, though, was the thought that Anna's story simply raised too many painful questions for Kay to be able to contemplate it for any length of time, never mind communicate it to someone else. It was hard to share in a person's enthusiasms once you had glimpsed what they had to exclude in order to exist.

Not that he saw anything more of Anna himself. He spoke to her once or twice on the telephone. Once or twice he hoped she might suggest they meet; once or twice he was disappointed. Mostly, though, he accepted her reading of the affair without complaint. Their night together had been subsumed into the constantly shifting pattern of their lives. Repetition was impossible, scarcely even to be desired.

Then, on the anniversary of Con's death, he bought a bunch of flowers from a stand outside the City Hall and caught a bus up the Falls to Milltown cemetery. Partly, of course, in the hope of finding Anna there. But only partly. He had to ask at the cemetery office for directions to the grave. One of the labourers interrupted his lunch to take him over. Drew would never have found it without him. A simple grey stone, the abbreviated forename, *Con*, and that was all.

A withered bouquet of roses, still in the florist's cellophane, lay on the clayey ground before it.

– Was he something to you? the man (*Joe*, he insisted, *call me Joe*) had asked as they walked down the aisles between the graves.

– It's a bit complicated, Drew said, striving for reserve, and his companion didn't press him further.

Joe said he minded the funeral well. Same day as one *over there*. Drew followed the direction of his nod to the end of the cemetery overlooking the motorway. The republican plot.

– Hunger striker, the other boy was, Joe said. You never saw a pair of funerals like it. One was as big as the other was small. And that one – (he nodded again towards the motorway) – was very big.

Joe filled a pipe with black tobacco, tamping it down with his thumb.

It was the woman at this one, he said, the wife or whatever she was, that he remembered most. He struck a match and puffed on the pipe, glancing at Drew through the smoke to check that he hadn't gone too far. Drew offered him an encouragingly blank expression.

– She, came, back . . .

Joe watched the bowl of his pipe, breathing in between each word, till the tobacco was evenly lit.

– . . . every day for weeks after the funeral. The boys here used to say she looked like she belonged in a grave herself, but that's the way the grief is with some people, you know? Though, to be fair to them, they had a point, she'd've given you the creeps all right. Like, there was this day me and another fella – Jamesie Power you called him, nice big fella, dead now himself – this day me and Jamesie found her sitting on a bench, dolled up to the nines as usual, staring at this dirty great spade lying on the ground at her feet. *What're you doing with that, missus?* Jamesie says till her, and here's her, she looks up at us a minute, all confused, then she starts to laugh. *Nothing*, she says. *Nothing at all.* And that was it, I don't think I've seen her more than three or four times in all the years since.

– When was the last? Drew asked.

– Me? Joe rummaged for a match. Two, three years, maybe? The caretaker, now, funny enough, the caretaker says he saw her only a lot of months back. One Sunday, let me think, in the spring, some time. That's right, it's always the spring you'd see her now if you saw her at all.

Of course, the spring when she and Con met, not the summer when he died. Drew knelt and counted the stems of the suffocated roses. Twenty. One for each year. He understood that this was where Anna had come the morning after he himself first met her.

– Thanks, he said.

– No problem, said Joe and left him in peace to lay his own flowers.

As Drew was leaving the cemetery, an army foot patrol was entering and spreading out among the gravestones. The dead too needed watching here. The dead *above all* needed watching here. Containing the dead, it could be said, was the beginning and end of policy in Northern Ireland. Containing the dead, it could even be said, was the whole rationale for the country's existence. But, whatever the policy or the rationale, the dead continued to leave their traces wherever you looked. They were there in the lilacs left annually on the platform of a suburban railway station, they were there in the small bunch of freesias tied to a bus-shelter on a quiet country road; they were there in the wreaths laid at the sides of disused barns and on the tops of hedgerows; they were there in the sudden efflorescence of nondescript city footpaths. They were every nowhere, not to be sidestepped, no matter how far to the side you tried to step.

And, paradoxically, only when he had accepted that could Drew reconcile himself to leaving again.

Because, even though this was the opening he had been waiting for, leaving was hard – much harder than he'd remembered. Perhaps because there was more *to* leave this time.

Drew was often up at Ellen's during what remained of that summer. Usually, by the time he was able to get away from the shop, his father was beginning to flag and could do no more than sit, mute and motionless, all the while his son was there. Given where they were starting from, however, just sitting together was movement enough. Indeed, after the years of constant fidgeting, stasis rather became Jack Linden. In his tireder, vaguer moments, it was true, he could seem almost shell-shocked, but in general he had the air of a man who against all the odds had achieved a sort of peace with himself. Not even his teeth (he'd been fitted with a new set after the stroke) bothered him now.

On one of these nights Drew was reading the paper on Ellen and Derek's back step, while his father sat nodding to himself, wise as Solomon, on a wrought-iron chair a few feet away. After a time, Drew saw his father's left hand grope across the table beside him for his notepad and pen. Drew flicked the newspaper straighter, making a screen between them. He considered it degrading for his father to have his exertions exposed to the public gaze in this way, the more so since, all too often, after a series of strangled grunts, the page he was attempting to write on wound up on the ground, crumpled in frustration. When next Drew looked up this evening, though, alerted by a stream of yeses, his father was beckoning him with a triumphantly flourished sheet of paper. Drew took it from him with some trepidation, hoping against hope that he would not have to hand it back again untranslated. He studied the page for what seemed minutes under his father's intent gaze, unable for the life of him to work out what the five spidery letters there spelt (though at least they were beginning to be recognisable as letters). Then all at once he realised he couldn't see it for looking at it. The word was not one his father had been in the habit of using to him in the past. The word was sorry.

Drew folded the page in half, then half again, then slipped it into his trouser pocket, but could find no words of his own to give in return.

His father wasn't the only one having to relearn lost skills.

Three weeks on, as he lay on the bed in the guest-house, staring at the ceiling, listening to Elvis Wesley in the shower, whistling the theme from *Sportsnight*, his father's note was still in his trouser pocket. Now, though, in a buff envelope in the pocket of the jacket hanging on the back of the bedroom door, there was also a reply. The reply said it had taken his father long enough to apologise. It said what he had done was wrong. It said a lot of other things besides; once he had started Drew had difficulty stopping. It said at the very end that he no longer bore his father any malice.

Drew had been carrying this letter around for the past two days, unable to bring himself to post it. He had lived with his grievance for so long now that he was reluctant to let go of it completely.

Some time around eight o'clock that evening, Drew's last evening in England before leaving for France, the thunderclouds dispersed and the downpour eased to a drizzle. There was hardly a breath of air in the room. Drew got up, put on his jacket, pulled his hair into shape and went out for a walk.

For a moment on stepping out on to the street, he could have sworn he heard the whine and rumble of a helicopter above the sound of the traffic. But, no, it couldn't be. He hadn't managed to shake the echoes of home yet, that was all. He set off towards a bar he and Melanie never went to, looking at the ground, watching his face loom over pimpled puddles in advance of him; then stopped, listening harder. Definitely a helicopter. He turned about slowly, scouring the horizon, and there it was, trapped, hovering, in the bar of blue between the rooftops off to his left and the gathering night. The genuine article too, by the looks of it, army-issue green. The pub was forgotten as he followed the helicopter's lure, through streets of ever-more downmarket boarding-houses and multiple lets, through a council estate of unrelieved wet concrete bleakness, across a dual carriageway bordered by shuttered shops and takeaways, over the remains of a mill, down one final residential street, partially gentrified, till he came out at a park crisscrossed by four paths, like the spokes of a wheel. Policemen in yellow reflector vests and rainproofs patrolled the perimeter. In the middle distance, behind them, great Green Goddesses and other, lesser military vehicles formed an inner ring about a cluster of beech trees, above which the helicopter balanced on a slender stalk of bluish light.

As Drew approached, a television reporter was pleading with a stony-faced police sergeant to be allowed in closer, while his cameraman took what footage he could through the park railings.

– What's going on here? Drew asked another bystander, an elderly Bangladeshi sheltering beneath a striped golfing umbrella.

– They're making safe a bomb, the man said, very correctly.

A bomb? In a park, in the north of England? Drew's gut tightened.

– Ever since the Blitz, the man says, the man said, indicating the police sergeant, it has been buried in there, unfound.

When he spoke, his teeth made a familiar clacking sound. Drew glanced at him under the umbrella. The man smiled out at him.

– Imagine, after all these many years, they're still digging them up.

He shook his head. The canopy of his umbrella rotated on its metal spindle, half a turn in one direction, half a turn back, spattering Drew's specs with raindrops. Drew took them off and rubbed the lenses with his cuff, blinking through the smirr at the balancing helicopter and the tea-coloured pools that had formed in the dips where the Green Goddesses had mounted the grass, feeling the knots in his stomach slowly resolve themselves. The television reporter continued to plead with the stony-faced sergeant, but to no avail. For want of anything better to film, the cameraman turned his camera on the onlookers. Drew instinctively rubbed his lenses harder. Himself, only more so.

The Bangladeshi's teeth clicked again.

– Imagine, all these many, many years.

On the way back to the guest-house, Drew passed a post-box and without breaking his stride fished out the letter to his father and posted it. After two days in his pocket, the envelope had become entangled with his overflowing sewing kit, and in the now near-darkness he inadvertently posted half of that as well.

Postscript

L ET ME SAVE you a journey. Next time you're in Belfast city centre, don't go looking for Bookstore.

Pamela Magill was right. Up to a point. The Belfast shop did close down, a fortnight before Christmas. The company, though, did not cut and run, as Pamela had predicted, but rather limped out when its entire Belfast stock was lost to smoke and water damage in an IRA firebomb attack. The Economy Minister, on a visit to Laganside, dismissed calls for government aid and suggested the media take up the issue of the twenty-four job losses with Sinn Fein. Sinn Fein said, in its actor's voice, that the job losses were indeed regrettable, but that the blame lay, ultimately, with the people responsible for the imposition of the border. Unionists said the border wasn't half strong enough and called too for more visible policing of the city centre security zone. Pamela Magill, asked on the local teatime news for her reaction, said it was a crying shame, and, as if to prove it, proceeded to cry into tens of thousands of front rooms as far afield as Dublin and the west of Scotland.

Drew had then been in Paris three and a half months. He had been there four and a half when his father suffered a second stroke and died.

It should have been a three-hour flight home including the stopover in London, but there was another war on now, in the Middle East, and what with the new improved high-profile airport security measures added to the everyday hole-and-corner ignominies of the Prevention of Terrorism Act, the journey to the far north-west took closer to five hours. The passengers had only the co-pilot's word for it when they left Britain behind and when they came above Ireland. The co-pilot apologised: visibility was poor all over today; the weather on the ground in Belfast was damp and drizzly.

Two women sitting along from Drew traded long-suffering sighs across the central aisle.

— Is it ever anything else? said one to the other, making conversation.